OUTWALKER RULES:

1. No technology
2. Be outside
3. Be hidden
4. Obedience to the gang

Also by Fiona Shaw

Out of Me
The Sweetest Thing
The Picture She Took
Tell it to the Bees
A Stone's Throw

OUTWALKERS

FIONA
SHAW

31 Beaumont Street
Oxford OX1 2NP, UK

Outwalkers
is a
DAVID FICKLING BOOK

First published in Great Britain in 2018 by
David Fickling Books,
31 Beaumont Street,
Oxford, OX1 2NP

www.**davidficklingbooks**.com

Hardback edition published 2018
This paperback edition published 2019

978-1-78845-001-0

1 3 5 7 9 10 8 6 4 2

Papers used by David Fickling Books are from well-managed forests and other responsible sources.

DAVID FICKLING BOOKS Reg. No. 8340307

A CIP catalogue record for this book is available from the British Library.

Typeset in Sabon by Falcon Oast Graphic Art Ltd, www.falcon.uk.com
Printed and bound in Great Britain by Clays Ltd, Elcograf S.p.A.

For Romy, Alex, Elodie, Bess and Emily

One

The Academy clock struck two. Outside it was the dead of night. Inside it was quiet at last. Quiet as it could be in a dormitory full of sleepers: every one of them made some kind of noise, course they did. Forty boys in forty beds. Forty boys, and their forty griefs. But just now even the ones who saw monsters in their dreams were quiet. Even the ones who'd cried into their pillows were asleep. Only Jake lay awake in his bed, eyes wide open, and listened.

The Mother had been round a few minutes before, shone her torch at each bed. The Father would be round in two hours' time. If he was going, then it must be now. Right now. The last boy left it too late and they caught him. He needed stitches in his leg from the dog bites.

You can do it. You can. Jake could hear his dad's voice inside his head, encouraging him.

–Go, he whispered, and he slipped out of bed, pulled on his plimsolls, grabbed his rucksack, wound a scarf round his neck, tugged his beanie down hard. Spare clothes bundled up beneath the covers made the shape of a sleeping boy, good enough to fool the Father's torch, he hoped.

Down on his belly, pushing his rucksack before him, he swam beneath the beds, pressing hard against the polished floor with his elbows and knees. He'd practised this.

Keep low, he told himself. Face to the ground.

Twelve beds to reach the door, in each a boy sleeping.

The dust was in his nose, in his throat, and he wanted to cough so bad it made his eyes water. Eight beds left, and something caught around his face. Another boy's dangling bedclothes, tangled round him like weed.

Sweat slicked beneath his clothes. He could see the door.

A sound. He stopped. There it was again. The sound of the door handle turning. He shuffled back under the last bed. The door opened; he could see a pair of slippers, pink ones: the Mother's. Why was she back? She was walking towards him, shining her torch at each bed. If she bent down just a little, she'd see him. Jake's heart was thumping so loud, he was sure she'd hear it. The torch beam swung across the floor. She'd stopped on the far side. Jake peered out. She was standing over a new boy's bed – Jake didn't even know his name. Now she was whispering, pulling the boy out. He was very small, maybe five years old. Now she was feeling the sheets, shaking her head, then grabbing the boy's arm and pushing him roughly, shoving him before her. Finally they were gone.

Not for long, though. They'd be back in minutes. Fast as he could, Jake swam beneath the last beds, and out the other side.

Maybe the Mother had left the sensor turned off? Jake looked up. But there it was, in the corner of the ceiling, its red light pulsing gently.

This next bit would be harder. If the rope held and he could get through the door quickly enough, he could fool it. It had been done. But if he didn't manage it . . . He felt the hair on his neck bristle. He'd seen another boy punished for trying.

And he'd have to leave the rope hanging there after him. The Mother didn't usually help boys in the night. Usually she just pushed them back through the door and left them to sort things out for themselves. The new boy might not even remember which his bed was, or know how to change a sheet in the dark. Didn't matter. He wouldn't get any help with it. Unless Jake was out of luck, and tonight was the one night the Mother decided to be kind. But he'd have to risk it. He was too far on to return. He wouldn't make it back to his bed unnoticed. This was his chance, and he just had to go.

He took the rope from his rucksack. He'd found it, along with a length of washing line, both coiled in the cobwebs in the groundsman's shed, and he'd hidden them in his trunk these past few days. There was a good twenty feet of rope, he reckoned. It should be enough. He'd practised for this as best he could. Tied a monkey's fist in one end – his dad had taught him the knot – and tied his Arsenal keyring to one end of the rope, to weight it.

A high shelf ran along the edge of the room, with boxes of old books stacked up on it. Jake wasn't interested in the books, but he was interested in the brackets that held the shelf up. In the dormitory's half-dark, he squinted up at the triangular space made by the bracket nearest the door.

He flung the rope in the silence of the sleeping room. It missed, and fell to the ground with a thud loud enough to wake the dead.

Jake froze. He could hear the Mother's voice from the linen cupboard, raised, angry. Had she heard him? If she caught him, he'd have six months on his tariff, no question.

–Go, Jake! he told himself. And he gathered the rope and threw it again. Tugged. It felt firm.

Somebody muttered something; a bed creaked; again he waited. But the room slept on.

His heart was in his mouth and his hands were damp.

Don't think on it, he told himself, and in a single movement, he reached up for the rope, grasped it firmly and swung, out across the sensor beam. The bracket creaked, just as he dropped down by the door. A few seconds longer and he'd have pulled it from the wall, crashed to the ground, woken everybody.

Better be right, JoJo, he thought, because it was JoJo who said the hubbing wouldn't work so well if you covered up your chip. JoJo, who'd never escape – not with his limp; not a chance.

Jake was out the door, past the linen cupboard and the Parents' room, into the corridor. He was running, fast as he could, quiet as he could, up on his toes, past the other dormitories, past the double doors that led back to the main Academy building, till he reached the far end and the small fire door he'd pinned his hopes on. It opened into a dim stairwell, concrete stairs in half-flight turns. No sensors, or not that he could see, and he took the stairs fast, one hand on the metal rail for balance. At the bottom was another door marked FIRE EXIT, with a broad iron bar for opening. Beyond the door, he'd be outside, into the grounds, and once he was past the watchmen, he was sure he could make it.

He pushed down hard on the bar.

The door wouldn't open.

He pulled the bar up and pushed it down again, pressing against the door with his shoulder. Still nothing.

–Come on, he said, because his escape couldn't end here. He had to get out. He waited for a moment to catch his breath, then using the stairs for pace, he ran the last short flight and barged the door, throwing his weight at it, and this time it gave and he hurtled through, tumbling over his feet on to the dark ground.

Lights glared on instantly, and he lay still, waiting for shouts and dogs. But it was quiet. He'd timed it well and the watchman was still on the far side of the Academy.

On to his feet, crouching low, he ran for the blackness.

Two

He used to be scared of the dark and his parents would leave a light on for him at night. A light to keep ghosts away. But the day before his tenth birthday they told him: tonight's the last time. And the next day, when he came home from school, they sat him down in the kitchen and they shut the curtains, turned off the lights, so it was completely dark. Then he heard them open the door and close it again and the room was silent.

–What are you doing? he said. –Where've you gone?

No reply, and he began to be scared. The door opened again and something small tumbled through, a black shadow of a something that scuffled on the floor and bumped against his ankles. But it felt soft, and real, no kind of a ghost, and summoning his courage, he put his hand down.

–Hey! he said, because the shadow of a something had nipped him with its sharp teeth, and then the light went on again and there it was.

A puppy. Black as the night, with golden eyes and soft fur, and the sharpest puppy teeth.

–He's yours, his mother said. –And once he's trained, he can sleep in your room at night.

–What'll you call him? his father said, and Jake knew that already.

–He's called Jet, he said.

*

The moon was next to full, but the sky was overcast and the night took him in. The dark, protecting night. Keeping his distance from the house, Jake made his way round to the front. His eyes had grown accustomed to the dark by now, and he could see clearly enough.

He heard a dog bark close by. Too close.

The watchmen are there to keep you safe, the Headteacher had told them. But Jake knew, they all did, that the watchmen were there to keep them in. Bushes lined the driveway to the house. Ducking down, Jake scrambled inside one. There was space enough between the branches. The moon shone down into his hiding place. The ground was rustly with dead leaves and he tried not to move at all. He put a hand in his pocket, took out a small package.

The dog barked again, nearer now.

The package was soggy, the 'toilet-paper wrapping' sticking in shreds to the bits of meat. Last night's dinner, and the night before. JoJo said they kept the guard dogs hungry, to keep them more vicious. Jake hoped the dog liked nuggets, and gristle. And he hoped the dog found him before the watchman did.

Now the dog was in the bushes, its padding paws, its panting breath. Jake glimpsed it black across the moonlight, then the snap of a branch and the dog burst through, a huge, muscled beast with sharp teeth and a square, violent jaw.

Jake's hands were shaking. He held some meat out before him, hand flat. The dog paused; its small eyes stared. It sniffed, nosed the meat, and in one gulp, it was gone.

–Here, Jake whispered, and he tumbled the rest of the package on to the ground.

The dog snouted in the leaves, and in two gulps ate the rest.

–Hey! Come, boy! The watchman's voice, just beyond the bushes.

–Don't give me away, Jake whispered. –Please.

The dog blinked, and cocked its head.

–Come, boy! The watchman's voice sounded just a few yards away.

And the dog turned and went.

–Found 'owt? The watchman was so close Jake could hear the sputter of his walkie-talkie.

The dog barked twice, and then it trotted away. Away from the bushes, away from Jake. And after the dog went the watchman, heavy-footed, clumping over the dry ground.

Jake wanted to shout with relief. He listened to the watchman's footsteps grow fainter and, soon as he dared, he climbed out of the bush on to the drive, and ran on.

Jake didn't think about his mum or his dad. He didn't think about home. He didn't think about the Academy either. He just thought about Jet. Jet would know he was on his way. Somehow he would know, and Jake must not let him down.

Veering off before he got too close to the front gate with its sensors, he made for the perimeter wall: concrete slabs and very high, ten feet at least, with glass on the top that shone in the moonlight. He'd already done a recce to find the right tree, but the night had changed things and he was sure he'd walked too far. He was beginning to panic when he found it again. It wasn't an easy one to climb, but it had one branch that jutted quite close to the wall and that's why he'd chosen it: the branch was close enough to jump from, if you were desperate.

He threw his washing line towards the branch. It dropped over on the first throw and he caught the free end and secured it with a slip knot. Grasping the line above his head, he twisted it once around his hand for a firm hold, braced himself, and put a foot up against the trunk. The line cut into his hand, but the rough bark held his plimsoll well. He managed to get a higher grip on the line with his other hand, and then to find a proper toehold in the corrugated bark with his other foot.

His hands hurt and the muscles in his arms and legs burned with the strain.

Just go, he told himself. *Go.*

Afterwards he couldn't say how he did it. Couldn't imagine doing it again. He'd read about men doing things they would never normally have been able to, when they were really really afraid. And women too. His dad liked those sorts of stories: he had a pile of them at home. Jake was good at climbing, very good. And he knew he'd gone into that zone – that's what his dad used to call it – where all you can see or hear or feel is the thing you've got to do.

He felt very calm, and he was very scared. But maybe you could be very scared and very calm at the same time.

He was climbing, hand over hand, when he heard a rustling. He stopped and listened. There it was again, the sound of someone pushing through the undergrowth, sounds of crackling and breaking.

He stopped climbing and looked down. The line was swinging, clear of the tree, and nothing he could do to hide it. He waited, the muscles in his arms tightening, his toes pushed in hard against the tree trunk. If he was silent, they might not come this way, but if they did, they couldn't help but see him. The rustling grew louder and his heart banged in his chest.

He still had a chance if there was only one of them. He

was close enough to make it to the wall. He'd jump and take his chances. He could see the bracken moving now and then there they were. Two of them.

Deer. He could see their eyes shining. He could see the white markings on their pelts. Then they must have smelled him, because they turned suddenly and disappeared again.

Jake took a deep breath and went on up to the branch. Ten feet up, straddling the branch, he untied the washing line and threw it over the wall.

–Stand up and jump, he said out loud. –You don't make it, you'll have to climb up some other way and do it again.

Before he could stop and think, he'd jumped and he was on top of the wall, grappling for balance, the glass slicing into his hands with a sharp pain that he barely noticed. He jumped down the other side and landed in the deep ditch that ran along the wall's outer side. Another time of year, he might have hurt himself. But the ditch was deep in early summer bracken and it cushioned his fall.

You're out! he told himself. *You've done it.* And only when he stood up did he see that his hand was sticky, and then that it was sliced along the palm. He bound his scarf round his hand and set off. It wasn't far to home: fifteen miles to Bridgwater, the first sign he saw said. If he walked all night, he'd be there in the morning.

And he did walk all night, ducking out of sight when he heard a car or a lorry. He grew hungry, and thirsty, but he kept his mind on Jet, and he kept on walking.

Three

Daylight came. Jake had reached the outskirts of the town. His hand was throbbing, and his feet hurt in the plimsolls, but there wasn't far to go. Harder to hide now, but with people on the streets and other children going to school, he was less noticeable.

He began to recognize places. There was the old swimming baths, closed down before he'd learned to swim. *There was Lidl, where Mum used to shop*, he thought, and then he checked himself. –Don't go there. Don't think about that.

A little further on and he passed the church, and the Coalition building with its blue-and-red flags. They'd learned about the flag in Reception. How there used to be two flags and two colours and how the Coalition decided to join them together.

He passed a food bank and the scan hub next to it. *We're looking out for you*, it said below the smiling face. And though he didn't think it made much difference, just in case JoJo was right, Jake pulled up the hood on his jacket and kept his head down as he walked past.

Another few streets and he'd be there and Jet would be waiting for him. The Hadleys had promised to feed and look after him and Jake imagined Jet lying by their fire, his smooth black fur shining.

–Hey, Jet, he whispered. –I'm nearly home. And he pictured Jet wagging his tail like he did when he was excited, nearly wagging it off, and giving those little yips.

The morning was cold, drizzle in the air, and everybody hurried along with their heads down. Nobody noticed him. He counted another two scan hubs, the news screens still blank this early in the morning. His neck prickled. It wouldn't be long before the hubbers found him now, but if he could just get to his street before they picked him up, then he could put his plan into action. He was heading for the Hadleys' house.

The Hadleys lived just around the corner, and he'd run errands for them and cleaned their car a few times. They were older than his mum and dad, but he knew they'd take him in, be his parents. They didn't have children of their own, and they'd told him often what a nice boy he was. How well behaved. How they wished they'd had a son like him. Jake used to take it for a joke, but Mr Hadley would say no, he was quite serious. Well, so now they could have him as a son and then he wouldn't have to go back to the Academy. Then he would be safe.

When Jake reached his street, he meant not to look at his own house. He had to walk past it, and he meant not to look. But it was too hard. He couldn't bear to see, and he couldn't bear not to, and when he got close, he turned and looked.

There was a board up outside:

TO LET
3 Beds. Unfurnished.
Apply carruthers@homeslocal.eng

They'd given him a trunk before they took him away.

–Plenty of space for a small boy's belongings, they'd told him. –The rest will be charitied.

The trunk was made of black plastic and they'd made him fill it with his clothes and his school books, a duvet, towels. But when they weren't looking, he'd put a photo of his mum and dad in there too, and an old CD his mother had in a drawer, and her green cardigan; and he'd put in his father's knife with the red handle and fifteen different blades, and his father's cap and his fisherman's sweater. Now he only had the photo and the cardigan and the knife, zipped deep in his rucksack. Everything else was left behind in the trunk at the foot of his bed in the Home Academy.

The gate was still broken, and no one had put the missing tiles back on the roof. His dad had been going to do that for months. The windows were dark, and Jake didn't look in. Down the side of the house he went, walking fast, round past the dustbin to the garden. Jet's kingdom. The grass was long and the flower beds overgrown. His mother would have hated that. Jake sniffed. Foxes.

–Never had foxes when Jet was here, he said to himself.

He allowed himself one long look down the garden.

–Bye, he said, then he turned to go. But there was a noise. A small whine. He stopped.

He knew that sound.

–Jet? he said, turning back. –Jet?

Another small whine, and this time he was sure. It came from the shed.

Jake ran over. It was padlocked and there was no window. Kneeling down, he put his fingers under the door, and there was his dog, nuzzling at his hand, whining.

–But they said they'd look after you, Jake said. –They promised.

He tugged at the door, but the padlock was firm. He could hear the clink that Jet's collar made, the name tag chinking against the buckle. He took out his dad's penknife, flipped open the biggest blade and dug it into the wood around the hasp, but it wouldn't give. Then he picked at the lock with the toothpick blade, but still the lock stayed firm, and all he could do was lean his head against the rough wood and promise to be back, to get him out of there.

–You and me always, he said, and Jet made small, sad barks in response. Jake tried to keep his voice calm, but finally it was too hard, and there in the garden, hidden in the long grass, he wept.

Mr and Mrs Hadley were eating breakfast. He could hear their voices and he could smell rashers in the pan. He put a hand to the wall. His head was spinning. Then, steadying himself, he knocked on the kitchen door. A figure approached, hazy through the frosted pane. He stood straighter, wiped at his face again, tucked his clothes in. A key turned, a bolt was pulled.

–Jacob! Mr Hadley sounded amazed. –What on earth?

–I'm sorry to disturb you, Jake said. –I'm very hungry. Could you give me something to eat?

Mr Hadley stared at him, then past him at the empty street. –Come in, then. Quick.

Jake took in the room as he sat down. Everything was as it always was. Shoes in neat lines on the shoe rack. Biscuit tin beside the toaster. Polished fruit in the fruit bowl, apples on one side, oranges on the other. Very different from his home.

They sat him at the kitchen table. Mr Hadley dropped

the blinds and turned off the computer. They put his plimsolls on the shoe rack. His wet socks made footprints on the floor. Mrs Hadley gave Jake a peck on the cheek, not like her normal hug, and he couldn't be sure, but he thought she had tears in her eyes.

–I'll put on some more bacon, she said. –No talking till you've eaten. Look at the state of you. I'll get you some dry socks. And you've cut your hand.

She cleaned the cut and put a big plaster on it.

–However did you do that? she said, and then she kind of waved her hand at him. –No, actually I don't want to know. But we might need to fetch something from the chemist.

–Pat, Mr Hadley said and his voice was stern. –We can't be seen to . . . And he didn't finish the sentence, but Mrs Hadley let go of Jake's hand.

She put a plate of food in front of him, with a glass of orange juice, and Jake ate every last bit of it. When he'd finished, Mr Hadley sat back in his chair and folded his arms.

–So, what's going on? he said. He didn't sound angry, but not friendly either.

–I ran away, Jake said.

–You ran away? From the Academy?

Mrs Hadley had put her hands to her head. Jake could see her, there by the cooker, out of the corner of his eye.

–I've got this plan. Also, I needed to see Jet. I promised my parents I'd look after him, and I thought he'd be with you, but he's in the shed at home.

–You shouldn't have done that, Mr Hadley said. –They won't like it if you do that.

–And the countryside, Mrs Hadley said. –You can't go running through the countryside these days, Jacob. It's much too dangerous.

–Mum and Dad took me for walks in the countryside, Jake said. –Nothing happened. The countryside didn't kill them.

The Hadleys looked at each other, but they didn't answer him.

–Anyway, Jet needs me, Jake said. –And it's like a prison in the Academy.

–You shouldn't talk like that either, Mr Hadley said, and Jake saw him glance at the computer, even though it was harmless; turned off.

–The Home Academy is your home now, Mrs Hadley said. –That's why it's called that. And you've got your Mother and Father there. That's where you need to be. It's the best place for you now.

She sounded kind. But she didn't get it, Jake could see.

–But I told you. Jet needs me, and I can't have him with me there. That's why I made the plan. Once you've heard it, and once you agree, then I won't have to go back.

Mr Hadley was shaking his head and he had a face as if Jake had done something bad. –You can't do this, he said.

–But you haven't heard the plan yet, Jake said.

–You have to go back, Mr Hadley said, and he was standing up, fishing in his back pocket for his mobile. –I'll have to let them know.

Jake was braced, ready to run for it, but Mrs Hadley put her hand on her husband's shoulder.

–At least let him tell us his plan, Simon. They'll be here soon enough.

Mr Hadley rubbed at his neck. –Not at all regular, he said. –It's set out very clear, what we should do.

But he sat back down, and Jake told them. They could be his parents. The Coalition said every child had to have two. They could be his now. He couldn't get to his grandparents because they were in Scotland. And the Hadleys didn't have any other children, so they'd get a son, and a bit more money. And he could go back to his school down the road, see his friends. And fetch Jet out of the shed.

That was it. That was his plan.

Jake looked up at Mrs Hadley. –What do you think? he said. –You'd have me as a son, wouldn't you?

But Mrs Hadley's face had gone sad, and Jake could feel everything falling away.

–We could keep Jet outside if you wanted, he said. –He wouldn't mind.

Because maybe that was a bit much to expect, to have Jet inside the house. They'd always seemed to like him before, patted his head, but in that careful way that people do who've never had a dog. Maybe that was why Mrs Hadley looked sad, because she couldn't say yes to Jet being inside.

Mr Hadley was shaking his head now, and he'd gone red in the face. He was pacing up and down, making the tablecloth flutter. Sweat patches had appeared under his arms, even though it wasn't that warm. Jake had a bad feeling in his stomach, and when he felt like that, pretty much always he was right.

–The Home Academy is the place for children like you, Mr Hadley said. –The tribunal said so. A proper Mother and Father and a proper education.

Jake shook his head. They didn't know what it was like in there. –It's a horrible place, Mr Hadley, he said. –They're not like my mum and dad at all. Not in a single way. And there are lots of sad children. And if you cry, you get sent to the safe room and you're locked in there on your own till bedtime. It's like Jet being locked in that shed where he's lonely and miserable. He hates it in there. He was whining.

Mrs Hadley put her hand across the table and patted Jake's arm. –You're getting to be a big boy now, Jacob. And you know, it's not your shed any more, dear. Not any more. Nor your home, I'm afraid. Do you know, there'll be a new family moving in tomorrow and they seem very nice. Friendly. They've got young children. And Jet will stay, because they'd like a guard dog, used to living outside.

–No! Jake said. He didn't mean to shout, but she still had her hand on his arm, like she was keeping him there, keeping him down. –He's my dog and he doesn't want another family. He wanted to shut his ears, keep their words out. They weren't meant to be saying these things. They were meant to be saying other things. Things that would give him a chair at their kitchen table and his own bed in the little boxroom next to the bathroom upstairs.

–Jet wants *me*, he said, and he pulled his arm away and shoved his chair back.

–Where are you going? Mrs Hadley said. –Jacob?

–Thank you for the breakfast, he said politely.

–You haven't anywhere else to go, Mrs Hadley said. –Sit down, Jacob.

Mr Hadley got up and locked the back door. –Right, he said. Nobody's trying to upset you. You just stay in here for a minute while Pat and me have a word.

Soon as they'd shut the door, Jake stood up, quiet as he could. He listened. Something wasn't right, with both of them out there and him in here and the back door locked. He could hear their voices, but not what they were saying. Then he heard, unmistakeable, the sound of the telephone keypad. They were phoning someone. And he knew that he had to get out of there, and fast.

He grabbed his plimsolls off the shoe rack, then paused. Walking boots. Mr Hadley's would be too big, but hers looked about right. Leather, thick soles. Jake wouldn't have been seen dead in them six months ago – they were mostly *pink* – but he was going to need boots like these now. Besides, Mrs Hadley wouldn't be using them these days, surely. Not with all the virus threats. She'd believe it all.

He pulled the boots on. They'd have him down for a thief now too, but not much he could do about it.

In the biscuit tin, he found what he was looking for: a red penlight keyring with three keys attached.

–Yes! he said, triumphant. He put the keys in his pocket and a half packet of biscuits in his rucksack.

There was a mobile in the biscuit tin too, in a pink case – Mrs Hadley's, with the PIN written inside the case. Jake was halfway to slipping the mobile in his pocket too, because there'd be cash on there and he could buy some food with it. But then he thought again. *Leave the mobile*, he told himself, because food or no food, if they didn't catch him by hubbing, they'd do it through a mobile.

He could hear Mr Hadley's voice from the hall. Then he heard his own name. Mr Hadley spoke it slowly and clearly and in full, as if he was talking to someone official on the other end: *Jacob William Riley,* he said.

Jake's heart missed a beat. No doubt then. The Hadleys had shopped him. He carried a chair over to the sink, climbed up quietly and opened the kitchen window. Throwing his rucksack ahead of him, he twisted into the window opening, first one shoulder, then the other. A moment to balance on the sill, and he was down in the front garden and running. Down the drive, past the car and on to the street.

Behind him he heard the Hadleys' kitchen door open and Mr Hadley's voice, a roar behind him:

–They're coming for you, Jacob William Riley.

Back round the corner he ran, no time to be careful, no time to hide his face even. Every minute counted. Through the broken gate, down the side of the house, across the grass to the shed. There were his tracks in the grass from less than an hour ago – still only *his* tracks, he was glad to see.

Jet had heard him, or smelled him, and he was already at the shed door, scratching, barking.

–Hold on, Jet. Quiet, boy. I'll have you out of there.

Taking out the keys on the red keyring, he found the shortest of them and slipped it into the padlock, and as he pulled the padlock free of the hasp, a tornado of black fur barrelled into him, knocking him backwards, down on to the grass, and Jet was there, licking his face, butting his head against Jake's, yipping loud.

Jake wrapped his arms around him and held tight. His cut hand throbbed, pressed against Jet's fur, and he didn't care. It was twenty-seven weeks and four days since he'd last hugged anybody. He pressed his face into Jet's fur and held him.

–Hey, boy, he said. –You and me always. Like Mum said. Like I promised.

But Jet felt different from before, and after a minute Jake stepped back from his dog and stared. What had the Hadleys done to him?

–You're half-starved, he said. The Hadleys hadn't looked after Jet at all. His collar was loose round his neck and the shine was gone from his fur. They must've barely fed him. They'd deserted him, just like they'd deserted Jake.

Back in the shed, he looked along the shelves. There were

the tins of dog food, just like always. He pulled back the rings on two, emptied them on to the floor, and watched Jet wolf them down. Then he refilled the water bowl at the tap and watched his dog drink.

He looked towards the bottom of the garden where the brambles tangled, and his mum had her compost piles and his dad had his sawhorse. He looked across the tall grass to the remains of his mother's vegetable garden. He would give anything to stay here and play with Jet, even just for a few minutes.

He heard the minibus before he saw it: a flash of blue and red as it passed the house. But he knew what it was. Where it had come from, where it was going, and who it was looking for, and in an instant he was on his feet. He took two tins of dog food from the shelf and stuffed them into the rucksack. Then, grabbing Jet's lead from inside the shed door, he took a last, quick look at his home.

–Time to go, he said, and with Jet at his heels he ran between the brambles to the gap in the fence and through.

Four

He was running, keeping Jet on a tight lead beside him, weaving through the supermarket car park, round parked cars, listening out for the minibus siren, expecting any minute to see it loom up in front of him. A whole life ago, he used to play out here. What to do next? Where to go? Mr Hadley's voice was still sounding in his head, booming and angry: *They're coming for you.* And they were, Jake knew. They were only streets away and they had him on their screen. They were coming to grab him, and he'd be taken back to the Academy, given years extra on his loan tariff for this and he'd never see Jet again. Jet would be locked in that shed and they'd treat him cruelly, and he wouldn't understand why.

–Stop it, he told himself. –Think.

Because there was something at the back of his mind, something someone had said that could help him escape right here and now. If only he could remember.

They talked a lot about escape in the Academy, the teachers and the students. –Don't attempt a departure. That's what the teachers told them. They called it 'departure' because escape made the Academy sound like a prison. But nobody was fooled. The Academy *was* a prison. So escape was what it was.

But it wasn't only the teachers. The boys in the dormitory didn't say much different. There was no point escaping because they just hubbed you and brought you back. Besides, they said, you'd have to be in the countryside, and that was where the virus was, and who wanted to risk getting cancer, or growing an extra head. They'd all seen the pictures. One of them told a story about a boy who'd escaped for two days before they caught him. He'd hidden in the river, breathing through a straw, but they still found him. He had to go up before the Headteacher and she added another whole year to his tariff.

Only JoJo had said different.

Jake pictured him: a small, geeky boy with big ears and a limp, who nobody paid any attention to. But Jake was paying attention now, standing stock-still beside a big, posh car, because JoJo had told them something else as well, and that's what Jake was trying to remember.

He slapped his head. –Think!

Then he remembered. Junkyards. That's what JoJo had said.

–Junkyards is where you can be safe, he'd told them. All that metal. It messes with the hubbing, all that magnet stuff. You get inside one of them, they can't track you.

–Cheers, JoJo, the boys had said. –No problem. And they'd laughed at him, because finding a junkyard was the least of it.

–Course, Jake said now. –The junkyard. And Jet wagged his tail like it was the best thing he'd heard in ages.

They were past the supermarket entrance, round by the vast blank walls to the back. This was where the lorries parked up to unload. They used to do stunts off the loading ramp, Jake and his mates. His mum had found out once and he'd got into trouble. Did he know how dangerous it was? But it was nothing to the danger he was in right now, and he'd have given anything to have his mum march down and shout at him and order him home.

But his mum was dead, and his dad was dead, and there was only him and Jet.

–Let's stop here a minute. I gotta catch my breath, he said, and he made Jet sit beside him while he hunched in the shadows between two huge container lorries. 'Eat English', it read on their sides, and there was a picture of a family eating a roast dinner. Jake stroked Jet's head. –Good boy, he said.

Then he heard it. The hub-van siren. It was playing 'Our English Shores', just one line of it, over and over: 'Our English Shores stand clean and proud, Our English Shores stand clean and proud . . .'

–That horrible song. That's what his mother had always called it. You had to learn it in Reception class, everybody did, and then you had to sing it every morning after Register, all the verses. In the Academy they'd stood at the end of their beds and sung it before breakfast every morning.

It was close, the siren. Too close.

–We got to get out of here. Now, he said. He tried to picture things. Where was the junkyard? On the edge of town, but which edge?

There was the siren again. He hadn't got much time. Minutes, maybe. He got to his feet and his legs nearly went from under him.

–It's no good, he said to Jet, and he shoved his hands into his pockets. A finger snagged on something sharp. A plastic edge. He tugged it out, and there in his hand was his school bus pass. Stuck useless in his pocket these past months. There he was in the photo, six months younger, or more, and grinning.

Grinning. That was weird. But it gave him an idea, and next thing he was walking, head up, dog by his side, round the edge of the car park. Like he had every right to, like he didn't have a care, like there was no hub van hunting him.

The bus stop was one of those semi-Perspex, see-through shelters, and he could see a couple of people stood waiting, staying out of the rain.

–Best behaviour, he said to Jet, and they went and stood there too. Jake tried not to look behind, back at the supermarket; tried not to see if they'd spotted him. His heart was thumping in his chest and he tried to calm his breathing. He shuffled up closer to read the bus stop news screen:

Virus inoculations held ready at secret location . . . Chief scientific adviser calls for volunteers . . . Deal brokered . . .

Jake tried to be less conspicuous. Not that it would matter if they'd got him on their hub screen. Couldn't hide then.

A man looked round at him. –You not at school? He didn't sound hostile, just curious.

Jake thought quickly. It must look odd, a boy his age, and with a dog. –My dog's sick, he said. –Taking him to the vet.

Jet looked scraggy enough for this to be true. The man shrugged.

And then Jake had a brainwave. –She said it's out by the junkyard, but I forgot to ask which bus. Do you know, by any chance, sir?

He didn't know if it was the 'sir' that did it, but the man got nicer then, and looked down the stop lists and told him he thought it was the number 37. The digital readout said the next number 37 was three minutes away.

The man went back to reading the news on the screen: 'Three arrested for virus violation' . . . 'PM hosts Allied Security Talks', Jake read.

His dad always used to tell Jake why the screens were wrong, but Jake didn't care any more. It didn't matter what his dad thought. His heart thumped hard as he and Jet waited on.

He nearly shouted with relief when the bus came. Three minutes on the dot, but it felt like hours. The doors opened and he climbed on, pulled out his pass. He recognized the driver. He was a real stickler. He often drove the school bus, but he didn't like kids.

Jake held out his pass and the driver looked at it, then back at Jake.

–Expired, the driver said. –A week ago.

From behind came the sound of a booming, tannoy voice: *Hub violation. Hub violation.*

Jake looked down at Jet, standing patiently by his side. He put a hand to his head, stroked his soft ears and the dog looked up at him and gave a single thump with his tail. Jake felt hollow. It was no good. The driver would have heard the tannoy too, and it wouldn't be hard for him to guess who it was shouting about. He couldn't escape. He could feel the tears at the back of his eyes. He didn't want the driver to see him cry.

He turned to get off.

–Where you headed? The driver spoke quietly.

–The junkyard, Jake said, turning back. –My dog's ill and my mum said—

The driver waved a hand at him. –I don't want to know.

Less I know, the better. Just get off when I say. There's a field, some horses. Cross the field and you'll see the junkyard.

–Thank you, Jake said.

–I'm not scanning your pass. And I'm sorry for your loss, lad, the driver said.

Jake stared at him. He didn't know how the man could know. But the words gave him a pain in his chest that was nearly sharp.

The driver gestured. –Go on then, he said. –Sit upstairs. Somewhere in the middle.

Passengers got on, got off, but none of them looked twice at the boy seated halfway along with his head down, pretending to doze; none of them even saw his dog, curled up on the floor by the window.

No talking, eyes forward, sit up straight, the teachers told them. The teachers sat on chairs at each end of each row, like a lot of vultures. He wasn't the only one crying. He could hear others around him. They were cross-legged on the floor in rows, maybe thirty children, in the middle of a huge hall. It was late, past his bedtime, and he could see one of the littler ones rubbing her eyes. She looked ready to fall asleep right where she was, there on the floor with the dustballs.

On a stage at the front was a lady in a black gown. She had long black hair and thin, sharp eyebrows. He found out later that she was the Headteacher. She was watching them all; he could see her eyes moving from child to child, and when she got to him, Jake saw that she looked at him for a long time.

–Welcome to your Home Academy, she said. –This is where you live now. Your only home. If you honour us and our rules, and if you honour your loan, and if you honour your country, then we will honour you. She pointed to the big wooden boards on the walls. Jake had seen these when he came in, with their golden lists of names and dates. –Then one day perhaps you will be one of these students, our Heroes.

Jake watched her talk. She paced across the stage to make her gown billow out behind her.

–You will feel homesick for a while, she said. –That's only natural. But the feeling will pass if you do as we say, and then you will understand that you belong here. Remember: *We watch you from the cradle to the grave.*

Jake listened to the murmur round the hall: everyone knew that one. You learned it before anything else. Before nursery rhymes, even. *Witch lady*, he thought. *My mum would've knocked you down, just like that.* He smiled because he'd never seen his mum hit anything. But he knew she would have, if she'd needed to.

Wish you could've clobbered something, he thought. *Maybe you wouldn't have died, then. Wish you could've, Mum.* And while the Headteacher went on with her speech, he cried inside for his mother and he cried inside for his father, his heart burning in his chest, and he didn't move a muscle and he didn't look away.

How long she talked for, Jake didn't know: they'd taken away his mobile, and his watch was in his trunk for safety. By the time she stopped, half the children were asleep where they sat. Loads of them would be too young to understand, anyway.

Jake didn't know if everybody had had their tribunal that day, like him. He didn't know which of them had a mum still, or a dad. Maybe some of them had brothers and sisters right here. There couldn't be many like him that had nobody. But when the Headteacher clapped her hands, as they all filed out, every single child looked alone.

When the bus driver shouted for him, he was drifting, half dreaming, and he sat up with a start to find that they were right out of the town now and the bus had emptied. Outside were warehouses and stretches of empty ground, fenced with barbed wire, full of weeds. No people here, leastways not that Jake could see. Him and Jet, they'd stand out like a sore thumb. *Good thing the Coalition had people scared of the countryside*, he thought, *cos at least it kept them away from places like this*.

–Over there, the driver said, pointing. There were the horses, heads down, grazing, and somewhere over the hill was the junkyard.

The bus door shushed shut, the bus was gone, and boy and dog stood alone.

It didn't take long to skirt the edge of the field, running between the trees, crouching low through the bracken. Then up the slope, and there ahead of them was the junkyard. A chain fence ran round the edge, topped with barbed wire, and there were signs: NO ENTRY. CAUTION: ELECTRIFIED.

–We ain't the first. JoJo must be right, Jake said to his dog, and he felt a faint hope somewhere inside him. Inside the fence he could see cars piled high. They looked like the cars in his old toy box, stacked in a heap like that.

–Get in there and we're safe.

But there was no way to get over the fence, so they had to get in at the front somehow, and fast. The hub police hadn't found him yet, but they would. He knew they would.

*

They hid behind a stack of rusted metal girders piled to one side of the gates, watching.

The entrance had high metal gates with jagged iron points. The gates were clamped shut across with a sign attached saying REPORT TO OFFICE, and underneath it an entry phone. There was a shed inside with a wonky chimney and a thin line of smoke rising.

–Don't think they'd let in a boy and a dog, Jake said. –Gonna have to be clever, Jet.

A lorry approached, and inside the shed a man pressed a button. Less than a minute for the lorry to be in and the gates closed again behind.

–Next lorry, we're in, Jake whispered to Jet. –Gotta be ready. Gotta move fast.

It wasn't long before the next lorry came, and he braced himself.

–Good lad, he whispered. Like a runner off the blocks. That's what his dad would've said if he'd seen him, hands flat to the ground, balanced on the balls of his feet, ready to run. His cut hand was throbbing, but he was listening so hard, waiting for the lorry to pull up at the gates, that he barely noticed the pain.

The lorry pulled up at the barrier, and the driver idled the engine while he got out to press the entry phone button.

Jake and Jet crouched by the lorry's rear wheels, then Jake heard the gears crunch and the lorry was moving.

–Keep in, boy, Jake whispered, –keep in. Because the lorry ran quite tight between the fence posts. Shielded by the lorry's flank, boy and dog were past the barrier, past the hut, and in.

Five

Busy with counterfoils and winches, busy shifting tonnes of clattering, clanking steel, none of the men noticed Jake and Jet slipping into the junkyard's shadows. They clambered in deep, over rusted bonnets and round heaps of twisted metal; and when Jake thought it was deep enough that no one would find them this far in tonight, he found a car with a roof still, and some seats left, and they climbed through the empty windscreen.

A Citroën Picasso, it was, and he took that for a good sign. His grandparents used to drive one of these; he'd seen it in his dad's photo album. *Might've been theirs*, he thought. *Might've been Dad sat here once, when he was my age*, and he let himself pretend for a moment.

Fishing out the biscuits, he divided them up with Jet. There were two tins of dog food left in his rucksack, but he was saving those. In case.

–Beggars can't, he said. –But I'll find you something proper soon. And some water, promise.

They curled up on the back seat and Jake slept, motionless, exhausted, one arm across his dog. When he woke, he'd make a plan. For now, they'd sleep safe. Safe as they could be in a junkyard with the rain pitter-pattering on the roof of an old, rusty car from a time he'd never known.

*

His dad used to say the hubbing wasn't as clever as they made out, and his mum would roll her eyes.

–A Coalition pumped full of its own power, his dad would say. –Thinking it can control us all. But the facts don't match the speeches.

–What facts? Jake used to ask. And he'd see his mum try and catch his dad's eye, to stop him saying more. But his dad would be pacing up and down now, and they both knew that only an earthquake could stop him.

–Number one. They tell you they can locate us at any time, anybody anywhere, from that little chip under the skin. But half the time they haven't got the manpower, and the other half, their tinpot hubbing technology doesn't work.

His mum shook her head. –Not true. That girl in Jake's class who got lost at the seaside. You remember, Jake? They found her because of her hub chip.

His dad waved his mum's words away. –Number two. If we had to, we could cross the border.

–But the border's closed, Jake said. –There's the New Wall across. We saw the photos. They told us about it in Citizenship. About the Faith Bombings, and the Scots attacking, and so we had to build it to keep ourselves safe, and how the Coalition put all the tech in it to keep it secure.

His dad shook his head, and Jake tried again: –What keeps us in keeps them out. Miss McCarthy said so. So we can't just cross it. Like we can't cross the Channel. Same thing.

–We can, his dad said.

–Jonathan, his mum said in her warning voice, but his dad shook his head.

–He needs to know. He's old enough.

–What do I need to know? Jake said, but his mum was

fiddling with her rings, wouldn't meet his eye. –What? he said again.

His mum put her hands flat to the table, as if she'd decided something. –All right. But you mustn't ever speak of this to anyone, not even your friends. Not even Josh or Liam.

–OK, Jake said. This felt serious. He could hear the clock ticking and his mum was looking at him with a dead serious face.

–Promise us, his mum said. –Say it.

–I promise, he said, and he felt daft, but his mum and dad weren't smiling. –Not even Liam or Josh, he added.

Then his dad took a deep breath. –The border's closed, right enough, he said. –Armed guards, all the rest. And yes, one of the men found guilty of the Faith Bombings was Scottish. But Scotland never attacked England. Several of the terrorists were English, for god's sake, but they don't tell you that at school.

His mum took over. –The point is, Jakey, the Coalition was looking for an excuse to build that wall. And the Faith Bombings gave it to them on a plate. They want us to think Scotland is full of terrorists. They want us to think the virus is really bad up there. Europe too. They want us to think that we can't get across the border, and it's true; the guards on this side will shoot if they see you try.

–But what you need to know is that you *can*, his dad said. –It might be dangerous, but you can. If you have to.

–And you could live with your grandparents in Scotland, his mum said. –They'll always look after you, Jacob. You and Jet. She'd used his whole name. Dead serious. –Because if you do go, it has to be both of you. You and Jet, always.

–Sure, Jake said, because why not? He wasn't going to

leave Jet behind ever, was he? Besides which, it wasn't like he was going anywhere further than the rec to play football, not any time soon. –But I wouldn't know them, he said. –I know they live in . . . Appletown, is it?

His mum shook her head. –Applecross, she said. –On the west coast. And your granny'll know you, even if you don't know her. You've never met your grandad, but your granny got a pass down here when you were five. D'you remember? And we had to visit the scan hub after school every day so she could report in as a visiting alien. *Visiting alien*, for god's sake, she said. –This was her country. Visiting alien!

–You'd recognize your granny, Jake, his dad said. –She looks like your mum, only not as pretty and much older.

His mum rolled her eyes. –She knitted you a sweater. You might remember that. You wouldn't take it off for weeks.

–Zigzags, Jake said, and his mum nodded.

–And my green cardigan. She knitted that too.

–So how come you're not worried about them getting the virus? Jake said, and his dad leaned forward, his face dead serious again. He was close as breathing to Jake, as if someone might try to listen in and he whispered:

–The truth is . . .

–Jonathan, his mum said again in her scary stop-whatever-it-is-you-think-you're-doing voice. But his dad went on.

–The truth is, you don't need to worry about the virus. Not here, not across the border. Not anywhere.

Jake laughed, because his dad had just gone weird now. –But you're working on the vaccine, he said. –Both of you. He looked across at his mum. –Mum? Tell him.

But she shook her head. –It's the truth, she said. –We are working on a vaccine, an antidote for something, but it's not for the virus. You don't need to worry about it. And it's best if you tell nobody about it, like you just promised. Nobody. Do you understand me, Jake?

He nodded, swallowing, because suddenly he felt scared.

–And if you do try to get to Scotland, it's got to be you and Jet, both. That's the second promise you've got to make.

–And you, Mum, Jake said. –We'd all go. Wouldn't we?

But they didn't answer him, which, when he thought about it later, was strange, because they had a thing about giving him answers.

–You and Jet, both, his dad said, looking hard at him, and Jake repeated it.

–Me and Jet, both, he said. He was properly scared now, and he looked at his mum for reassurance.

–Remember your promises, was all she said, and she stared at him until he nodded.

–Last thing, his dad said in a gentler voice. –You are everything to us. But you are nothing to the Coalition. They teach you 'cradle to grave', all that rubbish about how they're always watching out for you. Those pictures they get you drawing in Reception. Universal Credit so no one slips through any crack. Personal well-being budget. Don't believe it. When it comes down to it, we don't matter. Only good thing is: how much time are they prepared to spend hunting for any one of us?

That's when his mum put her hand down on the table. –Enough said, she said in her no-messing voice, and although Jake didn't know what his dad was talking about, after that both his mum and his dad seemed to pretend that it was all a bit of nothing.

–Go and walk your dog, his mum said, and when Jake looked back through the kitchen window, he could see them still talking.

*

The smell of food woke him. He checked his watch. He'd slept for four hours and he was weak with hunger, desperate with thirst. The smell was tantalizing.

–Sausages, he said. –It's bloody sausages. He would kill for sausages. Seriously. And like he understood, Jet sniffed the air and thumped his tail.

Jake listened hard. Everything was dead quiet. Not even the rain falling on the car roof. Nobody was hunting for him, he was sure, so he'd risk it and try to steal some sausages. After all, if he didn't find some food soon, he and Jet might as well give up now. He rubbed his neck. –Reckon their hubbing's not as clever as they say. Jo-Jo was right. And Dad.

He would leave Jet safe in the Picasso. Get to the shed. Steal some sausages somehow. Get back to the Picasso. Eat. Hole up till morning.

–Dunno how we'll ever get to Scotland, Jetboy. But we got to try. I promised them I'd try.

Although it was dark now, the sky had cleared and the moon threw a bit of light, enough that Jake could scramble his way towards the hut. He watched it for a bit, but the dusty little window was lit up bright and there wasn't anyone at home.

He wasn't in there for more than a minute. He took some sausages out of the pan, golden-brown, warm. Spread the rest around the pan a bit; took a handful of bread slices; some tins of spam and beans from a cupboard. Stuffed them all into his jacket pockets. Water was the last thing: an empty milk carton under the tap, top screwed on, and then he was gone, just pausing at the door to be sure no one was looking his way.

He divided the sausages and the bread equally between him and Jet, and both ate in ravenous gulps. He opened Jet a can of the dog food, and it went down the same way.

–Didn't touch the sides, he said. –You are one gurt lush dog.

Then a tin of beans, scooping them out with his fingers, one scoop for Jet, one for himself. And when the tin was empty, he filled it with water and held it for Jet to drink from, then stashed it in his rucksack afterwards.

The yard was quiet again, and with the moon behind a cloud it was dark as pitch.

Jake scratched Jet's head between his ears, the place he liked it, until Jet had had enough and shook Jake's hand away.

–Looks like we got away with it. Glad I got you, boy.

He leaned against his dog, breathed in the smell of his fur. It was the smell of home now. The only smell of home he had.

Sharp lights jolted him awake. He didn't know he'd even shut his eyes, but he must have slept again. The lights strobed across the Picasso and he ducked down further. They swung away and he glimpsed men with torches. Their voices were echoing and angry. Jet growled, a long, low sound, and Jake put a hand to his muzzle: a caution. The men hadn't seen them yet, but they'd find them soon enough if they didn't move. No time to think. He pulled on the rucksack, wrapped Jet's lead round his good hand, and slipped out of the Picasso's window. The voices and torch beams moved deeper into the yard, and Jake turned back towards the gates.

Crouching behind a stack of cars, he peered towards the shed. The shadow of a single man moved about: left to guard things, Jake supposed.

We stay, the junk men get us; we leave, it's the hubbers, he thought. Same difference in the end. He saw himself a hero for the day, the other boys crowded around, and then the years ahead in the Home Academy, his escape only a memory. And he saw Jet locked back in that shed, hungry, and mangy and unloved.

He stroked his dog. Felt how thin he was. Somewhere far back in the mountains of scrap metal, he heard the men's laughter. Then he made a decision. Got up and clipped the lead to Jet's collar and took Jet over to the shed. From inside there was the sound of the radio, a song playing, and a man's rough voice joining in. Then Jake slipped the loop in the lead around the shed door handle.

–Sit, Jet, he said. –Stay.

And before he could change his mind, he walked away, towards the gates. The hubbers were bound to catch him in the end, but they didn't have to catch Jet. Jake would end up back in the Home Academy, but maybe the junkyard men would keep Jet. Maybe they'd have him as a mascot. Maybe Jet wouldn't have to go back into that shed.

He didn't slow down and he didn't look back. It was the only way he could do it.

There was a button on top of a post off to one side to open the gates. He'd seen a man press it; it should be easy to find. If he was lucky, the gates would close behind him before the men returned and they wouldn't know he'd left the yard and he'd get a few more hours of freedom before he was caught. Each extra hour meant more solitary when he got back, but it would be worth it.

Behind him, the sounds of the search party grew louder. They were coming back. Shadows loomed in the grey dark and more than once he stumbled. The post must be close by, but he was panicking now. With his back to the gates, he stood still in the dark, his heart thumping.

Think! It was his dad's voice. They were at the climbing wall, and Jake was halfway up with no fingerholds above him, nowhere to go. You're not stuck, you've just stopped thinking, his dad said. Now calm down, and think.

The men sounded very close. He could make out different voices. He had to get out. Then he remembered the keys. He still had the Hadleys' keys. Fishing inside his rucksack for them, he felt the little penlight.

–Please work, he whispered, and he flicked it on. A thin bead of light lit the ground, and seconds later he'd found the pole with its button on top and pressed the button down. Slowly the gates swung open and as soon as there was a boy-sized gap, he slipped out. It didn't much matter where he went because the hubbers would catch up with him in a few hours' time. And anyway, he didn't much care about getting caught, now he'd lost Jet.

Shouldering his rucksack, he set off walking down the road. A half minute later he heard a thud that must be the gates closing and waited for any sounds from the yard. He stopped to listen, but everything was quiet from the scrapyard men. No shouts, even, at finding a dog outside their door.

The rucksack was heavy on his shoulders; it would be lighter without the tins of dog food. So, heavy-hearted, he started to unpack it. He was reaching inside when he felt something rub against his leg. Startled, he swung the rucksack and the something yelped.

–Jet? he said, and there Jet was again, tail beating from side to side, lead trailing between his paws.

–How'd you do that? he said, and he hugged his dog

fiercely. He feared the hubbers for his dog even more than for himself. But with his dog beside him, he didn't feel lonely. Maybe they'd catch him, maybe it would be soon. But with Jet there, he felt he could face anything.

–You and me, Jet, he said. –You and me, always.

They walked through the dead time of the night and the roads were empty. The rain had cleared and the stars were out; there was moon enough to see by. At first Jake strode, to get some distance from the junkyard. But nobody was coming after them, so he slowed his pace. He was too tired to move fast for very long. The cut on his hand was throbbing, but he was glad of it because it helped keep him awake.

They walked alongside the dual carriageway with its dead cat's-eyes, away from the town, keeping to the ditch, or walking slantwise along the embankment above, keeping out of reach of the car headlights. They needed a place to sleep, but it was too cold and too damp just to sleep outside. The warehouses and barbed wire had given way to scratty fields high in grass, or weeds, and every time a car approached, headlights sweeping the way ahead, before he ducked down, Jake hoped to see some shelter lit up: a shed, or a barn. But all he saw were sleeping sheep.

After a time there was a sign: *Services 1 mile*. And below, the images of a cup, and a knife and fork, and a WC sign and a table with a tree. Surely they'd find somewhere to sleep there. He could slip inside and go to the toilets and wash his face in hot water. That would feel good.

Twenty minutes later, the Services were just ahead. Lit up like a bloody Christmas tree, that's what his dad would have said. Jake reckoned the picnic area would be their best bet. He could see a shelter, a building of some sort.

They walked up the slip road towards a big roundabout.

No avoiding the lights now. Jet's black fur shone orange under the glow. There were no cars, so they walked straight across.

At the edge of the car park, he stopped and looked around. The Services seemed deserted. Just a few lorries off to the side, and half a dozen cars dotted about. The cooked air smelled of chip fat and fried meat. The picnic hut was on the far side. They could sleep there.

–Let's go, he said, and that's when they came. Racing across the tarmac, come from nowhere, three hub vans, sirens blaring. Lights hit the car park, seeking lights, brighter and brighter and above his head the roar and whirr of a helicopter. Jake stood paralysed. A voice blasted through the air:

JACOB RILEY. GIVE YOURSELF UP. THINK OF YOUR TARIFF. JACOB RILEY . . .

He ran. It was pointless – he couldn't escape – but still he ran, tearing under the trees, Jet tugging him on. He passed the picnic hut, picnic tables. But the hub vans had screeched up, and the men were closing in and the helicopter had him in its sights, the white lights strobing through the trees. Brambles lashed at his legs and his lungs were burning. Beside him, Jet strained forward on the lead.

–Jacob Riley, stop where you are. Stop, or we shoot the dog.

The voices sounded angry. Jake gripped Jet's lead and ran on. The helicopter lights took away every shadow, every hiding place. The trees ended just ahead, and beyond them he could see what must be a building site. Concrete half-walls, piles of rubble, metal bars, strutwork, great lengths of shiny tubing. The air burned in his chest. The hub men called to each other, and he thought he could nearly feel their breath at his neck. He ducked behind some rubble. A quick glance behind him. The men couldn't see him. Then he dived into the mess of concrete and steel, pulling Jet with him; nowhere left to run.

The blow was to the back of his head, so he didn't see it coming. A hard pain, and hands tugging at him, pulling him under. Then everything slipped away – Jet beside him, the men behind, the concrete, the hard light – and he was gone.

Six

The ground was hard and cold. He was lying face down, and his head was cushioned on something soft: a pillow maybe, except it smelled of the outdoors. Outdoors and something human, like sweat. He didn't open his eyes, but he could tell it was dark. There were small sounds, he thought maybe people moving about, and voices somewhere a little way off. But no sirens, no helicopters.

The back of his head throbbed. He remembered lights and loud noises, and something hitting him. He went to turn over.

–No you don't, a voice said, and hands pinned him in place.

–Let me go, he said, and he struggled to get up. But nobody answered him, and the hands kept their hold.

He was wide awake now and thinking hard. They'd be taking him back to the Home Academy. He'd be punished – a year, more maybe, on his tariff. '*Not punishment, Jacob; education.*' He could hear the Headteacher's voice. Soon he'd be back in the dormitory, back in that bed and the trunk at the end of it, and all the others would ask him how he'd done it, and how far away he'd got, and how'd they catch him. He'd be the big fella for a day, two days, and then it would be over, and he'd still have no mum and no dad, and there'd be nowhere left to go now.

Then he thought of the worst thing.

–Jet, he said, and he couldn't bear it, because they would put Jet back in that shed and they'd starve him again, and he'd die in there on his own.

He didn't mean to say Jet's name out loud, but he must have, because someone answered him this time.

–He's here. We'll give him back to yer, after.

And before he could ask who they were – because the voice was a kid's voice, which didn't make sense and so he wondered: *was he dreaming still?* because they'd hit him on the head, after all – before he could ask, somebody thrust something under his shoulders so they half lifted him off the ground.

–Hold him tight, a voice said, which sounded like a girl's, and all the hands gripped him harder. Then he felt something cold on the back of his neck; and then pain: the sharp, cutting pain of a knife blade. He cried out; he struggled; but he couldn't move.

–He's gonna be sick, someone said, and someone else held a cloth to his mouth.

–Pain in the neck, another voice said, and there was laughing.

–Let me go! he yelled.

–Strong now, boy, someone said and the blade cut him again, and there were fingers digging into his flesh, he could feel them pulling. Bile rose, but he wasn't sick.

–Got it. It was the girl's voice. –Keep the light still, she said, and now he could feel something pressing, and it still hurt a lot, still stung, but not like before. Not so as he wanted to kill someone with the feel of it.

–We can stop holding you down, but you've not to move, else you'll open it up. The girl sounded calm, like she was used to giving orders.

–What've you done to me? he said, but his mouth was so dry the words blurred together.

–It's glued, but you've got to lie still till I say so. D'you understand?

Jake lifted a hand to show he did, then he lay still, and then he must've slept.

Someone was giggling. There were fingers on his clothes, plucking. Fingers in his pockets. Someone was whispering. He flailed out, shouted, and they went away for a little. Something burned. Not a fire, but there was heat and he longed for cold water. For a river, or the sea.

It was quiet when he next woke. They'd turned him over and he lay on his back now. Pain beat through his neck and he didn't try to move. He just opened his eyes. It was nearly dark, but after a minute he could see that he was in a tunnel. The sides were made of stone with green stuff growing on it, and over his head the roof curved in sooty bricks. He could see light pooling at one end. A rough blanket covered him, scratchy against his hands, but he was cold, and despite the pain, he was hungry and thirsty.

–Hey, he said. –Any water?

No one answered him, but something scurried away, and soon after he heard voices.

They sat on either side of him, a girl and a boy. They weren't grown-ups, least he didn't think so, but not kids either. The boy held a torch that swung their shadows up and down the tunnel walls. The girl had a cup of water.

–Drink, she said, and she held it to Jake's lips. He knew her voice. She was the one who had ordered him held down. The cup was tin and the water tasted funny. Most of it slid down his chin, but he swallowed a few mouthfuls. –You can have some more in a minute, she said.

–Where am I? What've you done to me? Jake said.

The boy started to say something, but the girl interrupted him. Her voice was soft and harsh at the same time.

–We're asking first. You give us some answers, then you can have your questions.

They asked him for his name, and where he'd come from, and why he was on the road. They asked him if he'd got parents and he shook his head.

–They dead, then? the girl said, and he nodded. –Long time ago?

–September.

–Illness or accident?

–Accident. Both of them. A car accident on the way home from work.

–What about the dog?

Jake's heart jumped. They couldn't have hurt Jet. They *couldn't* have. –He's called Jet. He's mine since he was a puppy. I rescued him yesterday. They had him locked in the shed.

–He's a problem, the girl said. –We've got to find him food too now, and he could give us away, barking.

Relief flooded through Jake. –I've got tins of dog food in my rucksack. And after that I can find him food. And he's quiet when I tell him, always. Jake's voice was husky and his throat felt raw. –Anyway, I'm not asking you to do anything for him, or me.

–He can stay fer now, the boy said, and he turned and shouted something down the tunnel. They must have had Jet waiting outside, because almost immediately Jake could hear him, his claws scuffling at the tunnel floor, giving little yips of excitement.

–Whoa, easy, a voice said. A younger boy's voice, younger than the others. Then Jet was there, nuzzling Jake's cheek with his nose.

He stroked Jet's head, scratched his ears. –Lie down, Jake said. Because partly he wanted to show them how obedient Jet was, and partly he needed Jet to be still, on account of his neck hurting so much.

–Nice dog, the younger boy said, leaning in close. He kept flicking his hand across his face, like he was on his way to hitting himself, but the others didn't seem to notice. –We going to keep it? We going to eat it?

–Zip it, Davie. You'll freak him out. Shove off, the girl said, and the boy flicked his hand across his face a last time, gave Jet a last stroke, and disappeared.

Lying on his back, unable to turn his head, and with only the boy's torchlight, Jake couldn't see very much of his captors, and what he could see he didn't understand. They were wearing weird clothes, and parkas, and the girl wore a green beanie, pulled right down near to her eyes. The girl was pale like a ghost, her skin nearly white. And as pale as she was, the boy was dark, black skin and black hair. His hair was all matted up and in braids.

–Where's the grown-ups? Jake said. –Who are you?

It was the boy who answered. –I'm Poacher and she's called Swift. Because she's the fastest. And there ain't no grown-ups here. Not like you mean, anyway.

–What've you done to me? Jake said.

The boy – Poacher – leaned in towards him. He had some stubble on his face and his hair smelled – not nasty, just smelly. –Slow down with the questions, will yer? Only yer not giving us time to answer you. They had yer in their sights. Hub vans, helicopter, the business. Put the wind up them, yer must've. We rescued yer. Yer'd be back in your Home Academy by now if we hadn't.

–But how'd you know I was there?

–Chance, the girl said. –Just chance. You were lucky. Our lookout spotted you more than a mile off.

–If we'd seen 'em coming sooner, we'd have grabbed you sooner, Poacher said. –Near thing. That's why we had to do it straightaway.

Now Jake grew frightened. He touched the back of his neck. There was a bandage over the cutting they'd done, and his fingers came away sticky. –Do what? he said.

They didn't answer at once, and in that pause his fear grew huge, and he couldn't get his breath, and his skin went cold.

–What've you done? he said.

–We'd have told yer before, if we could, Poacher said. –But there wan't time. They'd have had you by now if we hadn't done it quick, and maybe they'd have got us too. Couldn't let that happen. So we took out yer hub chip. Stuck you with superglue. Works good. Better than stitches out here.

Jake's heart was banging so hard, he thought they'd hear it, sitting on each side of him. He was scared, and he was bewildered because he knew, everybody knew, you couldn't just take it out. Everybody had a chip for life, like everybody had a name. Even criminals. Even really bad ones. Cradle to grave. Even the King. Even the Prime Minister. You got it the day you were born, and it was with you when you died.

–I don't understand, he said.

–Simples, Swift said. –If we cut it out and then cut it in two, then they can't find you. Then no one can track you down.

–But it's mine, Jake said. –You can't do that.

Because your chip was how you got watched, for sure, but it was how you got looked after too. What if you got ill? Or needed school dinners? And what about when you were a grown-up and you needed a job, or somewhere to live? What about registering your mobile? It was true he was trying to escape from the hub vans and he didn't want to be caught. But if it was going to get taken out, that was his decision, not someone else's decision, someone he'd never even met before.

–I want it back, he said, and he knew his fear was there in his voice because he felt Jet shift beside him, heard the growl in his throat. But Swift nodded.

–OK, she said at once. –Shine it over here, Poacher, so dog boy can see. And she fished in her pocket. –Here you go.

In the palm of her hand was a bit of white plastic, cut into two, like the two halves of an old sim card. –Cleaned it up a bit, she said. –The blood and that. Anyway, you don't like what we've done, you'll be fine to get up in a few hours and you can take yourself off to the nearest hub post and tell your tale, and they'll fit you a new one, take you back in, send you back to your Home Academy.

–Yer gotta cut him some slack, Poacher said. –Got a lot to get his head around. Yer an' me been there too, once.

–There isn't time for slack, Swift said. –You know that. We shouldn't even still be here. It's only because of him. We need to be moving on.

Poacher put his hand on Jake's shoulder, just for a second. –Sleep again, dog boy, yer'll feel better tonight. Martha's put some moss on yer hand, on the cut. Was going nasty, but it's good now. We'll bring yer some food in a while. We ain't going anywhere till dark. But by nightfall, yer gotta decide. Yer want to come with us, yer want to stay here, whichever.

–You going? Jake said.

–Stuff to do. Poacher patted Jet's head. –Keep yer warm, won't he. Then he put his hands together like he was praying, gave a little bow, and he was gone.

This was the old dark again. The black tar dark of Jake's nightmares. The dark before Jet arrived, when sometimes, even with the light on the landing, he got too frightened and he'd run down the stairs and his mum or his dad would take him up again, tuck him in, kiss him on the forehead.

–Wish Dad was here, he said into the dark, and the dark seemed to swallow up his voice.

Somebody kicked his foot, broke his dream.

–Hey, dog boy. Poacher says eat this, and then you've got to stay or go.

Jake shook the sleep from his head. It was the younger boy kneeling beside him. He was dressed in denim shorts cut off below the knee and a pair of wellington boots and what looked like a donkey jacket with the arms chopped off. Round his waist was knotted an old waterproof jacket, and he too wore a beanie.

The boy held a torch in one hand and a plastic fast food tray in the other. He shone the torch at Jake's face, then swerved it away around the tunnel. –Far as I care, you can go, he said.

Jake could see the paper wrappings and cardboard folds, the yellow logo. He was ravenous and the food smelled good. He pushed himself up on one shoulder.

The boy set the food and a bottle of water down beside him. –It's for the dog too, he said.

Jake nodded. His neck hurt when he moved, but he wasn't going to show it in front of this boy.

The boy took a tea light from his pocket and struck a match, jerking it in towards Jake's face, and away, and the match went out. He struck another, lit the tea light, set it on the concrete and handed Jake the box of matches. Then he left.

The tea light picked out Jake's hands as he opened the food. It lit Jet's face and his twitching nose as he sat on his haunches, watching every movement.

–Even Stevens, Jake said. –Don't worry, boy.

There were two Big Macs, some McNuggets and a pile of chips. There was a doughnut and half a chocolate muffin. Ketchup had spread on to the doughnut, and one of the Macs had a couple of bites out. Jake grinned. His mum would've died to see them eating this stuff. But nothing had ever smelled as good.

He divided the food and put Jet's on the floor to one side. Then he tapped beside it to signal to the dog he could eat.

When they'd eaten everything, Jake drank a couple of slugs of the water and poured the rest into the plastic tray, set it down for Jet. He listened to his dog drink, the quick slap of his tongue. It reminded him of home. Jet's bowl in the corner of the kitchen. Jake was still thirsty, but Jet needed it more, and he did feel better for the food. Stronger. The pain wasn't so bad now.

He guessed at the time: maybe six o'clock. Not dusk yet, but not so far off. He had to think, to work it out, how long he'd been here.

It wasn't even twenty-four hours, and he'd been out of the

Home Academy less than forty-eight. But his escape, and Jet locked in the shed, and the Hadleys' kitchen: they seemed like years ago. Like another world. He'd thought he'd be a regular boy again by now, in a family, and with a mother and a father. Not his own mum and dad. But better than the Home Academy. Better than a dormitory, and a number on your clothes, and a bell to wake you and a bell for bed, and forty other kids, all of them as sad as you were. And instead he was here in a concrete tunnel, eating chucked-out food and not enough water, and a wound on his neck that was more than a wound, and he had to decide if he was staying or going.

–Devil or the deep blue sea, he said, and Jet thumped with his tail like he understood.

The boy in the donkey jacket was back. –Poacher says it's time, he said, and he swung his head for Jake to follow.

They were waiting for him under the trees. Poacher and Swift were the biggest, and there was another boy bigger than Jake but skinnier, and a girl that looked older; she had a rounded face and grey eyes that seemed to smile at him, even though she didn't know who he was. Then the donkey jacket boy – Davie, they'd called him – and another small one. He counted six of them, total. The bigger kids held long sticks and Poacher and Swift had knives hanging off their belts. Davie stared at Jake like his eyes were a weapon: they were green and unblinking. The littlest one didn't look more than five years old. Jake thought she was a girl, but it was hard to tell. She wore a pair of combats and a too-big hat with ear flaps and a too-big parka. Everyone looked at him except the little girl, who stared at Jet.

Jake tried to walk upright and look strong, but his legs felt wobbly and his neck hurt, especially when the rucksack bumped against it. The gang just stood and waited. Not angry, and not friendly either. So he got to a few feet away and stood, facing them. It was quiet under the trees, and warmer than the tunnel because the sun hadn't set yet. Somewhere there was the roar of traffic. It sounded like the sea.

–Decided? Poacher said.

They were all watching him, all waiting. Even the little girl, if she was a girl, even she was watching him now. He pulled Jet closer, so he could feel his dog warmth against his legs.

–I want to come with you.

And it was like everyone had been holding their breath, and now they all let it out. Two of the kids, the skinny one and Davie, did a high-five, and Poacher grinned.

Swift stepped forward. She hadn't smiled yet. –We've got rules, she said. –If you break them, you're out. We'll tie you up and dump you in a hub station.

Jake nodded, but she hadn't finished.

–The dog can stay if you feed it. She turned to one of the bigger kids, taller than Jake and skinny like a rake. –Ollie, your job to tell dog boy what's what. Tell him the rules. Make sure he understands. Then she turned away and was bending down, beckoning to the little girl.

Jake was scared of Swift and he only spoke because he had to. –Where are we going? he said.

Swift straightened and turned. –Where do you think? she said.

–I dunno. Because there's nowhere safe, is there? Nowhere you can go they won't catch you in the end.

–Nowhere in England, there isn't, no, she said. –Or Wales. And she crouched down again and called out. –Up you get, Cass. So she was a girl.

Cass ran over and Swift hoisted her on to her shoulders. Jake stared at her. Not England and not Wales. Course not. He heard his mum's voice in his head, what she called her stern voice, wanting him to understand something: *Your grandparents will always look after you. Always.*

–Scotland, he said. –You're going to Scotland, like me.

Swift shrugged. –Let's go then, she said, and she set off through the trees, and the rest of the gang followed.

Seven

Swift was at the front carrying Cass on her shoulders, and Poacher was at the back. The gang kept close together, one upon the other's heels. They walked without talking much, the only noise the snap of twigs.

Jake's legs had felt wobbly at first, but once he was walking, he felt stronger. He didn't know where they were going, or how long they'd be walking for, but it was good, for now, not to have to think, or decide anything. It was good just to walk behind Ollie, putting one step in front of the other until he was told to stop.

He'd walked in the countryside with his mum and dad, but never with anybody else. In fact, it was the first time he could remember seeing anybody walking in the countryside. People just didn't do it any more, and when his teacher had gone on about the virus, and rats and mice and stuff, and the poo being airborne, which they all laughed at till the teacher told them what it could do to you, and why you needed to stay away from fields, he'd kept very quiet.

Ollie was tall and gangly, with black curly hair, and he walked like a spider, like he hadn't grown into his legs yet. Jake reckoned he was maybe fourteen: older than him, but younger than Poacher. He wondered when Ollie would tell him the rules.

The sun dropped and night came. Jake zipped his jacket to the chin and kept Jet close. There must be lots of animals here, because he could feel Jet pull and start against the lead.

–Heel, boy, he whispered, and for a minute Jet would walk to heel, and then he'd smell something else and Jake would feel him strain again.

Swift took out a torch and the pace slowed. The torch-light picked out the trees, but it was difficult, at the back of the line, to see the roots and brambles. Jake stumbled again and again, and once he cried out at the scorch of pain from the wound in his neck.

–Give the dog some slack, Poacher whispered from behind. –Then you can follow him. So Jake let Jet trot ahead a few steps, the dog sure-footed, and then where Jet went, Jake followed, and he didn't stumble again.

They went on and on. Jake had no idea how long they walked for, if it was two hours, or four hours, or more. But the night went on being dark and the woods became fields, then back to woods, and still on they went.

Ollie dropped back beside him. –If a car comes, lie in the ditch, he whispered. –Lie flat on your belly with your eyes down. As soon as you see the lights. Then he said: –Poacher said I must tell you the rules. So are you listening?

–Yeah, Jake said.

Ollie's voice was down in the ground, it was so deep, and it was posh. Posh like government voices. Weird, this skinny half-boy and this deep-down posh voice.

–First of all, it's not a rule, but I don't like dogs. I was bitten by one when I was little. I have the scar to show for it. So I'd be grateful if you could keep your dog close to you.

–OK, Jake said. Jet wouldn't hurt anyone, but he wasn't about to wind this boy up and say so now.

–All right. These are the rules. We're Outwalkers, and you're still a bona fide.

–Bona fide?

–Our word for someone living inside Coalition rules. Outwalker gangs have different rules, and if you don't like them, then you stay a bona fide and you don't join us. Do you understand?

–So there are other gangs like you?

–Yes, but we stay apart. Too risky otherwise. And I don't know about other children. I've only seen grown-ups. The gang always comes first. So if you join us, and you break a rule, the leaders can kick you out. That's it. No questions, no second chances. Just out. And we have done it already, kicked kids out.

Jake stared at the lane. The tarmac black slid into the night dark. He didn't want to be left alone in this. –I understand, he said.

–There are four main ones, Ollie said. –Rule one is no technology. Two is be outside. Three is be hidden, and four is obedience to the gang. Say them back to me.

–No technology. Be outside. Be hidden. Obedience. Is that all of them?

–Yup. That's the lot. Rule one, no technology: that's for the same reason that we took out your chip. So they can't find us. No mobiles, pads, helmets, i-glasses, nothing. If you get found with anything, even some retro piece of iPhone crap, you're out. No questions, just out. We know you're clean – we've been through your rucksack – so keep it that way.

–No pad? Jake said. –Not even one for the group?

–Nope.

–So . . . Jake thought a moment. –No mobile means no money. How do we get stuff?

–Have to do without. Make do. Steal.

–OK, Jake said, but he didn't feel it.

–I was rubbish at scrounging when I started. Used to blush even thinking about it. I'm a very good thief now. So if I can do it, you can.

Jake grinned in the dark. –OK, he said again.

–Rule two: you only stop in outside places. Not in places that are part of things any more. You have to be outside and in the countryside.

–So how do we find places? Jake said. Because even on his own it'd be hard, finding a place to sleep every night, and there was a whole bunch of them in the gang.

–It's Poacher and Swift that decide. Poacher mainly, cos he's done it before, more than once. He's got a map of Outwalker routes and safe places. Paper map, of course.

–Done it before? Jake said, but Ollie went on.

–Rule three, he said, –is you've got to stay hidden. It's obvious why. That's why we sometimes travel in the night. That's why only Swift's using a torch now. We don't want to be seen. Four: you have to do what the gang says. If you don't want to do it, then leave.

Jake had been in a gang with his friends at school. They'd come to his house for tea one time. When Andy broke one of their rules, they'd kept him in the gang, because he had the best garden for playing in. This was completely different. They were all kids here, but it wasn't about playing any more.

–So, have you got any questions? Ollie said.

–Yeah, Jake said. He could hear the teacher's voice: *obey the notices, stay out of the countryside.* –What about the virus? Isn't anybody scared they'll catch it?

Ollie took a swipe at the verge. –Maybe. But I'd rather be outside and free and take that risk than give myself up to the hubbers. Anyway, if you don't like it, leave.

Jake remembered how his dad used to say you'd have to inhale rat poo for days even to get a rash. And his mum said it was a Coalition stunt to keep people out of the countryside.

–No, I'm cool with it, he said. –Something else: does the gang walk everywhere? Cos it's going to take a long time on foot.

–We're walking because of you, mate, Ollie said. –We were going to get a ride at the Services. But the hubbers were all over that place, hunting for you, so we had to make another plan.

Jake was glad of the dark then because he hadn't thought about what the gang was doing when it found him, and now he was ashamed and his face felt hot.

–Last thing, Ollie said. –You've got to have a skill. It's not a rule, but you can't be a full member of the gang without one. Little ones don't have to – that's only Cass; she's Swift's little sister – but you do.

–What kind of skill? Jake said.

–Something you can do better than anyone else. Something that the gang needs.

–I got no idea, Jake said.

–So, Poacher: he's got to Scotland before. He's been an Outwalker longest. He gets us into places. And he catches animals and he can make a fire without matches. Swift is the fastest runner, and quick with a knife and quick in the mind. She can look at the stars and maps – Poacher's got these old-fashioned paper ones – and work out which way to go. Don't know where she learned it. Then there's Martha: she's really good at doctoring, and she knows what to get in a chemist's. She knows about plants too, for medicine, and stuff you can eat, like nettles. Davie, he's a major techie;

dunno how since he was in an Academy for years. He knows loads of science. Science isn't much use for the gang, but he knows all about hub systems and that is useful. He's odd, twitchy, but you'll get used to him. Also he can sew things and mend clothes. He helps Martha with her doctoring too. And me, I'm a really good actor, though that doesn't count as a skill. But I'm the cook, and that does. I'm good at it too. You name it, I can cook it. Pavlova, drizzle cake, roast lamb, *risotto ai funghi.*

–What?

–It's Italian. My speciality. Not much chance for it so far, but I live in hope.

–But I don't know what I can do, Jake said, because they had everything covered. Everything he could think of. He felt Ollie's shrug in the dark.

–Not much use having you in the gang if you can't do something, Ollie said. –Nobody stays in without a skill, so you'll find one, I expect.

All night long Swift carried Cass on her shoulders. Each time they stopped, she would crouch to let her down so she could eat a biscuit, have a drink. Each time Cass would walk back to where Jake was and she'd stand and watch Jet, licking her lips, serious and unblinking. Not close enough to touch him, but closer each time. And she wouldn't move till Swift said to climb up again.

Three times they stopped and each time Swift and Poacher would check the compass, look at the map. The girl with the grey eyes and the round face, who must be Martha, brought out a packet of biscuits one time, and another time Poacher passed round a big bottle of orange squash. The third time, there was a sliced loaf.

–We be there soon? Davie said.

–Another hour, Swift said then. –Less, maybe.

–'Bout time, Davie said, but really quiet like it was just for Jake to hear, and he eyeballed Jake, then turned his back.

The last stretch they walked was on a railway line. It must have been a long time since it had been used, because even in the torch beam Jake could see trees and bushes growing between the rails, and grass high as his knees everywhere. After a while it dropped down beside a river – there was the glint of the moon on the water. Once a bird surprised him: a big owl, white-bellied, that bent its wings once and swept silent through the trees above their heads. But most of that night he was so tired, all he could do was keep his eyes on Ollie's back and keep walking. He just took one step and the next, and the railway line stretched on for ever.

–We're there.

Swift's voice took him by surprise. He looked up, and ahead in the lantern light he saw an old train. Three carriages, most of the windows boarded over with planks, sliding doors shut tight.

–How're we going to sleep in that? someone said.

–Gimme a minute, Poacher said, and he took the lantern and disappeared. A few minutes later, one of the boards was slipped from a window and Poacher beckoned from inside. One by one the gang scrambled in, and Poacher slipped the board back in place.

The carriage smelled of old carpet. Poacher had set a torch high up on a luggage rack, and it threw enough light for Jake to see all the way to the end. There were rows of red seats, two and two on either side of the aisle, and at the end a poster offering a FREE refill with your choc-choc muffin and a smiling lady holding one up. Swift spread a plastic sheet down in the luggage bay, put her jacket over it and tucked up the sleeping Cass. Jake watched the others pick places for themselves, curl themselves up on the seats, pull out a blanket.

–Lookout rota, Poacher said. –Swift's going first, then Martha, Ollie, Jake, Davie an' me. He took a timer from his rucksack and a wind-up torch. –One hour on watch. Anythin' strange, wake me. I'm going to sleep by the doors. Time's up, you shake the next person. He looked at Jake, still standing, watching. –Go on, dog boy, get yourself a sleeping place.

Jake lay down beneath a table. The floor was hard and gritty, and it smelled dirty. The timer ticked out the minutes. Someone whispered in their sleep. Outside, a bird shrieked. He put one arm under his head and the other on Jet's flank and closed his eyes. Sleep wrapped around him like a blanket and he slept.

Eight

They walked all that day, and the next, and the next. Not the actual daytimes. But soon as the sun got low in the sky and half through the night sometimes. Then up again soon after the birds' first calls, before the day had started even. They didn't go fast, but they went steadily, sometimes on paths and sometimes not. When they came to gates and stiles, there were the signs, same as always, tacked to every one of them:

WARNING: Virus Danger
Proceed at your own risk.
The Coalition accepts no responsibility for those who walk on this land.
In event of personal infection contact info@virtransics.org

Nearly always, Swift led the way, stopping often to look at her map. She'd set Cass down and do some stretches, drink some squash, but she never, ever complained, and she never asked anyone else to carry her sister. They walked between high rocks and through yellow gorse and through fields thick with tiny flowers. The weather had grown warm, and Jake tied his anorak to his rucksack. The paths were overgrown because nobody walked on them now, so Swift would slash with her stick to clear the way. She got stings and cuts all over her hands and wrists, but she never mentioned them.

Jake was used to walking in the countryside. He'd been for loads of walks with his mum and dad. They'd always told him the warning signs were just a bluff, and when Jake had said: –But my teacher says . . . they told him they knew better than his teacher.

–Look, his dad used to say, swinging his arm around in a circle. –Thanks to the Coalition, we've got it all to ourselves. Enjoy it, Jake. It's the only good thing to come out of it all.

On a walk, Jake knew what you were meant to be looking at because his mum was forever pointing things out to him. Sometimes he'd get annoyed at it, want to be left alone, wished he'd gone skateboarding, but mostly not. Mostly he liked it, even if he pretended not to. –See that hawk? she used to say. –Or that stream? And he'd look above the trees, or he'd see the thread of silver, and climb down the hillside till he could smell the peaty water, and scramble over rocks till he could kneel and dip his hand in and feel the cold water rush over.

But now they were walking to get somewhere else. Not to explore, not to look at anything. Just to move on, move on. They passed a stone circle; you could see it clear as anything. There was even a slanty board, faded writing covered in plastic to tell you all about it. *Look*, Jake wanted to say. But they didn't even pause.

One time the gang took a footpath he remembered taking with his mum and dad. That was creepy. He was keeping his eyes on the ground because the path was rocky and you had to pick your way, and when he looked up, the path had turned and they were in a gorge and he knew the place. He'd been here before, picnicked on a flat rock, and his mum and dad had got into a massive argument. He'd got bored and gone off, scrambled up the rocks. They were nice rocks to climb, with good crimp holds, and he found a cave up there – he could see it right now, the dark patch on the rocks – just big enough for him to sit inside and he'd waited till at last they'd stopped shouting at each other and shouted for him instead. He remembered how he'd made them call for ages before he came out.

The argument was always about the same thing. His mum said they had to stay and his dad said they should go, take their boy and go. Jake had heard it so often, he didn't worry about it.

But now, with the gang, he was glad to get out of there because it was horrible, remembering.

Each night they slept on borrowed floors, and they ate what they could find or steal. One night they slept in a gamekeeper's shed at the edge of some woods, and Poacher and Davie set traps and the next morning Jake woke to find Poacher shaking him.

–Gonna check the traps. We take yer dog with us, he can get some food too.

–All right, Jake said. But watching Jet trot into the trees between Poacher and Davie, he felt black fear rise, and while everyone else slept on, he sat and watched the woods and waited for them to return.

They were back inside the half hour, each of the boys with long sticks over their shoulders, and rabbits strung along the sticks, and Jet walking beside them.

–Breakfast, Poacher said. –But I gotta skin an' draw 'em first. You build a fire?

Jake nodded.

–Got his own breakfast, your dog, Poacher said. –Caught himself a rabbit. Damn quick too.

–Dog's more use than the boy, Davie said.

Jake stroked Jet's head. –Smart boy, he said. –He's never done that before.

–They got the knowledge in 'em, Poacher said. –Don't need no teaching for that. Just need to be hungry.

One night they slept in a barn full of machines, and Poacher took Ollie and Martha on a raiding party. Jake was sitting alone, back against a tractor wheel, when Davie came over. He stood in front of Jake till Jake looked up at him. He was doing a funny thing with his hand, flicking at his forehead like there was something tickling him.

–Hey, dog boy. Bona fide. I been wondering, Davie said. Flick went his hand.

There'd been a girl in Jake's class like Davie. Things came out of her mouth like she couldn't stop them; she used to slam her hand over her mouth, try to keep them in. Jake had steered well clear of her, because the things she said weren't nice, but mostly they were true.

–Cos you been with us a week now. A whole long week. An' I seen all the business with little Cass, an' it's very nice. Now the flicking had grown to a swipe, over and over, a kind of rhythm in it, like he was trying to make his own head turn, but his own head didn't want to. –She's got a sweet thing going there with your dog, but it ain't a thing. Least not your thing. Not your special skill. So what I want to know is what're you doing for us? Cos we been doing plenty for you.

Jake pulled Jet closer, put a hand down to his head. Jet had his ears half-flattened back. Out of the corner of his eye, Jake saw Ollie behind them, listening.

–Anyway, we're all waiting. Cos Ollie says he explained, 'bout the skill. Your skill.

–Yeah, he did, Jake said.

–So watch it, Jakey boy, Davie said, –cos we ain't your family, an' Swift don't give a toss about you. It's only Cass she loves. You don't prove you're worth it, you don't find yourself a skill, she'll keep yer dog, cos Cass is sweet on him an' that's a skill; an' there's the rabbits too. But you: you ain't no earthly use, an' she'll boot you out.

The raiding party came back with bags of scampi and chicken nuggets and frozen carrot slices and oven chips, lifted from the farmer's freezer. They made a fire in the woods and Ollie cooked the food on an old metal sheet.

Davie sat apart, hunched, his hands drumming a silent rhythm into the dead leaves.

–Davie. Martha held out a tub of food for him.

Davie went on with his drumming.

–Come on, Martha said.

His hands were going faster, lifting the leaves.

–Shouldn't do that, he said. –Rabbits is one thing. Chicken nuggets is another.

–Farmer ain't gonna starve, Poacher said.

Davie's hands drummed down on the leaves in a whirr.

–Nor thieves, nor the greedy, will inherit the kingdom of God! The words seemed to burst out of him, and the drumming stopped, and he slumped forward, stilled.

But Poacher was standing over him, and he grabbed Davie and rammed him against a tree. –You calling me a thief? he said, and his voice was scary and thick, and he spoke through his teeth.

–He who steals is a thief. Davie's voice sounded like a machine. Like something speaking that wasn't him. And it sounded matter of fact, not frightened at all.

Poacher had Davie by the collar, his fists under Davie's chin. He looked like he might kill him. Nobody moved. Jake held his breath.

–Poacher? Martha spoke very quietly, but there was something in her voice, something steely: Jake was glad it wasn't his name she'd said. And Poacher shook Davie away from him, like Davie was something dirty, and Davie fell down into the brambles.

–Keep yer god to yerself then, Poacher said, –cos he ain't got a clue about anything. And he took his food off the metal sheet and went and sat apart to eat it.

–Whoa, Jake said. –What was that?

–Happens to Davie sometimes. Like something he can't keep in. Like a pressure in him and he's going to explode if he doesn't speak.

–And what about Poacher? And Martha?

–They put Poacher's dad in prison for stealing, Ollie said quietly. –Money, not chicken nuggets. Poacher says it wasn't his fault. He says it was the only way his dad could get enough for the family. But anyway, that's how Poacher ended up in a Home Academy.

–What about his mum? Jake said.

–I dunno. He's never said he had a mum. But he had a sister. Older. She got sent to the picking fields. But she had asthma, used to suck on one of those machines, Poacher said.

–So?

–Pesticides in the picking fields: they're specially bad if you've got asthma. She got sent to the covered ones. It's worse under the plastic. Then she disappeared. Poacher reckons it killed her, cos he hasn't been able to find her.

–He must be very angry, Jake said.

–Yup, with the Coalition. He wants to murder the Coalition.

–And Martha? She was really quiet, but . . .

–Scary, right? Ollie said. –She always looks out for Davie. You want to be careful, getting into a fight with him, cos you'll have her to reckon with too.

The next night they were in a church and they had bruised bananas and apples from the bins behind a Co-op, and four carrier bags from the bins behind Cheung's Chinese takeaway. The seats in the church were all inside their own boxes.

–Box pews, Martha said. –They're really old.

They sat together in one of the boxes and Martha divvied out the food on a slab.

Swift set Cass down in another pew and fed her bits of food. But after a few mouthfuls, Cass turned her head away, and curled up on the hard wood.

Not enough for body and soul, Jake thought. Another thing his mum used to say.

When they'd all finished eating, Davie climbed up to the pulpit, pulled off his beanie, and opened the Bible. The pages crackled. Davie swiped a hand once through his buzz-cut and began to read. –Suffer the little children, he said. –Suffer them to come unto me, and forbid them not.

He spoke in a quiet voice, and it was like a cold whisper down Jake's spine.

Davie turned the pages and read out again. –Because the young will faint, he said, –and they will get weary, and some of them will even fall down . . .

–Shut it, Davie, Swift said, and she was on her feet, but Martha was there ahead of her, up the pulpit steps, her hand on Davie's collar, her face like thunder. She marched him up the church and through a door at one end.

–Why did he read that out? Jake whispered. –He must've known it'd make her angry.

–He can't help it, Ollie said. –But he's right. Cass is getting weaker.

Then Martha and Davie came out again, and Davie went and spoke to Swift, and after a pause, Swift nodded and they punched knuckles.

They each had a box pew to themselves to sleep in. Jake lay along the narrow pew, his arms tight to his sides. There were cushions on hooks around the box – they were kneelers, Martha said – and he used one for a pillow. Jet curled up at his feet, and when he closed his eyes, he could almost pretend they were back at home, in his old bed. He woke in the night to find a strange, cold arm across his face, but it was only his own.

Another night they found an old horsebox in the far end of a field, up to its ears in sticky grass and nettles. They slept head to tail like fish in a tin, and in the morning Poacher brought eggs, a pile of them snuggled in the hood of his parka.

–Still warm, he said. –Drink 'em down. Then we got to go. All those eggs gone, they'll be looking for us.

Jake ate them warm and raw, and they slipped down his throat like satin.

–An' the dog, Poacher said, and he broke them into Jake's cupped palms for Jet.

Only Cass wouldn't eat one, setting her jaw shut, her chapped lips set in a tight line. But Swift pinned her down. –You have to, she said. Cass twisted this way and that way, and her hair was full of straw, but Swift forced her mouth open and broke the eggs. Cass made no sounds, not a single cry, but Jake could hear her anyway.

Night-times, Jake dreamed of his mother again and again. She was there. He could see her. He could hear her. She'd call to him, or cuff his head like she used to, or grab and hug him before he wriggled free. Then something would wake him, someone crying in their sleep maybe, and he'd feel her disappear. He wanted to batter and shout out, he was so angry with her, because it was him who used to wriggle free. That was what he did, not her. And now she was slipping from him and he couldn't hold on to her.

He kept count of the days, making a new notch each morning on a stick he picked up on the first day with the gang: twelve days, thirteen. His boots rubbed and blisters grew on his feet, on his toes and on his heels. They made him limp and in the evenings Martha put plasters on them. He watched her face. He guessed she must be about Swift's age, but where Swift was hard and tough and wore combats, Martha seemed soft and gentle. She never shouted, not even when she was being scary, and when she smiled, there were dimples in her cheeks. The way she tucked her hair behind her ears – long, dark, curly hair – reminded him of his mum.

–We'll stop soon, she said. –Then the blisters will have a chance to heal.

–Why do we have to stop? he said, because he didn't want to. He wanted to keep on and keep on and get to Scotland and find his grandparents and sleep in a bed with Jet on the floor beside him. He didn't want to wait for anything.

–Because everyone's exhausted, she said. –And your blisters will get worse if we don't.

–I don't care, Jake said. –I just want to—

But Martha cut in on him. –If we don't stop soon, then Cass . . . She trailed off, and Jake remembered Davie's Bible reading: *the young will faint, and some will even fall down.*

–So where? he said. –Where can we stop?

–In an Outwalker place. You'll see, she said.

Nine

It was barely dawn when they left the river, quiet as foxes past the sleeping houses. Over the old bridge and up the hill and they came to a big stretch of grass with a church in the middle. It was the kind of grass that was mown and watched over.

On one side was a line of big old houses with spiked railings at the front. There were signs on the railings:

WARNING!
Keep Out
Dogs Patrolling
Armed Guards
Hubbing in Force on these Premises

His mum, Jake knew, had grown up in a house like this. Back before the partition, before her mum and dad went to Scotland. She said when she was little, ordinary people could live in one of them, whereas now you had to be rich, or in the Coalition Party. She said they didn't have railings or signs then, and when her friends came to visit, they just walked off the pavement and up to the front door and rang on the bell.

–Didn't have hub chips then, either, she told him. –Not when I first went to school.

–But everyone's got a hub chip, he said, because everyone did, even the Prime Minister, even Joe Pensari who played for Man U.

–But nobody did then, she said. –We had to learn a song at school and Mrs Anselm used to swing her yellow skirt when she sang. Mrs Anselm taught me when I was eight. So I know that that's when they first brought in hubbing.

Jake tried to imagine it, everyone going to get chipped, all at once.

–Must've had to queue for ever, he said. –All those people.

–They did the children first. That was why we learned the song: 'Quick, chip, and keep your child safe,' she sang, and she did a funny little dance.

–You just look silly, and it's not a very good tune, Jake said.

–But it was catchy. It got played all the time, everywhere. All over Twitter, all over the Net. Radio, TV, Netviews, everywhere. And it worked. Parents wanted their children safe. I understand that now.

–So you got chipped when you were eight, Jake said.

–Not immediately. Granny and Grandpa didn't like it, you can imagine, but . . . She shrugged. –Two years later it was made compulsory for children under eleven, so I was done then. I was just ten. And five years after that came the partition and the New Wall. Then it was compulsory for everyone. That's when we left, Jake's mum said. –A lot of people left then.

*

The gang walked on past houses with swings on the lawn. Family houses. In the porch of one house Jake saw a skateboard and it made his heart jump: a Santa Cruz, one of the expensive ones. He'd begged for one for years. He looked at the house, its closed curtains. There was a child in there, maybe a boy same age as him, dreaming in a bed, who had a Santa Cruz, and a mother and a father. He put the thought out of his mind and walked on.

About ten minutes later, Swift signalled a stop and the gang waited under some trees while Swift and Poacher looked at the map. Jake unshouldered his rucksack and leaned against a tree. He crouched and put his face into Jet's fur, ruffled his silk ears.

Cass stood near, her arms by her sides, licking her dry lips, like she did all the time. She did this every time they stopped – just stood, hands disappeared in the sleeves of her parka, and stared at Jet. Each time she got a bit closer, though, and this time she was nearly touching him. She had dark shadows under her eyes. She moved slowly and she didn't look like a child.

–You want to stroke him? Jake said. –Look, watch. And he crouched down and stroked Jet's back. He watched Cass's face, but it was like a mask.

–Cass doesn't speak and she doesn't smile, Ollie had told him. –She's got an illness and something bad happened to her because of it. It's why they became Outwalkers, her and Swift.

Jake waited, and slowly Cass put out her hand. He reached and took it, saw her fingernails bitten beyond the quick. –We stroke him together? he said, and she nodded.

Out of the corner of his eye, he saw Davie walk towards

them. –Don't forget, dog boy, he whispered. –Jet's ours now. But you're not.

Jake ignored him. –Gentle now, he said to Cass, and with her hand in his, he stroked Jet again. –Hey, boy, he said to Jet in a low voice, and Jet made a single thump of his tail. –See that? Jake said. –Means he likes you stroking him. And something crossed Cass's face that wasn't a smile, but it was something.

–Time to go. Swift's voice made him jump. He hadn't seen her come over, but he guessed she'd been watching. Watching Cass, and watching Davie. Jake watched her pick up the little girl and hoist her on to her shoulders. And he watched Cass lean forward against her sister's head, arms around Swift's neck. She didn't sit up any more; she didn't look like she could.

–Time to go, Jakey boy, Davie said.

–They'll never get you, Jake whispered to Jet. –Never. If they throw me out and I have to go, you're coming with me. We'll go back to that river and we'll follow it till we get to the sea. Then we'll find a boat, and stow away, and get to Scotland that way. Jet looked up at him, like he'd heard his thoughts and Jake pulled Jet closer, but he was scared.

The hospital had an iron fence around it, ten foot high and spiked on top, stretching as far as you could see, and every fifty yards there was a sign, hammered into the fence:

NO ENTRY, OR HUB VIOLATION
Report a Violation: Freephone:
@6456 321321

The signs were rusty and weeds nearly covered some of the fence; some had big purple flowers, while others looked like brambles. They passed the main gates and Jake could just about make out the board: *Frenchay Hospital*, it said.

It was a strange, forgotten place. Very quiet, like everything was holding its breath. Plants and trees had taken over. They grew out of everywhere: roads, walls, roofs. There were signs for 'Oncology' and 'Maternity' and 'Visitors', but green was twisted around everything so you almost couldn't see what was underneath.

Swift led, and Poacher followed behind, till the lines of buildings gave out and they came to a little roundabout wild with roses. Swift looked at her piece of paper, and turned right. Jake watched Cass, up on Swift's shoulders. She was slumped right forward now, her head bumping against Swift's head with each step. They walked past a long, brick building, graffitied into colour, net curtains still blowing from a window.

–You sure this ain't it? Poacher called.

But Swift pointed ahead with her arm and kept on walking. She was going so fast, it was hard to keep up; Cass looked like a rag doll, up on her shoulders, as if her body had no bones. Past the brick building, through a car park. 'Watch out for thieves', a sign said.

Swift stopped outside a house. *Must've been a really posh house a hundred years ago*, Jake thought. He watched Swift take Cass off her shoulders, whisper something. But Cass was floppy as a doll, eyes shut, head drooping. And Swift's face: he saw Swift's face then, and what he saw was fear.

The house must've had at least twenty bedrooms, and it was tall – three storeys – with high windows and stone leaves carved around the doorway. It had a load of chimneys coming out of the roof. From a distance it looked like it might still be lived in, but closer up and you could see there'd been a fire in there – the whole of the ground floor and the one above were burnt out, holes for windows, the bricks licked black all around them. No front door. The fire must have been a while back, because weeds had grown up through the windows and there were birds flying in and out.

–It's an Outwalker place, Ollie told Jake. –We can stay as long as we need to.

–Looks blinded, poor thing, Martha said.

–Looks skanky, Davie said, and quietly, just to Jake: –your kind of place.

In the hall, where the stairs used to be, there was nothing. Just a hole.

–Ladder's gone, Swift said. –Can't get up without it. Her eyes were wide and desperate. She had Cass cradled in her arms, and Jake hoped Cass was just sleeping.

–We could steal one when it gets dark, Davie said.

–No. Poacher took off his rucksack. He glanced back at Swift and Cass. –We got to be up there now. He studied his piece of paper, walked outside again and looked up at the house, beyond the burned-out windows, up higher to the second floor.

–Fire escape up the top. We kin get up that way. There'll be a ladder. I kin let it down from inside. Give us a leg up, he said, and Ollie went over and put his hands together.

Jake could always tell another climber when he met one. He could tell by the way that they looked at a wall, or a building, or a tree, and he knew already that Poacher wasn't a climber. *He won't get up there*, he thought, and he felt a rush of nerves.

–Why not? It was Swift's voice and Jake ducked his head. He hadn't meant to say it out loud.

–Not much for your fingers to get hold of, he said, but it wasn't that, because there was plenty. It was just that he knew Poacher couldn't.

–He has to, Swift said, and it was like she didn't care if Poacher knew how to climb or didn't.

Poacher had made it from the ground floor up to the first-floor window and he was gripping the lintel with one hand, trainers out to left and right, like a clown's feet on the narrow sill.

–Nicely. Doing all right, isn't he? Ollie said, and Jake saw something pass between Ollie and Davie: a look, an agreement, something.

Shifting his feet along the sill, Poacher felt above him with his fingers. He was searching for something, a pocket between the bricks to get hold of.

–Don't, Jake muttered. –Stop. Because Poacher wouldn't make it and Jake couldn't bear to watch. He crouched down, stroked Jet. Things looked different close to the ground. He watched a tiny spider freefalling from a dock leaf. Easy. He looked back at Poacher. He hadn't moved, and he wasn't hunting for holds any more. He was just holding on.

–Come on Poacher, Martha called out, which got Ollie and Davie going too, all of them calling to him that he could do it.

–Next stop, Everest, Ollie shouted, which got him the finger from Poacher. But when they quietened down again there was silence, and then Poacher's voice, which was small from up there:

–I can't.

It was like he'd punched them in the stomach, winded

them, and all their exhaustion came crashing down. Swift just seemed to crumple and fold over, Cass still in her arms, and Ollie had to grab her with all his skinny strength to keep her from falling. Davie sat down on the ground, his hands in his buzz-cut hair, tugging and tugging, till Martha put her hands over his and spoke to him in a gentle voice.

–Poacher, you have to. We have to get in, Swift said. Her voice was raw.

But Poacher wasn't moving, or barely. Just his fingers scrabbling over and over at the bricks. He was close to freezing, Jake could see it. Not with cold, but with fear. And once you froze, you were a lot more likely to fall.

Poacher would fall on to paving slabs. Hard stone. He'd probably break some bones. They'd have to take him to a hospital, and then it'd be all up with him. They'd put him in a Home Academy, and then the fracking fields, and he'd never get away.

Jake stood and called up. –Poacher, listen to me. He didn't look back at the others. –I'll get you down.

Poacher turned his head, seemed to listen.

–I'll tell you where the holds are and you'll be fine.

Poacher sat on the ground once he was down. Jake could see his hands and legs shaking. The gang all stood in different places, like they had nothing to do with each other, like they weren't a gang at all.

But if someone didn't get into the house, then they were all done for. There was only one thing for it: he knew he had to climb the wall. He took off his rucksack and unlaced Mrs Hadley's walking boots.

–Watcha doing, dog boy? Davie's voice was a snake,

sliding into his ear. –You fall, you're out, and they'll have you snugged back inside an Academy for ever.

–Porca vacca. Davie, leave him alone! Ollie said.

Jake didn't know what it meant, but he was glad of Ollie's support. He took his old plimsolls from his rucksack and pulled them on. He gave Jet's lead to Martha and took a single glance at Cass. She lay motionless, a small bundle of clothes in her sister's arms. He didn't look at Swift. She was too desperate, and it wouldn't help him now. He put his dad's penknife into his pocket, and touched his fingers to his mother's cardigan.

Be careful, Jake. He could hear her so clearly, her voice in his head, and he wished she could tell him not to climb it.

Soon as he started, soon as he was off the ground, his thoughts narrowed down and there was nothing else to think about except this piece of wall and its crevices and cracks and handholds, and him climbing it. It was easier than some of the routes he'd done on the climbing wall; easier than bouldering; and he was up to the first floor quickly. Boards covered the window hole and the bricks were black around it.

He looked back down at everyone. They were all silent and all watching him, all waiting.

He turned back to the wall, looked up. He'd plotted a route when he was on the ground, but now he was here, it didn't look as easy. He reached up with his left hand and got his fingers in between the bricks where the mortar had fallen out. Twisting his fingers, he made a finger jamb and looked for a toehold. A deep dent in one brick was the best he could find and, bracing his leg, he pushed his toes in. Reaching above for another handhold, he gave his weight to the holds he already had. Pain shafted through his blistered foot and he cried out.

–Be careful, Jake! It was his mum's voice again, from somewhere inside. He turned his head to get away from it and his body swung out from the wall so that he hung by one hand and one foot.

He heard the gang gasp. Scrabbling with his free foot, he found a toehold and then, up to the left, he saw a fingerhold. He felt clammy with fear, though he could feel the heat of the sun in the bricks.

He looked down. Swift sat on the ground now, Cass curled in her lap like a small animal, and the others stood with her like a proper gang.

You got to do it, he said to himself. *You got to.* Because the whole gang was depending on it. He reached above him, shoved his fingers into the hold.

He didn't know how long it took for him to climb the last few feet; it seemed like for ever. But as he lifted himself on to the second-floor sill, he heard the shout of voices from below. He looked down and they were cheering him, Davie and Ollie whooping, and Jet barking. So he gave them a thumbs up, then he turned and raised the window sash and climbed in.

It was so quiet inside it was like someone had blocked his ears up. Silence. Nothing moving.

The room had a load of beds in it, but they were strange-looking ones, made out of building pallets, and floorboards, and chunks of tree. And hanging from the walls, tied up to big hooks, were things that looked like beanbags. There was a line of hooks along the wall and some shelves. Blankets on one shelf and paperback books on the one below. Jake's parents had kept some paperbacks. There was a line of them on a shelf in their room. His dad said they'd still been able to buy them new when they were students. Jake had once tried reading one. It was weird, turning pieces of paper over. He'd seen it in films, but it was still weird, actually doing it.

On the bottom shelf was a line of tin cans with small holes punched in their sides, like someone had gone at them with a pair of nail scissors. He picked one up. It had a bit of candle inside. By the door was a sign taped to the wall:

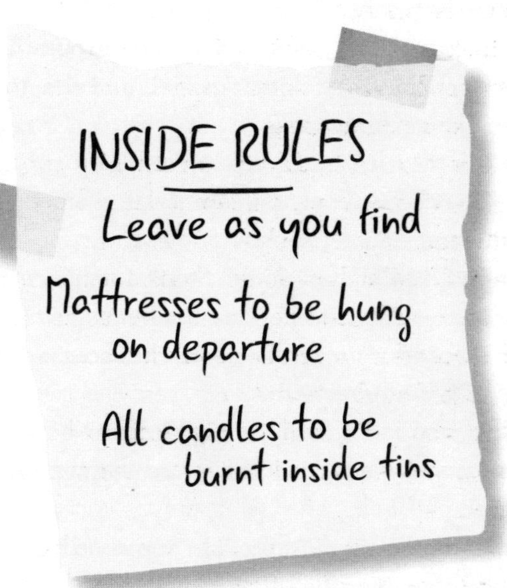

INSIDE RULES
Leave as you find
Mattresses to be hung on departure
All candles to be burnt inside tins

–Course. Not bean bags. Mattresses, he said to himself. And he guessed they were hung up to protect against mice, or something.

The corridor was dark and fusty. He tried another door. It was another huge room. For a moment he couldn't tell what it was for, and then he realized it was a kitchen. Or a sort of kitchen.

–Cool, he said, and he wished his old gang could've seen this, because this was to die for. The cooker was a barbecue built of old bricks with a window grille on top and a heap of wood piled beside it ready, and in the corner was a metal sink big enough to have a bath in. 'Boil water before drinking' it said on the piece of paper above. There were pots and pans hung off hooks on the wall and packing crates on their sides, stacked on top of each other to make a kind of cupboard. There were plates and mugs inside, and on the top there were more tin cans holding cooking utensils. Jake picked out a wooden spoon; you could see the chisel marks and it was lopsided. In another can were knives, made out of wood and stone, and one from a metal ruler. You could still see the inch measurements on the handle.

On the other side of the room was a big oval table. It was shiny and dark, like something out of the TV dramas his mum used to watch: a table from a hundred years ago. Maybe it had always been in the house. Maybe a big family used to sit around it, with lots of children and aunts and uncles and grandparents.

–Jake! It was Poacher's voice, hollering from outside. He'd forgotten for a minute: they were waiting for him down there on the ground. Jake ran down the corridor. Swift had told him what he should find. There was a door at the end, hammered together out of building pallets and lengths of plastic wood. Putting his hands between the pallet slats, he lifted it up, and there was the fire escape door. He pushed it open and stepped out onto the fire escape platform.

The ladder was covered in bird lime. He brushed at it, and it came off in clouds. Now he could see the ladder hinge. And, far below, the gang. Jet saw him and started barking, and Jake saw Poacher try to quieten him.

–Watch out! he called down, and shoving hard with his foot, he pushed the ladder out over the drop.

Moments later, and Swift was climbing up, Cass held tight to her in one arm. She didn't say anything as she came in, but she stared Jake in the eye and gave him a quick nod as she strode on down the corridor.

Davie was about to follow, when Jet broke free of Martha's hold, and before anyone could stop him, he was scrambling up the bottom rungs of the ladder.

–No, Jet. Down, boy! Jake called, but Jet didn't go down. He carried on climbing, his paws scrabbling on the metal rungs. Then Martha was there behind him, covering him as he climbed, and dog and girl climbed up and up together.

At the top, Jet ran at Jake, licking his face, his hands, and Jake thought that Jet must have known that he'd been in danger, climbing.

–Hey, boy, Jake said. –I'm fine.

Once everyone was up, together he and Poacher pulled the ladder back and refastened it.

–Good one, mate, was all Poacher said, and he followed Jake into the building.

Ten

Jake was standing at the kitchen window, staring at the trees, when they grabbed him. He didn't see them coming, and they tied his wrists before he knew what was happening.

They tied the scarf tight around his eyes so he couldn't see anything. Then they tied his wrists in front of him with a piece of twine, and his legs at the ankles. Someone pushed down on his shoulders, forcing him to his knees.

–Don't speak, Martha said softly. –And don't move.

And nobody spoke to him after that, though he could hear them whispering, and he heard their feet on the floor, and things being put down. There was the sound of a match being struck and the crack of twigs burning. A floorboard creaked, then there was silence for ages.

He tried to think. He'd got them in here, and he'd seen Swift's face, and her nod. But she'd marched straight on and put Cass to bed on one of the mattresses. Nobody had smiled. Nobody had said anything, or clapped him on the back, or high-fived him. Ollie hadn't even made a joke. It was strange.

He felt sick in the stomach. Maybe they didn't need him any more, now they were in here, and their plan was to wait till it got dark, then dump him outside a hub station.

Something sharp was pressing into his knee, a piece of grit maybe, and he shuffled a bit to try and dislodge it. He could feel sweat running down his back. They were going to kick him out and hold on to Jet.

Where was Jet?

–Jet, he whispered, and he listened for the shifting of paws, or the thump of a tail, but there was nothing. Silence. *No chance*, he thought. *No way you get him*; and he clenched his fists and set his jaw.

–Jacob Riley, stand!

He didn't recognize the voice, and he shook his head. He didn't want to make their job easier for them.

–Stand! the voice said again.

Jake shook his head, pulled his arms tighter to his body, waited for them to get hold of him, drag him off.

There was silence again, then a sigh. –You have to stand up yerself. We can't do it for yer.

He knew it this time. It was Poacher, but he didn't sound angry. More just a bit impatient.

It wasn't easy, with his hands and his feet tied. His first try, he fell on his face, got a mouthful of floor dust. When he was standing at last, he stood waiting, his heart pounding in his ears, heard the door creak, and then he heard Jet: his claws against the floorboards, his panting. What had they done to his dog? Hands were on him and fear was in his mouth. He had to swallow it down and he would have kicked out except that a small voice somewhere in his head said: *don't*.

Hands loosened the twine round his ankles and wrists, and other hands tugged off the blindfold. They stood in a line before him, the whole gang except Cass. Their faces were solemn and in the firelight he could see dark lines painted on their cheeks and a single circle on their foreheads. Poacher, Swift, Martha, Ollie and Davie. Beside Davie sat Jet, his lead wrapped tight around Davie's hand.

Poacher stepped forward, his hands in front of him barely an inch from his knife. He looked nervous, like he was about to do something terrible. Jake's heart raced. He looked at Jet. If he was quick, they could make a run for it. He'd grab Jet's lead and go for the gap between Martha and Ollie. Out the door, down the corridor. He was fast and Jet was faster: he could be down that fire escape before they'd decided what to do. He'd head for the bushes, and Jet would find the hole under the fence, or another one, then they'd go back to the river and on towards the sea . . .

–Jacob Riley, you have proved yerself today. And you've earned yer place as an Outwalker. We stand with you, and you stand with us.

Poacher's words came to him through a mist.

–What? he said. –What did you say?

–He said you've got your place. That was Swift and her voice sounded funny. A bit broken up. –You're not a bona fide any more. You're one of us now.

They crowded round him, and Martha hugged him and Davie gave him back Jet's lead.

–Respect to you, Davie said. –You done the stuff of which I spoke, and he put his hand out.

–But there's still one last thing we have to do, Swift said, and she nodded at Poacher.

–When we found yer, Poacher said, we cut your hub chip from yer and so you didn't belong nowhere. But today we'll give you a new mark and you'll belong with us.

Jake's throat was tight and he blinked a few times to clear his eyes. –What mark? he said.

–Show him, Ollie, Poacher said, and Ollie knelt down in front of him and undid the top buttons on his shirt. Yanking it down at the back, he bowed his head, so that Jake could see the narrow scar on his neck where his hub chip had been cut out. But there, below the scar, was something else: a small, tattooed circle with a dark dot at the centre.

–That's what, Poacher said. –Davie's gonna do it. Got a good hand with the needle.

–I'll do it designer quality, Davie said.

–The Outwalker mark, Ollie said. –Means you're properly one of us now. Not a bona fide any more, but an Outwalker. Inside the gang, and outside everything else.

Eleven

Over the next few days, Cass slept and Swift sat beside her, and the rest of the gang took possession of the house. It became their place, and they could do ordinary things in there: the kind of things Jake used to do without even thinking. They took down the other mattresses hanging on the walls, and they slept whole nights through on proper beds, beneath the heavy hospital blankets. They washed clothes and had baths. Not real baths, but still a sink full of hot water each, and soap and some shampoo that Poacher found. Martha cut everybody's hair. She even cut all of Ollie's black curls off.

–Go easy, Jake said, as the first curls hit the floor.

–No, cut it close, Ollie said in a curt voice. Then Jake remembered Davie's teasing a few days before. 'Such a pretty boy', he'd called Ollie.

Martha pointed at Jet with her scissors. –You can stop giving me advice and give that dog a bath, she said. –He stinks.

Jake hadn't even noticed, but the water went brown with dirt, and gritty, and Jet's fur went all fluffy after.

Martha collected plants and bits of bark and put them out to dry for medicines. Poacher put up rotas for foraging and they went out at dawn and at dusk with empty rucksacks and they brought back wood to cook with, and eggs and cheese and meat and proper vegetables – onions, potatoes, carrots – that Ollie cooked up into soup and stew.

–You cook like a dancer, Martha said, and Jake knew what she meant. Most of the time, Ollie's hands and his feet seemed like they were too big for him. His elbows and his knees got in the way when he was climbing, and he ran all knock-kneed. But cooking: Jake could've watched him for hours because Martha was right. When he was cooking, Ollie moved like a dancer.

On their third day there, Martha pinned another piece of paper next to Poacher's, and wrote at the top: *Needs*.

–Anything you need and you have to get in a shop, she said. –Write it down here.

–Like Wrigleys and chocolate, Jake said.

–No, not like Wrigleys or chocolate. Like safety pins, and blister plasters for the boy with the tender feet, Jake. You steal sweets, that's how you'll get caught, because they expect you to do exactly that. So don't.

Jake didn't know why she'd lectured him, till Poacher took him out foraging at dawn the next day.

–We gotta get you some spares, Poacher said. –Cos Martha's gonna take you with her when she goes to town. Be in a few days' time.

–What's spares? Jake said.

–Spare clothes. You ain't got any, you got to nick 'em. Clothes lines is good now it's nearly summer. Trousers, shirt, tie, sweater. Not a hoodie. You gotta be nicely dressed. You keep them folded in your rucksack and you only put 'em on before we go into a town.

–Shirt and tie? Jake said.

–Keeps yer neck hidden. Anyone sees a scar where yer hub chip should be, it'll put the wind up. Martha's tops to go stealing with cos they don't notice her. She looks too nice.

–But why me? Jake said. He could feel his heart racing. He hadn't been near people – ordinary people – since they cut his hub chip out. What if they guessed about him? –What if I'm no good at it?

–Like I said, Martha's tops. You do what she says, you'll be fine. But we gotta get you more clothes cos you don't look good. Poacher tugged at Jake's jacket, kicked a foot at his trousers. –You go in looking like that, they'll call in the hubbers straight off, arrest you for vagrancy.

The Santa Cruz was still there in the porch, and the house was asleep just like the last time, curtains drawn. Jake and Poacher made their way round the side, past the climbing frame, past the swing, their shoes leaving trails in the dew.

–Bingo, Poacher said, and through a window Jake saw a pile of clothes stacked neatly on the ironing board. –All ready for yer.

Jake checked the back door. –Locked, he said.

Crouching down, Poacher peered through the keyhole. –Easy. He took a piece of wire from a pocket and poked it through the lock till Jake heard the key drop out. Poacher pushed his hand through the cat flap. –There you go. He gave Jake the key.

Inside, Jake found a pair of black trousers, a white shirt and a blue V-neck sweater, all about his size, in the pile. They looked like school clothes. Poacher locked the door again from the outside and slipped the key back through the cat flap.

–They'll think it just fell out the lock, he said.

Jake glanced up at the curtained windows. A boy slept inside one of those rooms. *Could be me*, he thought. *Could be me with the garden and the swing, and a pad with all the games on it, and a mobile, and the Santa Cruz; and him out here, dead parents, scrounging other people's clothes, on the run.* There was the skateboard, leaned up against the porch, like it was the simplest thing in the world to own it. He took a few steps towards it.

–Don't. Poacher's voice was a whisper.

Jake paused, looked back.

Poacher shook his head. –Security powder, he said. –You get that stuff on yer, it won't come off. Not worth the risk.

Jake took a last look at the house as they walked away. In an upstairs window, somewhere behind the curtains, the other boy slept on.

Davie had set up a mending shop at the kitchen table, darning and patching and sewing. Soon as clothes were washed and dried, Davie did repairs. He sat near the window for the good light and shouted if you blocked it, even for a second.

Davie did the tiniest stitches Jake had ever seen, his hands so steady and so still; and the whole time he was sewing, Jake didn't see him flick at his forehead or swipe his hand across his face. He just looked calm. Really calm. *First time*, Jake thought. He watched Davie sewing. Noticed his fingers.

–How'd you keep your fingernails so clean? he said.

–See here? Davie said, ignoring the question. He was holding out an old T-shirt. It was a pink, threadbare thing with a faded picture of a kitten, and it had been sewn up before. –It's Poacher's. Check out the name.

Sewn into the neck was a name label, the kind you have to put into school clothes. It said: *Lily Brown*.

–Poacher's? Jake said. He didn't understand.

–Was his sister's, Davie said. –Lily, she was.

Jake stared at the T-shirt. It made him sad. Poacher's dead sister and just this scrap of a T-shirt left to Poacher. All of them, carrying their scraps.

Davie let down the hems on Jake's spare trousers, and sewed up a tear in the back of his jacket, where he'd caught it on barbed wire. He made a tie for Jake to wear with his spares.

–Poacher's orders, he said. You got to look like a good boy, Jakie.

Davie wrote down 'Strong White Thread' on Martha's Needs list. And he wrote 'New Needles' and 'Green Darning Wool'.

–Why green? Martha said. And Davie pointed at Jake.

–Cardigan in his rucksack. Got a hole in the elbow. Noticed it when we went through it, after we rescued him.

Davie had been nice since Jake got his tattoo, but he was like a firework. You didn't know when he'd be pretty, or when he'd go off in your face.

–I can darn it for you, we get the right wool. You won't know there was a hole, Davie said.

It was an apology, close as Davie would get, Jake knew that. But he shook his head. His mum used to wear the cardigan for gardening. He didn't want the hole mended.

–Leave it alone, he said. –And don't go looking through my stuff again.

Ollie made a draughts board from a piece of cardboard and taught Jake how to play. Ollie's fingers, long and spindly, moving around the counters, looked like spiders. At night they pulled the blackout blinds and everyone except Cass played card games in the candlelight at the table: Cheat and Happy Families. It was nearly three weeks since Jake had escaped from the Home Academy, but it felt like longer. This gang had become his family.

One night, Swift brought Cass to the table, and the little girl sat on Swift's lap, every so often licking her lips; she watched them play, but mostly she watched Jet. When he was close enough, she stroked him like she'd done with Jake. Even in the candlelight, Jake could see she looked better, the shadows under her eyes nearly gone, her lips less chapped, and when Swift won the most families, Cass clapped her hands together.

In the mornings, Jake took Jet outside and threw sticks for him. It was the first time they'd done this since before his mum and dad had died. They went out very early before the moon had gone from the sky. The dew was still like diamonds on the wild grass, and Jet ran trails through it.

–Wild dog, Jake would say to Jet with the stick in his hand, and his arm lifted, ready to throw. –Crazy dog. And Jet would turn and turn about his own tail, ears sharp, muzzle high, doing his dog dance.

Jet would have run all day, if Jake had let him.

On the fifth morning, Jet ran for the stick, and picked it out of the grass, and tossed it about like a live thing; and then something made him pause and drop the stick and lift his head, and stare at a patch of nettles.

Jake thought at first it was another dog.

It was a fox. A young dog-fox. Whip-thin, slender as an eel, its brush tipped with white.

Jet stood stock-still, ears up, tail back. Closer the fox came, only a few feet away now, its thick brush low, its dark ears flicking at every crackle of the grass, every wind shift. It lay down, paws in front, and suddenly Jake understood.

–You want to play!

Still Jet paused, and then he bounded at the fox, and the fox switch-backed away, sharp as lightning, and Jake watched them chase and zigzag through the grass.

A sound behind him – Poacher's soft step on to the fire escape – and the fox was gone.

–Could a' bitten him, Poacher said. –You should a' called yer dog away.

–They were playing, Jake said. –Just playing.

–An' the virus? Kind a' game would that be, ay?

And before Jake could reply, that the virus wasn't real, Poacher had gone back inside.

On their sixth day in the house, Ollie took Jake hunting for herbs. They found thyme – Ollie made him taste it – and wild rosemary growing near the house. The sun was high, and they took off their shirts and sat with their backs to the warm bricks.

–Shut your eyes, it could be Nice, Ollie said. –Could be Positano.

–Where?

–Somewhere hot and chic and foreign. About as far from here as I can imagine.

With the sun on his face, Jake shut his eyes. The air smelled sweet.

–So how come you know how to cook things?

–Best way to make sure you get enough to eat, Ollie said. –I'm always hungry. Low blood sugar: that's what my dad says.

–Low what?

–If I get too hungry, I get really faint. Literally, I can't walk. And I get very bad-tempered. So if I do the cooking, I can slip myself a bit of raw egg, or some cheese, or—

–So it's just a way to get more to eat than everyone else? Jake said.

–Well, no. Actually the blood sugar thing is true, but I know how to cook because of my father.

–Your father? He taught you? Jake opened his eyes. His dad couldn't cook for smoke.

–He's the best cook in the world. Better than any of the TV guys. Italian food's the best food in the whole world.

–Your dad's alive?

–*Porca vacca*, you're like the Inquisition. All these questions, Ollie said.

–Porca what? Jake said.

Ollie ran his fingers through his cropped hair, gave a shrug. –It's Italian, he said.

–So, is he? Your dad? Jake watched a beetle clamber over the ground between them. A hard shell: that's what they all needed.

–Yep. He is, Ollie said.

–What about your mum?

Ollie picked up a stone and flung it. He threw like a girl, with his elbow and his wrist, and the stone didn't go very far.

–You do it like this; it'll go further, Jake said, and he showed him.

–Thank you for the demo, Mr Man, Ollie said, and he picked up another stone. The beetle had climbed halfway over a stick when Ollie lifted the stone over it, held it like a weapon. Jake thought he was going to bring it down, crush it. But the beetle crawled on into the shadows. Ollie dropped the stone. –I've got my mum's eyes. That's what my dad always says. Her blue eyes and his black curly hair. Ollie's mouth was set in a line and his eyes had gone hooded. –I wish my mum was dead, he said. That would be better. You go in and her room smells like pee. They keep her clean and they change her, but it still smells. It's near where we live – lived, I mean – but that makes it worse. And she doesn't know me. Doesn't know anyone.

His fingers searched the ground for more stones. Now he was talking, it all came out in a rush.

–If my grandad hadn't paid loads of money, they'd have switched the machine off. Efficiency savings. But I wish they had. Switched it off.

–What happened to her? Jake said.

–It's because of what they did to my father. That's why she did it. But she shouldn't have because she still had me. I was still there, I watched her, and she did it anyway.

–But what did she do? Jake said.

–Jumped. Off a bridge over the M5. It's near us. They told me she was lucky to be alive, but she isn't lucky, not really. She's not really alive either.

It was a lot to take in. Jake tried to work out the right question. –What did they do to your dad? he asked.

–They put him in a detention centre.

Jake had heard about the detention centres. His dad had said they mistreated people in them, and his mum had told his dad to be quiet. –Why? he asked.

–He's Italian, Ollie said again, like that explained everything each time, and maybe it did. –He was all right in there for a bit. My mum got food and stuff in to him. But then they started hurting him. He wouldn't say how. He got a couple of messages out to us. He was in the centre a few months, then they excluded him. That's when my mum jumped.

–Excluded him? Jake said. –What does that mean?

Jake watched Ollie's skinny fingers pile stones up into a pile. –Sent him back to Italy. They won't let him in again, not even to visit my mother. Unless I can get out of England, I'll never see him again.

Jake understood. –That's pretty tough, he said. In the air, the words sounded thin, not enough, but Ollie nodded like he got it. –I'll never see my dad again ever, either, Jake said. –Or my mum.

They sat quiet then, in the sunshine.

–How did you find the gang? Jake asked after a while.

–Same way as you. They found me, Ollie said. He put another stone on the pile. –What about your parents, then?

–Dead.

–I know that. But recently? A long time ago?

–Six months ago. A car accident. Through a barrier on a bridge, and into the river. It was an electrical fault. They both drowned. Died immediately. That's what they told me at my tribunal.

–You in the car too? Ollie asked.

Jake shook his head. –They were coming home from work.

Ollie piled on a few more stones. Jake stared at the weeds on the other side of the yard, a mass of green and yellow, and scratches of colour here and there from the flowers. Poppies and other flowers that his mother could've named.

When they'd died, he'd been in a maths lesson, writing notes to Liam, waiting for the end of lesson bell. Just about everything else was blurred. The grown-ups talking around him, going in and out of rooms, pressing a hand on his shoulder or his head. He remembered Mrs Jennings, Liam's mum. She'd cried when she saw him, and said –Poor boy, poor boy; over and over.

There was a spider's web between two plant stalks, dead flies trussed into it. The spider was tucked in a corner. Jake blew at the web, watched the spider run to the centre.

–Where did they work? Ollie's voice broke in, made him jump.

–They're scientists. Jake corrected himself. –*Were* scientists. They worked for Co-Labs.

Ollie looked blank.

–You know, Jake said. –Coalition Wellbeing Laboratories.

–Top secret stuff?

–They didn't tell me much about it. Something to do with vaccines. Dad didn't like it at Co-Labs, though. They'd started arguing about it.

–All parents argue, Ollie said. –Mine did it in Italian, so I couldn't understand.

–Mine argued in the kitchen when I'd gone to bed. But I'd sit on the stairs and listen, in case it was about me. Mostly it wasn't and I'd go back to bed. But there was this one night, I dunno how it started. It wasn't long before the accident, and Dad was shouting, saying they should resign their jobs and leave England, and Mum was saying they couldn't, he knew they couldn't.

–They had good jobs, it sounds like, Ollie said. –Important ones.

–I suppose. Anyway, Dad banged the table. And he went on about how they'd been brought in to save lives and now look what they were doing. Wasn't much to do with vaccines, was it? And how soon it would be too late, and nobody would even know. And then Mum started in. I knew she was upset, cos she said his name, Jonny, like she always did when she was really upset: *Hush now, Jonny. You don't know that for certain, Jonny.* Stuff like that. Then they were both talking at once. Him saying he couldn't shut his eyes to it any longer, and her saying: *What else can we do? What else can we do?* Then she started crying, and after that I couldn't hear what they were saying, so I went back to bed.

–A vaccine? For what? For the virus? Ollie said. He'd stopped playing with the stones and he was sitting up straight and staring at Jake.

Jake shrugged. –The accident happened just after that, so I didn't think about it much.

–If your mum and dad invented a vaccine for the virus, then they were doing good stuff, even if it was for the Coalition, Ollie said. –But your dad said it didn't have much to do with vaccines.

Jake shrugged. –I can't work it out. Anyway, that's why I'm going to Scotland. It's where my grandparents live. I have to go there. That's what my mum and dad said to do, if anything happened to them. Me and Jet.

But Ollie was wasn't listening. –So how come their car went off a bridge? he said, half to himself. –Must've been somebody's doing.

Jake stared at him. –Why?

–Because there are no accidents, not any more, Ollie said. –That's what my dad told me. He said: *if they tell you I'm dead, died in an accident, died of a disease, don't believe them.*

Jake felt frightened, but he tried to shrug like he wasn't.

–Doesn't matter in the end, does it? he said. –They're still dead.

He closed his eyes. Flies buzzed. He could hear his

breathing, and Ollie's. He didn't want to think about it any more. He didn't want to think about it not being an accident. It didn't make any difference anyway.

In the kitchen, Ollie chopped the thyme and rosemary up fine and mixed them in a bowl with eggs and fried onions and cheese and left-over potatoes and some spinach Poacher had foraged the night before. He was dancing again, his hands swift and his shoulders turning. He took down the largest frying pan.

–Cut us some butter, Jake, and stick it in the pan. About a hundred grams.

–Hundred what?

–Hundred grams. About four ounces. This much. Ollie held up his fingers to show.

Jake cut the butter, tipped it in, and Ollie set the pan on the cooker.

–Ollie? Jake said. –Grams, and metres, and all that. That's from before the New Wall.

–Yeah. I know.

–It's against the law to use them, Jake said.

–Yeah, but it's what my dad taught me, Ollie said. –Kilograms and grams and metres and centimetres. It's what they use in Europe. Scotland too. It's how my dad taught me to cook.

–Dangerous, Jake said. –What if you'd said the wrong kind of measurement at school? They'd have reported it to the hub police.

–Well, I didn't. I was careful. And it was important for my dad. So back off, and melt that butter.

–The whole hundred grams? Jake said with a grin.

–The whole hundred. And tip it about so it covers the

base.

The pan didn't have a handle, so Jake did his best to hold the hot edge with a bit of towel. The pan was an old pedal bin lid – it had an upright edge and holes on one side where lid hinges used to be. When the butter was hot, Ollie tipped in the egg mixture. It smelled like home.

–Frittata, Ollie said. –One day I'll cook it for you properly. In Italy, maybe.

Twelve

On the seventh morning, Martha washed his hair again, then combed it and cut it even shorter with her nail scissors. When she stared at him, she had a furrow in her brow. His mum had had a furrow in her brow and she used to tell Jake he'd put it there: all the worry of a son. He wondered what had given Martha hers.

They chopped your hair short in the Home Academy, but Martha seemed to be cutting plenty more off; he could feel it.

–Go easy, he said.

–It'll be good for the birds, she said. –Their nests.

–I don't care about the birds, Jake said.

Davie was watching them, and laughing. –Be a number one soon, he said. –Could work in the fracking fields with that haircut. Might end up there, you get caught. Fracky boy, fracky boy.

Jake hated Davie's niggly voice. It made his skin itch, like some snitty insect bite. –Shove off, he said, kicking out at him.

–Don't jerk around, or I'll jab you with the scissors, Martha said, which just made Davie laugh harder.

–You've cut too much, Jake said, and he could feel Martha shake her head.

–The shorter the better. Makes you look obedient. Not like a boy who'd steal things.

Jake had emptied his rucksack out and scrubbed the mud off it, ready for the expedition. Martha gave him a second bag.

–You're a boy doing errands for your granny. It's her bag.

–It's got flowers on it, he said. –I'd never carry a bag like this.

–Stuff it inside the rucksack, get it out if you need it.

–Can I bring Jet? Jake said. –He's very obedient.

Martha shook her head. –We might have to make a run for it. I had to hide out in some toilets once. They'd have caught me if I'd had a dog.

Jake read his way down the Needs list:

Blister plasters
Biscuits (not choc) x 5
Vitamin pills
Calpol x 3
Ibuprofen x 4
Paracetamol x 4
Lip salve x 4
Salt
Bic razors
Safety pins
Scissors
SHARP KNIFE
Matches – 6 boxes
Wire cutters
String
Garden wire
Tampons - regular & super

COOKING OIL (OLIVE IF POSS)

Raisins

Biros

Pencil sharpener

fruit pastilles

Cass wellies. 12

STRONG WHITE THREAD

NEW NEEDLES

~~GREEN DARNING WOOL~~

Cass had put the wellies on the list. Swift had printed the words out in separate letters, and Cass had copied them out underneath in green felt-tip pen, tongue between her teeth. It took her ages and Jake had felt nearly sick with memory, watching her: he used to do that with his dad when he was little. They'd had a game about who could write best, and a line of M&Ms along the kitchen table. He didn't exactly remember how it went, but he always used to get most of the M&Ms.

–Remember, we only steal what's on the list, Martha said. –Nothing else.

Martha had sat over Poacher's map for an hour with Swift the night before, and then they'd shown him the route.

–Learn it off. Get it in your head, Swift said.

–Why can't we draw it on a piece of paper? Take it with us? Jake said.

–Too risky. You get caught, that would take them straight to us.

*

In the morning, Jake put on his spares. He washed his hands and cleaned his fingernails as best he could. Martha wore a skirt and an old-fashioned blouse with a bow at the neck, and she did something to her hair, Jake wasn't sure what exactly, but it fell around her shoulders in a pretty way. The sky was a dirty grey colour and she had a raincoat over her arm. They stood in the kitchen and Poacher and Swift inspected them.

–Sister and brother. What do you think? Martha said.

–Not bad. You got the same hair, Poacher said. He did up Jake's top button and pulled his tie knot tight to his throat. –It's your disguise. You gotta do it properly.

–Martha's the best, Swift said. –You do what she says, you'll come back safe.

Poacher gave them both mobiles. –For your cover. Look the business well enough.

And soon as Jake held it, he understood what Poacher meant, because it wasn't a real mobile, it was just pretend, a toy for a toddler, made of that soft plastic they could chew on.

They set off at ten. It would take them forty minutes to walk to the shops and Martha wanted to arrive mid-morning.

–More people out and about. Makes us less conspicuous.

Forty minutes wasn't so long, but five minutes in, it felt like for ever. They were walking down ordinary streets, in ordinary daytime. Jake hadn't been out like this since the day he'd rescued Jet.

They walked back across the common and past the church, then down the hill, and towards the house he'd taken the clothes from. What if someone came out and they recognized the trousers and sweater? What if the other boy saw him? What then? He could feel his heart banging in his chest and his hands were sweating. He looked away as they passed the house, stared down at the road, up at the far trees, anywhere except the house with the other boy and the Santa Cruz. But nobody came out of the house, and then they were past it.

When they got to the river, Martha stopped on the bridge and leaned over the edge, so Jake did too. It was a really old stone bridge with moss and ferns growing up the sides. He looked down at the water. It was clear and he could see to the stones on the bottom, and the bits of weed swaying in the current. He watched a fish nose its way through the weeds. This river had been his escape plan a week ago, before he became an Outwalker.

Martha threw a pebble into the water. –Do you know why you got chosen for this? she said.

–No.

–I'll tell you. It's because you're a watcher. You notice things. And a good thief is watching all the time, reading people's body language. Is the shopkeeper watching you? Does she trust you? Or is she about to call the hub police? What about the other customers? If you have to make a run for it, can you get out easily? Did you notice a back way? What about alleys, car parks, churches, markets? Places where you can lose people easily. I'm a good thief because I'm a good watcher, and a fast runner.

–Even in a skirt? Jake said, because it was funny to think of Martha legging it.

She grinned too. –Absolutely.

They crossed the river and walked down Frenchay Road. There were more houses now, and there were other people walking on the pavement, and cars going past. Ordinary, hubbed people, bona fides doing ordinary things, like going to work or shopping and visiting each other.

The back of Jake's head felt cold in the fresh air with all his hair chopped, and he had to stop himself putting his hand to it too often. He felt like he had a big sign on his head with OUTWALKER written on it in red capital letters. Surely people would take one look at him and know? The scar on his neck itched and he rubbed at it, pulling at his collar to get a finger beneath. His hair, his foraged clothes: none of it felt right. He hunched down as far as he could and kept to the inside of the pavement, running his fingers along brick walls and pebbledash, wanting to touch something fixed and solid.

Wish Jet was here, he thought, because Jet would be trotting along like he owned the place, sniffing at corners, lifting his leg on the lampposts, and then Jake could have pretended better too.

They'd been walking for fifteen minutes now and Jake's heart was still pounding. Two boys in school uniforms walked past and they looked at him, and they noticed something, he could see they did. He rubbed at his neck again.

–Stop doing that, Martha said.

–Those boys stared at me.

–You keep scratching at your scar, then someone really will notice something.

–It's itching, Jake said.

–I don't care. You've done it five times in the last five minutes. Don't do it again. And stop walking like an Outwalker. You're nearly hugging the walls and you're slouching. Behave normally.

–I don't know what normal is.

–Then pretend. Copy me. Else you'll get us both caught.

One of the most important rules of good stealing: never show your panic. Doesn't matter how scared you are, how much you think you stand out, how much you want to make a run for it. If you show it, people will think you're suspicious. If you look calm, people won't.

It crossed Jake's mind that he'd had Martha completely wrong. He'd thought she was this mousey, scared girl. But she had nerves of steel.

–You should be in films, he said.

–What?

–Cos you can act so well. I had no idea. I thought . . .

–What did you think?

He hadn't noticed before, but she was a real looker. That's what his dad used to say and his mum used to clock him round the head for it.

–Doesn't matter, he said, and he could feel he was blushing.

–Come on, Jake. Spit it out.

–I thought you were timid. Quiet.

She laughed and ruffled his hair, and he didn't know if it was Martha the Outwalker doing it, or the other one, Martha the thief.

The road got busier. More people, more cars. They passed a scan hub and a bus stop, a line of people waiting, talking to tablets, checking mobiles, doing ordinary stuff. A smiling pixelated woman on the bus stop's screen held out a plate of cupcakes. *Eat English*, she said, and she pushed the plate towards him before the picture morphed into a giant cockroach. 'Use Zeet to keep the Virus at bay', the headline read.

On another screen, a crowd of young men in green coveralls marched past. In the background there were bright green hills. 'Your Country, Your Future' this one said, and underneath:

Invest in your country's future.
Good benefits package.
join@frackforfuture.gov.eng

–Same old, same old, Martha said. I swear, they haven't changed the screens since I joined the gang.

They passed a corner shop. A couple of men outside it looked Martha up and down, the way his dad used to look at girls sometimes, and she did that normal thing girls do, which is pretend not to see them. But Jake didn't think anyone was noticing them especially, or not him anyway, and he began to feel more normal. He got his toy mobile out and pretended to check it for something.

–That's better, Martha said. –The mobile's a good prop. Don't forget to use it in a shop, like you're checking your cash.

They were walking side by side now, and she got her list out.

–We'll be there in a few minutes, so here's what we do. We do a recce first, to find the shops we're going to need. We start with the ones furthest away, and do the ones this end last, so we're always moving towards our escape. What works best is if one of us distracts the shop assistant. Asks them to look something up, for help finding something. Then the other one can do the stealing. Stay close: that's really important. So you can always see me, or hear me. And don't rush. You have to think you've got a perfect right to be looking around the shop for things you need. And you have to think that you're going to pay, so have your mobile out, make as if you're credit texting. Right up until the point where you don't. All right?

Jake nodded.

–So smile, Jake. Makes us look more innocent, in case anybody's looking at us.

Jake nodded again and widened his mouth in what he hoped was a smile.

–You've got to believe in your own story while you're out there, Martha said. –Like being an actor in a play. Else you won't be convincing. Remember, we're nicely brought up children, brother and sister, and we're out doing errands for our granny.

Jake shook his head. –No. That doesn't work. If I've just bunked off school to do these errands, they'll have hubbed me, tracked me down. They did stuff like that in my old school.

Martha nodded. –Fair point. She paused. –OK. Here's the story. Our granny's been in hospital, and she's still too ill to look after herself. But she's hit the efficiency threshold for her treatment till next month, and we're not a wealthy family. So they've sent her home . . .

–Yeah, Jake said. –That works. He could picture it now. Could imagine his own mum and dad doing this. –So the hospital has sent her home, and we're looking after her, best we can. Our dad's spending nights with her, and our parents are paying school absence fines for us to look after her daytimes and do her shopping. That's why the school hasn't hubbed us. So it's really important that we get these things, quick as possible, and get back to her.

–Good, Martha said. –Let's go.

The first shop was a doddle. The shop assistant wasn't much older than Martha, and Jake saw how his face lit up when he saw her; saw him look her up and down and up again.

He's gonna be thinking through his trousers, Jake thought. That's what his friend Josh used to say. First time, Jake didn't know what he meant and Josh took the piss when he asked. Josh had a big brother so he knew about these things. Anyway, Martha must've reckoned the same because she gave Jake the signal straight off. Jake could have stolen the whole shop and the boy wouldn't have noticed. He was asking Martha where she'd been all his life? And did she fancy a drink later? And was she really into DIY?

Jake could hear her start on about her sick granny. He grabbed a basket and collected what he needed – wire, string, wire cutters, sharp knife, matches, even needles and thread – then nipped behind a pile of paint cans and stuck the lot in his rucksack. Job done and he was out of there, and a minute later, so was she.

–Just walk, she said. –Ahead of me. But soon as they were round the corner and out of sight, she cracked up laughing. –He was about to ask me out. I could see him trying to get up the courage.

–Worth you taking all that trouble over your hair then, he said. –Like a secret stealing weapon.

They were on a roll after that. Superdrug on Fishponds Road: medicine, plasters, vitamin pills, tampons (Martha found those). Then past KFC to the Co-Op: cooking oil, raisins, pastilles, salt, all got.

–Up here, Martha said, and she led Jake round the corner and up a quiet street.

Jake was buzzing. –I can't believe we just walked out with all this stuff and nobody saw.

–Kids don't nick cooking oil or salt. Not usually. That's why they don't notice.

–It's like being a magician. It's like I've got eyes in the back of my head. I can see what people are going to do before they do it. I can tell when they're going to turn around and see me, when they're going to look away. I'm invisible, slipping things into my rucksack, then out of there like a ghost . . . Martha? he said; because she was looking around, as if somebody was there watching them, and there was the furrow in her brow again. –You all right?

–It's time to get out, Martha said. –I've got a feeling. It's a small place and we don't want to push our luck. We'll get noticed soon.

Jake got what she meant. A couple of strange kids wandering about when they should be at school would get reported to the hubbers pretty quick, no matter what story they had about a granny. The hubbers would run a scan, look at the CCTV and bingo: ghost kids. There on the CCTV, but invisible on the scan hub.

–Just Cass's wellies to get, Jake said.

Martha shook her head. –We need to go now.

Jake saw Cass at the kitchen table with the felt tip pen. It had taken her ages to write those words. That was her speaking, as close as she got.

–But she needs them, he said.

–No. We quit while we're ahead. Also, you're high on it, and that's exactly when you make mistakes.

There was Cass, writing out the words: 'Cass wellies. 12.'

–It took her ages to write them down, he said, but Martha had already turned away and she didn't answer.

They passed another scan hub, people gathered round the news screens. *Atlantic Alliance strikes deal on fisheries,*

Jake read on the first screen, and *Chelsea storm to 2-1 victory!* on the second. On a third there was a picture of a rubber boat with pieces of clothing in it. Jake could see a child's shoe, and a life jacket. *Three drown off Kent coast.* What had happened to the child? Jake wondered. He peered closer to read the ticker tape: *Coastguards rescue thirty drifting off Kent coast. Three die resisting arrest. All travelling without visas or exit documents. Hub police promise crackdown on illicit sale of rubber dinghies.*

But it was the third one that had the biggest crowd, and he dodged between people to see the headline.

Breakthrough in Virus Vaccine: Spectacular Trial Results

He pushed further forward. This was what his parents had been doing. This was their work.

Vaccination timetable brought forward, he read. *Inoculations ready for Christmas.*

–Jake! Come on! Martha's voice was quiet but urgent.

He read on down the screen, skimming the words as fast as he could. *Coalition Chief Scientific Adviser . . . extremely effective . . . 100% safe antidote to lethal virus . . . Pandemic averted . . . Free . . . compulsory programme . . . children and elderly first . . . inoculations ready before Christmas . . .*

He didn't understand. His dad had said—

–Jake! Martha's hand was on his jacket, tugging, so he turned away and followed her out. –What the hell was that about? she said.

–My mum and dad, Jake said. –They were working on the vaccine.

–So what?

–My dad said the Coalition was more dangerous than the virus.

–Dangerous man to know then, your dad, Martha said.

–But the screen said—

–We need to go.

Thirteen

Cass's wellies were waiting for him, in a big society shop just after Blockbusters. Right bang in the window, between a pile of kids' DVDs and a tray with a teapot and four King William Jubilee mugs.

–Martha, he whispered. –Look!

He wasn't completely sure about the size, but they looked near enough. Besides which, why not? He could grab them and be out in five seconds, stash them in the flowery bag before the door had closed. He'd walk away fast and they'd have done the whole list and Cass would have her wellies. Blue with white dots, size about 12. It was perfect.

–No, Martha said; but he was already going in. The shop assistant was on the far side, and she was talking to someone, not watching. The wellies were just there. Jake took out his mobile, made as if to text something and walked round the back of a rack full of old pairs of trousers till he was as close as possible to the window display. Martha was already walking away along the pavement. Last look at the shop assistant, and he slipped a hand between the DVDs and the teapot, lifted the wellies and slipped them in his bag. Then he was out of the shop and running to catch Martha up.

–Hey! Flower boy! The shout came from behind him and across the street and Jake glanced round. It was the boy from the DIY shop. –Tell your sister . . . the boy called, running after him.

–Oh no. Jake ran, holding the flowery bag close to his chest, the pretend mobile in his other hand.

–Wait up, flower boy! You're in a hurry.

The boy was calling out, making people turn. Ahead of him, Martha had seen the boy and started running too, dodging round the shoppers. She was fast and it was all Jake could do to keep her in his line of sight. Behind him, the DIY boy's shouts changed.

–Hey! Stop him! Thief! Hub him!

People were staring now, and Jake ran faster, his breath burning in his throat, his eyes swimming. He ducked between people, brushing against them. A woman called out, angry, as he ran by her, clipping her shopping bags with his hand, and he'd dropped the mobile, but he couldn't stop. Other voices were shouting after him, and he ducked and dived to escape.

Finally, just as he thought his legs would give out, the shouting stopped. He paused and gave a quick glance back: the DIY boy had stopped a way back. He was doubled over, out of breath, pointing towards Jake, and several people were standing with him, but they weren't running any more. As he watched, the DIY boy stood up and with three other men beside him, he started marching towards him. It was like being in a Western, except they didn't have guns. But the men had the hubbers to call on, and despite the stitch eating at his ribs, Jake turned to run again.

–Martha? he called, because in the time it had taken him to stop and look back, she had disappeared.

He had run beyond the shops now, into a street with houses and front gardens.

–Martha? he called, as he passed each house, but there was no reply. His panic rose. He wished he had looked at the map properly the night before, learned a few of the road names. He had no idea where he was.

Ahead were more houses, and then a church building rising up like a cliff. He ran towards it. *Coalition Family Centre*, the sign read, *All Welcome*. But there were spiked railings and the gates were locked. Not very welcoming.

Jake stopped, panicked. He needed to hide. He needed to find Martha. Where was she? He could hear footsteps behind him. The DIY boy.

–Martha? he called again, his voice coming out all quavery.

–Jake! Quick. Martha's voice was a hiss and it came from inside the railings. She'd got through a gap and was crouched in the bushes in the front of the Family Centre. Pushing the flowery bag ahead of him, Jake shoved his way in after her and threw himself flat down on the ground, his face pressed on to the dry earth.

Seconds later the DIY boy came running past, breathing heavily, then he was gone.

They just lay there. The ground below the bushes was shadowy, cut with dark green lines. It smelled of fox and old leaves. Jet would have liked it under there. Except for the distant sound of cars, it was quiet. Rain began to fall, a steady pattering sound. Jake's heart slowed to normal and the DIY boy didn't return. He tapped Martha's leg.

–He's gone, he whispered. Martha?

She didn't reply.

–Martha? he said again.

–Outwalker rule four, she said finally, her voice very quiet. –What is it?

–Obedience to the gang, he said slowly.

–And what happens if you break the rule?

–But they were right there, in the window . . . he said.

Martha squeezed through the gap in the railings onto the pavement and started walking back the way they'd come.

Jake followed behind her. –And Cass is little and she doesn't speak and— He stopped, feeling helpless. –Please, Martha.

She turned back to him, every quiet word like a blow. –Do you think I don't know all that?

–But, Martha . . .

–Shut up, she said. –We need to get out of here. She turned and walked on.

The rain was falling more heavily now and Martha had pulled on her raincoat. From behind, with the hood up, she looked like his mother, and it gave Jake an odd feeling in his chest to see it. They were going back a different way, up quiet roads of semis with scraps of grass at the front and wheelie bins and clapped-out cars in the driveways. Sheppard Road, Delabere Avenue, Symington Road. Martha seemed to know exactly where to go, and Jake remembered her hunched over the map the night before.

–Walk beside me, she said. –Looks suspicious if you're behind.

He caught up with her, walked alongside. The road was empty, just a few sodden pigeons pecking around some bins. They were the only ones on the street here.

–I'm sorry, he said. –I meant to do the right thing. I didn't think . . .

–No, you didn't. Her eyes were fixed on the road, and she sounded so angry Jake didn't dare say anything else.

The road ended and they were in a park. They passed a battered playground. No kids playing in the rain.

Jake felt ill. –Are you going to tell Swift and Poacher? he said.

–You put the whole gang at risk back there, she said. –Not just you, not just me, the whole gang. Including Cass. So yes, I am going to tell them.

Bile rose in his throat and he swallowed hard to keep it down. –Martha, please, he said.

She turned towards him. –Look at me, she said, and she swung him round by his shoulder. –I spent nearly ten years in a Home Academy. They put me in when I was seven. My brother was five. My mum and dad? They rendered them. That's all they've ever told me. I don't know why, and I don't know where they are, not even if they're alive.

Jake looked at her face. Her eyes were dark and unblinking.

–What happened to your brother? Jake said.

He saw her make this little movement with her shoulder, a flinch, as if he'd poked his finger into an open wound. She didn't answer him at first, and then she spoke in a distant voice, as though what she was saying wasn't really about her.

–We could write letters, but we only got to see each other once a year. Once a year for nearly ten years. They'd take a group of us girls from our Home Academy in a van to a Children's Centre, and bring our brothers from their Home Academy, and we'd have a day together. So . . . it was our visiting day. Our ninth. I was sixteen, Peter fourteen, and taller than me now. He looked just like our dad. Same eyes, same thing he did with his hands when he got excited. I'd got an escape plan, and it had to be that day because next year I might be in the picking fields, and the year after he'd be in the fracking fields and then it would be too late.

–I should have guessed something from his letters, but I didn't want to, I think. And I was a child, so how could I? What did I know?

She paused, and again Jake waited.

–He wasn't well, she said. –In the head. In the mind. He'd written some odd things in his letters, but I thought he was just having a laugh, because there was always normal stuff too. And if he was having a laugh, then he was surviving. That's what I thought.

–Anyway, he wasn't well that day. He was saying strange things. But it was our only chance to escape, so . . . I took him with me. I told him he had to be quiet. Told him it was really important. I held his hand and took him with me. Out the back of the Centre. Only I escaped, and he didn't. I was hiding in a dumpster, and I could see them. He was shouting. Calling out. That's how they found him. He couldn't be quiet. It took five men to hold him down . . .

She took a breath.

–And then they Tasered him. Just for fun. I saw it all. He was still afterwards. They brought in paramedics and they tried to bring him back. But he still lay there, no shouting, no waving his hand, no movement at all, and I could only watch.

Jake watched her. He felt dumb with horror. She went on, calmly, it seemed.

–Eventually they put a sheet over his head. I never even got to kiss him goodbye.

She put her bag of stolen stuff on the ground, and stood for a while, just looking at it.

–So I'm not going back there because of you, she said at last. –If you're thrown out, it's your own fault and you deserve it. My brother's gone and you're here, and you're not ill, and you're not like my brother, or Davie, and you've done something very stupid. If we're caught, we won't be able to escape again – they'll make sure of it. They've got Home Academies, special ones, for kids like us. Ask Poacher. Ask him what they're like.

–Martha, please . . . he said again.

–How long do you think Davie would survive in one of those places? Or Cass? She's ill too.

–I know she's ill. That's why I wanted to get her the wellies, Jake said.

–It's not wellies she needs, Martha said. She kicked at the bag on the ground. –It's not anything we can steal for her. She's got an illness of the blood. That's why they're in the gang, her and Swift. And every day that passes, she gets weaker.

–But I've seen Swift giving her medicine, Jake said.

–Yes. Swift brought it with her from the Home Academy. Broke into their pharmacy, took as much as she could lay her hands on. It helps a bit. Slows the illness down. But there isn't much left, and once it's gone . . .

Martha paused, wiped a hand across her face. She looked older than before. Then she went on.

–There is a medicine that can cure it. Not always, but sometimes. But it's above Cass's threshold. The Coalition won't pay for it, not for a child in a Home Academy. Standard treatment only, doesn't matter how ill you are, doesn't matter that you're a child. And of course they've got no family to pay the difference and get them first-class treatment. But if they can get to Scotland, then it doesn't matter if she's rich or poor. Doesn't matter that she's got no parents. Cass will get the best medicine. She'll have a chance.

–And if they don't get there?

–She'll die. In the gang, or in a Home Academy, makes no difference. But at least in the gang, they can be together. In the Home Academy, they were separated most of the time. Different dormitories for different ages. So if they got caught and put into another Home Academy, then Cass would die on her own. Martha looked across at Jake, waited till he looked back at her. –Did you think about that when you grabbed those wellies? she said.

He dropped his head. –I thought it was safe . . .

–And I knew it wasn't, and you disobeyed my order. That mobile you dropped – if somebody gives it in to the hubbers, they'll know we're something strange. Because what are you doing for money if your mobile isn't real? She picked up the bag. –We have to get on, she said, and she walked away from him.

Ten minutes later they were at the bridge. The water was dark and choppy with rain and the path beside the river looked lonely. Fifteen more minutes and they were walking up the fire-escape stairs. Martha knocked and Jake watched through the glass. Two figures approached, one tall and one small. The door opened and there was Swift and there was Cass.

–Go all right? Swift said.

–We got everything, Martha said, and Cass made a little jump and clapped her hands together. –But Jake needs to talk to you. I'll sort out the stuff.

I don't want to tell them anything, he thought. *I should just get Jet and go*. But when Swift opened a door and signalled to him, he followed her. And when she came back with Poacher, and they all three stood in the empty room, and Swift asked, –So what happened?, he told them.

–Right, Poacher said when he finished telling. –You done

what you done. He was fiddling with his knife, flicking the blade in and out. –You broke a rule. So now we got ter decide if you can stay; and when Jake looked over at Swift, she just gave this quick nod.

They made him stand outside in the corridor. He wished Jet was there beside him. He was probably with Cass. He leaned against the wall and stared at the wallpaper: little yellow birds and green leaves, only Davie had scraped the heads off all the birds in a long line along both sides, and the paper had brown bubble blotches that had leaked down from the ceiling, like the brown stew they served up in the Home Academy on Tuesdays that always spread across the plate and drowned the peas and dyed the mashed potato.

He could hear their voices, Poacher's and Swift's, but not what they were saying, and he wished again that he'd just gone.

–Stupid, he said, and he hit his forehead with his hand. He should have legged it with Jet. They didn't even want him in the gang.

–We're done. Swift's voice broke into his thoughts. She gestured with her head and he followed her back into the room. –Shut the door, she said.

He stood facing them. The rain had stopped and the sun had come out, shafting through the window, into his eyes. He could see the dust dance, but he couldn't see their faces. So he looked at the floor: wide old floorboards, the cracks between them stuffed with fluff and crud, painted round the edge with a deep, black border. This was it. They were chucking him out. His heart lurched and he set his teeth tight and clenched his fists in his pockets. If only they had let him stay . . .

–Gang's gotta leave tonight.

Jake looked up. –What?

Swift had turned her back to the room, and stood looking out of the window. It was Poacher who had spoken.

–Gang's gotta leave tonight. Cos o' you. When the hubbers find that phone, they'll hunt fer us. An' they ain't stupid, they'll find us soon enough. An' with you nicking the wellies too, an' the chase an' that: staying's too dangerous now. We gonna wait till it's dark, then go.

Jake bit his lip. His chest felt tight. Fear ran along his spine like electricity. But he met Poacher's stare and he didn't cry.

–I'll get Jet and go, he said.

Beyond the window the sun was still high. Hours till dark fell. He would fetch Jet now and they'd head along the river. They could put a good few miles in before dark. Follow the river far enough, it would take them to the sea, and then he'd get a boat to France, or Holland, or Scotland even, somehow. Him and Jet. Him and Jet always. To the death . . .

–You listening? I said yer still in, Poacher said.

–What?

–Yer still in – if yer want to be.

–But I broke the rule, Jake said.

–Yeah, you did. Swift turned back towards the room, towards Jake. –We've thrown kids out for less. You've put Cass at risk, cos she still badly needs to rest, and now we've got to walk again. You did the wrong thing, yes, but you did it for the right reasons. That's why you're still in.

–We ain't yer mum and dad making rules, Poacher said. –Do it again . . . And he drew his finger across his throat.

Jake nodded and looked down at the ground. He was blinking hard.

Swift's eyes were hard and her mouth was tight. –So, are you staying? she said. Jake nodded. –Right. You can go now. We've got stuff to sort out.

–I'm sorry . . . Jake said, but Swift lifted her hand.

–Yeah, she said. –We know. And don't go guilt tripping. It isn't wanted, and it isn't useful.

They left the house that night. Packed up their rucksacks, hung the mattresses back on the wall, shovelled out the ash, swept the floors, threw out the food they couldn't leave or carry.

–Gotta leave it in here like we found it, Poacher said.

–Where we headed? Davie said.

–Find out soon enough, Poacher said. –Be a long walk tonight.

Fourteen

They walked north straight through the night from the hospital, not stopping almost. Past houses shut up with sleep, and animals sleeping like stones in the fields. They walked in silence and Jake's mind drifted. He was on the climbing wall, finding holds, just climbing and climbing, with his father below. For hours they walked, and for hours he climbed in his mind. Only once he lost his footing. It was another village and it was a small, white house: nothing special; nothing to write home about. But as they passed the front gate, he smelled his mother's smell, her perfume. It was there, in the air, and he breathed it in and his feet went from under him. He fell headlong, crashing down on to the cold grit of the road.

They'd been in the woods for two days now. Found a place between high trees where the ground dipped and the bracken grew deep. They foraged in the high bins behind the Welcome Break for old food – trays of sushi, burger meat, packets of old salad, with Thousand Island sachets that Davie would squeeze neat down his throat.

–Milk and honey, he'd say, and tear away the strip on the next one.

On the first afternoon, Swift brought back two half-cups of Costa and a newspaper with the food.

–Here, she said, passing one cup to Martha. –They're

still warm. Left on an outside table. Get rid of the lid. It's where they drank from.

The two girls sat shoulder to shoulder, turned away from the gang. They talked in low voices, and they giggled. Jake hadn't heard them giggle before. They looked like the Year Eleven girls Jake used to avoid at school: the girls who used to tease the newest boys, asking questions that made Jake's ears hot even to remember.

The smell of their coffee: Jake closed his eyes. It reminded him of his mum and dad. He let his memory drift . . .

–Jake? Ollie's voice made him start. –The virus vaccine. That's what your mum and dad were doing?

Jake opened his eyes. Ollie was hunched over the newspaper, spread across the flattened bracken. He looked round, his blue eyes wide with excitement.

–Look. Here, Ollie said, pointing.

Jake crouched over to read:

VACPLUS VIRUS VACCINE HELD READY AT SECRET LOCATION

Volunteers Needed for Final Trials

Martha and Swift had turned back to the gang, no giggles now.

–Is that what your parents were working on? Martha said.

Jake shrugged. –A vaccine for something. They didn't tell me what. I'm guessing it was for the virus. But it must've been important, cos the day they died, these people came and took all their work files from our house. Didn't say anything to me. Not even that they were sorry about Mum and Dad being dead.

–Strange, Ollie said.

Jake shrugged again. The coffee smell. He saw his mum sitting in a deckchair and his dad giving her a cup of coffee, made all special like he did at the weekend, and his mum putting her finger in the froth and laughing.

–Listen to this. Martha tapped the column halfway down the page. *–Stun boats see off French aggro to rescue ninety migrants off Kent Coast, before picking a further fifty bodies out of the waves.*

–People drowning's nothing new, Ollie said. –My cousin drowned, trying to get out.

–But stun boats? Swift said. –They're new. We might have to get over the border by sea. Let's hear what we're up against. Read it out, Martha. All of it.

So Martha read the article out in a low voice, not to wake Cass, sleeping beside her:

–More than one hundred and forty migrants broke the law and ignored weather warnings on Thursday, cramming into rubber boats in an effort to cross to France. When French boats were sighted inside English waters, hub police quickly used state-of-the-art drone stun boats to apprehend the migrants and prevent the French from picking them up. Once stunned, many drowned because home-made life jackets failed to keep their heads clear of the high waves. The Home Secretary told reporters: "It is hard to believe parents will jeopardize, even sacrifice, their children's lives in this way. Our laws are clear and our borders are absolute. The safety of our people depends upon it. We will do all necessary to protect England. It is, of course, a tragic pity that so many children died during this operation."

–Cass wouldn't have stood a chance, Swift said. –The children don't stand a chance.

–We couldn't have got a boat anyway, Poacher said. –Cost a bomb an' we ain't got any money. An' yer can't nick 'em. Keep 'em in big hangars now with guard dogs and alarms and that.

Poacher showed them the emergency exit at the back of the Welcome Break, and Swift explained how to get past the CCTV.

–We've got two anoraks for it. You go in pairs and you wear the anoraks. Don't put the hoods up because if anyone's watching the screen that minute, it'll make them suspicious.

–So what about our faces, then? Davie said.

–Keep your head down. Take a mobile, pretend to be texting. Your eyes are the thing. They can trace them. And you feel like you're gonna twitch about, Davie, or blurt anything, get back here.

So in the small hours they slipped inside in pairs to use the Conveniences. The Conveniences reminded Jake of the Home Academy: cold lights, lines of basins, straggles of hair on white tiles. Machines sold condoms, and round balls you could chew to clean your teeth. Jake stood at the basins and squeezed pink soap from the dispenser and a dozen boys in beanies stared back at him in the long mirrors. Beside him, Davie swiped across his forehead once, twice, three times, and the mirrors were crazy with a dozen lost boys in a dozen sleeveless donkey jackets, all patched with tiny stitches.

But the hot water: that was good, and he put his hands under the tap again to feel it.

Swift took Cass and they weren't gone long, but she came back shaking her head. –Got given the eye by one of the cleaners, she said. –We can't go in again. We gotta get a ride soon, doesn't matter where to, else we're done for. They'll catch us.

The bracken was dry and soft in the place between the trees and it smelled like earth and almonds. When Jake woke again, there was the green of the bracken and Jet warm against his warm knees. Martha was shaking him.

–Your watch, she said. –Go get us a lorry. She gave him a quick smile too, like she'd finally forgiven him, and he was so glad he nearly skipped over to his watch.

Poacher had explained this to him. –What you got to do is check the lorries for our sign. A driver that'll give us a ride, he'll put a sign on the lorry.

–What kind of sign? Jake said.

–Ours. An' the lorry driver, he puts it on the licence disc. That's what yer gotta check.

–Risky for him, Jake said.

–Yup. Dangerous for him like it is for us. Fracking fields fer him, or the like, if he gets caught.

–But if we see the sign, we can get a ride, Jake said. –Did you get rides last time?

–There was only two of us, so it was easier, Poacher said. –We could get rides in the vans too. Never had to wait beyond a day. But there's too many of us now fer a white van, so it's gotta be a lorry. We want one goin' north, but we ain't gonna be too picky now. Too late fer that.

It was Jake's third watch, and this was the eleventh lorry he'd checked. Green with white stripes. Jake watched the driver head towards the Welcome Break. *Going for his dinner*, Jake thought, and his stomach growled. Once he was out of sight, Jake climbed down from his tree, picked up Jet's lead and clambered over the fence on to the tarmac. If anyone stopped him, he was just a boy giving his dog a bit of a walk; long car journey, that sort of thing.

Keeping Jet tight to heel, he walked across the tarmac.

The lorry was called 'Barbara', up there in fancy gold writing on the bonnet. Through the high cab window he could see photos above the windscreen of children, and a cat and a naked woman pinned up behind the driver's seat. The licence was tucked behind the lorry's second set of wheels and he had to peer in close to see it properly. It looked just like the others and he was already turning away when he saw the sign.

–Oh . . . he said out loud.

It was on the corner of the disc, and small enough that he'd nearly missed it. He looked again, in case it was an accidental mark: a bit of grime off the road, a smudge in the licence ink. But no. It was the sign. The same sign he had tattooed on the back of his neck. The Outwalker sign, there on the corner of the licence in blue biro: a circle with a dot in the middle.

–That's it, Jet, he whispered. –That's our ride out.

Fifteen

Poacher made them pack up the camp there and then.

–We gotta be ready to go soon as the driver gets back.

–But we don't know where he's going yet, Martha said. –He might not even be going north to Birmingham. He might be going anywhere.

–Don't matter. Swift's right. We used up our luck here. We go where he takes us. So we gotta eat what we can now, cos once we're inside that lorry, we dunno when we get to eat next. An' peeing, same thing applies. So go an' do it now in the woods. An' keep yer rucksacks by you.

Then he sent Jake and Jet back to their watching post.

–Soon as you see the driver, git over the fence and wander over like it's a chance thing that you cross his path. Tell him quick you seen the Outwalker sign. After that it's up to him to get us into the lorry.

So Jake sat and watched and waited. Jet had his ears pricked too, like he knew something was about to happen.

Off to the left, cars were driving in for fuel. He watched kids get out of a car and head into the garage shop, come out with packets of Haribo. He'd done that with his mum and dad, and never dreamed there might be a boy like him watching. An Outwalker boy.

–Come on, our man, Jake murmured. He watched for nearly an hour, and at last his driver returned, a paper and a Costa in one hand and a slab of something in the other.

He was a slab of a man too. Big hands, big belly, red face. Didn't look that friendly. Jake climbed the fence. Quickly he walked across the tarmac, making sure his path crossed the driver's.

If he'd got it wrong, this man could shop them all. There'd be a hub station in the Services. He could do it in two minutes.

As soon as Jake was near enough, he made as if he'd got Jet's lead tangled, and bumped into the man by mistake, and he said it out straight. –I saw the sign. We need a ride.

The driver acted cool as a cucumber. Didn't look at him, or slow down. Spoke to Jake in a quiet voice. –Follow me.

The driver unlocked the cab door. –Get in, he said, –and the dog.

Jake climbed inside the lorry cab and sat down underneath the picture of the naked woman. The driver swung himself up and inside, pulled the door shut and locked it.

–Right. You and how many more?

–Six more, Jake said. –And Jet; and he pointed.

The driver was shaking his head. –The dog's fine, but I can't take seven. It's too many. He took a bite out of his slab.

Jake stared out of the window. Poacher hadn't told him what to do if he said no. Would some of them go and some of them stay beneath the trees and wait for another lorry? Would Swift and Cass go? And Martha? He bit his lip and waited.

–How old are you? the driver said at last.

–Thirteen, Jake said.

–Thirteen, the driver repeated, raising an eyebrow.

–Nearly.

–Twelve then, the driver said, and Jake nodded. He saw

the driver look up towards the photos of the children. –You the youngest? They get you doing the dirty work? Checking out the lorries and that?

–It's not anyone's dirty work, Jake said. –And we all do it.

–All right, all right. The driver put his hands up like a pretend surrender.

–Except Cass, Jake said. –She doesn't do a shift cos she's too small.

–So how old is Cass, then?

–About five. Or six, maybe.

–Five? You serious? Jesus. The driver put his head in his big hands and Jake wondered if he was going to cry. But when he lifted up his head again, he looked angry, not sad.

–You got any adults with you?

Jake wasn't sure. Were Poacher and Swift and Martha adults?

–I dunno exactly, he said.

–First time I picked up kids from Michaelwood. So how long you been waiting?

–Two days.

–Two days! In those woods, I'm guessing.

Jake nodded.

–You must be getting desperate. And if I don't take you . . . But you understand, don't you? I've never taken more than two at a time. The more of you in there, the bigger the risk. He put a finger up to touch the photo of the small girl. –A single one of you gets noticed, it's the end of everything.

–I understand, Jake said.

–I've been doing this three years. Been lucky so far. Carried forty-seven people and not even my wife knows about it. Lucky and very careful. Coalition party member, signed up. Volunteer hubber. Look like one of the faithful, I do.

Jake knew the driver would have to make his own mind up. Knew there was no point trying to persuade him. No point telling him that the Home Academy was a cold prison that broke children into pieces, and Jet was all he had in the world. No point telling him that if hubbers got Cass and Swift, they'd be separated and he knew Cass would die.

He looked at the photos above the windscreen. One showed a woman at a table smiling, and the other was two girls in school uniform. They looked a bit younger than Jake, and they looked the same as each other. They had the woman's smile.

Jake waited. The driver was just staring at his steering wheel. His hands on his lap looked like two pieces of meat. Jake stroked Jet's head, felt the soft velvet of his ears. The driver had dropped his paper on the seat between them, and Jake read the headlines:

Europe threatens sanctions over zero tolerance immigrant policy

Virus kills fifty-two at religious rave

He squinched up his eyes to read the date: 23 May. Just over three weeks, that was all, since he'd escaped from the Home Academy. It was hard to believe. The Academy felt like it was years away.

The driver reached into his pocket, took out a handkerchief and blew his nose. Jake squeezed his eyes tight shut. His cheeks went hot. It was no good. He wasn't going to give them the ride. There were too many of them. The driver had too much to lose.

He put his hand on the door. –You can let me out. Thanks, anyway.

The driver looked round. His mouth was a thin line in his face, like he was pinching his lips together. –I'll take you, he said. –So listen up.

It would be about six hours, all told. He had to do two drops on the way, so they'd have to be bloody sure to hide before he opened the back. Muzzle the dog. Not a bloody sound.

–Should be into London by eight. Rush hour's over by then, shops shut.

–London? Jake said.

–Yeah, London. Where you hoping to get to?

–Poacher said Birmingham next, cos it's heading north, and he knows a place we can go there.

–It's London with me, or you lot got to find yourselves another lorry.

They waited just inside the edge of the wood, rucksacks on, ready. Swift had Cass in her arms and Jake kept Jet close against his legs. Nobody spoke. When Jake told Swift and Poacher where the lorry was going, he saw a look go between them.

–London, London! Davie chanted. –Catch us while they can!

–Might see the King! Ollie said. –Might see Big Ben!

But Poacher shook his head. –London's the wrong way. We need the north. We got ter go north.

–We can't stay here any longer, you know that, Swift said. –You said it yourself. We can't be picky now. Been lucky so far. With the weather, with the cameras. That cleaner giving me the eye. She'll have said something, I know she will.

–We got ter be patient. We got ter wait an' the right lorry'll come . . .

–No, Poacher. We're out of time. Doesn't matter how right the lorry is, if we've been caught. Locked up again. I'm not sitting here to get captured by the hubbers. We haven't got a lift to Birmingham, and we have got one to London.

–But . . . London. I bin plenty o' other places, but I ain't never bin to London, Swiftie. Got no knowledge there. An' it's too dangerous. I heard stories. Plenty of 'em. London's a terrible place.

–Going to be terrible here too, any minute now, when we hear those hubbers' sirens. It's better to be moving. We'll find our way north somehow.

Jake watched the lorry turn. It looked vast, like a house turning. Surely someone, another lorry driver, would wonder what it was doing? Wonder why it was reversing towards the woods? Red light lit the trees and the reverse noise made the birds rise into the air. The lorry stopped, its rear wheels touching the kerb, and the parking lights came on. The engine was still running and the driver was unfastening the rear doors. Then they were climbing the fence, moving fast in a single line. Across the strip of grass to the lorry, and the driver was helping them up, because there was no time to lower the tail lift.

–Up on top, and get to the front, the driver said.

Martha first, then Swift and Cass, each disappearing into the lorry's darkness. Two minutes and the lorry would be moving.

Jake climbed the fence. He dropped Jet's lead so the dog could shimmy under, and Jet gave this sharp yip Jake hadn't heard for ages, and he was running across the tarmac, tail high, lead trailing behind him like a whippy snake.

–Jet! Jake shouted. But Jet didn't stop, and on the far side Jake saw another dog, and he saw at a glance she was a female and in heat. No way Jet would listen if he just called. Still got his male pride, his dad used to say. Good lad. And his mum would roll her eyes.

Jake looked round at Poacher. He was standing there with the driver. –That dog gets back here now or you're gone without him, said Poacher.

Jet was sniffing out the other dog. He was doing that prance he always did with females on heat, his tail right up, excited.

–Come, Jet, Jake called, but he knew Jet wouldn't. He stepped away from the lorry.

–Get in, Poacher said. –Last chance.

But Jake couldn't leave without Jet.

–Let him fetch the dog. It was the driver's voice, and Jake heard Poacher start to say something, but the driver cut him off. –He fetches the dog, or there's no lift, not for any of you.

So Jake ran, paying no heed to who might see him, grabbed Jet's lead, pulled him away.

The driver didn't say anything, only gave him a short nod, and soon as Jake was in and Jet beside him, he slammed the doors shut, and a minute later the lorry jolted into gear, throwing Jake to the floor, and he lay there, out of breath, the lorry roar travelling through him.

After a while, his eyes grew accustomed to the dark. He was lying between two stacks of pallets that reached all the way to the roof. He looked up. The rest of the gang had disappeared, but they must be up the top there. Grabbing hold of a pallet corner, he was halfway to his feet when the lorry lurched, and he slammed into Jet and the two of them were tumbled on to the floor again. With his back against a pallet, Jake jammed his feet against the edge and braced himself. Beside him, Jet curled up, head pressed against Jake's leg. Jake stroked Jet's head, his soft fur a comfort in the cold, hard dark.

It was hard to guess the amount of time, but after maybe an hour Jake could feel the lorry slow down. He got to his feet, feeling along the pallets for a gap to slip through, or a handhold to climb with. The lorry came to a stop; outside he could hear gruff male voices. Someone slammed a hand on the side of the lorry, and it echoed inside.

–Help! he whispered. They were shooting the bolts on the doors now. –Help! he hissed again.

–Grab it! Poacher's voice said from above, and Jake saw two hands held down for him. He grabbed at them and felt himself pulled upwards.

–Come on, Jet, he urged, and he heard Jet scramble up beside him.

The rear doors opened and the driver's voice was shouting instructions to someone. Light flooded in and Jake flinched. He knew they were invisible as long as they kept low, but what if one of the men down there climbed up a little way? What if one of them sneezed?

An engine sound started up.

–Forklift, Poacher whispered. It came closer and Jake heard Cass's whimper and Swift's *sshh*. The gang lay there, scarcely breathing, as the forklift reached below the first line of pallets, lifted them up and away. Then the doors slammed them into the dark again.

–They could leave us a little light on, surely, Ollie said,

which set Jake giggling, and then Davie, and Martha. So it was a good thing the lorry moved off a minute later, because if one of the men had opened up the back again, they'd have found a pile of kids there sweating in the dark and laughing their socks off.

An hour later there was a second stop, and another line of pallets went. But it was ages till the lorry moved, and soon after it stopped for a third time and the driver opened the back doors a little way. There was the rustle of carrier bags, then the sound of the driver clambering in.

–Water, and bread, jam, bananas, cheese, peanuts, Haribo, dog food, he said. –Making good time so we'll stop for twenty and you can eat sitting up.

They climbed down from the top of the pallets and sat on the lorry floor to eat in the half-dark.

–Be long till we're there? Swift said.

–Depends on the traffic. Should still be there by eight. Any of you been to London before?

–No, Poacher said. He sounded angry, Jake thought.

–Big place, the driver said. –Very big.

–Bigger the better, Swift said.

–So d'you know where you're going, when I let you out? Last drop's to John Lewis on Oxford Street.

–Who's John Lewis? Poacher said.

–It's a shop, not a person, Ollie said. –A big one.

The driver nodded. –Department store. Got everything you could ever want in there, if you got the money.

–So we'll get out there then, Swift said, and she bent down to Cass, gave her another bit of banana.

The driver shook his head. –Shop'll be shut by the time we get into London, end of the day, but you can't stay in there. They'll have scan hubs all through the place.

Davie began to say something, but Martha kicked him.

–Wouldn't wanna stay anyway, Poacher said. –Stay out, stay safe. That's what we do.

–So where do other people go from John Lewis? Swift said. –The ones you've given rides to?

–One of the parks. Regents Park, Hyde Park. Or the Tube, I reckon. Bond Street, Oxford Circus, same difference. Doesn't pay to know too much, but I heard there's people like you in the Tube. Not on the platforms – only ever see mice on the platforms – but in the tunnels down there.

–Thanks, Martha said. –For everything; and the driver nodded back to her, and to Poacher and Swift.

–My sister, the driver said. –It's why I started with the rides—

But Poacher interrupted him. –Doesn't pay ter know too much, he said. –Fer us too. He put his hands together and bowed his head, which was his way of saying thanks.

The driver got it and did the hands thing back with his big sausage fingers. –Let's get on then, he said.

Sixteen

–Now! the driver whispered. –Two minutes, then the fork-lifts'll be over. Good luck.

–Go well, Swift said, and she slipped down out of the lorry, and the others followed. Jake was second out, with Jet on a tight lead beside him.

After the dark of the lorry and the hours lying flat, the lights dazzled and Jake's legs felt like jelly. He didn't know where they were, but it wasn't the time to stop and look. He just ran till he reached the wall. White breeze block. Rough. Cold.

–Where are we? Martha said.

–Delivery bay, Poacher said. –Didn't yer feel the ramp going down? We're underneath the shop.

–We're going out of the emergency exit, Swift said. –The driver said there's some gardens just behind the shop. We go through there first, then the Tube.

They ran up stairs, along a corridor, through double doors heading for the outside. There ahead of them was the emergency exit and Swift had her hand on it, ready to push. Through the glass, lit up by the street lights, Jake could see a line of buildings at a distance, and some railings which must be the park. He glimpsed a few people walking past. *Nearly evening, and they'd be going home*, he thought. *Lucky things.*

This was it. This was London. He was scared, but excited

too. He'd never been here before, but he'd seen enough of it on screens, and heard about it from Liam, when he came back from visiting his grandparents: Houses of Parliament, Coalition HQ, Buckingham Palace. Wembley. And people. Masses of people, everywhere.

–Down! Everyone! Swift's voice broke into his thoughts and he ducked, tumbling backwards into Ollie, yanking Jet's lead so hard that he yelped. –Hub police, Swift whispered. –Don't think they've seen us. Not a sound. And she pointed a finger at Davie.

The floor was gritty and smelled of cigarettes. The gang waited. Davie drummed silently on to the dirty floor, his fingers a blur, and he didn't speak.

Slowly Swift raised her head to the glass in the door, and slowly she lowered it again and shook her head. –Can't go out this way.

–So what now? Martha whispered. –We can't go back down to the delivery bay.

–Into the shop, Poacher said. –No choice.

Jake had never seen a place like it, not even in his dreams. It didn't look like a shop, least not one he'd ever been in. They were in a vast, half-lit hall full of shiny fridges and cookers, pots and pans and kettles and coffee makers. There were shelves piled high with plates and tea towels and mixing bowls, and every other thing you could imagine in a kitchen. Jake had never seen so many cheese graters and whisks and vegetable peelers, and funny gadgets.

–Amazing, Ollie said. –I could spend days in here.

–Sad, more like, Jake said. –Makes me hungry. All this stuff, but no food.

–Head fer the main stairs, Poacher said. –Find another

emergency exit, head fer a park. And he was off again and the gang following.

–A park, Jake whispered to Jet. –Then you can run; and he felt Jet's tail brush against his leg. He understood.

They moved quietly, the carpet muffling their footsteps, Swift at the front, then Cass, Poacher at the back. They passed a dozen tables, each one laid for a party with different coloured candles and napkins and plates and bright cutlery. In the middle of one table stood a silver tree, little unlit candles in glass holders hanging from its branches. Jake saw Cass stop and turn her head at it, her mouth open in wonder.

–Look, Cass!

Davie took a box of matches from his rucksack and lit the candles on the tree. The tree seemed to sparkle and glisten in their flames, and Cass clapped her hands. Davie sat down on a chair. It was like a throne, high-backed and painted gold. He picked up a knife and fork, and pretended to eat, the 'chink, chink' of the fork against the plate. Jake heard Cass chuckle, and saw Poacher turn, all in a moment. Then Poacher was yanking Davie from the chair, nearly lifting him off the ground by the collar of his donkey jacket.

–What're you doing? Trying to get us caught? He blew at the candles, snuffing out their flames.

–Easy, Poacher. Martha's voice was calm, but her grey eyes were wide. –He's only a boy.

–There's smoke alarms, fire alarms, prob'ly sound alarms too, Poacher said, but he let go and Davie fell to the floor.

Davie was twitching now, his arm coming up again and again, swiping a hand across his face, still grinning, but frightened too, Jake reckoned.

–Wanna stay in the gang, you shut it, Poacher finished.

Then he slung his rucksack back on his shoulders and went on.

They passed an escalator and next to it, a board with a long list. Jake read from the top:

Luggage
Haberdashery
Toys
Bedroom Furniture

He wasn't interested in Luggage and he didn't know what Haberdashery was. But Toys. Toys was a word from another universe. He'd have run up all the escalators there and then just to walk through that department. They'd have solarplex kits and worldcraft ones, he bet they did. He'd only ever had one kit. They were expensive.

–Jake! Come on! Ollie said, and he ran to catch up.

At the far end they found themselves in a big lobby, all bright wood and marble and metal. The floor was so shiny that Jet skidded and his claws clattered. There were lifts on one side and ladies toilets and wide stairs on the other, marble ones with a curving wooden banister. But it was another sign that got them all staring. In front of them was a high arch, tiled in white with little blue flowers, and a sign above in big gold letters: FOOD HALL.

The gang stared in through the glass doors below, and for a few seconds, even Davie was speechless. The room was decorated all around the edge with painted vines and birds, and from the ceiling great globes of glass hung down, which must be like a hundred glowing suns when they were turned on. On the walls were huge photos of children holding hands. Big children, and little children.

Like us, Jake thought. He looked round at the gang. And it was like he saw them, and himself, suddenly, like the lorry driver must have: a bunch of dirty-faced kids with filthy clothes and straggly hair and hunger in their faces.

–Is this for real? Davie said then. Because through the doors, below the big photos of clean, smiling children, they saw food beyond their wildest dreams. Real food. Cakes covered in icing, and chocolate, and cream; and pastries and tarts with fruit, and chocolates – posh ones with pink and purple bits – and sweets, and every kind of biscuit you could imagine. There were cheeses, and salamis, dozens of them, and whole chickens roasted. There were twenty different bowls of olives. Fruit glowed like jewels: raspberries, grapes, bananas, pineapples. There were samosas, and sausage rolls, and little tarts and big tarts, and meat on little sticks, and pork pies.

Jake had never seen anything like it. Somebody's stomach rumbled loudly, and Jet gave a little whimper. He had his nose in the air, sniffing and sniffing.

–This place stinks, Poacher said.

–What d'you mean? It smells wonderful, Ollie said.

Poacher shook his head. –Stinks o' money. Stinks o' the Coalition; and he was already turning away. –Right, let's get out.

–You're not serious, Davie said.

–It ain't safe in here, Poacher said. –An' we leave no mark, remember? That's a rule.

–We're safe as bloody houses till the morning, Davie said, pointing to the ceiling. –See that? That's cutting-edge hub tech, that is. They don't need any seccas walking round the shop with that stuff. Believe me, I know of what I speak.

Jake wanted Davie to explain more, but Poacher wasn't

listening. –We'll find food outside, he said, and he walked back towards the stairs.

–Wait, Poacher, Swift said. –Nowhere's safe. You know that better than any of us. But we're all hungry. Ten minutes. We can take ten minutes: it's no more risky than stealing out of bins, which is what we'll likely be doing tomorrow. So long as we're careful. So long as we don't make it too obvious.

Jake watched Poacher stop and turn around. He stared at Swift, then at the rest of them in turn, and there was a pause, like he was deciding. At last he nodded.

–I don't like it. But ten minutes, then we're out of here. On my whistle.

It was like the whole gang took a single, deep breath. Like they were standing on the edge of something, and then all at the same time, they swung the doors open and dived in.

Jake saw Ollie grab a handful of olives, and Poacher pull out his knife and cut through the plastic on a side of ham. *So much for being careful*, Jake thought. *If someone finds us now, we're done for.* Then he thought: *if someone finds us now, I'll be mega pissed off cos I haven't eaten anything yet*; and he ran to the nearest table and unwrapped something and took a bite.

Jake never dreamed he could eat that much that fast. It was mad. All you had to do was reach in under the glass for whatever you wanted. He ate pastries, and cake, and mouthfuls of salami, and something made of meringue and cream and raspberries. He didn't even like meringues. Three minutes in and his hunger was gone. Four minutes and he was full, but he kept on eating because when would he ever be able to eat like this again? Down the next aisle, he grabbed some chicken drumsticks and got a slab of red meat for Jet. That made him pause: watching Jet tear at the meat, his tail threshing the air. Up the next aisle and a movement caught his eye. It was Davie, waving a bottle, under a sign that read 'Beers and Wines'.

–Get over here, dog boy! Get some o' this, yer cruddy little orphan. Best place to be.

Jake ran over. Davie was chugging back from the bottle. It had apples on the label; another lay spilt on the floor and there was a smell that was sweet like apples, and heady. Jet sniffed at the liquid, put his head down like he was about to drink, but Jake yanked him back.

Davie twisted the cap on another bottle and took a swig. –Sweet 'n tasty. Do yer good, dog boy. Forget your sorrows. Your mum and dad swilling about in the water. Drink up and you won't even know you've lost 'em.

–Davie! Jake kept his voice low, but he couldn't disguise the panic. –You're drunk!

–Helps, you know? Davie held his hands out in front of him. –Look. No shakes. An' I ain't ticcing. Nothing.

–I don't care. If Poacher sees you . . . Jake whispered. He looked round for Martha. She'd know what to do for him. But she was nowhere near. He couldn't see her. So lifting a big bottle of water out of the cool cabinet, he twisted off the lid and pushed it at Davie.

–Drink! Now.

He grabbed a loaf of bread, tore it in half and pushed it at Davie.

–Eat!

Jake's stomach was churning now, watching Davie. He thought if he ate another thing he would be sick. But there wasn't much time left and he didn't know what his next meal would be, or Jet's, or when. He emptied some grapes out of a punnet and poured some water in for Jet. While Jet drank, he found bags of nuts, and biscuits, and bars of chocolate, and sweets, stuffing them into his rucksack. And reaching under the blue light of the meat counter, he took two more big pieces of steak for Jet, rolled them up in shiny white paper, and unhooked a tube of salami for himself. He cut the salami in half, zipped the whole lot in with the rest.

Pulling Jet with him, he jogged up past the fish counter, and down past Patisserie. There was Swift holding a bunch of bananas, and Poacher, tipping pork pies and samosas into a bag. There was Martha wrapping up some cake.

–Martha— he began; but then Poacher called: –Two minutes; and Jake remembered the thing he most wanted to find of all, in here. Raisins.

Up and down the aisles he hunted, and as Poacher called the minute, he found them. Strawberry-coated, the little pink boxes said: 'Goodies for Good Little Girls' on the label.

–Not my style, he said to Jet, –but Mum would be pleased, eh? And he stuffed a box into the last small space in his rucksack as Poacher whistled. Time was up.

Seventeen

Davie was drunk. Drunk as a lord. That's what Jake's mum used to say. So drunk he was falling over and giggling. So drunk that they couldn't leave the shop. So drunk he wasn't scared when Poacher went crazy.

In the lobby outside the Food Hall, Poacher and Swift went into a huddle. Jake leaned against the stair rail. He felt sick, longed to lie down. He watched Cass on the stair below him, back to the wall, knees tucked in, and Jet beside her, how she had her hand on Jet's back, her fingers dug into his fur, then stroking him.

–My mum used to shop here sometimes. Before, you know . . . Ollie whispered. –Used to buy proper Italian pasta. She said she'd bring me when I was older.

Jake was impressed. You had to be high up in the Coalition, or have a lot of money, to shop in places like this. It was like the total opposite of food banks. If you were poor enough, you got Universal Credit and your hub chip got you into a food bank; and if you were rich enough, it got you into places like this. You could only get in with the right info on your hub chip. It wasn't in the laws, and they didn't tell you at school, but everybody knew how it worked.

–My mum used to bring me back Spanish oranges, and marzipan fruits, Ollie said.

That was when Davie kicked off his wellies and started doing these slides down the lobby floor, taking a run-up and whooping, one end to the other, and back again. It looked fun. Jake would have joined in except he felt so queasy. But then Poacher stepped in, face dark as thunder.

–Stoppit, Davie . . . he said, and then: –Yer carry on doing that, I'll deck yer.

But Davie went right on.

–I mean it, Poacher said, and now Davie was chanting under his breath:

–Fight! Fight! Fight! – like they used to at school.

–Shut up, Poacher said. He was twice Davie's size, but Davie was too drunk to shut up.

–Fight! Fight!

Then Poacher brought his hand down, fast, in a hard blade of a blow and caught Davie down the side of his head.

Martha was there before Davie even hit the ground, and she drew a knife. She drew a knife, pointed it at Poacher, her grey eyes hard. –You touch him again, I'll cut you, she said, and Cass's hand paused in its stroking.

Poacher gave Martha this long look, but he put his hands into his pockets and turned away, and she put her knife back in its sheath.

Martha got Davie cleaned up in the ladies' toilets and he didn't look so drunk after that. But Jake wasn't surprised when Swift said, change of plan, they'd spend the night in the shop, head for the Tube in the morning.

–What about Security? Ollie said. –The seccas will have Tasers and stuff in a shop like this.

–Davie was right, Swift said. –Cutting-edge hub kit. Sensors activated by hub chips so they've got no need for patrols. We've got no hub chips, so I reckon we can sleep easy.

–Where are we going to sleep? Jake asked her.

–Where d'you think?

*

They climbed the silent escalators on all fours. Davie was shivering and very pale. He looked like he might throw up. He was muttering something under his breath and every minute or so he was doing his face swipe, three times always, like he was swatting a fly on his cheek, but angry and hard, so that he'd made his cheek red with it.

Jake kept his eyes on Ollie's trainers, just in front of him. The steel escalator steps were steep and cold, their sharp edges bruising his shins. With each step, they seemed to suck out his energy and by the time they reached the first floor, his arms and legs felt like lead. Beside him, Jet trotted from step to step, waiting each time for Jake to catch up.

Questions buzzed in and out of Jake's mind like little flies: When could they sleep? Why did Martha draw a knife? What if Swift was wrong about Security? How would they get out of London? What if they got to Scotland and his grandparents were dead?

What if they never got there?

The shop was quiet as the grave and high as a cathedral. It smelled different from any place Jake had ever been, like someone was pumping special air in that was scented with a little bit of different things all at the same time: perfume, and clean wool, and bread, and the air in the hills.

Four floors they climbed, to the top, then Poacher led them through stands of bathroom stuff, round the edge of Lighting and past Sofas until they reached the Bed Department.

A bed department, big as a football pitch, Jake reckoned. Twenty, thirty different beds set out there, big ones and bunks, beds covered with fake leopard skin and beds covered with roses. There were nightlights by the children's beds. A rabbit glowed pink in the shop's half-dark, and an owl shone blue and green. Just the sight of all of them had Jake yawning. And not just him: everybody was doing it, everybody except Poacher.

–Choose quick, an' stay close together. We got an early get-out, Poacher said. –I'm setting a watch. So don't get too comfy.

–Keep your boots and rucksacks close, Swift said. –In case we have to leave smartish.

Jake was given the last watch: 3.30 till 5 a.m. He pulled off his boots and loosened the laces, so they were ready to pull on quickly: Mrs Hadley's boots that he'd stolen that first morning of his escape. They looked pretty knackered now, but at least they didn't look like girl boots any more, all the pink gone to grey.

The bed was cold and soft with pillows piled three-high. The pillows smelled like clean clothes. They smelled like the wind. He lay back and the pillows rose around him in a white cloud and he breathed in the smell. He patted the space next to him.

–Hey, boy, he said, and Jet leaped up, did that dog-turning thing three times, lay down and was asleep. Jake was bone-tired too. But not sleepy. Too much going round in his head.

–The rabbit'll watch over us, Ollie said, and he made the nightlight wave a paw.

The bed warmed up and Jake shut his eyes, slipped one hand under Jet's side. It was like being back home. He kicked out his legs and swam deeper under the covers. He was drifting, drifting, and it was his parents' bed around him, as wide as the sea. He was swimming under the covers and he could hear his mum singing in the shower, and there was his dad's voice calling up from the kitchen.

–Jake! A hand on his shoulder, shaking him awake. He opened his eyes. –Your watch, Ollie said, shoving the timer at him. Ollie got into the next bed, pulled the duvet to his chin and closed his eyes.

Jake set the timer for his hour and a half, pulled on his boots, tied the laces. Then he sat back up in his bed, stacking a pillow against the headrest to lean against. He looked across the shop. He had a good view from here: he could see all the beds, through the Bathroom Department and the Bed Linen and the Lighting Department and right across to the escalator. There were the emergency exits. Before they'd gone to sleep, Poacher had shown them their get-out routes, the one to the left past the children's beds and the one to the right under a hundred different lamps.

–If yer have to make a run for it, keep crouched. Make it hard for 'em to see yer, Poacher had said. –An' the stairs, they got good banisters for sliding. Safe ones. We can git down faster than any adult that way.

Already the day was streaming through the skylights. Jake looked at each of his sleeping gang. They didn't look tough or hard right now. They looked like a bunch of kids tucked up for the night. Even Poacher. Even Davie. Kids who'd be shouted for in an hour and called to breakfast and sent to school with a pack-up box.

He'd always had a pack-up at school, and it always had the same things: sandwich, bottle of water, apple, crisps, biscuit, raisins. His mum was stricter than Liam's or Josh's and he didn't always get the crisps and she wouldn't let him have squash to drink. But then Liam and Josh never got raisins and the raisins were the best bit. Sometimes his dad would forget them, but not his mum. They'd be tucked in there, in a little twist of paper, and sometimes, if she was going away for work, she'd put a message on the paper: 'Eat up your carrots. I love you.' Or: 'Don't keep your dad up too late. Boys need sleep too. Love Mum.'

The sadness rose like pain, and he buried his head in Jet's fur. –Dad, he whispered. –Mum. And it was strange to hear the words out loud, because he never said them any more.

He didn't cry for long because he had to keep watch. So he wiped his eyes on his sleeve and looked across the shop, and back to the beds.

Ollie was still awake, watching him. –Can't sleep, he said. –Too strange in here.

–Yeah.

–You all right?

–Just missing stuff. Just wishing it was all ordinary. Like this was a sleepover and my mum was gonna make me a pack-up again. I looked for raisins in the Food Hall.

It sounded silly when he said it out loud, but Ollie only nodded, like it was a natural thing to hunt for, so Jake tried to explain.

–It's cos of my mum. Cos she always put them in my pack-up, on account of her great-grandpa. Five times great, she told me. Six times for me. She used to say each one. Great-great-great-great-great-great.

–Your mum sounds like fun, Ollie said. –So what about him? What's he got to do with raisins?

Jake checked Ollie's face again, but he wasn't smirking. He just looked curious.

–My mum used to tell this story, Jake said, –About how he got shipwrecked . . .

–Shipwrecked! Ollie sat up, bolstered a stack of pillows behind him. –For real? In a boat?

Jake smothered a laugh. –Keep your voice down, you're frightening Jet. Because Jet had growled and sat up. Jake patted him. –Lie down, boy, it's only Ollie; and he went on with his story. –Yeah for real. In a lifeboat in the Atlantic, and there were sharks, and men going crazy, and dying from drinking sea water, real adventure stuff. And after days and days, it was only my great-grandpa and another sailor still alive. And all they had left to eat was raisins, and then they were down to the last two . . .

Jake paused, looked around. Everyone was asleep, everything was quiet. He leaned back against the pillow and took a deep breath. They were safe here. Better in these beds than in a lifeboat for days.

–*E allora?* Ollie whispered, and Jake knew what he meant, even though he didn't understand the words.

–They got rescued, he said. –And my great-grandpa got married and never went to sea again.

–Else you might not be here hunting for raisins, and telling me this story, Ollie said with a grin.

–True enough.

–You know what I'd like to do? Ollie said. –Stay here for, maybe, a week. Hide out in the day till the shop shuts, then eat in the Food Hall, and sleep up here at night.

–Yeah, be nice. Jake yawned. He could fall asleep again right now at the drop of a hat.

–So did you find any raisins?

Jake rummaged and found the pink packet.

–The pink is not so cool, Ollie said.

–I'm giving them to Cass. She won't mind. And he slipped them into his jacket pocket to give her later.

–Imagine your grandpa on the lifeboat, and he opens the box, and the only thing to eat is these girly pink raisins.

Jake laughed at that thought and Jet gave another growl. –Ssh, Jet. I'm only laughing, Jake said.

–But I can top you for pack-ups, Ollie said. –My dad would put *pignoli* in mine for a treat.

–*Pignoli*?

–Little almond biscuits, chewy in the middle. They melt in your mouth. Ollie closed his eyes and he made a little chewing movement.

That set Jake off giggling again, then Ollie too, and the more they tried to stop, the worse it was, till they were laughing so hard they had to bury their faces in the bedclothes.

This time Jet's growl stopped Jake's laughter dead: a deep, low rumble that Jake could feel more than he could hear.

–Jet? Jake said, and a sliver of ice ran down his back. Jet's ears were flat to his head now, and his hackles were raised. Jake gestured to Ollie to be quiet. Then he heard them: men's voices, two at least, and getting closer.

–Stay, he told Jet, and he slipped off his bed. Two steps to Ollie's and a hand over his mouth too.

–Got our own sharks now. Two of them, probably got Tasers and batons. On the far side. Be here in less than a minute.

Ollie's eyes widened and Jake took his hand away.

–Seccas? Ollie said.

Jake nodded.

–*Porca vacca*, Ollie whispered.

Jake's mouth was dry, but he kept his voice calm. He was thinking fast. –No time for us to escape. Not all of us. So we've gotta be decoys.

–Us? Let ourselves be caught? Ollie said.

–Yup. Maybe. That's all Jake said, but inside he was

raging. If the gang got caught, it would be their fault, his and Ollie's, but mostly his. And he'd rather be dead than that.

–No! Ollie's voice was a whisper, but it had the force of a scream. –I can't do it. I'm going to be sick. And I have to get to Scotland. I have to get to my dad.

The men's voices were louder. Tasers could fire from up to a hundred feet away, and they could take out three people in one go. Three people before reloading.

–Swallow it, Ollie! Jake kept his voice to a whisper. –We do this, or everyone gets caught. When I say it, run. You go that way, he pointed, –and I'll go this. Jet stays with the others. We make some noise so that the men chase us. Duck and dive as much as you can. But don't head for the emergency exit, cos that's the way the others'll go. Try for the escalator.

–Have we got a chance? Ollie said.

Jake shrugged. He'd got no idea. –Long as we're running, we're free. He hitched Jet's lead round the bedpost. –Stay, boy, he whispered. Then he got hold of Ollie's arm, pulled him to his feet. –Go!

Ollie stumbled off, then Jake was up and running the other way, taking no care now to be quiet, and the men were after them, shouting to each other, crashing through the displays.

Jake ran to the far side, cutting between dressing gowns and slippers, swerving and switch-backing round stands of coloured towels. Behind him the thud of a secca's boots. Maybe he could cut back and get down to the floor below. That would keep his secca busy. Diving under a rack of nighties, he crouched low for a moment, tried to catch his breath. Flowers swirled around his head.

–Stop where you are! Get down on the floor.

The shout came from the other side of the shop. Jake looked over to see Ollie shoved to the ground, a Taser pressed to his neck. Turning back, he saw a flash of moving colour in the far corner: Poacher's beanie, disappearing through the stairs door. The others had got to the stairs unseen. They had got away.

Jake set off again. The others had got away and he felt like he could run for ever. Like he was quicker and smarter than anyone. He'd get to the escalator and slide the rail down to the next floor, and from there to the next, and all the way to the ground floor and be out through an emergency exit and then he'd find the others, cos they wouldn't have gone far, and they'd have Jet with them – wouldn't they? – and they could plan how to rescue Ollie.

He didn't see the man till too late. Didn't see the Taser raised. The slug struck him in the shoulder, piercing through jacket, sweater and shirt, piercing through to his skin. He was on fire. His shoulders, arms, legs, all of him. He fell to the ground, muscles spasming. Pain rushing through him.

–Hello, sonny! a man's voice said, then everything went dark.

Eighteen

His head hurt, and his arms and his legs, but his head worst of all. It felt chopped up.

Jake opened his eyes. He was lying on a floor. It smelled of old breath and smelly shoes. Flicks of dust, bits of Pringles, a Haribo wrapper.

He wanted the pain to stop and he wanted to sleep. He just wanted to go back to sleep. His fingers felt fizzy, and he realized he was lying with one arm beneath him. Slowly he tried to turn over, to get more comfortable, but his body didn't seem to be working properly.

–Jake! Ollie's voice, scared.

Jake shut his eyes again. Something had happened. He'd been running, and there'd been a voice, and then what? Ollie was scared, and he was on the floor.

–I thought they'd killed you, Ollie's voice said. –Till you started groaning. I thought you were dead.

–What's happened? Jake said, but he couldn't get his mouth to work properly and his words came out slurred and quiet.

–They caught us. They locked us in here.

–What's happened to me? Jake said.

–They zapped you. Fired a Taser at you and you just dropped. So they dragged you in here, and me after you. Locked us in. Two seccas.

It was coming back to Jake now. The chase, the running,

the escalator just out of reach, Ollie getting caught. Then pain. Like a hundred forks jabbing, twisting into him, taking him out at the knees.

–Just us? Jake said.

–Dunno. It's just us locked in here. The seccas, they were asking me what was my name. They searched our rucksacks, took all the food. Took my dad's scarf too. Only thing of his I had. I didn't tell them anything, but they've gone to get a scan hub. And they're gonna put it to our necks, and then what?

Ollie was panicking, Jake could hear it in his voice.

–Cos they'll get no reading, Ollie said, his voice rising, –and then they'll pull down our collars and see. Our scars. See we've got no chip. See the Outwalker sign.

Jake needed to get up. He couldn't think, lying flat out on the carpet and Ollie's voice yabbering on. –Gimme a hand, he said. He felt weak as a baby, and his legs and arms were like jelly. Ollie pulled him up and he managed to stand.

They were in a poky little room. No windows. Just the desk and two chairs and an ancient-looking laptop, like the one his dad kept in a box in the loft. Feeling steadier, he walked across the room. He tried the door handle, but it was locked top and bottom.

–I've done all that already, Ollie said. –And checked for grilles, loose floorboards.

–Not like the movies, Jake said. He thought about Jet. Surely someone, surely Swift, would've grabbed his lead and got him out? –The seccas didn't say anything about the others? he said.

Ollie shook his head.

–Then Poacher will have got them out, Jake said. He'll have got them to the Tube, I bet. So if we find the Tube, we'll find the others. Jet will be safe too.

–Shut up! Ollie said. –Shut it about the others. He was white as a sheet, his eyes opened wide. They were like pieces of blue glass; they were holes of fear. He banged his hand down on the desk. –And shut it about your dog. We're locked in this room and we're not going to find the others, or your dog. They're gonna come back with a scan hub and they're going to send us back to a Home Academy and we'll be locked in isolation for weeks and be in the Home Academy till we're grown-ups and then we'll have to work off our tariff till we're old, and—

–Ollie, stop! Jake shouted, as loud as he dared. And then, more quietly: –Get a grip. They mustn't see we're scared.

–Scared. Ollie's voice was quiet and flat. –You ever been in isolation?

Jake shook his head.

–I did two weeks, Ollie said.

–What happened?

–Nothing. Nobody shouts. Nobody touches you. They put you in this room and leave you there. Everything's soft. Soft walls, soft floor. Soft food, soft voices. No dark. And at first you think it's OK. Nice even, after being shouted at and ordered around. But it's terrible, and you don't know if it's day or night, and then you don't even know which way is up or down. I begged them to let me out. Said I'd do anything. And after that . . . He looked at Jake with that wide, scared look. –You scream, but the walls eat the sound.

Jake didn't really understand why it was so terrible, but he could see Ollie's fear. He tried to think. They must still be in the shop, and still on the top floor too, because Ollie said they dragged him straight in here. He reckoned that once they'd been hubbed, the seccas would get rid of them to the hub police quick as possible. And that would be their chance, he reckoned. Make a break for it when they were in the shop maybe; or before they got put in the van.

–We've gotta make a plan, he said.

But Ollie wasn't listening to him. He was staring at the door.

The seccas barged in like they were ready for war. Body armour, helmets, loads of stuff hanging off their belts. One of them locked the door and the other put a red and blue box on the table.

Jake's heart sank. He knew what it was. They used to bring a portable scan hub box in for Citizenship classes, and you'd all line up and the teacher would put the chip reader to the back of your neck and scan your hub disc. When the scan light glowed green, you could look at the screen and see the infopage about you. Only this time, when the secca did it, there'd be no green light and the infopage would show a blank.

Next to him, Ollie was breathing in quick, shallow breaths.

Jake watched the secca lift the scanner hub out of the box and turn it on. A few seconds and it was live.

–Gonna get you two back where you belong, the secca said. He lifted the chip reader out of its padded compartment and rummaged in the box for a cable.

Jake couldn't watch. He looked down at the scratty carpet. –Get on with it, he muttered.

The secca was still searching, opening different compartments, unzipping side pockets. –Cable's not here, Jimmy, he said. –Go get the spare. You'll be quicker than me.

–You watch these two then, Jimmy said, and he gave the boys a hard-eyed stare. –Any funny business, you'll be goners. Specially you, he said, pointing at Jake, –cos twice in a day, it kills people. Heart attack. And he tapped his Taser holster in case they weren't completely clear about what he meant.

The other secca made the boys sit on the floor. He pulled out a chair and sat down astride it, one hand on his Taser. Reaching into his pocket with his other hand, he took out a packet of Wrigleys, folded a couple into his mouth. The spearmint smell made Jake shut his eyes against the knot of memory: his mum hunched over the computer. She always chewed Wrigleys when she worked, and in the last weeks before the accident, when she never stopped working, that's what he could smell when he came home from school, and went up to bed, and came down in the morning.

–So come on, the secca said, –what you doing anyway, holed up in here? How come you didn't get picked up by the scan hubs?

Jake stayed silent, but Ollie started making a noise, like he was clearing his throat. Jake looked round at him.

–Shut up! he mouthed, but then Ollie began to cough, a rasping, hacking cough, and he went red in the face.

The secca picked at his teeth. –Pat him on the back, he said. –I won't shoot.

Jake patted Ollie on the back, but the cough got worse and now Ollie was gasping for breath.

–Can't . . . breathe. The words seemed squeezed from Ollie's lungs. His face had gone purple, and his body heaved, as if he was trying to drag the air in.

–Shit, the secca said, and now he was bending over Ollie, banging him on the back.

–Water, Ollie gasped, and he fell forward.

–Lie him down, the secca said. –Keep his airway clear. Pull him over, come on.

Jake was pulling as hard as he could, but Ollie was unconscious. A dead weight. The secca took Ollie's arm and yanked him over and Ollie lay slumped on the floor.

Jake's heart was racing. He slapped Ollie's face, listened to his chest. Nothing. He slapped his face again. –Come on! he said. –Come *on*! He didn't want to say Ollie's name aloud. Then he turned, furious, to the secca. –He's not breathing. You've killed him.

The secca was on his feet and shaking his head. –I ain't taking the rap for this, he said. –Just doing my job. Not me that Tasered a kid.

And he took a last look at Ollie on the floor, and was gone. The door swung open behind him.

In the silence of the room Jake could hear the sound of his blood beating in his ears. Ollie was lying dead on the floor. His eyes filled with tears. –Wake up, he whispered to Ollie. –Please. Wake up! Come on!

Ollie opened his eyes. –Sweet, he said in a normal voice. –You really care!

Jake stared, open-mouthed. –You faker, he said, and he laughed then, relief flooding him like sweat. –You bloody brilliant faker! he said.

–Told you I was a good actor, Ollie said. –Just came to me.

Jake clatted Ollie round the head, and got to his feet. –I owe you, he said. –Now let's get out of here.

Slinging his rucksack on his shoulders, he went to listen at the door. It was quiet outside. Everything in him wanted just to run for it, out the emergency exit and into the green of that park. But his brain was working fast now, and he reckoned the seccas would be using the stairs.

–Head for the escalator, he said. –Keep down.

He inched the door open and peered out. Rows and rows of school uniforms hung up like ghosts: grey pinafores and white shirts and grey trousers. But no sign of anybody.

–Let's go, he said.

They were nearly down the first flight when they heard the secca. He was roaring with anger, boots clattering on the escalator steps. Jake glanced back. The man looked deadly angry, Taser out ready, and he was gaining on them.

–Gotta go faster, he called to Ollie.

–Yeah, we could fly, Ollie called back, and that's when Jake had it. Of course. The handrail. Top to bottom of the tall building, a straight stretch at the side of each escalator, the well in the middle plunging all the way down to the ground. His mum had banned him from sliding banisters after he'd smashed into the hall table and knocked out a tooth. But now he could hear her voice in his head and it was telling him: *Slide! Go!*

It *was* like flying, and he could smell the friction burn on his jacket sleeves and feel the heat on the inside of his legs. Everything in him was braced to stay balanced. If he lost it, he'd be done for.

There was no way he could slow down at the bottom, and when the handrail dropped away he tumbled backward on to the ground, and Ollie on top of him. Scrambling to their feet, they made for the next rail down. Ollie went first this time and Jake was about to follow him when a movement caught his eye. Two floors above him, the secca had copied them. He looked like a rhinoceros astride the narrow rail, and he was going faster than them. Fast enough to catch them up.

The secca was already down to the next landing. He'd got his Taser in one hand now, ready to fire, fingers round the trigger. Jake had to do something or the secca would be there.

There wasn't time to think.

–Watch out! he yelled.

It seemed to happen in slow motion. The secca looked round. Then he stuck out his Taser arm and lost his balance, windmilling with his arms. And then . . . then his body tipped sideways, over the sheer drop on the escalator's edge, and he fell. Down. Down the well, down past Ollie still sliding, down and down and down to hit the ground with a dull thud and the shrill sound of a hundred bottles breaking as his body smashed against a perfume stand.

By the time Jake got down, Ollie was kneeling by the secca. He had his fingers held to the man's neck – checking for a pulse, Jake guessed. Then he saw Ollie give the man a little shake, like Jake's dad used to do in the morning to wake him up. But this man wasn't going to wake up. Ollie must know that really, because nobody could lie with their head twisted round like that, and be alive.

This man was dead.

Jake gagged. Perfume bottles were smashed all around the secca and their scents were so thick in the air Jake could almost see them. They stuck in his throat and made it feel sore, just from breathing.

He watched Ollie stand up and turn away from the body. He was white as a sheet again. Then Ollie leaned forward.

It must have been everything he'd eaten in the Food Hall, the whole lot. Jake had never seen anyone be that sick, and when there was nothing left to throw up, still Ollie was heaving. But there wasn't time for Ollie to sit down, or even for Jake to find some water for him. They had to get out of there.

–We gotta go, Jake said. –Come on. He put a hand on Ollie's shoulder, but Ollie was shivering and grey-skinned. He needed to sit down, away from the dead secca and the perfumes and the glass, and he needed someone to put a blanket round his shoulders and make him something warm to drink. Jake had seen his mum do that. But he couldn't do that for Ollie now.

–We killed him, Ollie said. –If we hadn't . . .

–We've gotta go, Jake said again. –Now. The secca's dead, nothing we can do. They'll be here any second, and they'll blame us for his death, doesn't matter what happened. Doesn't matter that it wasn't our fault. They'll lock us up.

He pulled at Ollie's arm, but Ollie shook him off and turned back to the secca, put his hands together, closed his eyes and began muttering under his breath.

–What are you doing? Jake said. Then he understood. He hadn't seen anyone pray before, except onscreen.

When Ollie stopped, he still looked a grey colour, but his eyes were brighter. –Let's get out of here, he said.

The boys ran headlong down the short flight of stairs towards the emergency exit.

–Been here before, Jake said. He looked through the glass: no hub police this time. He could see a park across the road, entrance right across from the shop. That's where the lorry driver had told them to go: the park, and the Tube. Behind them, he could hear voices shouting – muffled now, but in a few minutes, maybe sooner, someone would come charging through that door, hunting for them.

He pushed down the Exit bar. He heard a bell go off behind him, but the door swung open and they were out.

Nineteen

Jake hit the pavement running. It was busy with people. Men in smart suits, women in high heels carrying pad cases, all on their way to work – Jake could smell their cleanness. The men had slicked hair and the women wafted perfume.

At least we smell like them! he thought.

Their faces were closed in, most of them plugged into their mobiles, or wearing i-glasses. Some were invisible beneath umbrellas, though it was barely raining. None of them looked at the two boys who'd tumbled out of the John Lewis emergency exit. Weaving between them, ducking the umbrella spokes, Jake reached the kerb with Ollie close behind. Get across the road and into the gardens fast, before the seccas tracked them out of the shop – that was his one thought for now.

He looked round at Ollie. He was still pale, and wobbly on his feet, and Jake could see that if he didn't sit down very soon, he'd fall down.

–Come on, Ollie, Jake said, and he grabbed Ollie's hand and ran straight into the traffic.

Cars braked and a cyclist yelled, –Out my way! You want the hubbers?

But Jake didn't stop running. They were across and into the park, except it wasn't very big. He glanced at a sign: *Cavendish Square Gardens*. There were a few trees, some benches, clipped hedges, neat flower beds. A statue of a man on a horse. But the gardens were too small, there was nowhere to hide. He glanced back towards the department store.

–Uh-oh, he said, because the emergency exit door was wide open and he counted three, four, five seccas muscling on to the street. Big men in black gear, and all of them holding Tasers and batons. He saw people staring at the guards, then looking away. He saw the guards looking over to the gardens.

–I've gotta sit down, Ollie said. –I can't walk any more.

Pulling him by the arm, Jake half dragged him to the far side of the gardens. He glanced back again. The men were crossing the road, waving their Tasers at the cars to force a stop. Where could they hide? If he'd been alone, he'd have climbed a tree, or run out of the gardens and down another street, but there was no way Ollie could do that.

Jake sniffed. There was a smell, a foul smell coming from somewhere. He looked around. Nothing to see except some grass and a path and railings. Beyond the railings what looked like a small rectangle of space. They walked towards it and the foul smell got stronger.

–It stinks, Ollie said. He was right; it did. Now they were closer, Jake saw that the rectangle of space had a set of filthy stairs leading down to a door with a big padlock on it. His heart leaped. In front of the door was a heap of rubbish: dirty cardboard, takeaway bags, twigs, leaves, food wrappers. The smell must be coming out of that pile. Something dead, he reckoned, but he didn't want to think about it too carefully, because that pile of rubbish was their only chance. There was nowhere else to go.

–Hold the railing, Jake told Ollie. –Put your foot in my hand. And before Ollie could say anything, he punted him up, so that Ollie pretty much fell into the stairwell, tumbling on to the pile of rubbish. Without pausing, Jake jumped down after him, and before Ollie could say anything, he put a hand across his mouth.

–Don't say anything. Just lie down, he said, and he gave Ollie a little push, to show him he was serious. Dead serious.

The smell was so thick he could've cut it with his penknife, and the perfume smells on them made it even worse. Jake gagged, clenched a fist to keep his nausea down. Pulling at the cardboard, he tugged it over Ollie. It was damp and clammy in his hands. He threw a couple of takeaway bags over the top, and you couldn't see that there was a boy underneath.

–*Porca vacca*, it's disgusting, Ollie whispered. –I can't breathe.

–Shut up! Jake whispered back. –Move an inch and you'll never see your dad again.

Then he lay down beside Ollie and, fast as he could, pulled the rubbish over himself. One bag gave way, and his fingers sank into something soft and cold and he wanted to scream, and if he hadn't heard the guards' voices calling out, he'd have been out of there, with its foul smells and dead things.

The boys lay like stones. Jake breathed through his mouth, small shallow breaths, so as not to gag, but he could taste the dead smell even so. Moments after he'd got himself hidden, there was the sound of heavy boots and then a man's voice, angry-sounding, just above them, talking into his mobile.

–You find 'em, you bring 'em to me. He was my partner four years. It's me got to tell his wife and kiddies.

Jake gulped. The dead secca had a wife and kids. Course

he did. And they were blaming him and Ollie for the secca's death. Didn't matter that it wasn't their fault. If they got caught now, they probably wouldn't make it back alive to a Home Academy anyway.

–Yeah, static crew's checking the CCTV, just had a text, the voice said. –They're gonna get some mugshots out on the public screens. Yeah, OK.

Jake willed him not to look down. The seconds seemed like hours till he heard him shout across again.

–Nothing here. Just rubbish, takeaway skank. Stinks. We'll head for Harley Street or Dean's Mews. We'll catch 'em pretty soon if they've gone that way. The scan hubs'll pick them up.

The seccas must've gone and it was quiet after that, but the boys still waited another half-hour before climbing out, first Jake, then Ollie. Only as Jake leaned down to give Ollie a pull-up over the railings, and Ollie's foot pushed aside one stretch of cardboard, did Jake see where the stink had come from. A dead dog with black fur stared from a dustbin sack. Its head rolled sideways: its eyes were gone and its lolling tongue was covered in flies. For a split second, a chasm opened and the world went dark.

–Jet!

Ollie looked down. –It's not Jet. It's a different dog. Pull me up!

Because, of course, it wasn't Jet. The dog had been dead too long to be Jet. Jet was somewhere in London with the gang, and he was safe with them. Wasn't he? Jake took a deep breath to slow his heart and took hold of Ollie's arms to drag him out.

It was still early morning and the gardens were quiet. The seccas were gone and other people were busy going to work. Jake looked out at the buildings beyond. His mum had promised to take him to London one day. They'd visit the museums, and ride on the Tube, and climb to the top of the Shard. Now he was here, and all he wanted to do was get out. It was his fault: he'd found the lorry with the Outwalker sign. The lorry heading in the wrong direction. They never should have taken it, cos this city was evil. It didn't care about anyone, and it hated them. It hated Outwalkers. That's what he felt.

The buildings around the square were huge, white and brown and grey, a hundred, a thousand panes of glass staring coldly back at him. Although the air was warm, he shivered. There was still rain in the air, but it wasn't that. These buildings didn't care about a couple of lost boys, they only cared about themselves.

–I don't like London, he said. –Sooner we're out of it, the better.

–Sooner we're out of this square too, Ollie said. –I heard them. They think we're murderers. They'll keep hunting.

They walked quickly to the gate at the top end of the gardens, the end furthest from the department store. Just inside it, Jake spotted a water fountain. He washed his face and hands as best he could, then he refilled his bottle. Finally he had a drink. The cold water was delicious and despite his hunger, despite his fear, he felt revived.

–Get some of this, Ollie, he said. –Best water I ever tasted.

He turned round. Ollie had slumped down on to a bench just inside the gate. He looked bad. His skin was still grey, and his hands were shaking.

–I can't go any further, he said. –It was that guard falling, and then being sick. I've got nothing left in me. I'm sorry. It's my blood sugar . . .

–You'll get us picked up straight off, looking like that, Jake said. He could feel the panic in his body. If he didn't do something fast, it would overwhelm him, and then where would they be?

Ollie needed somewhere to rest, somewhere out of sight and away from dead dogs. Jake could see that. Somewhere under cover. But where? He looked around at the empty gardens and the tall buildings. What were they going to do? Pushing Ollie down on to a bench, he crouched down to him.

–Stay here. Just for a minute.

Leaving the gardens, Jake crossed the road. He had an idea. There was scaffolding up one of the buildings, and stretched across the lowest scaffolding was a sheet of blue plastic twelve feet high, as if they'd started to wrap the building up. He couldn't see any builders. Maybe they were on another job; his dad said that's what they did all the time: two jobs at the same time.

A bottom corner of the plastic was flapping, and when Jake knelt down, he saw that if you lifted it up you could slip behind it, if you were nimble. Space enough for a couple of boys, anyway. So Ollie could rest there while Jake went foraging for some food.

Course it was a risk: the builders might turn up, and need to climb behind the plastic for some reason. But it was less of a risk than Ollie staying in the gardens. The guards would be back; or someone would get nosy about the boy sitting on a bench during school time and phone in to the hubbers, or ask too many questions. Then they'd match Ollie's fingerprints to the fingerprints on the dead secca, and they'd match his DNA.

Jake didn't think Ollie would survive getting locked

away. Ollie made out to be very grown-up and cool about things. But he wasn't. He was a kid who desperately needed to find his dad.

Jake imagined this happening. It would be like the scene in the olden-times movie his mum made him watch once because it was her favourite when she was a girl. The children wore olden-times clothes and ran after old steam trains, and at the end the biggest sister walked along a station platform, and her missing dad appeared through all the steam and she ran to him and he hugged her so hard he lifted her off the ground. That's how Jake imagined Ollie finding his dad again.

Ollie was off the bench when Jake got back, and standing beside a map board just inside the gate. His eyes were shining.

–I found a place— Jake began, but Ollie interrupted him.

–Look! he said, and he pointed to the map board. –Look!

The map showed a criss-cross of streets, with names and numbers, and yellow blocks of buildings, and small patches of green. YOU ARE HERE was written on the green patch in the middle of the board.

–*Cavendish Square Gardens*, Jake read.

–That's where we are now, yes. But look hard, just above. What do you see?

Jake looked. All he could see were streets, and more streets. –Come on, Ollie, we need to be out of here. Now.

But Ollie wouldn't be hurried. –Look at the Tube stations, he said.

There, above the red Bond Street Tube sign, Jake saw it: another circle, scratched on to the plastic surface, and in the middle of it, a small dot.

His heart leaped. –Nice one, he said. Now they knew where Poacher and Swift and the rest of the gang would be. They could head over there as soon as Ollie was strong enough to move again.

They made a den for Ollie behind the scaffolding and plastic. He lay on the ground with his rucksack for a pillow.

–One of us needs to stay near the gardens, case the gang comes back here, Jake said. –I'll be quick as I can. I checked out the bins in the gardens: no food. But you need to eat, and soon. So I'm going to find a food bank.

Maybe it was lying down that did it, but Ollie had gone scared again. –What if the hubbers get us before we find the gang?

Jake took off his jacket. –Here, put this over you. Makes you look more like a heap of old clothes, less like a boy.

–That other secca, he got a good look at us. They'll find us on the CCTV. I saw the cameras in the square. Ollie put a hand on his rucksack pillow. –And my dad's scarf, the seccas took that, remember? So they'll give that to the sniffer dogs and the dogs'll sniff me out, even in here.

But Jake wasn't listening. –I know I can't get in without a chip, he said, –but there'll be people coming out with bags full of food and I reckon one of them'll give me something.

–And what if the gang don't wait for us? Ollie said. –What if they aren't at Bond Street Tube? What if they leave London before we find them again, what then?

Jake didn't have an answer. That was the scariest thought of all and it frightened him too. But if he really thought the gang had gone, then he'd just sit down with Ollie and not get up again.

–I won't be long, he said. –And I'll bring back food. Sort

out your sugary blood thing. I promise. Then we can get to Bond Street and down into the tunnels and we'll find them.

He knew how scared Ollie was, being left there on his own, and too weak even to make a run for it, but they didn't have a choice.

–Gimme your hand, Ollie said. They bumped knuckles, and Jake left.

Twenty

Jake had never been into a food bank, but he knew how they worked. If you were poor, the food bank scan hub would know it, and it would let you in. You went there each week and you got given bags of food. His mum had explained it to him, and he'd seen the food bank buildings in the town, with their huge red and blue FB above the entrance, and the queue of people waiting outside with their red and blue bags. Because if you didn't have the right bags, they wouldn't give you the food, his mum said.

–The Coalition looks after you cradle to grave, Miss McCarthy taught them, and she showed them pictures of olden-times starving children. –Nobody in England need go hungry now.

Some of the kids at school brought food bank vouchers for school dinners too. They got different dinners from everyone else. Grey stew with white bits floating, and mashed turnip and grey mashed potato, and pink blancmange. And they had to eat it all up, or else. Sometimes voucher kids missed playtime because they hadn't eaten their dinner. Once a girl in his class sat in front of hers until going-home time, and the teacher put it in a plastic box for her to take home. The ordinary school dinners looked really nice, but his mum wouldn't let Jake have them.

–Can't change the system, but as long as there are voucher kids, you're having a pack-up for lunch, she told him.

He scanned the streets. Food banks were usually in busy places where everyone would see them. And they always had tall red and blue flags flying that you could see from way back. But the buildings in London were so tall he'd never see any flags, and these streets were too quiet. The longer he left Ollie, the more likely Ollie would get caught. He needed to be fast. But he didn't want to catch anybody's eye, and he didn't dare run. So he walked, as fast as he could, reciting the street names back to himself under his breath to make sure he could find his way back.

He noted a flagpole, a red crane, a clock hanging out into the street, a flower shop, an oval blue sign on a wall. He paused to read it.

Leopold Anthony Stokowski, Musician, it said.

Must be an old sign, Jake thought, because nobody would get a sign on the wall now for being a musician. Then a boy's voice called out.

–Hey! Lamer!

Before he could stop himself, Jake turned. He'd never heard that word before, but he could guess what it meant. A group of boys in school uniform were standing outside a school on the other side of the road and staring at him. They were about his age, and they didn't look friendly.

–Ain't you got any pals? On your own? The voice was hard.

Jake carried on walking. He wished he had Jet with him. Or Ollie. Or the gang. This lot wouldn't make a peep if Swift and Poacher were here.

What if they haven't waited? The thought came in at him like a poisoned arrow, its barb piercing his skin, its poison spilling into his bloodstream, sapping his strength. He looked over his shoulder. Two of the boys were walking towards him.

One of them shouted again. –Where you from, weirdo? You from Europe? You some lame Euro Peean?

He'd have to run for it. But his legs felt weak. He didn't know if he could.

Brrrrring!

The bell made him jump. Then a woman's voice, not loud, but penetrating. He knew she was a teacher: –Carlos Edgars and John Lee. In. Now!

Jake glanced back. The boys had stopped dead. They were turning. He took a deep breath and he was away safe.

–You! Boy! The teacher's voice again, but this time she was talking to him. –Shouldn't you be in school?

Exhaustion washed over him. The teacher was standing on the kerb with her hands on her hips. She was angry. But when he looked at her, he saw her face change.

–Come here, she said more quietly. –You look like you need some help.

Now she looked kind. Like she'd put an arm round his shoulder and get him some hot food, a cup of sweet tea. She'd ask him how he got those cuts and scrapes, and why he was so exhausted. And then she'd phone someone and it would all be taken out of his hands.

He wanted so much to cross the road and let her fetch him in. Tell him he could be a bona fide again. Tell him what to do and where to go. Look after him.

He didn't think about Ollie lying on the ground, waiting for him. He didn't think about anything. He just wanted an arm round his shoulders.

He walked towards her.

You and Jet, always. It was his mum's voice, inside his head. Him and Jet. He'd promised her.

He took another step. The teacher was waiting.

You and Jet, always. There it was again, his mum's voice. If he crossed the road now, he'd never see Jet again. Somewhere in this city, Jet was waiting for him, and they had to get to Scotland, because he'd promised his mum.

He shook his head and turned away from the teacher, and walked on up the street. A minute later he was at the top of a massive road, traffic roaring, and there on the corner red and blue flags flying, a food bank. *We're looking out for you*, the sign said below the smiling face.

–Yes! Jake whispered, and he punched the air with relief.

At the entrance, he could see the scan hub and a woman checking a pad screen as each person went in. The hub light lit green as each of them walked past. There was a line of people queuing, like always, their red and blue bags flapping around in the traffic wind. And they looked just the same as they used to back home: poor and patient. A few had their eyes down, looking at their mobiles, but most were staring up at the news screen.

A photograph filled the screen. A man holding two small children by the hand. He was smiling out at the camera. Something about the man's face was familiar, but Jake couldn't place it. Then the LED ticker tape spattered across the bottom:

Heroic security guard . . . Father of two Gregory Miller . . . murdered in John Lewis, Oxford Street . . . Ruthless duo occupied store overnight . . . still at large . . . Police warn: pair armed and dangerous . . . Do not approach . . . Any information leading to their arrest, text INFO to: 07721 . . .

Jake wanted to run away fast. What if one of those people looked at him and guessed? What then?

Don't run, a voice in his head told him. They haven't

even said it was children. Nobody's looking at you, and you need food. He reached back to pull up his jacket hood, make himself invisible that way. But the voice cut in again: No, don't do that either. You pull your hood up, people will wonder why you're hiding. But you're just a boy outside a food bank. That's all.

So with his hood down, and walking, not running, Jake went round to the exit.

People left quickly with their bags of food, like they couldn't get away fast enough. Finding a spot in the shadow of a big building, Jake watched them from a distance: a steady stream of people hurrying off. He just had to choose the right person. Someone who looked kind. A bit of food to get Ollie on his feet again, and get them both to the Tube: that's all he needed. Then they could find the others . . .

But what if the gang had gone? What would him and Ollie do then?

Angrily he pushed the thoughts away, but they were there in his head, those fears, barely out of sight, just waiting for him.

He counted the people out. Five, ten, fifteen people.

Come on, he told himself. Get on and do it. He went and stood just a few feet away. He could see in from here: could see the guard stood just inside.

Then, gathering his courage, he went up to someone.

–Excuse me, he said.

The woman was about his mum's age. She wore jeans and a jacket with little blue hearts on it and she had lots of bags, so he'd guessed she must have children, and he thought she had a nice face. He glanced quickly down at her bags. There was a sliced loaf at the top of one, and he could see tins in another and a carton of milk.

–We got separated from our parents, he said, –and we're very hungry. The woman stared at him like she didn't understand. So Jake tried again. –If you could spare a few slices of bread, or a tin? Any tin? I've got a penknife, I can open anything . . .

She'd stopped when he spoke to her, and he could see the guard looking their way. *Come on*, he thought, *before the guard comes out*. The woman beckoned to him, and he took a couple of steps closer. Maybe she'd give them a tin of beans and a tin of fish. Maybe she'd give him a swig from the milk carton.

Leaning forward, she whispered, so only he could hear, –I know what you are. You're an illegal. We've been warned about you. Disgusting, your parents are, sending you out like this.

Jake stepped back. The woman's mouth was twisted into a thin line and she was staring at him like he was something evil.

–They're not, Jake said. –You don't know anything—

But she cut him off with a shake of her head. –Lucky for you I'm in a hurry, else I'd take you and report you to a hub post myself.

And with her bags on her arm swinging in at him, she reached and grabbed him by the ear and wrenched it round so that he fell to his knees with the pain, despite himself.

–They want food, tell them to go on the Universal, like the rest of us.

She let go of his ear and walked off.

Before he could run, before he even could get to his feet, the guard was over to him. Jake tried to roll away, tried to resist, his fingers scrabbling at the pavement for something to hold on to, but she was much stronger than him, and she grabbed him by the arm and pulled him into the food bank. He wriggled and turned, trying to get free, but her fingers were like iron.

She bent close to him and whispered in his ear, –I can handcuff you if you prefer it, she said. –But they're not nice to wear, even for small boys. So I suggest you come quietly, lad.

Her voice was worse than her grasp, and Jake's strength deserted him and despair filled his veins.

–Now don't make a sound, or else, the guard said.

People stared coldly at him as they walked past with their bags of food. Pulling him into a side room, the guard pushed Jake down onto the long wooden bench that ran down one side and shut the door.

–Don't move, or I'll cuff you, she said.

On the other was a wall of metal lockers. Taking out a bunch of keys, she unlocked one and swung the door open. Despite his fear, Jake gasped, because the locker was stacked high with food. Chocolate bars, cakes, fish tins, tins of fruit. Cartons of juice.

–Not a sound, remember? she growled. –Gimme your rucksack, and he watched her stuff it with food: a packet of KP nuts, some bread rolls, a couple of tins of fruit, two cartons of juice, three slabs of malt loaf, two chunks of Cathedral Cheddar, two packets of biscuits, a box of Mr Kiplings and two bars of Fruit & Nut.

–Now I'm going to take you out like I've punished you. Keep your head down and rub your eyes like you've been crying. Don't run. Walk. And if anyone asks where you got that food and you so much as mention Euston Road food bank, I'll swear blind you held me up with a knife and stole it from me. Do you understand?

Jake nodded, and she grabbed him by the scruff of his jacket and pushed him in front of her, out of the locker room and back into the corridor where people were still leaving with their bags of food.

–Get out, she said loudly, her voice sounding rough and angry, –before I report you to the hub police, and she shoved him out of the exit.

Jake kept his head down all the way back to the scaffolded building. It was raining now but he didn't care. Glancing round to make sure no one was watching him, he slipped behind the flapping plastic.

But Ollie had gone.

There was nothing in the space behind the scaffolding except a heap of old clothes in one corner.

–I said I'd be back. And I said I'd find food, Jake said. –You just had to wait for me.

Tears pricked at his eyes, and he took a kick at the pile of clothes.

–Ouch!

Jake jumped at the voice, and then as he watched, the pile of clothes untangled itself.

–You didn't need to kick me, Ollie said, sitting up. –I thought I should disguise myself better. He rubbed his elbow. –Least it worked, I suppose.

–I thought you'd blinking gone and left, Jake said, and he took a swipe at his friend.

Shadows passed by on the outside of the plastic and the two boys froze. When they'd gone, Jake pulled off his rucksack and unzipped it like a magician with a rabbit.

–Breakfast, like I promised, he whispered. –Look!

And he grinned to see Ollie's face.

Twenty-one

They ate inside the sound of falling rain. Not just any rain, but thunderous, heavy drops that slammed into the pavement and ricocheted back against the plastic sheeting like bullets. The storm took the light from the sky and the air grew cold, but with food to eat, the boys didn't care. When they'd eaten their fill, they packed the remainder into rucksacks. Jake pulled on his jacket, felt the rattle of the raisins in their box, somewhere deep in the lining.

–Ready? Jake said.

–Yep. Tube's not far, Ollie said. –I checked on the map in the gardens.

Jake pushed aside the plastic and looked out. The street was empty. –You first then, he said.

Ollie was a different boy with food inside him, and Jake, having to run three steps to Ollie's long-legged two, was glad it wasn't far to the Tube. Within a minute he was soaked to the skin, but at least with the rain coming down so hard, nobody looked twice at two boys running. Ollie turned left down a long, narrow street lined with smart shops and cafes, and at the bottom, he stopped and pointed.

–Bond Street Tube, he said.

And there it was, the Tube entrance lit up, blue and shiny through the rain, on the far side of a huge street, pavements packed with people. Just a stone's throw away.

Ollie turned up his collar. –Keep your neck hidden. Don't want people seeing our scars.

Jake had never seen so many people, everybody rushing, clipping and cutting across each other. The crowd looked solid, no way in, but Ollie had disappeared already, eaten up by it. So Jake took a few deep breaths and followed him. It was like stepping into a vacuum, all the air sucked out. Faces in their mobiles, minds somewhere else, people caught him with their bags, swung their umbrellas into his face. Ollie was ahead of him, already disappearing, and he tried to catch up, but the crowd was so strong he felt himself pushed against the road barrier, felt the breath squashed from his body. His head felt dizzy and he was slipping down towards the grey pavement slabs, gasping for air.

Then a hand was on his collar, pulling at him, and Ollie was there, his lanky length shielding Jake from the crowd, standing firm against it. –You all right?

Jake gulped deep draughts of air. He nodded.

Ollie put out his hand. –Hold it till we get to the Tube, he said. And then, seeing Jake's expression, he rolled his eyes: –Get over yourself, or stay here. Up to you.

Jake didn't know how Ollie did it. He seemed to weave around people, find gaps where there weren't any, and a minute later they were inside the Tube station. It was as crammed as the street outside, with crowds of drenched people standing around, eating street food, waiting for the rain to stop. Scan hubs were mounted on the walls above people's head, and reflexively Jake pulled his collar up. Slowly the boys made their way through the people, inching closer and closer to the ticket barriers.

Nearly back to the gang. Nearly back to Jet. As long as

the gang hadn't left already. Jake shook the thought from his head and ducked out of a wet umbrella's way.

Along the walls, screens showed adverts for *Les Miserables* and Coca-Cola. Above them, the red ticker tape news bulletins spewed out:

. . . Coalition to clamp down on illegals . . . scientists testing virus antidote . . .

They were close to the barriers now. Jake watched people hold their mobiles to the swipe pads on the silver posts; the barrier opened, and the moment the person was through it closed swiftly behind them.

Nice one, Jake thought. *We can't buy a ticket because we haven't got a mobile. But we can't get caught because we haven't got a chip.*

He tapped Ollie on the shoulder and pointed to the barriers.

But Ollie didn't respond. Instead he pointed to high on the wall, to the ticker tape feed. Jake looked up.

PM promises greater security against outlaw swarms . . . US President in surprise interest rate decision . . . outlaw gang murder London security guard: police close in on suspects . . .

Round the station the ticker tape spooled: *police close in . . . police close in . . . police close in*, on every side.

–We have to get out of here, Jake said quietly.

–But we haven't got mobiles, Ollie said. –We can't swipe.

–We can slide under. Just do what I do, Jake said; and before Ollie could say another word, he crouched low, then dived beneath the barrier, head between his arms, fingers laced in front of him, sliding on the tiled floor. Seconds later, he was under and up on the far side and people were staring at him, taking photos. They were waving at the hub camera, and the hub camera was turning slowly towards him. He looked back. Ollie was shaking his head.

–Come on, Ollie, Jake said.

Behind Ollie people were pressing in, impatient. Jake saw him take a deep breath, put his hands together, close his eyes.

He's praying, Jake thought.

Then, with a little shout, Ollie dived.

They were halfway down the escalator when the hub police arrived at the top, lights flashing, tannoy booming: STAY WHERE YOU ARE. STAND TO THE RIGHT. DON'T MOVE. The escalator ground to a halt and people stood frozen to the spot.

Jake's first instinct was still to make a run for it. It would be risky to shoot at them: too many other people in the way. And if they ran now, they could head for the nearest platform, jump down at one end, run into the tunnel, take their chances. Better that, surely, than stand here and be caught. He was ready to give Ollie the signal when Ollie nudged him.

–I know what you're thinking. Don't do it. Take a look. There are tons of them.

–But . . . Jake said.

Ollie shook his head. –We haven't got a chance.

Jake glanced round. A crowd of hub police jostled at the top, all of them weaponed up. Helmets, black gloves. And as he watched, they started pushing their way down the escalator stairs, three lots of hub police on the three parallel escalators. Somewhere a baby started crying, its wail echoing off the tiles. Any second now and it would all be over. He gritted his teeth and gripped the rail.

He felt Ollie lean forward into him. –You've been a proper friend, Jake, he said quietly. –I won't forget, whatever happens.

The hub police were steps away now. Jake could hear their grunts, could hear people's cries as the police trampled past them. Shoulders hunched, he kept his head lowered. You didn't look around. You didn't watch what was happening to someone else, in case it happened to you. But this was happening to *him* – and the man on the step below him, and the woman on the step above Ollie: they would look at their shoes, or their phones, or anywhere else they could, when the hubbers arrested two boys. Any second now.

JoJo used to say the police pulled zip ties too tight on purpose, specially on kids. There was a boy in their Home Academy who JoJo said had been paralysed that way.

Jake took a deep breath. He could smell aftershave, and sweat, and apples. Why could he smell apples? He made himself feel the smooth rubber of the escalator rail, nudged his boot toe between the ridges on the escalator step. His last minute of freedom. He wanted to store the memory, even if it was here, in this underground place, and in London.

He wouldn't see Ollie again, or the gang. Or Jet. He'd never see Jet again.

The baby went on wailing.

Then the hubbers were there, pushing past Ollie and shoving Jake backwards, jamming him up against the rail. A hand gripped his shoulder, tight enough to bruise, and he felt the cold plastic of a baton shoved under his chin and lifted and pressed up against his throat, forcing his head backwards.

The tannoy blared: DO NOT MOVE. HUB POLICE EVENT. DO NOT MOVE. HUB POLICE EVENT.

A hubber stared back at him, her face only inches away from his. She was close enough that Jake could see the bags under her eyes, a livid scar across her cheekbone. She was close enough that he could smell her oniony breath, and he could see her eyes, which were his mother's eyes, true brown, but not kind. And he was close enough that he could see he wasn't what she was looking for. Her eyes tightened to slits, and she lowered the baton and spoke into her wire.

–Bond Street, escalator two, twenty yards. It's a boy. No girl found.

She let go of him like he was something dirty, which come to think of it he was, and ran on down the escalator stairs, other hub police at her heels, and they were all gone as fast as they'd arrived.

Jake stood, dazed. People were staring at him, but he didn't care. He was still free. He felt Ollie leaning forward again.

–They were looking for a girl, Ollie whispered, his voice high-pitched with relief. –Not us.

–One girl and all those police. She must've killed a lot of seccas, Jake said, and he was laughing; he couldn't help himself, even though it wasn't funny.

–It'll be us soon, though, Ollie whispered. –They'll have us on CCTV everywhere, the shop, the gardens, the streets, and they'll be close behind now.

Still everyone stood on the three escalators, hundreds of people in three lines standing in the middle of nowhere, waiting. Then the tannoy voice again:

SECURITY ALERT OVER. PLEASE ENSURE YOU HAVE ALL YOUR PERSONAL POSSESSIONS.

The escalators jolted to life and the boys were swept along in the crowd of people pushing down the steps to the trains below.

They'd been searching the platforms for nearly two hours and Jake had almost given up hope when Ollie finally found the Outwalker sign. The trains rumbled under their feet with a gathering roar, the thunder on the rails, the rush of warm, old air, the blast of headlights as they came out of the tunnels. They'd checked every nub of chewing gum, every scratch, every bit of graffiti, and found nothing. At least the hub police had disappeared, and nobody paid any attention to two scruffy boys. Nobody noticed that they never got on a Tube train. Nobody noticed that they didn't have mobiles, or wondered why they kept their jacket collars turned up, even in the fuggy warmth of the station. Sometimes Jake thought he glimpsed figures like them in the crowds pushing on, flooding off the trains: dirty-skinned and filthy-clothed, eyes shifting and lurking. But no children. Never their gang.

The sign was scratched on to the side of a vending machine: a circle no bigger than a bottle top, and inside it another tiny dot, dinted firmly into the silver metal. Jake ran his finger over it. If you didn't know, you wouldn't even notice it. But this was their lifeline. This was their hope. If they hadn't gone already. If they hadn't gone.

Jake looked down to the end of the platform just a few yards off. A sign showed a bolt of lightning:

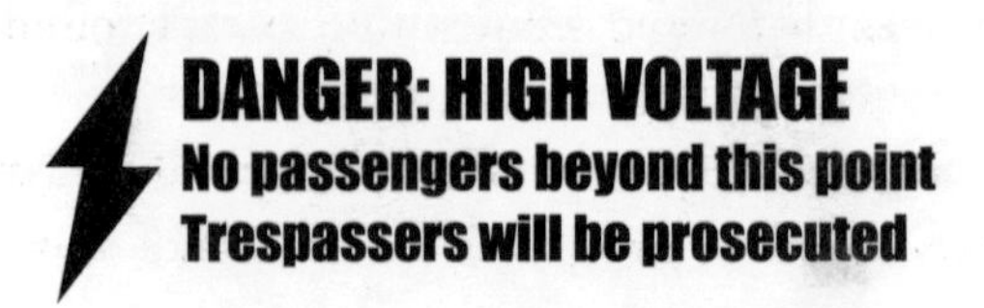

DANGER: HIGH VOLTAGE
No passengers beyond this point
Trespassers will be prosecuted

That's where they had to go. They had to step round the sign, past the barrier, jump down onto the gravel beside the lines and run into the pitch-dark of that tunnel.

–Don't look like you're looking, Ollie muttered, and Jake turned back towards the platform. But a train was approaching, the rush of used-up air, and nobody was watching them. STAND CLEAR OF THE APPROACHING TRAIN. STAND CLEAR, went the tannoy voice.

Another minute, the train pulling out, and they'd be down beside the track and running. Running towards the gang. Running towards Jet.

If the gang hadn't gone.

If they hadn't gone.

Butterflies flicked in Jake's stomach. The gang might be close now. Really close.

The Tube doors opened and people flooded out, shouldering forward past them, jostling into the carriage till they were packed tight as fish in a tin. KEEP CLEAR OF THE CLOSING DOORS, and with a suck of air, the doors shut across the coats and bags and damp umbrellas and the Tube pulled away. Jake looked up at the noticeboard:

1 Stanmore 2 mins
2 Stanmore 4 mins

–Every two minutes, Ollie said, and Jake could tell he was thinking the same thing. Two minutes. That's how long they had to run into that darkness. Two minutes before the next train was there, and what if they hadn't found a way out of the tunnel by then?

The boys leaned against the platform wall and watched another train arrive, fill up and depart. Jake was scared.

More scared than he'd been since his parents died. Escaping from the Home Academy, climbing up the outside of the house, being zapped with the Taser, being hunted by the hub police: none of these was as frightening as this tunnel. Fear sapped his strength, so his legs were shaking and his arms felt weak.

–I'll go first, Ollie said. –Gimme your torch. Soon as we're out of sight, I'll flick it on. Ready?

Jake shut his eyes. He pictured his grandparents and a house by the sea. He'd seen a photo once. He thought of Jet and the gang. Ollie's hand was on his arm. –All right, he said.

The next train pulled out, leaving the platform nearly empty. A glance from Ollie. This was it. Vaulting the warning barrier, they jumped down beside the rails and walked fast into the tunnel.

The ground was rough and Jake could feel the sharp hardcore through his boots. He moved carefully, following in Ollie's steps. The tunnel smelled of dirt and rubber. It was hot. Ollie was coughing. The noises from the platform had disappeared the moment they were inside the tunnel and all Jake could hear now was a low hum. As they followed the curve, the darkness sucked them in and Jake put a hand to the tunnel wall to steady himself, running his fingers along the bricks. The soot was thick, and soft as feathers. It was dense. Ollie turned on the torch and a thin beam of light hit the wall beyond them. Something scurried across the beam, black in the black dust.

–What are we looking for? Jake said.

Ollie shook his head. –Don't know. Anything.

Banks of cables snaked along the wall beside them and blackened girders curved like ribs around the tunnel.

–Which rail's the electric one? Jake said, and Ollie shook his head again.

Jake's heart seemed to be beating very fast and he tried to get deeper breaths. He could taste the filthy air in his mouth and at the back of his throat. The hum on the rails was growing louder, it was pulsing, and he could hear a rumble that must be the next train. Like a beast in its cave, it sounded, just waking up. But they hadn't been walking more than a minute, surely. They must still have another minute till the next train came.

Keep a hand on the wall, keep a hand on the wall, he told himself. We'll see the way out soon. There will be a way out. Sweat prickled his skin. This was the dark of all his old fears. This was the dark for real.

Ollie was walking faster, and the torch beam was jagging from side to side, touching the black walls of the tunnel, striking the cold silver steel of the rails.

–I can't see, Jake said, but only to himself. The hum of the rails was in his chest now. The boys started to run, stumbling through the dark.

Better to die near someone. That was his thought, like a voice in his head, and he saw his mum and dad in the car together, imagined them, eyes open, holding hands, beneath the water.

Ahead of them, the tunnel straightened out, stretching away in a straight line, and now, at its farthest point, Jake saw a beam of light.

The train!

It came so fast towards them, its headlights lighting up the tunnel dark, and in seconds the hum became a roar, filling Jake's head, sucking the air from his lungs, dazzling him.

–JAKE! A voice was screaming somewhere, and Ollie

was grabbing him, pulling him sideways, and he fell hard to the ground as the train thundered past, a blur of steel and red, and it was quiet again, quiet again, quiet again, except for the train's beat dying away on the lines.

Jake lay still, winded. His pulse was banging in his ears and something had happened to his leg.

–Where are we? he said.

Ollie shone the torch around. They were in some kind of passageway. It seemed to be cut out of the rock, stretching away into the ground. Its walls were as black as the tunnel's and at the furthest reach of the torch beam, near the top of the passageway, was a small, whitewashed O sign. Turning the torch on himself, Ollie grinned and made a whoop of triumph.

Jake put his fingers to his leg and they came away, gritty with dirt and sticky with blood.

–I was a dead man back there, he said. –You saved me.

–Give me your hand, Ollie said, and he pulled Jake to his feet. –You all right? He shone the torch on to Jake's face, making him blink. –You don't look great. You got black smudges all over, and to be honest, your face looks grey underneath.

–I'm fine, Jake said, and he nodded to be more convincing. –Besides, you look just the same. Black smears, all that.

–Let's go then, Ollie said. –Cos they must be close by. We'll find them any time now.

And Jake didn't voice his fear, the fear he knew Ollie had too, that they wouldn't find the gang. That they'd have gone already.

The passageway stretched down deeper underground. They might have been walking to the centre of the earth. Jake lost all sense of space and time. His body hurt and his mind was scared, but he kept as close to Ollie as he could, and put one foot in front of the other and kept on walking. Once, as they turned a corner, someone disappeared ahead of them. He was sure it was a person, but it was gone before he could be sure.

–D'you see that? he said, and Ollie had looked back at him with wide, scared eyes.

Eventually the passageway opened up: a vaulted space, brick-walled and half-lit with thin, fluorescent strips.

They stood in the middle of it, and looked around them.

–What is this place? Ollie said.

A long wooden bench ran the length of one side with wooden lockers beneath like the ones in school for where you put your shoes. At the far end, three tunnels led away out of sight. They were numbered: 62, 63 and 64, and Tunnel 63 had a yellow triangle sign and a zigzag arrow with a cartoon outline of a man lying down beneath it and some words Jake couldn't make out. He sat down on the bench.

–The others must've come through here. Maybe they left something. Like a sign for us, he said.

It was good to sit down. He was suddenly very tired.

–Maybe, Ollie said. –If they had time. He was walking round the edge. –Smells like the river, he said. –One of these tunnels. Smells mouldy. Don't like it. I want our gang. Even Davie. He sat down beside Jake. –What if . . . He shook his head. –No. They'll come and find us. They're my family. Our family.

Jake was watching the man on the sign. He was getting up from under the arrow and he glowed in the grey fluorescent light. The man was standing up in the sign now, and turning his head, beckoning.

He shut his eyes. He was too tired to move.

But the man was still there, behind his eyelids, and he was calling to him.

–*This way. Come and join us, Jakey.*

It was a voice Jake knew, like he knew his own name.

–Dad, he whispered.

–*We'll hold your hand*, said his mum's voice. –*Keep you from the dark. Always. Always.*

Down that tunnel. That's where they were. Clear as day, and alive.

Fighting his exhaustion, Jake stood. The black walls shimmered in front of him. He took a deep breath, to drink as much as he could of the warm air. His legs were shaky and he felt hot. Burning from the inside. Hot as anything. The air from the tunnel drifted towards him. It smelled fresh now, not mouldy at all. It smelled of trees, and reeds, and the wind.

–*Come on, Jakey*, the voices said. They knew about the river. They were in the river already, waiting for him.

He walked towards Tunnel 63, towards their voices. The river would cool him down. The man in the sign was waiting. He smiled at Jake, a kind smile, and beckoned, and Jake stepped into the tunnel.

Jake hit the floor with a crash, headlong, the side of his face against the concrete, smelling its bitter, dank smell. He smelled the river and he smiled, because there was his dad and there was his mum, and he felt the grit of the ground against his cheek, and someone was holding his legs, pulling him backwards, and he could hear Ollie's voice, muffled, like it was underwater. Then everything was quiet.

Twenty-two

A long way off, a dog was barking. Something brushed across his forehead and Jake swiped at it. Everything smelled of soot.

–*Porca vacca*, you're awake! That was Ollie's voice, but so loud that Jake put his hands to his ears. His arms felt heavy as stone and a pulse of pain throbbed across his skull. He opened his eyes. Grey light, then Ollie's head, his face, looming in. Dirt was smeared over his face, and his breath stank. The room stank, and everything was loud.

–Quiet, Jake said. –So thirsty. His voice was rusty, hoarse, and his tongue was stuck to the roof of his mouth.

Ollie sat back on his haunches and laughed. –You've been away with the fairies. Burning up, hot as hell, and shouting crazy, crazy stuff. He reached into Jake's rucksack and pulled out a carton of juice.

Jake made to sit up, but something was cutting into him, pinning him down. –Gimme the drink! He reached up to his chest and felt rope tight across him. –What've you done to me?

Ollie's face was serious. –Tied you to the bench. Had to. You were heading down that tunnel. The one with the danger sign. I had to drag you back, wasn't easy. You were so strong, and so crazy. Shouting and shouting, saying your mum was there, your dad, and Jet. So I tied you up. Found some washing line in your rucksack. Only way to keep you safe. You've been out for *two days*, Jake.

While Ollie unpicked the knots, Jake tried to think, but his head was a fog. Where was the dog? Was it Jet?

–You've been ranting nearly the whole time, Ollie said. –Loud sometimes, whispering sometimes, like you were talking to someone, but not me. Just once you were quiet, and that's when I thought you were for it because you went limp, like a dead man, but your eyes were still open. For hours, Jake. Hours and hours.

Jake licked his lips. They were cracked and sore. –I need water, he said.

–Two days, Jake. You've been out for *two days*. I thought I was going out of my head. Tried to get some juice into you, but I reckon most of it went down your neck.

Ollie passed Jake the carton of juice, and leaning up on an elbow, Jake drank it down, the whole thing. Ollie was shouting at him not to finish it, it was the only drink they had, but Jake couldn't stop.

Then something else pushed into Jake's mind. His mum and dad. They'd been here; he could still feel his mum's hand on his hair. They'd called to him, and he'd wanted to go.

–Where are they? He grabbed at Ollie's jacket. –Where are they?

–Get off. Ollie pulled away, stared at him. –Who?

–My mum and dad. They were in Tunnel Sixty-three. They wanted me to go with them. Where are they?

Ollie pulled the washing line out from under Jake. He shook his head. –It was a fever dream, he said. –A wish. There's other people down here. I mean, not our gang, not that I've found yet. That must be what you heard, because I heard them too.

–No. I saw it for real. You weren't here, and they were, and they called me. My mum had on the scarf I gave her for her birthday. The one with blue and red sailboats.

But there was a line in Ollie's forehead, and he looked sad. –Your parents are dead, Jake. You saw them in a dream.

Jake sat up, head spinning, fingers fuzzy. He looked across the space and felt his mum and dad slip away from him, fainter and fainter, and then they were gone.

Gone again.

He could feel it in his chest like a pain, the feeling he had, the sadness.

Ollie filled Jake in on his lost time: Ollie's exploring, the options they had. Tunnel 62 ended at a locked gate, and Tunnel 64 at a river.

–But it's not a river we could cross, Ollie said. –It's like a torrent. I can't see how the gang could have crossed it either. And it's dirty. Really dirty. There's stuff in it, stuff like from your toilet, and dead things. And I saw rats. Big rats.

–What about Tunnel Sixty-three?

–Last one I went into. I know it was your fever, but I was spooked when you saw your mum and dad down there. The torch was giving out, so I couldn't see properly, whether there were Outwalker signs. Anyway, I nearly fell over an edge of the ground – like, the ground just stopped. Disappeared. I couldn't help myself, I yelled out.

–So how deep is it? Jake said.

–I don't know. That's when the torch died.

–Maybe we can get down with the washing line, Jake said. –Even in the dark. Drop a pebble to hear the bottom, give us an idea of how deep it is. Secure it at the top and . . .

Ollie was shaking his head. –We'd be mad. We don't even know if it's the right tunnel. He'd been euphoric when

Jake woke up, but now his voice was flat and dead. Dead as the light in this place, flat as its old air.

–But maybe my parents appearing is a sign, Jake said. He knew it wasn't logical, but they'd been so real. His mum had been wearing her silver starfish earrings. His dad's chin was stubbly, like he hadn't shaved that day.

–Stop there, Ollie said, –because now you're really scaring me. We are not going to drop down a black hole because you saw your dead parents in a fever dream.

–So what then? Sit here and die of thirst?

–No, we go back up. Back the way we came, soon as possible. Out of the tunnel, back through the station. Ollie was putting on his rucksack as he spoke, like he'd made up his mind.

–But the others must have gone somewhere, Jake said. –You're sure we can't cross the river?

–It'll drown us and spit us up god knows where. Miles away, probably. If they've gone in there, then they're dead. And if we go in, we'll just be some drowned boys nobody knows and they'll bury us in a grave with no name.

A shiver crawled over Jake's skin. He saw the dead dog in the pile of rubbish, could feel the smell of it in his nostrils. What if Jet . . . ? But he mustn't think that, and he shook the thought away.

–We gotta try and get across, he said. –We might drown, but we're dead boys, deffo, if we go back the way we came. Good as dead. You saw the screens same as I did. They're hunting for us up there, on the streets above our heads, Ollie. For you and me. Not for the gang. For you and me. We're murderers now. If we go back, they'll catch us, and hub us, and lock us away in one of those Home Academies for really bad kids and we'll never get out. I'll never see Jet again, you'll never see your dad, we'll never see the gang. He slammed his hand down on the bench with frustration. –Come on! Think! He was yelling, but he couldn't help himself. They couldn't come all this way just to turn around and hand themselves in.

He stood up, and felt his legs go from under him, grabbing the bench just in time to fall back down on it.

–*Stupido*, Ollie said. –You haven't eaten for two days. He rummaged in his rucksack and found a slab of malt loaf. It was sticky and sweet and it made Jake feel sick. But he swallowed down a chunk. *You'll feel better for some food.* His mother's voice, but only in his mind this time.

–Ollie? he said, because he didn't want to hear his mother's voice now. Not his mother's or his father's. He didn't want to be sad, and he didn't want to think on dead things. Not dead in any river. Maybe this was it, this room, and him and Ollie; and someone would find them years from now, just skeletons left inside their clothes.

He shook his head. Bad thoughts.

–Ollie, he said again, louder, wanting to tell him he wasn't mad at him really, that they could still get to Scotland, just the two of them, that it would be all right.

But Ollie didn't answer. He was on his feet, and walking over to the tunnels. *Walking like a boy who's seen a ghost*, Jake thought, and his skin prickled.

–Ollie, he said once more, his voice urgent.

Ollie stood at the entrance to Tunnel 64 and stared into the black. –Listen, he said, and faint, very faint, Jake heard a dog's bark.

Twenty-three

Jet came hurtling with his lead trailing, a black fur bullet. Tearing past Ollie, he knocked Jake backwards, licking his face, then stepping back and barking at him, like he used to bark at squirrels, and his tail whipping from side to side. And Jake grabbed hold of him and held on, because Jet felt like the difference between life and death.

Poacher and Martha came out of the tunnel, blinking. Poacher was scratching at his dreads like he couldn't believe what he was seeing. They stood and stared at the two boys, and Jake and Ollie stood and stared back. Then Poacher got this huge grin on his face, punched the air. Ollie whooped, and Jake, and then Martha was hugging them like they were her own boys, which maybe they were, in a way, and it all started Jet up with his barking again.

They'd brought food and water, which was musty-tasting, like it had sat around too long.

–It's safe, Poacher said. –Boiled.

Martha had brought her medicine bag, and while Ollie described Jake's fever, she cleaned the wound on Jake's leg and dusted it with sweet-smelling powder and covered it with a big plaster. She rummaged in her rucksack. –Chew this. She gave him a dried strip of wood. –Willow bark.

Then everyone tried to talk at once, Jet too, till Poacher clapped his hands.

–Later. We gotta get going. We found you, is what

matters. But we gotta git out. These tunnels ain't a way through London fer us. Too dangerous. So you two stay here, Jet too, rest up some more. We kin leave yer the water. An' Martha an' me'll go fetch the others. Be back in less'n an hour. Then we kin head out, whole gang, back the way you came in . . .

–No, Jake said. –We can't.

–The tunnels are making Cass sicker, Jake. No fresh air, no daylight. It's like a tomb. Martha's voice was gentle, but firm. –She needs to be above ground, else she won't—

–Not the same way. We can't go out the same way we came in.

–What? Why not? Poacher was tapping his boot, impatient to go.

Jake tried to think, but his brain was still addled from his fever.

–Because we killed a man. Ollie said it, his voice a whisper.

Poacher and Martha just stared at him. Then Martha sat down, hands either side of her on the bench. –You what? she said.

–He fell, Jake said. –From an escalator when we were escaping. We didn't mean for him to die.

–But he wouldn't have fallen if he hadn't been chasing us. He'd still be alive, and he's got children, Martha. He's got children . . .

–Ollie, stop. Poacher gripped Ollie by the shoulders. –Sit down, afore yer fall down; and he pushed Ollie down on to the bench beside Martha. Then he turned to Jake. –What happened? Tell it short.

So Jake explained, as quickly as he could. About the seccas, and the scan hub machine and their escape. About how the secca chased them down the escalator and lost his balance, and crashed to the ground. About how they went to see if he could be alive, but how his head was twisted round the wrong way.

–So they think we did it, Jake ended up. –The hubbers, and the seccas. They're hunting for us up there, masses of them, all round Bond Street Tube, and there'll be pictures up and descriptions by now, everything. That's why we can't get out the same way.

Poacher only took a moment to think, eyes on the ground, hands in his dreads, then he nodded. –Right, let's go, he said. –All of us. Back ter the others. We gotta find another way outta the tunnels, an' fast.

They went down Tunnel 64, keeping close, Poacher first, then Ollie, then Jake and Jet, and at the back, Martha. Poacher's torch lit the path ahead and Martha's from the back took the edge off the darkness and made shadows on the walls.

–Your dog, Poacher said. –If it wasn't for him, we wouldn't'a come. Yesterday he started up with all this whining an' pawing, like he could smell you, or hear you, dunno how. An' we ignored it, but then there's Cass giving us these sad looks. So we followed Jet, an' it took us a bit of here and there, few wrong ways, but yer dog was sure every time, an' here we are.

Jake held Jet's lead and every so often he would bend and touch Jet's fur, and every so often Jet would push gently against Jake's legs.

Down the tunnel went, slanting deeper and deeper into the earth, heading for the river. Alongside them banks of wires snaked. You could just see their colours through the dirt: red, yellow, purple, green, white. The tunnel walls got damper. They glistened green, and from the walls hung white, pencil-long stalactites. They came to a vast chamber hollowed out of the rock, and hammered into a corner a long metal ladder. At the top, a narrow walkway.

–Didn't spot that when I came down here before, Ollie said.

Poacher stopped and shone his torch down. Below them, a dark river ran. Jake could taste the air.

–Breathe through yer mouth, Poacher said. –Smell kin make yer throw up.

The black water roiled and turned. Something was alive in there.

–Eels, Poacher said. –Big 'uns. Bite you bad an' taste good. Get a good price for an eel.

Jake didn't like eels. Teeth that pointed inwards, and too black and slimy. He'd heard stories about eels that could kill you. But they swam for thousands of miles just to lay their eggs, and nobody knew how they did it. Made getting to Scotland look like a vicarage tea party. Jake grinned. That's what his dad used to say, whatever a vicarage was.

Away from the river the tunnel led upwards. Here, the walls were painted again, and there were working lights that buzzed like bees. Cobwebs hung around them like candyfloss.

–Close now, Martha said, her voice excited.

They got to a riveted metal door with a round metal wheel as a handle.

Using both hands, Poacher turned the wheel, and they stepped over the door rim and out.

A white-tiled hall, brightly lit. Escalators leading upwards. Big faded poster adverts on the walls. Jake looked around, panic flooding through him. What had they done? Why had they come here?

–You mad? You brought us up to the Tube station! he said.

But the escalators weren't moving, and there were no people. No passengers. And now he looked more carefully, he could see there was dust over everything here too. The place was echoing and empty. It was wrong. Something creaked behind them and he turned, ready to run. A door opened in the wall beneath the escalator and there was Davie, hurtling at them, and behind him Swift with Cass. They were all grinning, even Cass with those blisters on her lips.

Davie did a kind of dance around them, his arms flying about, till Martha told him to stop. So he grabbed Ollie's arm instead, swung it up and down. –Lost, an' now you're found. Dead, an' now you're alive. He grabbed Jake's and did the same. –Din't reckon to see you again. Not at all. Then he beat a tattoo on Jake's shoulder with his fingertips. –Got a bit to tell you, Jakey boy. Seen a bit down here last couple o' days, Jet and me both, ain't we, Jet?

–Good to see you, Swift said, and she clasped their hands. She was smiling, but Jake saw how pale she was and how tired, her eyes red-rimmed. –Now we can get outta here. Head north. She crouched down, eye-level with Jet, scruffled his neck. –Good one, Jet, she said, which made Jake proud. And Cass, in her too-big parka and her blue wellies, walked up to Jet and patted his head.

Jake buried his face in Jet's fur. –Clever dog, he whispered.

–So what is this place? Ollie said. –Cos it's weird. He'd climbed up the escalator steps, and when he spoke, his voice echoed round the hall.

–Guess, Martha said. –Listen. I'll read out one of the

posters. Star Wars the force awakens. Director's cut in 3D, Real 3D and Imax3D. December 18, 2015.

December 2015! I don't understand, Ollie said. –Why've they got that one up? That movie's from way olden times. It came out before my mum was born. There's been six more since then. I can name them for you, and their cast lists, and their directors, and producers, and–

–'S all right, Poacher said. –Think we kin live without it.

–But I don't get it, Jake said. –Are the posters real?

–Yup, Swift said. –Been there a long time. Ever since things stopped here.

–What d'you mean, stopped?

–It's a dead station, Davie said. –A ghost station. So cool. They shut it after the Faith Bombings. Dynamited the entrance. Abandoned it. So it doesn't exist any more, not officially. This ain't Bond Street, Jakey Boy. It ain't a station to anywhere, so nobody's going to come down the escalator.

Another poster caught Jake's eye. –Listen to this one, he said, and he read it out in a pretend deep voice like the ones on the screen ads. –Experience the wonder of the Channel Tunnel! A dream weekend in Paris. Travel in luxury on Eurostar and visit the romantic capital of the world. Tickets from just £90. Let the adventure begin!

–We got enough adventures already, Davie said. –Don't need no more.

–Yeah, but a train from England all the way to Europe? Unreal! Ollie put his hands together, like he was doing a prayer. –But it'd solve it for me. I wish! And the others laughed.

–So if this station's dead, then how come the lights are on? Jake said.

–Because nobody up there knows that they are, and

nobody up there knows about us, Swift said. She was pulling on her rucksack.

–About our gang, you mean, Jake said.

–Swiftie, tell him, Poacher said.

–About any of the gangs, Swift said. –It isn't hub police that are the danger down here.

–There are other Outwalkers down here? Ollie said.

–No, not Outwalkers, Swift said. –You'll see soon enough. She zipped up Cass's parka. –Anyway, let's go. Sooner we're out of here the better. Sooner we're out of here an' out of London, sooner we'll be on our way north. Scotland. And she dipped a little kiss to the top of Cass's head, picked her up and walked towards the door that led back to Tunnel 64. –Come on then, she called back.

–Swiftie, Poacher said again. –We can't. Not that way. They're hunting for Jake and Ollie up there. They're saying they murdered a man.

Twenty-four

Swift sat down on the escalator, Cass beside her, parka still zipped to her little chin. She didn't look at Jake, or Ollie.

–That was our only way out, she said in this dead voice.

And then it felt like a fog that came down over them. Jake could almost smell it, almost taste it. He looked round at Poacher, at the others. They'd all sat down around Swift and Cass, two steps up, two steps down on the escalator. Martha was shivering, Poacher zipping his jacket higher, though it wasn't cold. Jet must be feeling it too, because he was pressing against Jake's legs, and he had his tail tucked under him, like he did when he was scared.

–There must be other ways out, Ollie said. –Up the top of the escalator, or down there; and he pointed to the tunnel that led away beneath the *To the Trains* sign.

–There ain't, Poacher said, and he ticked the answers off on his fingers. –Up there is blocked off. Dynamited. Down there is a pile o' other gangs . . .

–Why can't we ask them for directions, then? Jake said. –We don't want to stay; we want to get out.

Poacher's laugh echoed round the escalator hall. –Sweet, that is. Ain't it? We kin just ask nicely an' they'll show us the way. Blimey, Jake, ain't you learned anything yet? We ain't asking them cos they ain't offering.

–How come the hub police haven't rounded them up, if

there's so many? Ollie said. –They must know they're down here.

–Hub chips don't work down here, Swift said.

–An' mebbe they are catching 'em, Poacher said. –Davie's heard rumours. People disappearing.

–That's horrible, Jake said.

–Could be the hubbers is picking 'em off, just a one here an' a one there, or could be they're killed by other gangs. Mebbe the hubbers reckon it's easier leaving most of 'em down here, outta the way, long as they ain't a threat. Long as they ain't makin' no secca jump from any escalator.

Even under the dim light, Jake could see the fear on Ollie's face, and he caught a glance from Swift to Poacher. It wasn't like Poacher to be sharp like that.

–Anyways . . . Poacher said, and he put up a third finger. –Third reason we're stuck here: if yer want ter travel over any gang's patch, yer gotta trade wiv 'em. Only way we kin ask them fer help is . . . He rubbed his fingers together. Jake's dad used to do that with his fingers when something cost a lot of money. –We gotta give 'em passage fees, innit? Cos none of them ain't Outwalkers. More likely cut yer, soon as look at yer. Else they ain't gonna help. Gonna do the opposite when they see we're kids.

–Trade with what? Jake said. –We don't have mobiles, or pads. No money . . .

–Most valuable thing is food, Martha said. –Only problem is: we've got next to none left, and what we have got: well, you'd need to be hungry to want to eat it.

Ollie had his hand up, tried to say something, but Poacher waved him down, and Jake saw Ollie roll his eyes and do something with his hands that Jake guessed was from his dad. An Italian thing.

–Bought food ain't the only thing ter pay with, Poacher said, ignoring Ollie like he hadn't seen it. –Plenty I could poach. Rats, mice, eels. Crabs too, white ones on the walls above the river. I don't fancy 'em, but they get a good price. Only problem: someone catches you fishing on their patch, hunting on their patch, ain't no hub police, no anyone to stop 'em . . . And he ran his finger across his throat. –So, bein' straight up wiv yer. Our gang ain't got the strength ter be down here much longer; nodding slightly towards Cass. –No sky, no sun, no proper light. Dunno day from night. An' cruddy air what fixes in yer lungs, each breath. So once you've told us what happened to yer, we gotta make a plan. Ain't gonna be easy, but it's got ter be whatever's best fer the whole gang.

Jake glanced round at Swift. Her face looked blank and she was staring down at the escalator step. He couldn't tell if she was listening or not. Cass was nestled into her side.

Again Ollie tried to say something, and again Poacher waved him down.

–Tell us what happened when yer got caught, Poacher said quietly.

Jake and Ollie told it between them, from when Jake got Tasered to when they heard Jet barking in the tunnel. It was three days since they'd been in John Lewis and there was a lot to tell. But it was only when Jake told about the food bank that he got interrupted.

–So have you still got some food? Martha said, and the excitement in her voice was like electricity, and it was touching Swift and Poacher: it was there in their faces too, and the fog lifted, just like that, like they could see beyond their knees again.

–That's what I was trying to tell you, Ollie said.

With the others looking on, Jake and Ollie set two malt loafs, and the Hob-nobs, the box of Mr Kiplings, a chunk of Cathedral Cheddar, the bar of the Fruit & Nut and the tins of fruit down on an escalator step like a shop display.

–Thought we had three malt loafs, Jake said. –And there was another chunk of cheese.

–You were out for two days, Ollie said. –I had to eat something. I stared at the Fruit & Nut for hours. You should congratulate me that it's still there.

Jake put his hands up. –Respect, Ollie.

But even with the bar of Fruit & Nut, it didn't look like so much when they got it out. Still, it was high-class stuff for trading, Jake was sure of that. He could've scarfed the whole lot, he was so hungry. Hungry and very tired.

He looked up at Poacher, at Swift, waiting for them to say something, but they were looking at Davie.

Davie shook his head. –Ain't enough. Need a lorryload to cross everybody's patch.

–Yer sure? Poacher said.

–I just said. Davie got to his feet. –Not a chance.

Jake let Ollie tell the rest of the story. Exhaustion was washing through him like water, sluicing through his mind so that it was difficult to think, difficult to remember clearly.

–But when the seccas look at the CCTV, they'll see it was an accident, Martha said. –That the secca lost his balance. Just fell.

–It don't work like that, Martha. Poacher's voice was angry. –Don't matter ter the seccas what's true, do it? Easier ter blame lowlifer kids, cos that's what they'll call yer.

–And that's why we can't go back up to Bond Street,

Ollie said. –Cos that's where they'll be looking hardest. We'd walk straight into their arms.

There was silence again, but it wasn't a nice one. Above him on the escalator Jake heard someone shifting their feet. Someone coughed, and when Jake looked round, he caught a glance from Swift to Poacher, saw Swift give a shake of her head. A tiny shake, but it was there. Martha, sitting above them, was making patterns in the dust. She wasn't looking at anybody, but her face looked grim, the kind of grim Jake's mum used to look when she was going to tell him off. The kind of grim she'd looked after he'd grabbed Cass's wellies. When Jake looked back down towards Ollie, he was looking as worried as Jake felt. Jake wondered if he'd had the same thought: what if Poacher and Swift just saw them as a problem now? What if . . .

–So in John Lewis . . . Swift spoke into the silence. –When the seccas came . . . which of you was on lookout?

Jake's stomach lurched. He'd hoped no one would ask.

–Which of you? Swift said again.

–Me, Jake said quietly.

Swift looked at him, and it was hard to meet her eyes. –What happened, Jake? The rest of us asleep in the beds, and the whole place quiet as a tomb. How come you didn't spot them earlier? Warn us earlier?

–They came up from behind— Ollie began, but Poacher put his hand up.

–We wanna hear it from Jake.

Jake stared down between his knees and his eyes swam out of focus. He wished he wasn't here. He wished his mum and dad weren't dead, and he wasn't in this gang, and he was an ordinary boy whose mum told him stories, and who went to school and had a gang of friends to play on the rec with. He wished he was a boy who went home when it got dark, and for whom the scariest thing in his life so far was being frightened of the dark. It was warm down in the dead station, but he felt cold to his bones. He shivered.

–Tell us the rest, Jake. Then we kin decide what we do, Poacher said.

Jake looked up and tried to focus. Their faces were fuzzy, but he knew that everyone was waiting for his answer. It felt like there was a stone in his throat, and he swallowed, but it didn't go.

–When the seccas came, I was thinking about food, he said finally.

–Food? Martha said. –But you can't have been hungry, not after the Food Hall.

–It was about stuff I miss.

–Thinking doesn't explain it, Swift said.

The heat rose to Jake's cheeks, and he stumbled with his words. –Thinking and . . . and talking. To Ollie. So I didn't hear them, didn't see them till it was too late.

Another pause, and then Swift again. –So because you were talking, you nearly got us all caught. And you got Tasered, and now we're stuck down here, under thousands and thousands of tons of London, with freaking scary gangs down every tunnel, and we can't get out . . .

She hadn't raised her voice, but he wanted to put his hands over his ears to stop any more of her words getting in.

–But they're only looking for you, Swift said. –Not for us.

Shock, then silence. Swift's words cut into Jake like swords. She was right. He looked at Ollie, but Ollie was staring at the wall adverts, though Jake didn't reckon he was seeing much. Ollie looked like Jake felt: his skin was greeny white and his eyes wide open, like he'd just seen the scariest beast and it was sat there amongst them, ready to open its jaws and destroy him.

Jake remembered Ollie talking about his dad. Best cook in the world, he'd said. All his love, all his longing had been there for Jake to see. All his hope. And now, any minute, the gang might destroy it.

–Jake? Martha's voice was gentle. –What were you missing?

Martha's voice was gentle. *Maybe she'd understand*, Jake thought.

But before he could speak, Swift banged her hand against the side of the escalator.

–Come on, dog boy! What food? What were you missing so much? You nearly got us all caught. You've driven us down here. You've got the seccas on our backs. You've made it a hundred, a thousand times harder for us to get north. To get to Scotland . . . She glanced at Cass, snuggled in beside her, then went on. –Do you know what a Taser would have done to Cass?

Jake felt his face flush with shame. It would have killed her. Jarred her small body so hard with its violence, her heart would have given out, and then Swift's heart would have given out too. All his bravery since then was like dust when he thought of the danger he'd put Cass in.

Swift was on her feet, her face a mask of contempt. –In fact, don't bother telling us, dog boy. I've had it. If Tunnel Sixty-four, and Bond Street Tube, is the only way out, then I say we leave the two of you here and head there now. You and Ollie: you're gonna have to take your chances, and good luck to you.

Somebody gasped – Jake didn't see who – and the gang

was on its feet, and everybody saying different things. Swift saying to come on, they should get their stuff, leave now, and Davie drumming with his fingers like no tomorrow and calling out – Go! Go! Go! And Martha saying no, and Poacher calling –Sit down. Sit down.

Jake stayed sitting, one hand on Jet's back, and he could feel Jet shaking; Ollie had his head in his hands. Chasing through Jake's mind was a single sentence: *I've killed the gang.* And he wished that the ground would open up and swallow him.

Then Swift shrugged, and zipped up her parka. Her face was all lines: mouth tight, eyes narrowed, cheekbones sharp. But as she bent to pick up Cass, Cass slipped beneath her arms and now the little girl was climbing down the steps, one small hand up to the rail to steady herself. Two steps, then a third. Swift stared at her little sister, mouth open. Then stopping on the step above Jake's, Cass hunkered down and put her arms out round Jet's neck and leaned into him.

Jake kept his eyes on his dog, and he waited for Swift to be there, loosening her sister's hold, putting her arms around her, lifting her away.

But Swift stayed where she was. Sat down again, dropped her head into her hands. Everybody fell quiet. Even Davie stilled his fingers. When at last Swift looked up, Jake noticed the black rings below her eyes; noticed the exhaustion written across her face.

–All right, we stay, she said, –and whatever comes next, we face it together. All Outwalkers. One gang.

When everyone was quiet, Martha asked her question again. –Jake? What were you missing so much?

And he would've hugged her right then, except it would

be embarrassing. But because he knew she would understand, he answered her.

–Raisins, he said.

Silence.

–Raisins? Poacher said.

Jake nodded. There was more silence.

He looked at his knees and waited. Someone made a strange noise, a kind of snorting noise, and he looked up. It was Swift. She was choking; no, she was laughing, and the others were joining in, Ollie too. All of them sitting there and laughing so hard, they were crying, and finally he was laughing too.

–So we nearly lost our cook – an' we nearly lost our climber . . . Poacher spoke between his gasps . . . –on account of raisins. On account of some dried fruit.

–Not a good raisin fer anything, Ollie said, and it was so daft that everybody laughed, even Cass, chuckling silently into Jet's fur. When Jake caught Martha's eye, she winked at him, like she wasn't only laughing at him. Like she understood him too.

Finally they quietened, and Martha passed the water bottle round. Swift turned to Ollie and Jake.

–There's stuff you need to know down here, about the other people.

–We thought we saw others, Ollie said. –And heard them. In the shadows.

–They're not Outwalkers, far as we know. They're illegals. Loads of gangs. Call themselves lowlifers. Grown-ups, mostly. And they aren't trying to get anywhere. This is it, for them.

–They live down here? Jake said.

–There's kids born down here, Poacher said. Long as

you stay down deep enough, you can't be got, cos hubbing doesn't work down here. They say there's one who's been down since the Faith Bombings. Got skin white as milk, hair white as snow. They's all kinds o' weird, Davie's seen 'em. He's bin our scout so far . . .

–I only know about the ones near us, Dave said. –Catchpitters, Friners, Line Kings, Eelers. Catchpitters got the best gear cos they make it out of stuff they scavenge from the catch pits. Rubbish, mostly, that people drop when they're waiting for Tube trains. Food wrappings, bits of plastic, hats, gloves, jewellery, whatever they can find. Some o' them is party people from above, but most is down here fer good.

–Catch pits? Ollie said.

–Trenches between the Tube rails, Davie said. –To catch the leapers.

–Leapers? Jake's head felt fuzzy with all this new stuff.

–You know. People who . . . jump. You know! Davie said impatiently. –To kill themselves? But it doesn't always work. An' mostly the catch pits catch the stuff people drop in there, sometimes by mistake, sometimes on purpose. Different gangs control different territory. So round here is controlled by the Circus, he continued. –But up near Kings Cross Tube, where we gotta get to next, it's a different gang, calls 'emselves the Line Kings. Then there's the Friners going east. They're on the run from interning. Europeans, mostly. They got a name for eating bugs. Cooking 'em up in oil. Lots of cockroaches and yellow scorpions from the tunnels on the Central Line.

–Enough detail, Davie, Martha said. –Ollie's going to be sick.

And it was true, Ollie had gone very pale, and he was shaking his head.

–You don't look so brilliant, either, Martha said to Jake, sitting down beside him, putting her hand on his forehead.

Her hand made him jump.

–You all right? she said, and he nodded, but there was this lump in his throat because the last time anyone did that, it was his mum. Then Martha took her hand away and rummaged in her rucksack, and though it made his throat ache and his eyes ache, he wished she would put it back.

She brought out a small plastic bag with some dead leaves inside.

–You've still got a temperature, she said. –Chew one of these. Stop you feeling so hungry too.

Jake sniffed. –Mint?

She nodded.

He leaned back against the escalator side and chewed. The mint was comforting.

–He needs to lie down, Martha said, –else he'll be ill again. And you, she said to Swift. –If you don't sleep now, you won't be able to look after Cass.

–Prob'ly ain't gonna be our easiest day tomorrow, Poacher said. –An' we should all sleep if we can.

Twenty-five

It was like coming home. The thought took Jake by surprise. It was a feeling he hadn't had for a long time. It didn't matter that they didn't know how to get out of here, let alone how to get to Scotland, it was still like coming home, and not just to Jet. It didn't even matter that the gang had so nearly split down the middle. What mattered was that it hadn't, and now it was even stronger.

Dizzy with tiredness and hunger, he lay down on the cardboard in the abandoned room below the abandoned escalator. Behind him was an oily, dusty mass of machinery and cogs. He could smell it as he lay. Turning around three times, Jet lay down at his side. If Jake moved his fingers, he could touch Jet's paw, feel the soft leather of its pad. On the other side of Jet lay Cass. She was tucked into a cocoon beside her sister, beneath the escalator cogs, just one hand out, resting like a blessing on Jet's back. The others slept close by. His gang, in their den, for now.

Above them hung the two vast barrelled engines that Swift said had once driven the escalator round, those steps climbing and dropping, climbing and dropping. And stretched out above the engines, like a strange silver sky, was the escalator belt, slanting from high up on the left down almost to the ground beyond Jake's feet on the right, little dashes of light coming through the slats. *They looked like stars*, Jake thought.

No daylight, hundreds of lowlifer gangs with no laws to stop them, and they were on the run from the Coalition. But this was their place, their burrow, just for now, and at last, despite his hunger, he fell into a deep sleep.

Jake started awake. He was stiff from the hard ground, and cold despite the fuggy warmth of the Tube station. He felt clear-headed again, and very hungry. It was a hollowed-out kind of hunger, like his fever had consumed everything in him, but that wasn't what had woken him. He listened: Jet's paws were twitching, making small scuffling noises on the cardboard bed – dreaming of rabbits, that's what his mum used to say – but it wasn't Jet either. Then there it was: a steady beat, like a drumbeat. Footsteps? He listened on. The sound was getting fainter now and he lay back. But as he closed his eyes again, it began to get louder, and still louder, a thump-thump noise, till it sounded like it was directly overhead.

He got to his knees. Who was on watch? He should wake Poacher. What if it was a hubber? What if they had come down here, after all? It could be the woman hubber with the scar. She'd recognize him straight off. She had a baton, and a Taser, and she'd be able to call in support. More hub police, armed to the teeth. The gang wouldn't stand a chance. They'd shovel them into a van and lock them up to rot in a Home Academy, one with lots of safe rooms, and they'd each be put in a different one, locked away on their own. And Jet would be sent into kennels, or shot, or . . .

–Stop it, Jake, he whispered to himself. Because it was probably nothing. Just the weird sounds in this place. Probably mice, or rats. And the gang was tired. Everybody needed sleep. He lay down again and shut his eyes.

Above his head, the thump-thump went on. But it wasn't rats or mice. It wasn't just the creaky sounds of a dead escalator. Last time, he'd been too late to warn the gang. He wouldn't make that mistake again. Feeling in his rucksack for his penknife, he flipped the main blade open, and with a whispered 'Stay' to Jet, clambered round the sleepers, pushed open the door into the escalator hall and crept out.

Crawling along the side of the escalator, he looked across the hall to the far side. It was empty, as far as he could see. Above him, the drumbeat noise continued. It was getting quieter again, moving away up the escalator steps. That meant whoever it was, it was only one person. And whoever it was, was going up at the moment, so probably had their back to him at the bottom. So Jake should look round the corner now, before they turned to come down again.

Knife in his hand ready, Jake peered round. No hubber, no secca. Just a small figure in wellington boots, scruffy donkey jacket reaching nearly to his knees.

–Davie!

From the top of the escalator, Davie turned and grinned. –Listen up, he said. –I got a plan!

The dust lay thick on each step and Jake swept it with his arm and sat down, Jet beside him. Poacher sat above him, bleary-eyed. He'd been hard to wake.

Something rattled in the lining of Jake's jacket, and feeling with his fingers through the pocket hole, he found a little box and pulled it out. Cass's pink raisins. The box was bashed about, the pink gone grey, the writing worn off. He'd give them to her when she woke, watch her face.

Davie's plan was simple: find a gang he called the Surfers. Parley with them. Pay them a passage fee. Escape.

–That's it? Poacher said. –It ain't much.

And Davie shrugged. –What choice we got? No more food nearly.

Which was true, Jake thought. *No choice.*

–Stop with the pacing, Poacher said. –Yer gonna wake everybody.

Davie looked wired. He looked like he was about to do something crazy. He stopped pacing but started drumming with his fingers, a small thub-thub sound.

–So what's with Surfers? Poacher said. –Cos you talked about other gangs, Catchpitters, Line Kings, Friners, but you ain't said next to a thing about Surfers before.

–It's the gang we gotta be cool with, Davie said. –They got a leader, he's a legend. Been down here for ever, that's what they say. Fearless too. Surfers is the ones see everything, know everything.

–Yeah, but what are they? Poacher said. –Like, why they called Surfers? An' why you ain't spoke of 'em before? He sounded cross, but Jake reckoned it was only because he'd got woken out of his sleep.

Davie's eyes were shining. –Surfers ride the Tube trains. He made a movement with his arm like a wave. Lie flat on the Tube roofs. Toughest of the lot, an' crazy, an' scariest too. That's what I bin told. I ain't talked about them before cos they got no territory, no patch, so I reckoned they ain't no use to us. But most all o' the gangs let 'em through, long as they don't stay long. So – I bin thinking. Then I got it. The answer. The Surfers are the only ones know the whole place. All of it, not only the Tube tunnels, but the other tunnels too: water tunnels, electric tunnels, tunnels fer shit, tunnels where the rivers go. They're cool with danger, cos surfing, you can get sucked off, or hit by cables, walls, signals. And they get high on it. I heard tell, when a Surfer gets killed, they do 'em a final journey, an' they strap 'em, their body that is, to one of the Tubes, ride with 'em all the way from one end o' the Tube map ter the other, then they have a bonfire.

Poacher shook his head. –So cos they know it all, they're gonna help us? He didn't sound like he believed any of it, but Davie didn't seem to notice.

–Yup. Listen. There's a meet gonna happen.

–A what? Jake said.

–A meet. All the gangs are gonna go, be in the same place, same time. There's gonna be music, an' food an' booze. It's what they're all telling about.

–So what? Poacher said.

–So with loads o' them out the way, I figure that's our chance to get out. Now we got Jake and Ollie's food, we got passage fees. Not much, but enough ter pay *one* gang. So we go an' parley with the Surfers, just them, cos they could get us the whole way out . . . Davie did a little drum roll against the escalator side.

–But if they've got no patch, how are we gonna find them?

–I bin told where they're hanging. It's a hard climb, but it ain't far from here. 'Cept they ain't gonna be there long, cos they ain't any place for long, so . . .

Davie's pause hung in the stale air. Poacher had his head in his hands, fingers pushed into his dreads, thinking, and the others waited. Then he put his head up.

–So if we go, we gotta go now, Poacher finished up.

–Yeah, Davie said. –Only thing is, Jake's the climber an' I've got the info. It's gotta be just me and him.

*

Poacher woke Swift and she went and sat with him in a huddle halfway up the escalator. She didn't like the plan, Jake could tell. She was up and down, looking away and looking down. But by the time they stood up, she'd agreed to it.

–Now you gotta eat, Poacher said, and he fetched food.

–Took us hours to find, Swift said, a warning in her voice, so Jake kept quiet. It was horrible, festering food scrounged from the bins on the Tube platforms, picked out from the stuff thrown out by the food stalls in the stations. But he was so hungry, he wolfed everything: ham gone shiny-green at the edges, a squidgy black banana, two hamburger buns, bled with ketchup but no burger, cold noodles orange with sweet 'n sour, squashed to a solid block. But it didn't stop him imagining the Cheddar cheese and the chocolate and the tins of fruits packed into their rucksacks for the Surfers.

–Last Supper, Davie said, and Poacher told him to shut it.

–Listen now, Poacher said. –This ain't pretty but if one of you gets— He stopped and looked down at his feet, like he was embarrassed. Jake listened to the distant thrubs and tick sounds coming from somewhere above, or below them. Poacher cleared his voice and went on. –Yeah, so if one o' you gets hurt, anyway, then the other one's gotta go on. Cos it's the only chance we've got of getting out. Any of us . . .

–And if you two aren't back here in two hours, we're coming looking, Swift said.

Twenty-six

Davie took the lead. He knew the way to the Surfers' den. Least, he said he did. A lowlifer had told him where it was this week. He'd drawn a map on the wall: an arrow on the slant, another pointing straight down. That was it. It didn't make much sense to Jake.

A few minutes into their journey, the only feeling Jake had about it all was a bad one. It seemed like they were travelling to the centre of the Earth, and that was not a place he wanted to be. Course he knew they weren't, not literally. He'd done the Earth with Miss McCarthy in geography. He knew the Earth's crust went on for miles. He knew they were only walking through tunnels made by men. But down here, underground, with the bricks and concrete and soot and cables, in the hot, dead air, he felt very scared. He felt like the weight of the whole city might come crashing down on them at any minute. What if they never got out again?

But hardest of all, much harder than his hunger, or his fear of being so far underground, was leaving Jet. As they'd walked away, Jet had set up barking, the kind of shouty bark he did when he was unhappy. Jake had looked back once and wished he hadn't. Because Jet was leaning forward, braced against his lead, and Poacher was yanking him back.

Then Davie took them through a door and down some kind of service tunnel, and Jet's barking got fainter and fainter, till Jake couldn't hear anything beyond his own breathing. Deeper they went, and the hot air smelled of earth and metal, till they came to another riveted door. It had a sign on it: a picture of a figure falling backwards and in big letters the words: WARNING: RISK OF FALLING.

Davie had his hand on the door lever. –You ready? he said. –Cos I reckon we got to the straight-down arrow bit. And before Jake could reply, he'd swung the door lever, and they stepped through.

The sight made both boys gasp.

Coming from above them and dropping away below them was the biggest hole Jake had ever seen. It was lit with dim electric lights, but when Jake looked up, he couldn't see the top of the hole and when he looked down, he couldn't see the bottom. It was as wide as a house – his old house, anyway – and its curved sides were banded with riveted metal that gave off a greeny gleam. There was a smell of metal in the air; metal and damp. Down one side stalactites dripped from shining crystals and glistened in the flickery light.

They were standing on a metal grid walkway, a safety rail running along it at waist height.

–Whoa! Jake said, looking down at the black. He could feel his heart speed up, till it was racing in his chest, and his hands were sweating so much he had to rub them on his trouser legs. –So what now? Cos even your Surfers can't jump down there.

And Davie pointed to the far end. –Behold the ladder set up on the earth, and the top of it reaching into heaven. And behold the angels of God climbing on it! he said, but his voice was tiny and scared, and when he looked round at Jake, his eyes were big as saucers.

The walkway wasn't hard to walk along, but each time they took a step they could feel it bounce slightly. Davie's knuckles were white, gripping the handrail. But it wouldn't matter how hard they held the rail if the walkway came out of the wall. They'd still fall to their deaths, and no one would know, or ever even find their bodies. Jake shook his head to get rid of the thought. *Breathe*, he thought instead. That's what his dad would have told him.

–Breathe deep, he said to Davie. –It'll help.

When they got to the end, he saw there was a latched gate set into the safety rail. A metal ladder, set vertically into one side of the hole, dropped away beneath the gate, just reaching another walkway maybe twenty feet below.

–We're climbing down that, aren't we? he said, and Davie gave a small nod.

–Surfers' den is six ladders down. They told me: there's a rope hanging and a wooden ledge, is how you can tell.

Davie's voice sounded tight, like it was difficult to get the sounds out. Jake couldn't see very well in that light, but he reckoned Davie had gone very pale.

–It's why you gotta be the one with me, Davie said. –Cos you ain't—

–Scared? Jake said. –Of climbing down that ladder, no safety harness, no nothing? I'm way past scared. He could hear his dad's voice in his mind, over and over: *Always clip on before climbing. Always clip on before climbing.*

–If one of us falls . . . Davie said.

–He's mashed, Jake finished.

–If one of us falls, Davie said again, –then the other one has to go on an' find the Surfers. Has to go on an' do the trade. Else the whole gang's gonna be dead with him. Agreed?

Always clip on before climbing, went his dad's voice in his head. –Shut it! Jake whispered.

–You what? Davie said.

–Yeah, agreed, Jake said; and he wondered how long it would take to hit the bottom. A few seconds. It'd be quick probably.

Davie stared down over the safety rail, his beanie pushed back on his head. Sweat glistened on his brow. –Bit of a long drop, down there, he said in a quiet voice. –Yer dog'll be blooming sad if you fall.

–If you fall, it'll kill Martha, Jake said. –So don't, OK?

–Ha! Very funny, dog boy, Davie said. He was trying to be cool, but his voice was choked. And then: –She be that sad, d'yer think?

–Yeah, Jake said. –She would.

Davie seemed to think about this for a moment, then he shook his head.

Jake's dad had taught him rules about climbing: about who went first, about what you should do and what you mustn't do. But the rules didn't matter now, because Davie was shaking and ashen-faced, and the longer they stood looking at that black hole, the bigger it would become and the more terrified they both would be; and they couldn't go back, and they had to climb down into it. So he pushed all the rules out of his head, had to push his dad out of his head too. And instead he took Davie by the shoulders and told him what to do.

–You gotta stop drumming, he said, because Davie was beating a tattoo on the safety rail, –else you won't be able to grip properly. –All you've gotta do is copy me. Keep breathing, and take your time. Don't rush it.

Jake got on the ladder first, crouching, hands gripping the sides, reaching down into nothing till his foot found the first step. The ladder shook slightly with his weight, and he could feel the tug of his rucksack, heavy with food, pulling him away into thin air. His mouth was dry. He licked his lips, took two slow breaths. *Focus on the climb. Don't look down.* His dad's voice again. If he put his hand out, he could touch the tunnel wall, break off one of the stalactites. He stared at the ladder: the cold metal lines, the corrugated surface of the rungs. Now he was on to it, feet on the rungs, hands gripping the uprights, his nerves steadied. He climbed down a few rungs to give Davie room to climb on.

–It's OK, he said, –easy does it; and quietly he talked Davie on to the ladder. Davie was muttering below his breath, and Jake could feel the shake in his hands through the ladder metal. But he was on, and every so often, Jake heard him take a proper breath.

Slowly they started climbing down. Jake made himself concentrate, because it was simple, this ladder climbing. But one slip and he'd be dead. Scarier still: one slip from Davie, and they'd both be dead, cos if Davie fell off that ladder, he'd take Jake with him.

He could feel Davie above him: the slide of his foot on to the next rung, the shift of his hands down the ladder, his breath.

–Breathe steady, Jake whispered. –You're doing grand. Keep your eyes on the tunnel sides.

A minute, two minutes, and they were down the first ladder, Jake feeling the stretch between the rungs where the first ladder ended and the second began.

–Down one. You gotta feel down for the new one. Careful, Davie.

–Steady Eddie, steady Eddie . . . Davie's words chasing each other, faster and faster.

Jake could feel Davie's foot search for the new ladder rung, and miss, and strike the tunnel wall . . .

Below them, a thousand feet of deadly air.

–Take it slow, take it slow. Steady, Davie. Because he mustn't panic. He mustn't.

–Steady Eddie, steady Eddie . . . Davie's voice was rushed; scared.

–Shut your eyes, Davie. Jake made his voice strong. –Shut them. Imagine this ladder is near to the ground. You're just coming down to the ground, and it's no distance. Now feel with your foot . . . that's it.

Four more ladders, they had, but Davie had found his footing, and he wasn't twitching, or shaking, and he didn't miss his footing again. Then they were there: the rope and the Surfers' ledge: a narrow wooden platform stretched over the abyss like some weird diving board, and behind it, set into the tunnel wall, another riveted door. Jake swung out on the rope and stepped down on to the platform, and Davie followed close behind.

Jake knelt down on the platform, felt the sturdiness of the wood beneath him. Relief ran through his muscles like quicksilver. They'd done it. He pushed from his mind the thought that they'd have to climb back up the ladder too. Gripping the rail that ran round the tunnel, he dared to look below him. They must have climbed down a hundred feet, but the tunnel below dropped another thirty and he still couldn't see the bottom.

–Playground stuff, Davie said. –We good to go? But Jake could see the sheen of sweat on Davie's forehead, and when they bumped knuckles, Jake could feel the tremor that ran through his arms.

The door opened with a push, and the boys stepped through into a narrow tunnel lit in pools by small lights set on the ground.

–What the— Jake said, because the tunnel walls were covered, every inch, with graffiti; and as Jake stared at it, he saw that the pictures rose and fell along the walls like waves, and that the colours were all the colours of the sea.

–Surfers, deffo, Davie said, grinning. –You all right to do the talking? Be better, cos my mouth goes off all over.

–Sure, Jake said, and he walked through the waves to the door at the end, and with his heart chasing through his chest, pushed it open and went in.

The room was a din of noise. Jake didn't count, but there must have been twenty or more Surfers in there. They were all in hoodies and old trackie bottoms, and all padded up with leather on the knees and elbows. Davie's description flashed across his mind: they rode the train roofs, of course. That's why the padding. They wore workmen's boots, and baseball caps, and the ones without caps had short haircuts. It was hard to tell the men from the women.

–Top o' the world, Davie muttered. Jake looked round at him. Davie was grinning. –Top den, eh Jake?

A brazier was burning in one corner, and Jake could smell food cooking and burnt toast. Tacked up on the wall to his left was a huge map, with a line of LED lights set out on the ground to light it up. It was a Tube map, but woven around the Tube lines, other lines were drawn in, and there seemed to be a hundred other places marked on to it, besides the Tube stations. Along the length of the opposite wall ran a bank of dead consoles, dead screens above them: the room must have been a control room once. Underneath the console desks, Jake could just make out sleeping figures, caterpillars in their sleeping bags. From the ceiling hung long blocks of dead lights. String had been looped between them, and washing was drying. All this Jake saw in his first glance. And in the moment before the boys were noticed, and everything stopped, Jake saw a room full of people doing ordinary things: cooking over the brazier, a man shaving with a tin can of water, people eating. Two Surfers looking at the map, pointing. Someone bandaging another's foot. An argument going on.

The boys stared in at the room, and then the room fell silent and stared back, just the sound of a lowlifer cough rasping somewhere. Jake listened to the sound of the brazier, the crackling of the fire, listened to the cough, and waited. His heart was beating as hard now as when he'd stood at the top of that ladder.

–What've we got here? The voice came from the far side of the room, a deep voice that sounded like it knew it was in charge. –Who – are – you? The words were spoken slowly, then more silence.

Jake bit his lip. His mouth was dry. He tried to make his voice sound strong, but it came out small and childish. –Gotta speak to your boss.

There was a moment of silence, then the whole room burst out laughing. Heat rose to Jake's face, and for two pins he'd have turned and gone.

–Steady Eddie, Davie murmured. –Steadfast, steadfast; and Jake was very glad that Davie was there with him.

When the room quietened, the deep voice spoke again, and Jake saw who it belonged to: a tall man dressed in the same Surfer clothes. On his hoodie, a jag of silver lightning, and where the other Surfers had short hair, he wore a blond ponytail beneath his cap. He looked a bit older than the rest, and it was clear that he was in charge.

–You made the ladder. Respect, boys. But you're on our turf now and we need an explanation. And he beckoned them over to where he stood, beside the giant map.

The Surfers made way for the boys, and they crossed the room to where the tall blond leader stood.

–Let's hear it then, he said.

The room had gone back to what it was doing, by the time Jake finished his story: a group of kids escaped from a Home Academy van, and got down here by mistake.

The blond Surfer ground his boot toe into the floor, thinking. Then he fixed Jake with a stare.

–Nice story, and for what it's worth, I believe you. You look green enough to have escaped only yesterday. But so what?

–We ain't— Davie started to say, and Jake elbowed hard to shut him up.

–We've got good food in our rucksacks, Jake said, –and we'll trade it with you, if you'll help us get out. We heard about the meet. We thought maybe it'd be easier then?

–The meet? the blond Surfer said, and something shifted in his face, like he'd thought of something. Then he was silent, thinking. Jake waited. Davie had started twitching, beside him, fingers tapping against his leg, and Jake could hear him swallowing sounds, trying to keep them in.

–Why should we do a trade at all? the blond Surfer said. –What's to stop us just taking your food off you, and picking you both up, and holding you over that big, big hole, and letting go? Nobody would ever know. You'd be bones. Dust. Eh?

He was waiting for an answer, but Jake didn't know

what to say. And Davie was silent too, thank god, only his fingers beating their beat a hundred times a minute.

–All right, maybe this one'll be easier. Why should we believe you? the blond Surfer said finally. –There's people disappearing from the tunnels, some of our own included. Getting picked off. Means there must be an infiltrator down here. Now, you don't look likely being kids, but you could be spies, for all we know.

–Spies! Spies for who? The exclamation came out before Jake could stop it. He could have kicked himself. He didn't want to stay silent, but he'd spoken before he thought, and now the Surfers would think he was stupid. The blond Surfer stared at him, the hardest stare Jake had ever had, like he was trying to see into Jake's mind. And then just when Jake thought it was all up, he laughed. Put his head back and laughed, and the whole room, like it had been waiting to see which way he'd go, laughed with him.

–Just kids, he said.

Ten minutes later and Jake and Davie were setting off back. Their rucksacks were empty, and in his pocket Davie had instructions on how to get to the meet. It was happening that very night, and the blond Surfer had been clear: they had to go there first, and by a certain time, otherwise no deal. That's where he would come and find them. Davie was high: fist-pumping, zippy high.

–Knew it! Knew it was gonna go good. Surfers are the business: I'm gonna be like him when I'm older. Ponytail, the lot. Scotland! he shouted, and it echoed up and down the dark hole.

They found Poacher and Swift still sitting where they'd left them. And in the split second before they were leaping down the escalator steps, Jake saw despair in their bodies, in their faces.

–We thought . . . Swift said. –We didn't think . . . And then Jake felt her arm across his shoulder and she laughed. Swift laughed!

–Tell us, Poacher said.

Twenty-seven

They told it by turns, sitting high up on the steps, to be away from the others still sleeping below, and Poacher and Swift listened without interruption to the end. Only half-way through Swift got off the steps and started pacing the escalator hall, to and fro, one side to the other.

Poacher shook his head. –Credit, both of yer. I couldn't a' done it; and Jake felt proud, because he knew it was true. Poacher looked down to Swift then. –Ain't it right, Swiftie? But she didn't stop her pacing, and when she spoke, it wasn't to congratulate.

–So we go to the meet, find the leader, the blond Surfer, then the Surfers show us the way out. But if we don't go, they don't show us. That's the deal, isn't it? She looked round at Jake, at Davie, waited. Jake nodded, and she went on. –And you've given them all our passage-fee food, so we have nothing left now to negotiate with. That's true. Again Jake nodded, and a cold feeling ran through him, because he didn't understand Swift's anger.

Poacher stood up. –Stay here, he said; and he went to join Swift on the hall floor.

The argument was nearly the worst Jake had ever heard. It was like the ones his parents had, the months before they died. And then he thought: *course, cos it's life and death again.* And then he thought how long ago it seemed, another world, when he was that boy, with his mum and dad, and sitting on the stairs, listening, in his pyjamas.

Swift was shouting now, a quiet, fierce shouting:

–I don't trust them. I don't trust him, whatever Davie says. However much he promised. We all go, we all get robbed, or killed. There'll be pills and poppers, and some white brew cooked up out of old skins, and everybody'll be packing something, cos everybody does down here. You think I'm gonna take Cass into that?

Poacher shook his head. –The Surfer says it's the only way . . .

–And what about lowlifers disappearing? That's what Davie said. Different people from different gangs disappearing. What d'you say about that?

–I dunno, Swift. But the Surfers are as freaked by it as any. Some o' them have gone missing too.

–We trust a Surfer! Swift snorted. –We do the most dangerous thing we can think of cos Jake and Davie say we should trust a blond Surfer . . .

–If we ain't gonna trust what he says, why'd we give them all of our food? We ain't gonna get any more like that. We ain't got no more stuff to trade with, 'cept ourselves. Poacher was almost shouting too. –An' we ain't gonna trade ourselves, no way.

–But a meet? We leave this den to head for a meet?

–A meet that every single lowlifer's gonna head for. You heard them. It's our best chance. I ain't a betting fella an' we ain't got much to stake. But I'd put the lot on going.

–You know, well as I do, what'll be going off there, Swift said, scorn in her voice. –Drink, and mandy. Our gang: it's kids. They're in our trust, Poacher.

–So we get there, wait for the blond Surfer, an' we leave.

You heard it all like I did. When the meet's happening, then we can make our break, cos the other gangs won't be guarding their patches. The Surfer's gonna guide us out.

–Davie's a kid, Poacher. Jake's a kid. They don't know what a meet's gonna be like.

It was like nobody else was there for Swift and Poacher. Like they'd forgotten about him and Davie listening to every word. Like they didn't see them any more. Swift was so angry she was slapping her hand against the wall, against a poster. Jake could read it: *Brexit: The Musical.*

–They got in with the Surfers, Poacher said. –Got their trust. You heard them tell it. The Surfers believed their story. Our story. It's our best chance.

–So let the other gangs go to the meet. If they aren't guarding their patches, we can make our break on our own, without the Surfers' help.

–No, Poacher said. –We don't stand a chance on our own. We'll be lost in these tunnels. Die in them.

–For god's sake! Swift slapped the poster so hard the sound echoed around the room. She hissed at him. –Take Davie and Jake, take the others, and come back for us. Cass and me, we'll keep our rucksacks packed and ready.

Poacher shook his head. –No, Swiftie. We might need to move very fast. Won't be time ter come back. We got more chance if we're all together. Stronger that way.

–And this blond Surfer? Swift's voice was high, stretched thin, like she didn't believe what she was hearing from Poacher.

–We gotta trust him, cos we got no choice. How long d'you think we're gonna last down here? How long before a couple o' crazies gets wind of us, an' that we're kids, an' marches in an' takes everything we got, or worse? He shook his head again. –An' don't forget about Jet. A dog's gotta be valuable down here too. Might eat it or keep it for company, either way we ain't gonna be able ter stop 'em. I ain't saying that out loud to anyone, but it's what I got going on in my head . . .

Jake felt his stomach drop. Jet! He felt dizzy with rage. Poacher had forgotten he was sitting up there listening. Jet too . . .

–An' if they take everything, we ain't even got our knives ter defend ourselves, or kill ourselves a rat or an eel. Can't get north. They ain't Outwalkers down here. They'll chuck us out of our den, and we'll starve to death in one o' them service tunnels an' they'll kick our bodies into that river. Crabs'll pick our bones good and clean.

–Come on, Swift said, her voice softer, – not everybody's out to get us.

–Don't need everybody. Just need *one*. Now it was Poacher's turn to pace. –I dunno who's running the meet. Mebbe it's a thing they do down here sometimes. Crazy party to make people remember they're alive. I ain't wantin' ter put us in danger more'n we have to, but it's our only chance. An' if the blond Surfer is true ter his word an' they guide us out, then we kin move on north again. Git Cass to a hospital, eh? He paused a moment. –Swiftie, he said, and now his voice was quiet and sad, but somehow it carried more force than all Swift's shouting. –We ain't got no choice.

Davie went up front with Poacher, calling the way. Tunnels, staircases, long long slopes; huge drops away down concrete shafts, ladders Jake had to lift Jet up. Crazy landscape, like something from an old film. Jake smelled burning, like the tang of burning rubber, and sometimes a stink like rotten eggs. And everywhere the black dirt, soft as velvet. And everywhere the warm, old air.

–Smells like rotten breath, Martha said.

Sometimes they heard shouts, sometimes other noises, violent noises. Jet huddled in close to Jake, his tail between his legs. –Hey, boy, Jake would whisper, and he'd put his hand to Jet's head or pat his back.

–Lake of fire and sulphur, Davie said. –Beasts an' false prophets an' torment.

Ollie was muttering behind him, and once he leaned forward and whispered to Jake: –This crazy, or what?

Jake shrugged. How could he know? But he wished they had never come to London. Never come down into this horrible underworld.

They came to another dead station and walked the narrow trench between the rails.

–Gang territory, Davie called back, pointing to the platform, and Jake saw, now he was looking, mattresses stacked beneath the Eastbound sign and a pile of cans. –An' where we're walking, that's the catch pit, Davie said. –Lucky they're all at the meet.

Jake had no idea where they were, or how deep beneath the city. It seemed to him he'd been down here for months, not days. He longed for light, and clouds, and sun and the darkness of the night, not this underground darkness and the grey strip lights. His breakfast with Ollie behind the scaffolding had happened in a different universe. One with a sky and rain, and trees and buildings, and a north and a south. Poacher said they might get out of here soon, but what did he know? The black dirt was in Davie's lungs and Jake was sure he could feel it in his own. They would die down here and no one would know and no one would care.

Once they walked through an empty room with a desk and an old-fashioned light. A sign on the wall said 'Quiet Please'. Sometimes Jake saw things moving: a rat clambering over a mattress. Cockroaches scuttling. Once, he thought, a person, slipping away through a grating at the corner of his sight. They came down a short ladder into a long room lined so deep with boxes there was only room for one person at a time down the middle. *Security Archives*, Jake read on the sides. Numbered box after numbered box. When they reached the far end Jake could feel a pulse of sound, coming from below his feet.

Ollie nudged him. –D'you feel it? he said. –Meet's through there, Davie said.

He was pointing to a door with a sign on it:

PLEASE CHANGE SHOES OR APPLY PLASTIC COVERINGS

Davie was handing out something blue, something flimsy and plastic, from a box next to the door. –Gotta put these on. Cover our tracks.

The gang followed Poacher through the door into a corridor, their blue feet rustling. The pulse was stronger here, nearly tipping over into sound. Wherever it was, it was very loud.

–Jeepers! Poacher stopped so suddenly the others nearly fell over him. He ran a finger along the wall. –It's clean, he said.

But it wasn't just ordinary clean. This corridor was clean like when Jake's dad had cleaned the bathroom clean, and it was lit with proper lights like you saw in shops, with coloured shades. There were doors off the corridor and the signs on them looked new too. 'Emergency Exit', one said, and Jake could see a spiral staircase going upwards through the glass panel. On the floor were shiny blue tiles and there was a lemony smell in the air. There was no black dirt.

–Look, Davie called. –Full of richly things.

He was peering on tiptoes through a glass door pane. Jake looked through. It was a shop, shut up now because it was night time. Jake could see a stand of postcards, and rows and rows of model trains. There was a counter with boxes of pencils and gig sticks, and bouncy balls and sweets, and a lift to bring you down to it on the far side. 'This way for the street', a sign above it read. Another sign on the wall read: 'MailRail Museum'.

–So where now? Poacher said, and Davie pointed to a final door. –That's where it's happening. Down there. Sodom an' Gomorrah, ain't it; and Jake saw Martha put her hand on Davie's shoulder.

Through the door, another spiral staircase. Louder and louder the noise got with every step down, pulsing through the metal stairs, throbbing in their ears, until they reached another, smaller door. Swift held Cass tight in her arms. Jake wrapped Jet's lead around his wrist. Davie was drumming on his thigh.

The sign on the door said 'Engine Repairs'. Poacher looked back at the gang.

–Partner up. Martha an' Davie, take this side. Jake, you and Jet go with me an' we'll take the far side. Swift, you got Cass too, so you an' Ollie best stay here by the door. Check out newbies, check out who's leavin'. Only reason we're here is ter find the blond Surfer. Only reason, remember? He's the one gonna git us out a these tunnels and north. So stay sharp, eyes peeled. He'll have Surfer gear on, hoodie, trackie bottoms, white knee pads, an' a ponytail. Right, Davie? Jake?

–Only Surfer with long hair, Davie said.

–Right. Cos we ain't staying a minute longer than we have to, Poacher said. –If we gotta go, I'll whistle, or Swift will. An' if we ain't signalled, then it's half an hour an' we leave anyway, out this door. Understood?

He pushed the door open.

Twenty-eight

The room was huge and crammed with people – a hundred, two hundred, more, Jake didn't know, because he couldn't see the end of it. He couldn't believe so many people lived down here beneath the city.

The music was so loud now that it felt like being underwater, and he wanted to run out, or put his hands over his ears. He felt Jet's growl, rather than heard it. Jet's hackles were raised, and when Jake put a hand to his head to reassure, he felt him flinch. The sooner they were out of here, the better.

The people were lowlifers, all of them, no mistaking it. Their clothes, their hair, the way they walked, half-stooped as if they were still crouched down, and most of all the colour of their skin: their hands were grimy, and their faces looked grey, like they hadn't seen the sun in years, and everywhere he heard that cough, Davie's cough, a dry, rasping sound. Some people were dancing, but most were standing in clumps. Some of them were smoking something and it hazed the air, a musty, sweet smell, mixed with the smell of sweat. Drifts of heat seemed to wash across and everyone was drinking from bottles of water and he wondered where they'd got them, and if that meant there was food somewhere too.

He followed Poacher to the far side of the room. The music was quieter over here, and he could nearly hear what people were saying. Further down he glimpsed a trestle table. That's where the bottles of water came from: it was piled with them and people were grabbing them like they were in a desert, chugging them back, chucking the bottles in a dustbin. That was weird, because it sounded like you didn't get anything for nothing down here, so someone must've paid for those and brought them in.

He was about to tap Poacher on the back when a group caught his eye. Surfers. He searched among them but he couldn't see the blond ponytail.

How had they all ended up down here? A few looked ancient, but lots of them didn't look much older than Poacher or Swift. Maybe they'd escaped from Home Academies too. They were passing round water and a little plastic bag, the kind of bag his mum used to put carrot sticks in for his pack-up. The bag was full of sweets, it looked like, and he watched each of the lowlifers take one and swallow it down with a glug of water.

–You want? A girl (she wasn't much more than a girl) was offering him a sweet. She was wearing a long mac, the kind his dad wore to ride his bike in the rain, though it wasn't going to rain in here. Jake didn't know which gang she belonged to, but she had a soft voice and a kind smile.

–Go on, she said. –One for you, one for your very nice dog, and she handed him two of them, a blue one and a pink one, and a bottle of water. –Plenty more where these came from, little boy.

–Thanks.

Her fingers were black, her nails broken, and her eyes were like dark holes. –There's a Surfer messiah down here, she said. –Gifts galore.

–Yeah? Jake said. –What's he look like? Is he here?

But she went on talking like she hadn't heard him. –I heard he's got a golden halo an' everything. An' brought us manna from heaven, enough for every tribe. See everybody? And she swept her arm around to include the whole room. –So eat it, sweetie. Babes in these deep dark woods don't turn down treats when they're offered.

Her voice was all drifty-dreamy against the noise, soft on his ears. And he didn't know what manna was, but he had the sweet on his tongue, and it tasted bitter, not nice at all, when a hard grip on his arm pulled him sideways and a voice hissed in his ear:

–Spit it out.

Poacher tugged him away, pinching his ear. A sign above his head said: 'Rules Before Operating Heavy Machinery' and another said: 'No Smoking'. Then Jake felt Poacher's fingers in his mouth, feeling for the bitter sweet, and he threw it on the floor, a blue blob in blue spittle.

–Rinse yer mouth and spit, Poacher said, handing him a bottle of water. And when Jake had finished, he shook him by the shoulders. –These are drugs, Jake, he hissed. –Mandy. They ain't sweets. They just give 'em to you?

–And Jet. Gave me one for Jet as well. Poacher put his hand out and Jake handed him the pink pill. His hands were shaking. He felt like he did after nearly slipping on a climb.

Poacher dropped the pill on the floor and stamped on it till it was powder. –They're dangerous fer kids. Proper dangerous. Kill dogs, probs.

–It's the blond Surfer handing them out, Jake said. –I'm sure of it. The girl called him a messiah.

–Are you sure? Did you see him?

Jake shook his head.

–Mandy for free, Poacher said. –No wonder they think

he's like a god. An' the bottles o' water? Who's payin' fer that? He shook his head. –I don't believe he's gonna help us. This whole thing stinks. The meet, everythin'. He dropped his head, scratched his dreads, and when he looked up, he looked scared. –Swift was right. We shouldn't a' come here. Somethin's gonna happen. Something not good. An' if you're right an' the blond Surfer's handing out the mandy, then he's a part of it. We gotta get out. And he gave a sharp whistle.

Poacher moved fast, fast as Swift, and it was hard to follow him. He was soon out of sight. Keeping his eye on the far door, and ducking and diving between the crowds Jake stumbled behind, keeping Jet tight to his legs. His rucksack bumped against his back and sweat trickled down. He'd have killed for another drink of water, but there wasn't time to stop.

More people were dancing now, tying clothes around their waists in the heat of the room, and the lights had gone down. The music seemed mellower too, more like a band off one of his mum's old CDs. Maybe Poacher was wrong. Maybe this was OK, all of this, and it was Poacher being crazy, not everybody else. It all looked chilled to him, even Poacher, loping ahead, and if there was free water and free mandy, he'd bet there was food too somewhere. Gangs with different kinds of clothes were all dancing together, in pairs, in little groups, all mixed up together and their territories forgotten, like in a dream. Like the soldiers in the old war that his teacher told about who got out of their ditches because it was Christmas, both sides, and played a game of footie.

The scream stopped him in his tracks. A girl's scream, sharp, and then gone. A girl's scream, not an adult's.

He looked back, and between the swaying dancers he

saw her: a flash of black hair, a wild glare. A tall man had her in an arm lock, his hand a bar across her mouth, and she was fighting him, twisting and turning, but he had her tight. Jake shouldered his way closer. Now he could see the man clearly. Now he could see the lightning zigzag on his hoodie and the blond ponytail that whipped across his back as the girl struggled.

–The blond Surfer, Jake murmured.

The Surfer was saying something to the girl, tight-lipped, and the girl was shaking her head. Jake couldn't fully see the girl's face, but he could see enough to know she was no adult. Older than him maybe, but younger than Swift and Martha. And he could see that she didn't stand a chance against the Surfer.

Twisting her head free, the girl yelled out, –Let me go! Help! Gaz! Checker! He's going to hurt you!

She was dressed in Catchpit gear – black denims, black jacket scratted with tinfoil and plastic and crisp packet colours – and there were some Catchpitters right there, but their eyes were big as saucers and they watched it all like they were on a different planet. Whichever ones were Gaz and Checker, they didn't make a move to help her.

–Let go of me, the girl yelled. –I've seen your plan. I know what you're going to do. You won't get away with it! Gaz! Help!

But the Catchpitters turned away, shaking their heads, and the blond Surfer got his arm clamped down and silenced her again. Jake was close to them now, close enough to hear what the Surfer was whispering to her.

–Now now, little girl. Your friends don't want to know. You don't matter to them, not when they've got free treats. But your mother's been very very upset . . . she's had us searching all over London, such a waste of our time, far more important things to be doing, so we ought to get you back to where you belong . . . The Surfer was grinning, a wide smile full of shiny white teeth . . . –but then again, if you've seen things, then we don't want you telling anybody else what's going on down here, do we? Might ruin future plans too. So maybe we'll lock you up somewhere comfy for a little while. I think your mother would approve, as long as she thinks you're safe. Then he reached into his pocket and fished out a plastic bag full of mandy and shook them onto the ground. –Be happy, he said, and where nobody would help the girl, now there was a mob pushing and shoving to get the mandy: Catchpitters, Friners and others Jake didn't recognize, scrabbling for the pinks and blues and reds.

Jake stared. This was the Surfers' leader, the man who'd said he'd get them out. They'd paid him for it with the last of their food. He'd promised them. But he was hurting this girl, wrenching her arm round, twisting it behind her. He was holding her prisoner. Anger boiled through Jake. The blond Surfer was a big man and Jake knew he didn't stand a chance. Besides which, he had Jet, and he didn't dare let go of his lead.

–Poacher! he yelled. He looked around. Where was he? –Poacher! he yelled again.

Slowly the blond Surfer turned towards him. He had a hard look on his face, like a question and an accusation all at once. Their eyes met, and Jake saw recognition flash across the Surfer's face. Still holding the girl, he'd taken one step towards Jake when Poacher came from nowhere.

Poacher saw it all in a flash. He gave one sharp wolf whistle, then folded his fingers into a fist and crunched the blond Surfer straight in the face. Jake felt the blow, heard it, almost as if Poacher had hit him instead. The Surfer had let go of the girl and was on the floor, hands to his face. No way he was going to lead them out of the tunnels now. Because whatever he'd been threatening the girl with, he was their only chance to get out of here, wasn't he? And Poacher had made him mad.

Jake's heart was thudding in his chest. Now what?

–Get her out, Jake! Poacher shouted, because the Surfer was back on his feet fast, hands to his face, blood pouring from his nose.

–You frigging lowlife illegal, he roared, making a grab at Poacher.

The girl just stood there, paralysed. Jake got her by the wrist and pulled her.

–Come on! he shouted.

He didn't look back, just ran, gripping her wrist and Jet's lead. This time the crowds seemed to part for them, boy and girl and dog, and they got to the door in no time. The gang was all there, and seconds later Poacher too, his face and hands covered in blood.

–You OK? Martha said.

Poacher nodded. –But the other fella's not feeling so good. We ain't stayin' fer dessert.

They hid in the shop. Crouched down behind the postcard racks and the trays of toys and sweets, silent, waiting. They were invisible, if anyone looked through the glass. As long as no one opened the door. The girl was crouched beside Jake, her breath still coming in gasps. He didn't dare move his head, so he could only see her foot. She was wearing black trainers, classy ones. The kind you saw in the adverts, but never got in the shops in his home town.

–Ssh. Swift's quick command.

Jake listened. Heavy footsteps coming closer. Someone running down the corridor. He looked at the ground, like he'd be less visible that way. He could feel the fear in the gang. It was like a heat behind the eyes, like dizziness. The footsteps reached the door. Stopped. They could hear the man's ragged breath. Jake stared at the floor, hand on Jet's muzzle, not moving. Then the footsteps again, moving away, getting fainter.

Another minute, no one moving, no one making a sound, and still everything was quiet. Only the distant thump of the meet music.

Swift went to the door, looked through the glass; inched the door open, checked the corridor.

–It's clear.

Jake felt relief flood through him and he leaned back against the merchandise trays. He watched Martha pull on a MailRail cap, which made her look like a little kid. He watched Davie fill his pockets with packets of Love Hearts.

–Love with all yer heart, Davie murmured. –It's in the good book; and he winked at Jake.

Swift nodded to the girl. –It's clear, she said again. –You can go.

Jake watched the girl out of the corner of his eye. She was sitting quite still, one hand in a pocket, the other fiddling with something on her clothes, one of the weird bits of crisp packet or something, since it made a rustling noise.

–What if I don't want to? the girl said.

Jake looked round. You didn't speak against Swift unless you were Poacher. Ollie had his mouth open, and even Davie was staring at her, but the girl was pouting.

–Go, Swift said again. –Back to your Catchpitters.

–They're not mine, the girl said. –They don't want to know.

–They're stoned, Poacher said. –Free mandy. Free pills. That's why they don't wanna know.

–But don't you want to know why there are free pills? And that man. I have to stop—

–No, Swift said, interrupting her. –Poacher did the right thing, pulling that guy off you. But that's it. Job done. We don't want you with us and we don't wanna know about the info.

–But it's important. If I can't rescue them, there are going to be others. The Coalition— the girl said.

–Not interested. Swift chopped her off. –What's interesting to us is getting out of here, and that's got a whole lot more difficult since Poacher punched our guide in the face. You with us is going to make it even riskier. For starters, you're chipped . . .

–I'm not, the girl said.

Swift went on as if she hadn't heard her . . . –so we leave this room and then you're on your own.

–I'm not chipped, the girl said.

Poacher snorted. –Yeah, right. And this ain't England.

–Everyone's got a chip, Martha said. –Even the King.

–Uh-uh, the girl said. –That's what they tell you. If you get born high enough – Royal Family, Coalition minister: they don't chip your children. Anyway, I'm not, and I don't want your help.

The girl's voice was new to Jake. She spoke like they did when his mum put the radio on. Maybe it was how they spoke in London, or maybe she was just very posh. She was clean too. Cleanest person he'd seen down here so far.

But if she was very posh and very clean, what was she doing down here?

–You ain't complained about getting my help so far, Poacher said. –That blond Surfer had hold of yer good an' proper till I punched him.

–He's not a Surfer, the girl said. His name is Noel, actually. She shuddered. –He works for my mother.

Jake wondered who on earth this girl's mother was, but Swift didn't seem to care.

–Whatever, she said. One thing we know now is he's as much a Surfer as you're a Catchpitter.

–I *am* a Catchpitter. They inducted me and everything. I've done four catchpits. Only Piccadilly Circus left to do and I'll be a full gang member . . .

Jake heard Davie snort behind him.

–Jake, Poacher said. –Check her neck.

The girl looked like she was going to protest, but Jake parted her hair and gently pushed her head forward. Her hair smelled nice. Lemony. He stared. It should be just there, on the left. Everybody in England had one, a little scar there, a tiny white line on the skin of your neck where they'd slipped in the chip. Every single body. They told you that at school: everybody, even the Royals, even the Prime Minister, because everybody needs to be looked after equally.

But her neck was smooth. No scar, no nothing.

He put his fingers to it, felt for the telltale hard edge of plastic below the skin. Nothing. It was freaky. He pulled away, and the girl tossed her hair back, as if to say, Get your hands off me now.

–No chip, Jake said.

Davie gave a low whistle. –No cuts or tattoos. Biblical. Freaky.

Jake saw Poacher and Swift exchange looks.

–Have you thought about how you're getting out of here? the girl said.

–We had a plan till you happened. And it's none of your business, Swift said, putting her arm around Cass as if the girl might be dangerous to be near. –So git.

–Because Noel will have those stairs guarded. The girl went on as if Swift hadn't spoken, nodding towards the green emergency exit sign in the corner. –And every other rat-run near here. She was talking fast, urgently. –He'll have brought in the troops, everybody, cos—

–So we'll git the lift, Poacher said, interrupting her. –Scan hub won't see us. Ollie? Go an' press the button. And Ollie was getting up when the girl spoke again.

–I wouldn't, if I were you. They'll have someone waiting at the top, he'll see the lift button light up, and *boom*! She made a sound like a little explosion. –*They've* got you.

There was a silence, as if nobody knew what to do or say. Jake had never seen Poacher or Swift like this: like they didn't know what had happened and didn't know what to do next.

Then Poacher sighed, like he was giving up something. –What's the rat-runs? he said.

–So, the girl said, as if she'd been waiting for someone to ask, –the rat-runs are your paths and passages. They know about them all, and mostly they'll leave you alone in them. That way, they know where you are, after all. Look, I don't mean to be facetious. The truth is, we could help each other now. I need to get out too. I have to stop Noel somehow.

–Who's 'They'? Poacher said.

–The Office of Covert Surveillance, the girl said. –Part of the Home Office. You know, the government. The Coalition.

Of course, they didn't know that I was down here, not till just now, and that will change things, somewhat. Because that man – she gave a little shudder here and Jake didn't know if it was acted or real – now he's seen me, he will do everything to get me back to my mother. Otherwise it won't only be his job that's on the line.

–So it's you they're hunting now, not us, Swift said.

Jake shut his eyes against the man falling in his mind, the thud he made at the bottom, the stink of broken perfumes. He saw the ticker tape feed spooling round the walls of the Tube station: '*police close in . . . police close in . . .*'

–The Coalition doesn't know, doesn't care about us, Swift went on, –but if you're telling us the truth, then it makes you dangerous to be near.

–Maybe, the girl said, –but they'll still have all the exits covered, and anyone coming up is going to get arrested, checked by the hub police. Even people that aren't important. The girl looked down at her hands – was she checking her nails? – and Jake noticed that they were painted purple.

Martha was frowning, forehead furrowed like someone older. –So why don't you go back to your mother? she said. –Since you've got one. More than most of us down here has got.

–Because I can't, the girl said in a hard voice. –She's . . . But she stopped herself. She turned to Swift. –Let's do a deal. You let me stay with you until we're all out of London and I'll get us all out of here. I'm in a hurry too.

–Don't listen to her. Let the hubbers pick her up, Martha said immediately. –If she's so important, they won't hurt her.

The girl turned her back on Martha. –Deal? she said again to Swift. –Then we can go our separate ways. Believe you me, I wouldn't be suggesting this if I could think of an alternative. But you seem to need to get out of these tunnels, and I have to get out of London.

Jake listened to the girl in amazement. She spoke like a grown-up, and not just any grown-up. She spoke like, he didn't know, like the Home Academy Headteacher, or someone on the TV going on about Coalition stuff.

Swift and Poacher swapped glances again, and Poacher glanced over at Davie, at Jake. –That Surfer dishing out mandy, he was the one was gonna git us outta here, wasn't he? he said.

They both nodded.

Poacher turned back to the girl. –Deal then, he said. –Gimme yer rucksack. I gotta check it.

The girl passed it to him, and he rummaged through.

–Few bits o' clothes, notebook, he said and he handed it back. –Now gimme yer mobile.

–I've already turned it off . . . the girl said.

–Give it to me. Poacher held out his hand.

–And I can take out the card, the girl said, but Poacher shook his head.

–Give it. Gotta keep us all safe as we can.

Reluctantly the girl took her mobile from her pocket. –Be careful with it. It's got very important information on it. Evidence. Important for everyone, I mean. For you, and for all of them, in the meet, and you have to listen to me . . .

Poacher nodded. –Yup, he said, unclipping his penknife, and flipping the card out of the back of the mobile, he cut it in two.

The girl gasped. –You can't do that! I need to tell people . . . You need . . .

Placing the mobile on the floor, Poacher stamped down

hard. Jake heard the crunch of split plastic and the girl's cry of anger. Picking up the mobile pieces, Poacher dropped them in the bin behind the desk. He pushed one half of the card beneath the bouncy balls, and the other half under the Love Hearts.

–That was mine. My evidence. I need it, the girl said. –You don't understand how important—

But Poacher shook his head, interrupted her. –Ain't got time fer *important* right now. We gotta git outta here smartish, so you gotta change yer gear, cos he's looking fer a Catchpitter. They all will be. An' he's looking fer long hair. Poacher nodded to Jake. –You're near enough same height. Give her yer spares. Stash her gear in yer rucksack, hers ain't big enough. Martha, cut her hair.

–Not my hair! the girl said. –I'll change my clothes, but not my hair. I'll put it up. You've got no right. You *can't*!

But Martha had already taken out her scissors, and before the girl had even finished protesting, she'd cut fast across the shiny black.

Jake heard the girl's gasp, watched her put her hand to her head. She looked much younger with her hair cut. Poacher passed her an old beanie from his rucksack.

–Case yer wanna cover it, he said.

The girl took it from him as if it was dirty, which it probably was, but she put it on. She hid behind a stand of pencils and pens while she put on Jake's spares.

Davie gave out little packets of Love Hearts while the girl got changed. –Gotta love yer neighbour, he said. –Eat my heart.

'Be real', Jake's first one said, and when he put it in his mouth, it reminded him of car journeys and his mum and dad talking in the front.

Davie gave an orange Love Heart to Swift. –'I'm sorry', she read out.

Once the girl was changed, Martha gave her a paper bag she'd taken from behind the till. –It's got your hair in it, she said, and the girl took it and Jake saw her bite her lip.

–That Surfer fella'll be back pretty smartish, when he doesn't find us up there, Swift said. –So how do we get out, posh girl?

Twenty-nine

The girl led the gang through a door signed 'MailRail Museum', each of them clicking through a turnstile, onto a narrow platform. But it wasn't like an ordinary Tube platform. It was narrow and there were no vending machines, no adverts. Just a sign on the wall that read:

- **SEAT BELTS TO BE WORN AT ALL TIMES**
- **KEEP HANDS INSIDE CARRIAGE DO NOT LEAN OUT**
- **PASSENGERS TRAVEL AT OWN RISK**

And the train, a little way down the platform, wasn't like an ordinary Tube train either. The carriages were more like wagons, and they were low and narrow with *MailRail* painted on the sides, and there were benches to sit on, with barely room for two people to each wagon, and little doors, and seat belts, like in a car. At the front was the engine with a dashboard of buttons and switches.

–Used to be for the post, the girl said. –It's been a tourist ride since before we were born. But they revamped it recently. I went on it with my mother, the first day it re-opened.

–That's how we escape? Martha said, and the girl nodded.

–I sat in the engine and got to start it. I can do it again.

–Where's it go to? Poacher said.

–I don't know, the girl said, –but it'll get us away from here.

–Everyone in then, Poacher said. –Quick.

The girl climbed into the engine space and the gang scrambled into the wagons behind, Swift and Cass just behind the engine, then Ollie, then Jake, with Poacher, Davie and Martha in the back three.

–Let's go, Poacher said.

Jake gripped the side. He looked ahead to the tunnel. It looked barely high and barely wide enough for the train. The girl's hands were moving over the dashboard, but nothing happened. Again and again he saw her press a large green button on one side, but still nothing. *Come on*, he thought. It was so quiet, you could hear a pin drop.

Poacher leaned forward. –Get it moving. His voice was low, but Jake could hear his impatience.

–I'm trying to, the girl said. –Last time I just pressed this button. She sounded bewildered, amazed that something wasn't going her way. –I pressed it, and the engine started, the roof came up and over, and the driver pulled this lever and . . .

–Listen! That was Swift. Jake listened, and there was the tickety-tick click of the turnstile, once, then again, and again.

There were running footsteps. Jake froze with fear. But it was Davie – he was out of his seat, out of his wagon and running down the platform. Yanking open the driver's door, he shoved the girl over. Jake could see his hands moving over the dashboard, almost as if they could read it.

The gang waited, breath held, and in the quiet Jake heard voices from the direction of the passage and coming this way. Come on! he willed Davie.

–Done it! Davie's voice seemed loud enough to wake the dead.

–What about the roof? the girl said.

–Ain't got time to find the button. Just gotta keep our heads down, Davie said. –It's two-hand control to start the engine. Just gotta sort out a couple of other bits. When I say so, press the green button, he told the girl. –Not until. And the girl nodded.

The voices were getting louder. Jet gave out a low growl. Jake kept his eyes fixed on Davie's back. Come on! he willed again.

–Gotcha! There was no mistaking that voice.

Jake couldn't help himself, and pulling his hood up to shield his face, he turned back to see. At the top of the platform stood the blond Surfer, blood on his face from Poacher's punch, and two hubbers: a man and a woman. The man wore a baseball cap with a big 'H' on it. The woman Jake recognized. She was the one who'd shoved her baton under Jake's chin on the escalator. The one with the hard eyes and the scar. They were all holding Tasers. There was a moment's pause, long enough for Jake to see the triumph on the blond Surfer's face, and then all three were running towards the train, towards the rear wagon.

That's where Martha's sitting, Jake thought. Martha was tough, but she wasn't a fighter. Jake had seen how she held a knife. His heart beat hard as he watched the one in the cap, the fastest of them, reach the train, and he clenched his fists in terror. –Come on, Davie! he almost shouted.

–Go! Poacher yelled.

Davie's shout burst out. –Now!

And the train lurched forward. But the hubber had

grabbed the wagon edge, his black-gloved hands reaching towards Martha.

Jake put a hand to his face. He could hardly bear to watch. –Come on! Come on! The sounds came out through clenched teeth. Through his fingers, Jake saw Poacher reaching over his seat, but the tunnel was too low for him to climb back; and he saw Martha lift her rucksack up in both hands, lift it above her head, her face fierce below the MailRail cap. The train was moving forwards now, faster and faster, accelerating, throwing Jake against his seat belt.

From the front came the girl's voice: –Heads down! Heads down! Because any second now and the train would be into a tunnel, and as anyone could see, there was no room between the train and the tunnel roof.

Jake snatched another look back, in time to see Martha bring her rucksack down with full force on the man's head.

–Yes! he hissed, fist clenched, willing her to be strong against this man who would destroy them. He pictured Martha, that day they'd gone stealing together: fierce, and wise, and deadly, if she had to be. He held her in his mind's eye as if that could protect her now.

He heard Swift's voice, and Poacher's, shouting for her too. But they were too far from her to help, and now the man reared up again, roaring with rage, his arms round the rucksack, and he was pulling Martha up with him as the train reached the tunnel, the two of them standing up together in the rear wagon, arms locked around Martha's rucksack in a terrible embrace.

–Get down, Martha! Poacher yelled. –Get down!

The tunnel loomed, like a huge black mouth, and just in time, Jake ducked down, laying his head next to Jet's as the train roared in. But above the train's noise he heard a cry, and he felt the train lurch, like a split-second pause, before the roar filled his ears and the train thundered on into the dark.

Warm air, oily-smelling, rushed past, pulling tears from Jake's eyes. Martha! He couldn't see a thing, but he could feel the tunnel roof rushing past. It must be only inches from his head. He put a hand to Jet's back and he didn't know if it was him or Jet that was shaking.

On and on the MailRail rushed, through endless tunnels, and all Jake could do was hunker down, keep his hands in and hope Davie knew how to stop it. They must be there soon, wherever there was, and then they could get to Martha. He'd do anything for her. Anything. Surely she would be all right. Surely she would . . .

The stop was as sudden as the start, a screech of brakes, the stench of burnt rubber. There was a yelp from Jet, and Jake was thrown forward again, then silence. Jake sat up and looked around. He patted the seat, and Jet sat up beside him, leaned in. There was lighting here, big, dim blocks of electric light high up on the walls. They were out of the tunnel and into a bigger space, a kind of station. Signs on the wall said *King's Cross* and *MailRail*, and there was dusty machinery on the platform. It didn't look like anyone had been here for a very long time. Not bona fides and not lowlifers either. Around him, he could hear the rest of the gang beginning to move too.

He stroked Jet's ears. –You all right, boy? Jet thumped his tail.

Davie climbed out of the engine space, grinning from ear to ear, and the girl after him. –Yes! he said, and he high-fived the girl, who didn't look like she'd ever done a high-five before. –You been here before, right?

–Not exactly, the girl said. –They took us back to the shop when I did it. But of course I know King's Cross.

Jake stepped out onto the platform with Jet, and there were Ollie, and Swift and Cass, all of them looking like he felt: shaky but unhurt. Poacher got off, near the back. Only one missing was Martha.

–Martha? Swift called. Her voice was high, fearful.

They watched Poacher walk back to the final wagon, watched him look in over the side door. They saw him staring down. Then they watched him take a step away from the train, something odd about the way he was moving. Watched him pull off his beanie and stand still a moment. Then he leaned forward and was sick.

–Martha! Swift set Cass down on the platform and ran for the rear of the train, swift as her name, past Jake, past Ollie, past Poacher. Opening the wagon door, she was stepping in and stooping down, and Jake held his breath, as if somehow Swift with all her power could make Martha be all right. But when Swift stood up, as slowly as she'd run fast, her arms were empty in front of her. And as she turned, Jake saw her face. It looked hollow, and it was white as chalk.

–What's happened to her? Ollie whispered, but for answer Swift only shook her head.

Poacher's face, Swift's face: Jake knew what they meant. It was something about the eyes. The two hub police that told him about his mum and dad: they had had the same look. And there was that same silence after, which was more than a silence; it was a void, a hole, a blackness that you couldn't see the bottom of, that pulled you in.

–She's dead, isn't she. Ollie spoke the words as a statement.

–The hubber wouldn't let her go, Poacher said. –She couldn't get down, an' the tunnel . . .

Now Davie was running to the back, his mouth open wide in a soundless scream.

–No, Davie! Poacher said. –Don't look . . .

They caught him, Poacher and Swift, before he reached the back of the train, and held him away. Held his silent screaming, pounding, desperate body, while the rest of them stood paralysed, and watched.

Jake couldn't have moved, even if he'd wanted to. His body was lead. Arms, legs, head, everything. Martha was dead. She'd died, but they'd got away. And if he'd been in the last wagon, he'd be dead now instead of her.

–Not died, he muttered to himself. –Killed. *Murdered.*

Poacher and Swift brought Davie back down the platform, and the rest of them followed. Davie didn't try to run again, but he was rocking, back and forward, and chanting over and over: –Lo, though we walk through the valley of the shadow of death . . . lo, though we walk through the valley of the shadow of death . . . lo, though we walk . . . And swiping hard at himself. Not a flicky movement, but a hard, slapping one against the side of his head, over and over.

They sat, all of them, on the gritty ground, and nobody knew what to say or what to do. Swift wrapped her arms around her little sister, and buried her head in Cass's hair. Jake saw she had a smear of blood on one cheek.

–She's just lying there, Poacher said, –an' she's all . . . He shook his head. –I can't . . .

Jake didn't know how long they all stayed like that. It might have been minutes, it might have been hours. He felt cold, but he didn't cry. There was a rumbling sound above them. It grew louder, then faded away. A few minutes later there was another.

–Right. Swift let go of Cass. –This is hard. Probably the hardest thing we'll ever do. We have to go, cos that Surfer, the hubbers: they won't be far behind. And we can't let them catch us. Not now. Her eyes were shiny with tears, and she swiped them away with her fists.

–But leave her like she is? For them to find? Poacher said. There was horror in his voice.

–What choice have we got, Poacher? We can't bury her, can we? Swift took a scrap of paper and a pencil out of her rucksack. –She's got to have her whole name. Otherwise, with no hub chip, no one will know who she is.

Poacher shrugged. –Them knowing can't hurt her now, he said.

A movement caught Jake's eye. It was the girl. She'd sat down a little way off from the rest of them. Now she stood up and walked over to where the MailRail equipment still lay: gantries and metal cages and winches; black boxes on wheels ready for the mail that never came any more. Jake could see that the girl was looking for something. Then she reached down into one of the boxes and came up holding some brown sacks. Jake could make out the words 'Royal Mail' on the side of one. Pulling the beanie off her cropped hair, the girl stuffed it into her pocket, took a water bottle from her rucksack and walked to the back of the train. The gang watched her. She walked slowly, like they'd walked at his mum and dad's funeral.

When she reached the final wagon, she dropped the sacks and her rucksack and pulled open the half-door. She stood there a moment, just looking. Jake could see that she was biting her lip, and saying something to herself, though he couldn't hear the words. Then she bent down and, as Jake found out later, moved Martha's body, laying her out on the wagon bench as best she could. Zipping open her rucksack she took out a T-shirt, and poured some water on to it. And taking a deep breath, she knelt in towards Martha's body.

–What's she doing? Davie said.

–She's cleaning off the blood, Swift said, and she shook her head. –I should be doing it, but . . . And this time Swift let the tears run down her face.

They watched the girl in silence. Five times she stood back up, wrung out the T-shirt, poured on more water and knelt in to Martha's body again.

Finally she picked up the sacks, and though he couldn't see, couldn't bear to see Martha's body, Jake understood now what the sacks were for. The girl was covering Martha with them. Giving her a kind of burial. When she had finished, she came over to the gang. She carried her rucksack in one hand, and Martha's MailRail cap in the other. How had it stayed on her head? How was the cap still there, and Martha not?

–Here, the girl said, and she gave the cap to Swift.

Thirty

They laid a packet of Love Hearts on Martha's body, and they wrote on a piece of paper:

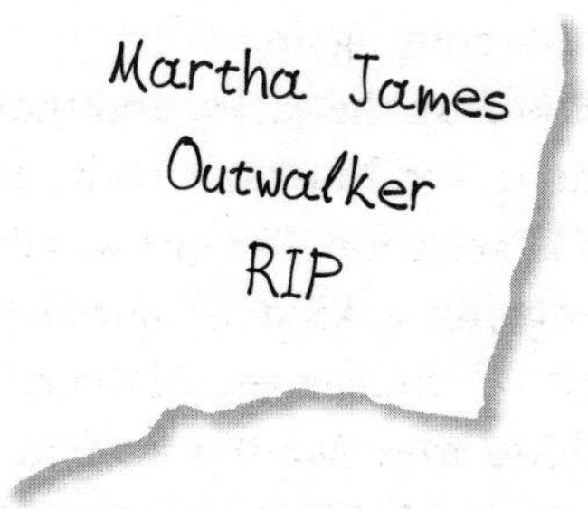

They left it next to the Love Hearts.

Thirty-one

Poacher took out the malt loaf, the very last of their food, and cut it into chunks with his penknife. He gave a chunk to everyone, even Jet. And when Davie said he couldn't eat, Swift made him.

–You think Martha'd want that? she said. –You eat it, Davie. It's all we got. If we don't eat, we'll get too weak to go on. You think Martha'd want that?

The girl still sat a little way apart and ate hers too.

Poacher hadn't cut the loaf like Martha would have. All the chunks were different sizes. Jake chewed his piece and the malt loaf stuck in his throat. He watched Swift squat down and cut Cass's piece into tiny bits and feed them to her like she was a baby bird.

–Right, Poacher said. –We gotta work out what ter do. He beckoned to the girl, and to Swift, and they got in a huddle. The rest of them waited in silence on the platform. There was nothing left to say, and they didn't know what to do. Davie and Cass sat on the ground, and Jake and Ollie stood against one of the parcel bins. Ollie's mouth was set in a thin line and every few seconds he banged his hand against the bin rail. Although he didn't say a word, Jake knew he was angry.

–D'you reckon we'll escape? Jake said, and Ollie shrugged. It was a pointless thing to say, because how would Ollie know, but he wanted to distract him.

Jake watched the huddle, the nods and head shaking. Poacher and Swift were asking the girl questions and she was doing most of the talking.

–She might help us. She knows London really well. She said so, Jake said, which got another shrug, and a glare too, this time.

Then Poacher summoned them over. –We made a plan, he said. –This girl here says if we kin get up outta the Tube from here, she kin get us outta London.

The girl nodded. –What I've suggested— she began, but before she could say any more, Ollie broke in.

–What, like she got us on that train? Like she got Martha killed? The words spat from him like stones and Jake saw the girl flinch.

–Yeah, Martha would be alive if it wasn't for her, Davie said. –She'd be here now . . .

–We don't want your suggestions, Ollie said, and his voice had gone hard, and posh like the girl's.

–Shut it. Both of you, Swift said. –Martha's death: it's not the girl's fault.

–But we wouldn't have got on that train— Ollie began, and Swift interrupted him.

–No, we wouldn't. We'd have gone up in that lift like sitting ducks and they'd have us in a hub van by now, or worse. She got to her feet. –Poacher's right. They'll be hunting for us. We've got away, but now we have to find a way out of here, and fast.

It was a warren of tunnels and rooms, so everyone went in a different direction. Davie found a lift, big enough for a whole wagon, but Poacher said it was too risky. There was a Gents with toilet roll and soap. Jake washed his hands and face and the water ran grey and grey and then clear. He would have kept his hands under that shiny stream for hours if he could have.

Jake and Ollie found a control centre, knobs and dials on the walls, and office chairs. Jake brushed the dust from one and sat down and pushed off. His dad used to do that, whizz him on the office chair, make it spin till Jake was so dizzy, turning and turning, he'd fall down if he stood up. He pushed the chair round with his foot and shut his eyes. He could hear his dad's laugh, feel his hand on the chair back . . .

A dog's bark. Jake opened his eyes, waited for the room to settle. Jet was barking at a tall grey door. Jake looked round at Ollie, and his face showed what Jake felt. What if there was something bad in there? Something dead.

–*Porca vacca*, Ollie said, shaking his head. –Your dog. You open it.

The handle was stiff and Jake had to use both hands.

He could smell the air even before he had the door open. Not the dirty air of the tunnels, and not the smell of something dead or rotting, but fresh air. Air that had birds flying in it, and clouds and rain and sun. He breathed deep and felt it like an ache in his chest.

Then he saw the staircase.

–Hey, he yelled. –Jet's found it!

The spiral staircase was thick with dust and old cobwebs, and orange with rust. It seemed to go up for ever, turning and turning as far as you could see. They climbed as quietly as they could, their footsteps clanging softly. Small blocks of emergency lighting, crusted with dirt and dead flies, lit their way. Red rust showered down with each footfall. Poacher went first with the girl behind him and Swift was at the back, cradling Cass in her arms. The rust fell down like soft rain, and with each footfall the smell of the fresh air grew stronger.

–Stairway to heaven, Davie said quietly. –Might find Martha at the top of it.

Thirty-two

Just do it. Just climb.

Martha underground.

Martha lying dead.

Martha found by the blond Surfer.

One step, and the next, and the next, and don't think, don't imagine.

Martha being slung in a van.

Martha lying in the dark.

Martha alone.

Stop it! Jake was yelling inside his head, and outside he was climbing, everybody was climbing, like they were all still a gang together, like it mattered.

He listened to Ollie's voice, beating quiet and steady.

–Eighty-six, eighty-seven . . .

He sounded normal. He sounded like nothing had even happened.

–Shut it, Ollie.

–Eight-nine, ninety . . .

–Shut it, Jake said again.

But Ollie went on and on, till Poacher called them to a stop. –Sit down, he said.

–Two hundred and four, Ollie said in the same flat voice.

Jake sat down in the red dust and shut his eyes. He felt Jet's head on his lap, and he stroked Jet's ears. Davie was drumming on the staircase, a hard, angry rhythm.

Poacher's voice was hoarse, like he'd been shouting, or crying all night, which maybe he had, just silently. –All of yer, drink some water. Halfway up, I reckon. Cos once I pop the lid up there, we gotta go fast . . .

–I ain't leaving. That was Davie's voice.

–An' we go in pairs . . .

–I ain't leaving, cos Martha ain't dead, Davie said. –I ain't seen her dead. Not properly. He got to his feet.

–Davie, you go with Jake . . .

But Davie was scrambling past Jet, pushing past Jake, fighting to get down again.

–Going back for her, he said.

–I saw her, Davie, Poacher said. –She's dead, and then to Swift: –Stop him.

Jake saw a rush of movements: Davie pushing down, and Swift's arm raised, and the flash of a knife. He saw Cass turned away into the wall, her eyes scrunched shut.

Swift held the knife out so it was just touching Davie's chest. –Can't let you go, she said. –Cos they'll catch you, and you'll lead them to us. They'll make you.

That was all they were, Jake thought. They weren't a gang. They were just a group that didn't dare let anyone go.

–Frisk him, Swift told Ollie, and Ollie patted Davie down and took away his knife, and pushed Davie down on the step next to Poacher.

Then Poacher went on like nothing had happened.

–We head for the freightyard. Break in there an' jump a train going north. Girl knows where the yard is, an' I done freight before. Getting on and off's dangerous, so you got to be super-careful. Look fer Outwalker signs. An' do what I tell yer.

Davie giggled. –Bye bye, Martha . . .

–Shut it, Poacher said.

–Sleep well, Martha. Never mind.

–He's lost it, Ollie whispered. –Dangerous to keep him, dangerous to let him go.

–Doesn't matter, Jake said to himself. Because they were just a bunch of kids and it was too hard, looking out for each other, and it was too hard, losing each other. He looked down at Jet. –Doesn't matter what happens.

–Can I say something? The girl's voice took Jake by surprise. He'd been lost in his own thoughts. Her voice sounded squeaky, like someone rubbing a balloon. –Because there are a few facts that I know and you don't . . .

–And we don't need to hear them, Ollie said. His voice had an edge Jake had never heard before. –You've said enough to Poacher and Swift already, and you're not part of our gang. Soon as we're out of London, you're on your own.

–Button it, Ollie, Swift said, but the girl shook her head.

–I don't mind. I know I'm not part of it, but I suggest we all try to act like a gang, at least till we're clear of London. Then we're less likely to get caught.

–She's right, Swift said. –We stop being a gang, we do their job for them. She looked upwards to the girl. –Tell us quick.

The girl cleared her throat. –So, I know that the hub police use heat sensors on lots of freight trains to catch people like you. She paused, then corrected herself. –Like us.

Jake felt mutinous. Ollie was right. The girl wasn't one of them and she was trying to weasel her way in. That's why she cleaned Martha's face and everything. But he wasn't fooled.

–Which is why you have to jump on at the very last minute, the girl went on, –after they've done their checks.

And as I said, I know where the nearest freightyard is.

–Why should we believe you? Ollie said. –You said you could start the MailRail, and you couldn't.

The girl looked at Poacher.

–All right, Poacher said, like he was giving her permission. –Tell 'em who yer ma is.

–She's a minister in the Coalition, the girl said. –Borders are her responsibility.

–Ooh, Davie said. –Get her with her important mother.

–So what? Ollie said.

–So I hear things.

–Nice, Ollie said.

The girl ignored him and went on. –They catch stowaways every year. Lots. And they're not kind to them. Fracking fields, picking fields, big tariffs, that kind of thing. The stowaways try to get out on the Tunnel freight trains, because that's the quickest route into Europe. We shouldn't even think of going near those.

–What Tunnel? Jake said.

–The Channel Tunnel? the girl said, as if it was obvious, doh.

–It's been closed for ever, he said angrily. –Dynamited before we were even born. After the Faith Bombings. We got taught it in history. They showed us photos.

–Oh no. The girl shook her head. –No, it isn't. You see . . .

–Enough, Swift said. –We ain't got time. But the Channel Tunnel ain't good for us anyway, cos we're going north.

–Like I said, freightyard. We go in pairs, Poacher said, deciding. –If we have to run fer it, stay in yer pair if you can. The girl an' me'll go first.

*

The top of the stairs just happened, no signs, only Poacher banging his head against something very hard, his curse echoing back down the steps towards the rest of the gang.

–Ready? Poacher said, rubbing his head.

He waited for each of them to answer. Acting like a gang, whatever they felt like inside.

–Be quick, but don't run, he said. –Running looks guilty. Let's go then.

Pushing up with his shoulders, Poacher slid the manhole cover to one side and climbed out. Seconds later and they were all out, squinting, feeling the outside air fresh on their faces, looking about, ready to run.

Jake stared up into the night. He wanted to eat the air, it was so good.

There were no tannoys, no hub police. It was night-time – of course it was, Jake had forgotten that – and they were in the middle of a big, floodlit square that glistened black in the rain. On one side, a Tube sign glowed red and blue in the darkness. There were a few small trees in big pots, but nothing much else to hide behind. But the only people Jake could see had their heads down and their umbrellas up, and they didn't seem to notice a small group of kids arriving from nowhere.

He looked around. Along one side was a wide, yellow-brick building with two enormous arches of dark, shining glass, and at the top, a clock lit up that read 12.30: gone midnight. Along the other side traffic still streamed past, a dazzling mass of streaky light.

–King's Cross station, the girl said. –Follow me. And she was already walking off, when Swift called out.

–Jake! She was pointing.

Jake turned. Down a third side of the square was the

biggest news screen he had ever seen, reaching up into the night, and in the middle of the screen was his face, peering out from inside his hood:

WANTED in connection with violent death of security officer
WANTED for abduction of young girl
At large in London
DANGEROUS. Do not approach
INFO: text 010
REWARD offered

The words shone out into the dark. Everyone would see them. Everyone would see him. Heat rushed to the back of Jake's neck.

–How did they get the picture? he said.

–The escalator, Ollie said. –When they stopped us. Look. You can see it in the background. That hubber. She must have had a camera.

–She was at the MailRail too, Jake said. –With the blond Surfer. Same woman.

–You sure? Swift said and Jake nodded. He felt sick. Someone only had to take his photo and text it to that number, and the hub police would be there in minutes.

–More reason fer us to get away fast then, Poacher said. –Keep yer face covered.

Jake looked over to where the girl stood waiting. In the rain in the dark, dressed in his clothes, Poacher's beanie pulled down over cropped hair, she looked small and harmless. He felt a surge of anger.

–They wouldn't be after me, except for her, he said.

–She's too dangerous for us. See – *abduction of young girl.* That's *her.* We leave her here, then they won't want us so badly.

But Swift shook her head. –We promised her.

They left the square in their pairs. Poacher and the girl went first, then Jake and Davie, up the side of the station. They kept their eyes away from other people and walked like they knew where they were going.

–Keep your hands in your pockets, Jake told Davie. –So they don't see you drumming. Looks weird. Might get us noticed.

But nobody looked at them. One man smelled of beer, and another smelled sweaty. A woman rushed past so close that Jake felt her coat tails brush against his legs, and she smelled like his mother, her perfume. He gasped and looked round, but she was gone already into the darkness.

The rain was heavy, and as they came round the corner they hugged close to the wall for the little shelter it gave. A few people were slumped inside bus shelters, their faces lit up by the ad screens, but otherwise the street was empty. Cafes and tanning shops, shuttered and dark.

Jake was frightened now, feeling the cool, rainy air on his face like a smack, every time he looked up or out. There was a price on his head, and if they caught him . . .

He reached down to Jet, patted him. –Stop it, he told himself. –Panicking won't help.

At least it was raining. There was nobody to see them. Nobody to notice a wanted boy. He tried to breathe more evenly, slow his heart down.

At the far end of the road, through the railings, he saw the trains all put to bed for the night, their blue and red paint shining under the station lights. His mum told him she'd got trains from King's Cross all the way to Scotland when she was his age. She told him that before the New Wall went up, you'd be sitting in your seat, looking out of the window, and you wouldn't even know when you'd crossed the border. One minute you were in England and the next you were in Scotland.

–Wasn't there even a fence? Jake said. –Didn't they say something over the loud speaker?

And she said no, there wasn't anything, no they didn't make any announcement, that it was just normal, people did it all the time, the same as going to Wales or Devon.

–But we're lucky to have the New Wall, Jake said. –It's kept us safe. Mrs Martin says lots of European countries would like to make a wall like ours, only they can't cos they're not islands and Europe won't allow it.

–Does she, his mum said flatly, which was what she said when she didn't agree.

She told him that in the month before the New Wall, train tickets to Scotland got sold on the black market for £50,000 a ticket; that on the last day, the trains got mobbed.

–I don't think people really believed it would happen until then. The Wall, I mean. And the Coalition denied all the stories. Managed the English Internet, so people couldn't read, couldn't see . . .

–What d'you mean? Jake asked. –Managed?

–Censored it. Controlled it, like they still do. They must have had it planned for ages. My family, me and your granny and grandpa, we'd moved up to Scotland six months before. We had to leave our house unsold. Couldn't bring out much money either. In Scotland the stories were everywhere. On the Internet, on the news, on people's lips. Everyone had seen things, survived things. People locking themselves to carriage tables, hiding in train toilets, crammed in so tight some people suffocated.

–To death? Jake said.

His mother nodded. –You're old enough to hear some of it now. It's your country's history. Children stuffed into suitcases, parents asking strangers to take the cases to Edinburgh and leave them on the platform. They'd rather risk their children's lives, risk that kind of fate, than keep them in the new England.

She was sombre now, going on.

–People crushed to death against the barriers, trying to storm the last trains out before the New Wall. I remember in the news: a young woman, didn't look much older than me, pregnant, dead. Hub police pulled people off the carriage roofs. They used tear gas in one train, fired it straight into the carriages. They said on the English news that there had been a riot. They said there were fifteen people dead, three of them children. But the Scottish news said it was sixty-two people.

She looked angry and sad together.

–Five hundred and seventy-nine people died in the Faith Bombings. It was terrible. But the Coalition killed more than that in the year they put up the New Wall.

–So why did you go back to England then? Jake said. –If that's all true?

He remembered how his mum had stroked his cheek then. –It is all true, she said. –And I knew I might never see my parents again. But your father and me, we were childhood sweethearts. All our growing-up years, we'd managed to stay in touch, me in Scotland, him in England. I went back because of your father.

*

–Jake! Hurry up.

Davie's voice started him out of his thoughts. He looked around. How had they got here? He couldn't remember the last few minutes. On both sides of the road he saw steel-bladed railings topped with razor wire, and security lights blasting the dark as they went past, flooding the night so that everything shone in the rain, which fell in sheets of silver.

The rain had soaked in everywhere. Inside his jacket, down his legs, so that his trousers stuck to them. His feet were wet inside his boots. Ahead, Poacher and the girl were crouched close to the railings, pushing at the sharp steel blades, and before Jake could see how, they disappeared through.

The Outwalker sign was scratched on to one of the railing posts, the small circle with the dot in the middle.

–How did they do it?

Davie crouched down, pressed each of the blades in turn till he found the point.

–Lo, thou shalt breach the fenced places, he said. –Ready? And he pressed. A section of the railings hinged down, leaving a space just big enough for them to climb through. Once they were through, the railing snapped back, so you'd never have seen the place.

Buckled concrete stretched like a sea ahead of them, and beyond it long lines of metal containers, and beyond these, a train. Poacher and the girl had run across already, and were crouched between two containers.

–Like Moses crossing the Red Sea, Davie said. –Watch me. And before Jake could reply, he'd set off. The security lighting robbed him of his shadow, and he looked very small under its glare, running flat out. He was nearly across when he stumbled, and crashed to the ground headlong.

Davie! Jake yelled inside his mind, and he set off running, Jet on his lead beside him, running low too, like he knew in his dog mind that they mustn't be seen.

Davie was on his feet again by the time Jake reached him.

–You all right? Jake whispered, and when Davie turned, he saw that one side of his face had been scraped raw on the concrete, grazed from his eye down to his chin. Blood and rain trailed down his cheek.

–Bad one, Jake said. –Need to get that seen to.

But Davie shook his head, and as if in a trance, he dragged his fingernails down his face, pressing them into his bloody cheek. –Shouldn't a' left her. She's on the far side an' the sea's closed over again, Jakey. She's on the far, far side.

–You gotta run! Come on! Jake said. Because they needed to move, get out of the floodlights. Behind them, Jake could hear Swift and Ollie climbing through the railings, their whispering voices.

Davie pressed his fingers harder, and his tears ran into the blood.

Jake took him by the shoulders. –Don't do this. Least not for Martha. You gotta cross the sea for her. You've got to do good to yourself, not bad. That's what she'd tell you. He looked around. Any secca could see them here, clear as day. –Remember what Swift said? he whispered. –We've got to be strong. He pulled Davie's hand gently from his face. –Come on now; and he took Davie with him out of the security light and back into the darkness.

Thirty-three

The train was stacked with shiny new cars, wagon after wagon of them, ready to leave. From the loading certificate on the side of the wagons, its destination was Tyne Yard, Gateshead, due to arrive at six o'clock the following evening. Poacher told them the plan, and when the train started slowly to move, they were ready. Poacher ran first for the back of the train, the next to last wagon, crouched low, climbing up between the wagon rails. And one by one they all followed, Ollie, then Swift, pulling Cass up on to the platform. Now Davie was on and it was the girl next, Jake and Jet the last to go.

The girl was running, girl-style, arms out, Jake and Jet just behind her, and Ollie and Davie were grabbing at her to pull her up. But she stumbled and fell to the ground, her feet tangling in Jet's lead so that she took them both down with her. It was only for a moment, and they were up and running again, but it was long enough because the train was gaining speed now.

–Come on! Ollie yelled, reaching out with his long, thin arms, but they couldn't reach him.

–Next one, Jake shouted, and he didn't know if the girl had heard him, but he was sprinting beside the final wagon and grabbing the rail and pulling himself up on the standing platform.

–Up, Jet! he called, and his dog was there in a single

movement, graceful and easy. Then it was only the girl left, running in her stupid posh trainers, mouth wide, running her guts out. This girl who thought she was so much better than them, and who didn't know how lucky she was. Besides which, she only cared about herself. Only did that stuff for Martha to get in their good books. All this flashed through his mind in the space of a second, and the thought that came after: no one would know if he left her here, and no one would care.

But he took a deep breath, and gripping hold of the rail, he leaned out from the wagon. –Gimme your hand, he shouted. –Come on! And then she was gripping him, her nails digging into his skin, still running, her breath coming in gasps, and somehow, from somewhere, he found the strength to pull her up till she was lying beside him, sobbing and heaving for breath.

The rain whipped at Jake's face and the wind cut through his wet clothes. They were out of the freightyard already, lumbering through the city, gaining speed. Dark houses, glistening streets, hub flags, ad boards rushed past.

They'd made it. They were on a train and they were heading north, heading towards the border. They'd done good, like Martha would have wanted. Soon they'd be out of London, and – Jake crossed his fingers, wished inside his head – out of England.

Anger still ran through him like electricity, but he turned his mind away from it and gripped the cold steel rail and stared out into the night.

He pictured his granny and grandpa. Figures standing by a house with the sea in the background. That was the photograph his mum had kept on her chest of drawers. But now in his head they both turned his way, like they were waiting for him.

–We're coming, he murmured, and for the first time he let himself imagine it. Him and Jet walking into the picture, walking towards the house, towards the figures; he imagined his granny catching sight of him, her hand on his grandpa's arm, his grandpa shielding his eyes to see, taking a step forward. He imagined how he'd break into a run then, and how they'd hug him tight, and how Jet's tail would be nearly wagging itself off because he'd know who they were too.

The city lights blurred in Jake's eyes and he blinked the tears away. He stared forward through the dark to the next wagon, but he couldn't see any of the others. He looked the other way, down to where he'd left the girl.

The girl had disappeared. The air roared in his ears as he made his way past all the sleeping, shiny cars, up the jolting wagon. Jet kept close to his legs and when he went to pat him, he could feel him shaking, so he crouched a moment and held Jet's head gently between his hands and spoke quietly to him.

How could the girl have disappeared? He didn't care about her, but he didn't want her to be dead. Specially not since he'd half killed himself, pulling her up on to the train.

–Hey, he called. –Where are you?

Lights from the sleeping city came and went as the freight train trundled through, and Jake could see a bit here and there. He scrabbled under the cars and peered between them, calling for the girl. Right to the end of the wagon they went, him and Jet, till he was staring down at the rail track spooling out from underneath him, disappearing into the dark. He walked back down the wagon on the other side and was nearly giving up his search when he heard something.

–Here. I'm here.

Her voice was faint, like maybe she was hurt, or trapped somewhere. He peered below the car. Nothing. Tying Jet's lead to the wagon rail, he scrambled up on to the bonnet and scanned along the car roofs.

–Where are you? he called again.

–Where d'you think? Her voice was louder this time and then a movement caught his eye. Crouching down, he stared in through the car windscreen, and there she was, grinning.

Grinning at him. He'd been searching, scared, and she was grinning.

Jake opened the back door for Jet, then pulled open the driver door and thumped down into the seat. He was angry. So angry, he could taste it.

Behind him, Jet's claws slithered on the plastic seat covering. He turned around himself and settled down to sleep.

Jake sat back, shattered. The girl was still smiling, sitting there with her posh trainers, and no chip ever, and her bright shiny voice.

–I didn't want to get out and wave at you, in case anybody saw me, she said. –It would have been awful, after everything, if we got caught because I'd waved . . .

–Yeah, awful, Jake said.

–So I just kept on shouting and waving. But it was funny when I could only see your legs. I couldn't help laughing. I'm glad you've found me. You do look very tired.

Then finally Jake couldn't stop himself. –You think you're so clever. His voice was shaking, he was so angry, and he spat the words out. –You'd have been captured, or hurt, if we hadn't rescued you. And I know what Swift said about Martha's death not being your fault, and I know you did that stuff for her afterwards, with the water and the sacks and everything, but—

The girl stopped laughing. Jake stared out through the windscreen. Nothing to see except the dim shape of the car in front. It was weird, being in a car that was travelling, but going nowhere.

–Go on, say it, the girl said.

–OK. You know what's the biggest difference between you and us? Jake's voice was vicious, and he didn't care. –It's not where you live, or your expensive clothes, or even you not having a chip, ever.

He flicked the switch on the overhead light. He could see her now.

–The biggest difference is, you can go back home, he said against the choke in his throat. –The hub police would just take you home, and your very important mother, and maybe you've got a dad too, well, they might be very angry with you and everything, but they'll still have you back. You might not like it, but it's there, and it's yours. All of us: we get caught, it's a Home Academy. That's it. Locked in. Secure rooms. Prison.

He knew he was going to regret it, but at this moment he wanted to hurt her like he hurt.

–Jet's my only family in the whole of England, he said, –and if I get caught, I'll never see him again.

He stopped and flicked the light off again. He'd said his piece. On the back seat Jet had woken up and he was turning round and round, like he always did when there was an argument. Jake reached back and stroked his velvet ears.

The train rumbled through a sleeping town, the street lights flicking against the dark.

The girl was still silent. She pulled Poacher's beanie

off her head and put a hand to her chopped-off hair. Jake watched her. She looked like she was trying to decide about something. Then she put her hands flat out in front of her.

–You don't know my name, she said finally.

–What? Jake said incredulously. He'd had a real go at her, laid into her, angry enough to spit in her face – and all she was worried about was him knowing her name?

–My name, she repeated. –You haven't asked me what it is.

–Is that a joke?

–No. She looked affronted. –But you would have asked, if you thought of me as a real person. If you respected me for who I was.

–Real person?

–Yes. Not just someone who's posh. Someone who's had all the luck. At least, that's what you think. *I* respect *you*, you know.

Jake shook his head. –I don't believe it. You sound like a blooming Citizenship class.

–I know all your names. Jake, Ollie, Swift . . .

–Yeah, all right. Jake put his head in his hands. This was unreal. Unbelievable. He half wanted to laugh. How had he ended up on a wagon with her? The anger surged again and the half-laugh died in him. –When we get off this train, I won't have to see you any more, so no, I don't care what your name is.

The girl looked down at her lap.

–What I care about . . . He stopped. The words hurt. –What I care about right now is that Martha is dead. I care about Jet, and my gang, he said. –I care that that Surfer and Scar woman are hunting us, cos they killed Martha already and if they killed us, they wouldn't care . . .

He couldn't see her face, but he didn't care what she thinking.

–and no, I don't care about you. I don't trust you. You've had your little adventure now, so go home. You can tell your posh friends about it. Go on, jump off when the train slows down. Tell anyone who your mum is, they'll get you home safe.

–I can't, the girl said.

–You jumped on, so you can jump off. I'll help you, if you like.

–I can't. I found a memo on the kitchen table. Yesterday. An official one, and . . .

Jake banged a hand down on the steering wheel. –Hang on. You happened to find a Coalition memo on the kitchen table? He couldn't keep the disbelief out of his voice.

–It was on the top of my mum's work papers, so I took a phone pic of it, the girl said. –That's why I went to the meet.

–You're going to tell me next it was marked *Top Secret*.

–How did you know? She sounded surprised. –That's what made me read it. Normally my mum's work stuff looks so boring. I could've shown it to you with its Coalition stamp and everything, if your Poacher hadn't smashed up my mobile. Anyway, how did you know it said *Top Secret*?

–Because *my* parents— Jake began, and then he stopped. Why was he even talking to this girl? –Doesn't matter. I don't care about the memo, or your mum. He turned to Jet, clipped the lead on to his collar. –Nice story, but I'm gonna find another car.

–You don't even know what it said. The girl's voice had gone high-pitched, like girls' voices did when they got cross.

Jake reached for the door handle.

–And if you get out now, I'll never tell you, she said. –We'll get to Newcastle and I'll tell Ollie instead.

–So tell Ollie then, he shot back. –This isn't a game.

–No, the girl said, her voice dead quiet, –it's not a game, you're right. And I'm not playing. I wouldn't be trying to tell you if I wasn't desperate. I'd much rather tell it to someone who treats me like a proper person. Not like a bad joke. But I haven't got any choice.

Jake wanted to shout at her. It was his gang who weren't thought of as proper people. It was them who were the rejects, not her. Locked up in Home Academies, living as Outwalkers. But something stopped him. He didn't want to feel this angry. He was just tired, and he wanted to find his grandparents and stop Outwalking. Nothing else was important.

He took a deep breath. –I do think you're a proper person. Just . . . you've had a very different life. He didn't sound like he meant it, but it was the best he could do.

She shook her head. –Not that kind of proper. What I mean is . . . She put her hand up against the window glass. When she spoke again, she was hesitant, stopping and starting. –All of you – dead parents, Home Academies, illness. You wouldn't be doing this if you hadn't lost so much already . . . Leaving your country, leaving anybody you've ever known, and you don't even know what will happen if you do get across the border . . . Compared to you, I haven't suffered anything. Not like that. And not my best friend dying like that. I can't even imagine . . . She ran her finger down the window. –That's what I mean.

Jake stared into the darkness. She sounded like she meant it.

–But it's not a game for me either, the girl went on,

–and if you won't take me seriously because I'm posh, and because my parents aren't dead, then you're more stupid than I thought.

She scratched the back of her neck, then fell silent. Jake pictured Martha cutting her hair off. It must have been a shock. He could see that.

–I don't know why my mum bothered having kids, the girl went on. –She's never at home. She only cares about her Ministry and her stupid briefcase.

–What about your dad? Jake said, because despite himself, he was curious. What made a girl like this want to escape?

–He's not around much either, but at least he's not going to hurt anyone. He just writes about Shakespeare all the time.

–What d'you mean, hurt someone? Jake said. –Someone in your family?

The girl turned round and stared at him like he was daft. –No. Not in my family. I'm talking about the memo, of course. The memo you don't care about. What it says: it's sick. I was out of the house straight after reading it, but I couldn't get down to the lowlifer tunnels because there were seccas everywhere, masses in the Tube, and I had to hide out. So the meet had started by the time I got there, and you saw what was happening. Noel handing out mandy like Smarties. Everyone chilled, stoned. I told them about it, showed the Catchpitters the phone pic I got. But they wouldn't listen. Checker just laughed. And Gaz: Gaz was my friend.

–So what's your mother going to do? he said.

–It's not just up to her. She always goes on about how she's part of a team that's part of a bigger team, that's elected by the whole country. So what she does: it's done for the whole of England, and by the whole of England.

The girl couldn't have seen Jake's face in the darkness, but she must have guessed at what he was thinking.

–It's like she's saying that nothing's her fault. No responsibility because she's only doing what her team has agreed.

–Yeah, Jake said.

–I think she really believes it, though, and I do get it, the girl said. –I understand her. But when it's something that's really wrong, really terrible: then I don't think there's any excuse. Doesn't matter if someone else orders you. Doesn't matter if your team all agree. Her voice was shaky now. –My mum. The Coalition: what they've done, there's no excuse, and my Catchpitter friends. They were nice to me. Gaz was smart, really smart, only he'd never had a chance. And Checker was kind.

She stopped and fished in a pocket, blew her nose.

In the last few minutes the dawn had come as a thin bar of low light, and the rain had stopped. The girl had turned her head away and was looking out of the window. Jake saw trees, a church steeple, a barn, black against the rising light. He wondered how it would feel, to know your mother had done something bad. Something really bad. He thought how lonely the girl looked. And he thought that maybe he'd judged her wrong.

–Shouldn't judge a book by its cover, he said.

–What?

–Something my mum used to say. She used to read a lot.

–She still read books? Actual books? the girl said.

–Yeah. Gently he tapped her shoulder. –My name's Jacob Riley, he said. –What's yours?

She turned back towards him, and in the dawn light he saw that she was crying. –Aliya Khan, she said.

Jake put out his hand. –Pleased to meet you.

Aliya swiped her tears away, cleared her throat. –I'm not crying now because you asked my name nicely, she said. –I don't cry. Not normally.

–OK, Jake said.

–In fact, I don't know when I did last cry.

–It's fine. Plenty to cry about, for both of us.

Then Aliya told him what her mother had done.

Thirty-four

–They're going to kill lowlifers, Aliya said in a matter-of-fact voice. –Use them for an experiment when they know some of them will die from it. That's what the memo said. So the meet last night: it was a trap to catch them, and Noel – the one you called the blond Surfer – he and my mum are at the centre of it.

Jake gasped. This was worse than he'd ever imagined. Lowlifers were invisible people. Next to nobody knew they were there, living underneath London, so nobody would care what happened to them. They didn't matter while they were alive, and it wouldn't matter to anyone if they were killed.

It was horrible. He pictured the Surfers' den: all of them looking up to their leader, and he was going to betray them all.

–But Noel, he's the Surfers' leader, he said. –I saw him in their den. That's his life. Not someone employed by the Coalition. And you said your mother was in charge of borders. What's that got to do with a bunch of stoned lowlifers underneath London?

–Noel's both, Aliya said. –It's called deep cover. He is the Surfers' leader, but he's also a spy. He used to turn up at our house at funny times, report to my mum. I didn't know where he did his spying, but I do now, and he knows that I know. That makes me very dangerous. He can't kill me, because of my mother, but he can kill you, and he will if he catches you. You should have been part of the experiment, and now your gang knows too much. Specially with me in it.

Jake shut his eyes. It was a lot to get his head around. He was bone-tired and he wanted, more than anything, to sleep. He wanted to stretch out in a clean, empty car, put his arm across his sleeping dog, and close his eyes to everything. But now Aliya had told him this, he needed to understand it all.

–Listen. Can you remember it? The memo?

–Scorched on to my brain, she said, nodding. –I've got one of those memories. Don't understand it, but I can remember it all. Luckily, since you lot smashed my phone.

–So we could write it down. Show the others. You got any bit of paper?

She rummaged in her rucksack. –My school planner? Not going to need it now, am I?

On the cover in gold letters, her name: *Aliya Khan, Year 9, Westminster Academy.*

–Posh, Jake said. –We didn't get paper at my school. He flicked through for an empty page, slipped the pen out. –Ready.

And in a steady voice, Aliya told him what had been written on the memo and he wrote it down.

Primary trial, Vacplus nano-microchip
anti-viral vaccine

cc. Rt Hon. Caro Fielding; Rt Hon. Ina Khan

Sample: lowlifer population
Sample size: 250–350
Delivery date: 29.05–30.05
Start: 23.00 hours

Location: sub-Covent Garden Tube station.
Inoculation measures ready: delivery team on critical footing
Nanotoxicologists on red alert
Venue: established
Exit routes managed
Aftercare measures ready
Anticipated attrition/death rate: 20%
Authorization cleared
Media management activated

Signed: Noel Knight (Virus Management Facilitator)

Jake read back over what he'd written. He didn't understand it all, but he understood enough. It was horrible. They were using lowlifers to experiment on. A death rate of twenty per cent. Twenty out of every hundred people. That meant fifty deaths last night. More. That was enough to know why Aliya was so desperate to warn the Catchpitters.

But something was niggling him, something he'd seen a few days ago. Then he remembered: the newspaper Swift had found in the motorway Services. There had been an article about the Vacplus vaccine.

–The newspapers said they were looking for volunteers to test the vaccine, he said. –But last night . . .

–Last night they were drugged, Jake. They couldn't have volunteered.

She was right, he thought. He remembered the girl with the dreamy eyes, the gangs all dancing together. The people at the meet weren't in a state to say yes – or no – and mean it.

–Now do you see why I can't go home? said Aliya. –My mother is part of this.

Jake checked his watch. –Eight hours since we left the

meet. They'll have done it by now. Kept the whole thing underground, I bet, so nobody knows about it.

–I couldn't make them listen to me, Jake. There were tears in Aliya's eyes. –They didn't believe me when I said the Coalition knew they were down there. We have to warn people. We have to let people know. It's the only way to stop it. Her voice rose in a sob. –Fifty of the people we saw yesterday will be dead now. Gaz might be. I couldn't make them listen! Her fist thumped the car window in frustration.

Jake felt cold with horror, but he had to know more. –But why? –Because nobody cares about lowlifers. My mum thinks they're worthless. Like vermin. She hated it when she found out I was friendly with some Catchpitters.

–How come? Where did you meet them?

She shrugged. –At a gig. They were wearing this cool gear and I got talking to Gaz and . . . But they're not like my mum says, not at all. They're amazing. I had to keep it secret cos she'd have grounded me. She didn't even know I'd gone to the gig. She thought I was at my friend's house. She'd have locked me in my room every day after that if she'd known. So I got really good at lying to her.

–Why does she hate them so much? Jake said.

–Because they aren't honest, or hard-working, and they don't contribute anything. It's not true, but that's what she says. So she must think it doesn't matter if some of them die. Aliya's words came out choked with sobs.

Awkwardly he put his hand on hers. A government that could do this to people . . . and her mum part of it. What would it be like, to have a mother like that?

–My mum and dad were working on a vaccine too, he said. –Least I think they were. But they wouldn't have given it to a single person if they'd thought it might kill them.

Aliya didn't move her hand from under his, but she was crying more quietly now. –Lucky you, she said bitterly.

–Yes, he said, and he felt it. Even though his parents were dead. At least he didn't have to be ashamed of them. Then a question came to him. –But why is the Vacplus vaccine so dangerous? He looked again at his page of notes. –Why would it be likely to kill so many people?

–Because I don't think this is only about a vaccine, Aliya said. –I think it's about population control. That's part of my mum's brief as Borders Minister. Otherwise, why is she involved? Vaccines aren't part of her job.

Population control. It sounded so clean, so planned. Jake forced down his horror. Carefully he tore the sheet of notes from the planner, folded it and tucked it into his rucksack.

–When we get off, let me do the talking, he said.

Jake took the first watch while Aliya slept. She pushed her seat back so she was nearly lying down and she was asleep in seconds, her breathing slow and even. For the first time in ages, Jake was alone with his thoughts.

But there was too much on his mind, and his thoughts zigzagged with exhaustion, between his mother and Aliya's, between the MailRail train and this chugging freight train. He imagined his old friends Liam and Josh dressed as Surfers, drugged and dying in a Tube tunnel, he saw Martha smiling and then serious. He could feel her hands in his hair, washing it before they went stealing, and he saw her leaning over the old stone bridge, telling him that he was a watcher. Like her.

He shook his head. He'd slept, he was sure. Checked his watch. Two hours still until he was to wake Aliya.

–Don't think, he told himself. –Just watch. He pinched

his hand, bit his lip to stay awake, and stared through the window and between the wagon rails.

The sun shone on golden fields and small towns, junkyards and reservoirs and farm houses, level crossings and cars, and horses and cows and people. Jake counted church spires and he counted wind turbines. He saw miles of polytunnels, and he saw green picking fields and lines of tariffed pickers in their blue and red coveralls crouched down, barbed wire fences around the field edges. Boys for fracking fields, girls for picking fields. That was how it went. The jobs that nobody wanted. That's where the Home Academy children got sent, everybody knew.

His stomach rumbled and he tried to remember when he'd last eaten. There was no food left in his rucksack, only a few mouthfuls of water in a bottle. He looked round at Jet. He was sleeping, tail tucked round his legs. Aliya had turned towards Jake in her sleep, and she lay now with one hand underneath her cheek. The other still held Poacher's beanie. The train pulled past a block of trees and sunlight pulsed in lines across the wagon of cars. Aliya's eyelids flickered, but she didn't wake. She looked peaceful, for now. Gently he touched her hair. It was warm with the early sun. He bent towards her. Her hair smelled sweet. A thought rose, a bubble in his mind. He could kiss her, just there, on the top of her head, and she'd never have to know. He bent closer.

The train slowed, a pulling back motion, the smell of rubber, and Aliya murmured something, moved a little in her seat. Quickly Jake pulled away and sat up straighter and looked out of his window again. Heat rushed to his cheeks. What was he doing? Why did he even think that? –Stupid, he told himself.

Once the train stopped and a man walked past, tapping

onto a pad. Jake couldn't see his head or his feet, only his middle. He was sure the man couldn't see him, but he slouched low in his seat and held his breath. He didn't wake Aliya and the man walked on.

His turn to sleep finally, Aliya on watch. He tilted back the passenger seat, put his hands beneath his head for a pillow. He wondered if she'd watch him while he slept. He wondered if he wanted her to. He was tired. So tired. His face was close enough that he could breathe in Jet's dog smell. The same smell he'd had as a puppy, the smell of home.

–Jake. We're there! Aliya was shaking his arm. –Look! There's the Angel!

Jake groaned. He didn't care what was outside the window, he didn't care about anything, if only he could sleep some more. But he turned and peered out, eyes bleary, only half-focused. The train was moving at a snail's pace and they were in a broad valley with hills on both sides. Early evening sun shone over twenty or more railway tracks that twisted away like spaghetti, weaving round huge grey warehouses. Container wagons sat on the tracks like giant blocks of Lego.

On the nearest hilltop, just above the train, a huge metal figure glowed in the sunlight, rusty red, with wide, oblong wings. Below, cut into the hillside in broad red letters, its name: COALITION ANGEL. The statue was even bigger than Jake had imagined it. It reached as high as a house: two houses.

–It's enormous, Jake said.

–Do you know why it's called that? Aliya said.

–Course, Jake said. –Everyone knows that. Because everyone did. You got taught it in Year Four and Year Five and Year Six. Jake's teacher had read it to them out of the

Cohistory book. About how the Battle of the Angel was the last battle in England's entire war on terror. And how, after all the Faith Bombings in the cities, the last Faith Bomber was tracked to this valley. And how the best hub team in the country confronted her in the shadow of the Angel, and all she had to do was pull the pin on her explosives and she'd have blown them all away. And she pulled the pin, but she only blew herself up.

–You can see the shrapnel damage, Aliya said, and it was true, you could. The Angel was dented and scarred and one wing was buckled in the middle. The Coalition had left it like that on purpose, so English people would never forget the horror of the Faith Bombings, or the wonder of England's deliverance.

His teacher had said it was the Angel that protected the hub team, and that was a miracle, and that's why they decided to change the statue's name, from the Angel of the North to the Coalition Angel.

–Do you believe it? About the miracle? Jake asked Aliya.

–Do *you* believe it?

Jake shrugged. –I did when my teacher told us the story. But I don't trust anybody now.

–So whose side d'you think the Angel is on today? Aliya said.

Thirty-five

They were off the train before it came to a halt, running for cover, crouching down in the weeds. Jet strained on the lead, pulling Jake forward. The weeds smelled of fox, and for a split second Jake was back home, at the end of his garden, playing in the long grass with his dog.

–Keep low, he whispered back to Aliya, and she gave him a thumbs up, but she looked scared. Ahead of them, Poacher and the others were making their way, single file, towards an old wooden warehouse building.

Some way off, men were working. Jake could hear occasional shouts, but they didn't sound urgent. The men weren't hunting for a gang of children, or for Jake.

Not yet, anyway.

They followed the others, running parallel with the warehouse until they were crouched behind a pile of rubble, waiting their turn to run across an open stretch of concrete about the width of a tennis court. Away in the distance Jake could see the men loading wagons now, using a big crane.

–When it's your turn, look straight ahead and just go, he told Aliya. –Don't look round at the men, not even a glance, and don't stop and start. He waited for her to tell him she knew it all, but she only nodded and bit her lip a little.

She wasn't very quick, but she got across, and Jake and Jet came after her, running round to the far side of the building. The others were there already, a little huddle of kids catching their breath, taking a moment before the next thing.

Jake pictured the Angel, watching them. *On our side so far*, he thought.

He felt as if he'd been doing this for ever: escaping, running, climbing, hiding. Finding empty buildings, abandoned rooms. Eating left-over food. Sleeping in forgotten places. He wanted to stop somewhere. To stay and not to go. He wanted to belong.

He tried to bring to mind his grandparents by the sea, and the house behind. That was closer than ever now, but it didn't seem real any more.

–A'right? Poacher clapped Jake on the arm, patted Jet.

–Poacher! Jake said. –Some stuff you need to know, about the virus, the meet . . .

But Poacher had his hand up. –Not now. We need to get inside quick. Door's locked here, but the window's not, an' I reckon Davie'll fit, just about. So we're gonna punt him up an' he kin pull the bolts fer us.

–It's important, Jake said. –Really important.

He heard Jet growl, but it was Poacher he kept watching, because he saw the black rings below his eyes and he saw how Poacher's fingers danced on the handle of his knife. Poacher was as exhausted as he was, and when he was tired . . .

–I said not now, dog boy. Poacher's voice was angry. He looked over at Aliya, jutted his head at her. –You kin leave us, soon as we're outta this yard. We done our side then.

Jake could see her form a reply, and he willed her not to answer. But Poacher had already turned away, and now Davie was punted up to the window, pulling it open, slipping round and inside it like an otter – Jake had seen them on a screen once, how they moved, smooth like oil – and then Jake heard Jet's growl. Heard it properly, because it hadn't stopped, Jake realized.

Jet was growling at something Jake couldn't see, something down the far side of the warehouse.

–Jet! Jake called, but Jet went on standing, paws planted, hackles raised, growling. And Swift had noticed, and was picking up Cass; and Ollie, who ran to the warehouse doors, banged on one.

–Davie! Open the doors! And Swift was calling too.

Jake headed for the warehouse corner, fishing for his penknife, and then he saw it. A huge, grey dog trotting towards them. A sleek-headed, muscled brute, studded collar, ears pinned back, lips in a snarl, eyes blazing. It paused, sizing him up. Jake clipped the lead on to Jet's collar, flipped open his penknife. Then he shouted round to the others: –Guard dog! Get inside! Fast!

The dog lunged forward, running full pelt, all the power of those bunched muscles hurtling at them, saliva whipping across its cheek, teeth hungry. And Jet had squared up, feet planted foursquare, angry, hackles raised along his back. He gave a long, low growl.

Behind them, Jake heard the sound of metal on metal, Poacher calling instructions, urgent, to Davie.

–Come on! Jake pulled on Jet's lead. Because they needed to run. Now.

But Jet stood his ground. He wouldn't move. The dog was nearly on them. Jet's ears were flat to his head, his tail high and still, except for the faintest electrical quiver at its tip. Every ounce of him was focused on the guard dog. Every ounce of him ready.

Jake glanced back. Davie had the warehouse door

cracked open, and they were squeezing in, only Ollie and Poacher left outside.

–Come on! Jake said, both hands pulling on Jet's lead. The guard dog was close enough, Jake could see the whites of his eyes.

Then the dog leaped.

It leaped, jaws wide, straight for Jake's throat. And in that same split second Jake felt the lead whip from his hand and Jet had launched himself at the guard dog.

Everything was turmoil, and fur, and sound, and the two dogs were up on their hind legs, twisting and lunging, snarling and yapping, biting at each other, their teeth bared. Jake watched with horror, but he couldn't get near enough to pull Jet away.

And then the guard dog got Jet. Got him on the back, by the scruff, sank his fangs in, and Jake saw Jet's body give with the shock, the force of it. The guard dog was throwing Jet one way and then the other, blood spattering the ground. The dog was tearing at Jet's flesh, his saliva frothing pink with Jet's blood, and Jet was weakening under the force of the bigger dog, Jake could see it.

Jake stepped forward, his penknife held out in front of him. If he could just get close enough to use it. But the dogs were rolling on the ground now and he was scared he would miss the guard dog, scared he might plunge the knife into Jet.

Maybe Jake had distracted the guard dog, and so maybe the dog weakened his hold on Jet. Or maybe Jet was waiting for his moment, Jake didn't know. But in that moment of Jake stepping forward, somehow Jet found the strength to shake free. He gave a last yelp, whipped around and sank his teeth into the guard dog's neck.

It can't have been more than thirty seconds, but it seemed

like for ever, Jet holding fast, teeth sunk deep, and the guard dog turning this way and that, blood pouring from his neck, his movements slowing and slowing. Only when the guard dog lay absolutely still, when his body had become soft as a puppet, did Jet let go, collapsing into a bloody heap beside him, and the two dogs lay on the dirt ground, both of them motionless.

Carefully Jake stepped forward, penknife in hand. But the guard dog lay in a glistening red pool, and his eyes stared out at nothing.

Bending to the ground, Jake slid his arms beneath his dog, and lifted him up, and walked towards the warehouse doors. Jet's eyes were closed. Jake wasn't sure if he was breathing, or not. His neck was a mess of blood and froth and fur. He put his face to his dog's warm side. Could he hear a heartbeat?

–Don't be dead. Jake spoke into Jet's black fur. –Please don't be dead.

Poacher's voice broke in. –Jake! Get in here! Now! And gently Poacher lifted Jet from him and took him into the warehouse. And Davie had hold of Jake's arm, his green eyes wide, and he pulled him inside and slammed the door shut.

–Yer dog saved you, dog boy, Davie said.

Stumbling over to where Poacher had set Jet down, Jake sank to the ground. –Jet, Jake said quietly, and it wasn't his imagination, he did feel Jet move. Just the slightest of movements. He was alive. But he didn't lift his head, or beat his tail.

–Drink, a voice said. Swift's. A bottle of water beside him. –We'll use the rest to clean Jet's wound. You, and she pointed at Aliya, –your T-shirt's cleanest, it's in Jake's rucksack . . .

Swift went on talking, and Jake understood what she

was saying, but he wasn't listening. He was praying. Or maybe not praying, because he'd never prayed, but he was pleading with something, or somewhere, not to let Jet die.

–We ain't got boiled water an' we ain't got antiseptic. Medicines all went with Martha, right, Davie?

–Yeah. All gone, dog boy, Davie said, and he sounded sorry about it.

–But it's gonna *look* better when it's cleaned up, Swift's voice went on as she ripped the T-shirt, poured water over a piece of it. –Hold him now, Jake heard her say, –cos it's gonna hurt him like crackers when I do this.

And Jake felt Jet rear, his head snapping round at them, at him and Swift and Davie, and Cass too, because she had sat down on the floor and put her hand on Jet's back: all of them holding him down.

–Now you got to keep this pressed against the wound. Swift handed him another piece of the T-shirt. –To stop the bleeding.

Jet's wound was severe and the bite had gone deep into his shoulder. Without proper treatment, the wound would become infected, and then . . . Jake pressed the piece of T-shirt to the bloody, matted fur on Jet's neck and it grew wet beneath his fingers.

–He's shivering, Davie said, and he was shaking his head to and fro and to and fro. –Martha . . .

–Shock, Swift said. –Gotta keep him warm. Gonna have to move him very soon. Her hand on Jake's shoulder was gentle. –Poacher and Ollie have gone to find a place to hide. Or a way out. Because as soon as they find that guard dog, they find us.

Jake was trembling again. Aliya was talking to Davie, putting her hands on his hands, and a thought came to Jake that this was what Martha used to do. Swift was opening her rucksack. His eyes felt wide with horror, and his chest was tight and his throat was dry. This couldn't be happening. Not Jet. Not Jet. Not Jet.

He hadn't noticed Cass get up. She placed a blanket carefully over Jet's body and sat back down again. It was her blanket, the one Swift always covered her with when she slept. They sat quiet. The warehouse was dark, stretching out behind them.

Jake listened to Jet's breathing. It was very rapid. Then, behind him, he heard footsteps.

–Ain't no way out 'cept through those doors, Poacher said. He was out of breath and covered with dust. –No loose boards, nothing. Low ceiling, so there's a floor above, but no ladder up, or stairway, or lift. Nix.

–And nowhere to hide, Ollie said. He pointed a thin finger behind Jake. –Shelves right to the end and stacked tight with old luggage. Suitcases.

Jake turned. He saw what Ollie meant. From floor to ceiling, the shelves were jammed full.

–Suitcases? Aliya said.

Ollie looked at her like he hadn't noticed her before. –Wheelie bags, rucksacks, laundry bags, carrier bags. Crates too, and cardboard boxes, or what's left of them. Maybe rats ate them.

–Whatever yer can stuff stuff into, Poacher added. –All got labels, special Coalition labels, names an' addresses. Thousan's of 'em. Scottish addresses mostly.

–So do you think they've been abandoned? Aliya said. –Or . . .

Ignoring her, Swift turned to Poacher. –Is Ollie right? Nowhere to hide?

And Poacher nodded. –An' the seccas'll be here soon, looking fer their dog.

Swift motioned to the gang. –Sit. An' you, listen by the door, she said to Aliya. –You'll be going home soon. Adventure over. You can write it up in your diary, show it to your friends.

–She's not . . . Jake began, but Aliya shook her head, and he swallowed his words.

Poacher ran his fingers into his dreads, looked down at his feet. He looked around at them. –Seccas'll be here any minute. Might be last time we're together, so just listen. Cos being as I'm yer leader, I'm speaking now. We got a long way together, proper Outwalker gang. We got close to the border . . .

Jake looked around. Everyone knew what Poacher was talking about. Even Cass. Maybe especially little Cass. Swift had both hands around her sister's shoulders and there were tears in her eyes. He couldn't believe it. Couldn't believe that that was it. That the whole journey, everything they'd gone through, would end suddenly, here in this cruddy warehouse stuffed with lost possessions. That Martha's dying had happened for nothing at all. Ollie's face was blank, no expression. Davie was doing his drumming, both hands. He had his eyes screwed shut. Jake touched Jet's head. It felt hot, like he had a fever.

–But they got us in their sights and we got nowhere left to hide, Poacher was saying, –an' no way out this warehouse 'cept these doors. So we're gonna give it a go, as a gang, but . . .

–But what about her? Jake said, nodding towards Aliya. –She's told me things about the virus, and the Coalition. Important things, and she's not one of them.

–Not one of us either, Swift said. She licked her finger and ran it through the dust. Then she crouched before Cass and painted a circle on her forehead. –Outwalkers first, all of us. They can't change that, whatever. Chip us again, separate us, lock us up, tariff us and send us to the fields, they can't change it. Outwalkers for ever.

She licked her finger again and painted the circle on her own pale forehead, then everyone else did the same. Jake remembered his ceremony: the gang in a line, their faces painted, his own face painted too. He put his finger to his neck and felt the small circle tattoo, just below his chip scar.

Inside the gang and outside everything else. That's what it meant. I won't ever forget it, he thought.

Then Aliya was running towards them, eyes wide, pointing back to the door. She spoke between gasps. –They've found us! They're outside. I could smell him. His perfume. Then I heard them. Him and her.

–Who? You heard who? Poacher said.

–Noel, Aliya said. –The blond Surfer. And your Scar woman. From the Tube.

Thirty-six

Behind them, the grating sound of the warehouse doors being opened, and voices. Angry voices.

They walked between the high shelves, trying to hide. Swift took the front, carrying Cass, Poacher the rear. Jake carried Jet, wrapped in Cass's blanket, till his arms burned with the strain, then Ollie took over.

–You don't like dogs, Jake whispered. –First thing you said to me.

–I like this one, Ollie whispered back.

Davie coughed. The low chest cough he'd had since the Tube tunnels. Jake could hear him try to swallow it, to keep it in.

Deep between the high shelves, Swift stopped them and they stood close, catching their breath, listening. The seccas were getting closer.

–Be ready to draw yer knives, Poacher said quietly. –On my signal. Then he put his hand on Jake's shoulder, nodded towards Jet. –He gets caught, he'll die. You know that, don't yer? And he'll die alone . . .

Jake looked at Poacher's face. It was gentle. What was he saying? Then he understood and something crawled down his spine.

–You think I should kill him, he said slowly.

–Be kinder. He'd die quick, Poacher said. He pulled his knife from its sheath. –You could use mine. Sharper'n yer penknife.

–It has to be you does it. This was Swift speaking. –So he dies held by the boy who loved him. And you gotta decide now. Cos we ain't got any time to spare.

Jake took Poacher's knife, hefted it until it sat properly in his hand. He looked at Ollie, holding his dog, but Ollie wouldn't meet his gaze; his blue eyes were fixed at something above Jake's head. He couldn't look at Jet and his legs felt like jelly; he tried to think, but blackness filled his mind.

Then at last he looked up.

–No, he said.

It was like the whole gang had been holding its breath. Swift gave a small nod, and Poacher took back his knife. Jake went over to Ollie and Ollie gave him his dog.

–I'm sorry, Jake whispered. –Couldn't do it.

In the near dark, the gang waited. Nobody moved; even Davie's drumming fingers were still. The silence was more terrifying than the noise. Where were they?

Jake was so scared, he felt numb. As if his body wasn't his, and the thoughts he was thinking were about someone else. *Maybe they'll kill us all*, he thought, *everyone except Aliya*. Jet first, then Cass, cos they were the weakest. Because no one would miss them, or care, or even know. He could imagine Scar woman and the blond Surfer giving their report. Some lowlifer intruders killed by mistake; didn't know they were kids until too late.

That way, at least he'd never be separated from Jet, and at least Jet wouldn't have to suffer any more.

–Shit! The blond Surfer's voice, and only a few feet away.

Jake whipped around. Where was he?

The gang stayed silent, listening. The blond Surfer was just the other side of the shelves, and he wasn't alone. Jake could hear them whispering. The gang crouched motionless.

Although she spoke quietly, Scar woman's voice carried clear as a bell. –They're here, I know it. Tasers ready, everyone.

They heard the clatter and bristle of seccas checking equipment, making ready.

–Draw knives, Poacher said quietly.

This was it.

A shudder ran down Jake's spine. He wiped his hands on his jacket. He was sweating with fear, braced, ready to attack.

From nowhere a figure was amongst them: a big, bearded man in boots and black clothes.

He raised his hand.

Quick as her name, Swift stabbed out hard with her knife.

But the knife struck air and with a single movement she was disarmed.

Poacher drew back his knife arm, but the man had him by the wrist in a pincer hold. Leaning forward, he whispered in the deepest voice Jake had ever heard, –Follow me. Keep it quiet.

Then he was moving, quick as an eel, away from them already, twisting himself through a gap in the shelves.

And Poacher didn't hesitate. Taking up Jet in his arms he whispered: –Follow him. Go!

Twisting and turning between shelves, clambering over boxes, squeezing through spaces, they followed the man in black, leaving behind the shouts of the seccas, leaving behind the blond Surfer and Scar woman.

Jake lost all idea of where he was. Cobwebs clutched at his hair, spiders skittered over his face. Dust was in his nostrils, so he breathed through his mouth, tasting the warehouse's old, sad air with each breath.

They reached what seemed to be a corner, where a sheaf of thick, dirty electrical cables dropped from ceiling to floor. The man stopped and turned. He was older than Jake had realized, deep lines scored around his eyes, his mouth, his hair caught back in a wild grey ponytail beneath a Newcastle United cap.

–My ears ain't so good. Listen out and tell me what you hear.

The gang listened, motionless.

–They're further off, Davie said. –Scar woman is giving an order. Can hear her voice.

–So then, the man said, –I'll be up first an' let down the creel for the dog and the wee lass. Ye'll not manage them safely without.

He pulled the mass of cables out from the wall and stepped behind them. Hidden behind the cables was a rusty metal ladder pinned to the wall. It reached straight up to and through a small hatch in the ceiling. And they all went up the ladder – Cass, then Jet, lifted in a big wicker basket that the man let down for them.

The roof space was big and empty. Light came in a little from the sides. Broad wooden boards were spread in a path over rafters to the far corner.

Little piles of white gleamed in the gloom. A clatter of wings and a dart of black, flitting and jagging around them and out again, fast as the wind. Cass covered her head with her hands, and the man whispered.

–Don't be scared. It's swifts. Fledgers in the nests. He reached into the basket, gathered Jet in his arms. –Bad hurt, eh? Safer if I take him across here. Then he gestured to the gang to follow him. –Careful, he said. –Boards is noisy. Don't want 'em hearing us.

They trod as lightly as they could, but still the boards creaked. Jake's thoughts tumbled in his mind. What if this man was one of them? He had Jet. What if he was taking them straight to the seccas?

–*Attenzione!* Watch it! Ollie's whisper broke into his fears. He'd stopped in his tracks and was listening. A voice below. Jake's skin prickled: the blond Surfer. He was speaking on a mobile as he walked and his voice came up clear as day to the gang.

–The children? Close to retrieval. Got an extra eighty hubbers on it. Northumberland on high alert.

Behind him, Jake heard Davie's cough again. The blond Surfer went quiet and they all stopped in their tracks. Had the Surfer heard him?

Jake swallowed. He caught Ollie's glance. His heart was so loud, thumping in his ears, maybe the blond Surfer could hear that too. Everyone's heart thumping. All eight of them up there, and the man and Jet, just above him.

Then the blond Surfer spoke again. Yes, they'd take care with the girl. They knew who she was. The others: dispensable, yes. Home Academy fodder, absolutely, fracking fields. He knew what he'd do with them, scummy lowlifer kids.

Jake breathed out and grinned. The blond Surfer had no idea. Now he was moving on, out of earshot, and after a minute they walked on across the boards.

The old man pointed to the corner and Jake saw that the bricks had been removed here to make a hole just big enough for a grown man.

–We drop down here. Mattresses groundside to break it. I'll catch you, far end.

–We jump? Poacher said, but the man shook his head.

–We slide. Best if I take the dog again, and with Jet in his arms, he hooked his legs over the hole and was gone.

Fast as he could, Jake followed him, pushing himself out over the dark drop till he slid-fell down and down, to land with a soft whump on the ground. Now he saw it was a builder's chute, made of bottomless dustbins, set at its ground end into a lidded skip.

Already the man had laid Jet on the ground at the far end and Jake sat by him as, one by one, the rest of the gang came slithering down. Swift carried Cass high in her arms and Cass was smiling when they landed.

–Fun, eh? the man whispered, and he lifted a flap on the farther end of the skip. –Not far now. Keep close. Keep low. And he picked Jet up in his arms again.

–Who are you? Where you taking us? Swift whispered, but the man only shook his head.

–Later, he said.

Outside, they turned this way and that, zigzagging between stacks of containers, round splintered, tumble-down sheds, till Jake lost all idea of where he was. Crawling beneath an old wagon, they froze, hearing men's voices just above. More seccas. They came so close Jake could smell their cigarette smoke. He heard one of them hawk and spit. But the old man was ducking to the side, bringing them away through the high weeds and the gap in the barbed wire fencing, and more weeds that grew sweet and sticky above them, trailing scratchy over Jake's hands, over his face, until at last the old man stopped beside a derelict car, half-hidden in the undergrowth.

–In here, the old man said, and he crawled in through the open car door and disappeared.

Jake was bewildered. He followed at the man's heels and suddenly there was no car inside, no seats, no nothing, just a hole in the ground, boarded out, with the earth packed hard below, and narrow steps into a tunnel. Half-falling down the steps, Jake protected Jet as best he could, bruising his shoulders, his arms, an elbow against the tunnel sides. Then he got to his feet and walked along; it was high enough to walk if you had your head bowed. The others followed behind. A minute later he felt the tunnel rise and ahead of him he saw the old man climbing out.

They were in a small brick room, high walls, small, dirty windows, broken concrete floor. One by one the gang emerged, everyone so smeared with dirt and sweat you couldn't see the Outwalker marks on their foreheads any more. Swift, carrying Cass, looked exhausted, her face white as chalk, and Davie was coughing, and when Aliya came out, Jake saw that she was shaking and she'd gone very pale.

The old man had gone to the far end of the room and he was fishing up towards the ceiling with a hooked pole. Catching a small ring, he tugged to bring down a ladder.

–Home, he said.

But Poacher shook his head. –You don't tell us who you are, an' what you want with us, we ain't followin' you up there. We got weapons.

The old man walked back towards them slowly, hands by his sides. Instinctively the gang all put their hands on their knives, ready. But when he was a few paces away, the old man stopped and bent his head forward, swinging the ponytail down over his shoulder. Pulled his shirt down to expose his neck. There, visible, was the narrow scar line where the hub chip had been cut out, and just below it a tattoo: a small circle with the black dot in the middle.

–Name's Ralph, he said.

Thirty-seven

The room above was long, with windows all the way down one side, and the evening sun was flooding in, washing across every surface so you could see the dust dance. They stood as if in a trance until Ralph brought the ladder up, replaced the boards in the floor. Then he posted Poacher at the window as lookout.

He turned back the covers on the bed and nodded at Swift. –Tuck the wee one in here. To the others he pointed to the floor. –Sit quiet.

Jet lay still beside Jake. Jake felt his nose, his ears. They were hot. He stroked Jet's head. –Hey, boy, he whispered, and Jet opened his eyes, but he didn't raise his head, or wag his tail.

Jake looked around. Facing the bed was a line of long wooden levers sticking up from the floor, some photos stuck above – people, children maybe – and beside the levers, a chair with clothes thrown over and shelves with books. In the farthest corner was a small packing-case table, on it a notebook and a massive pair of headphones, and a black box with dials and wires.

At the other end of the room, where Ralph was busy with something, stood a sink and a cooker and a small table. Pots hanging on the wall, a jug with wooden spoons, a towel hanging from a nail, a line of little jars, bunches of leaves hung up along a wooden pole. Ollie was over there already, and Ralph was taking vegetables out of a box, showing Ollie packets of things.

Along the walls, below the long window, there were shelves made of boards and bricks, filled end to end with crates, each of the crates with a number painted on. And in the middle of the room stood another table, the longest Jake had ever seen. And like the ladder, it was made from wood that looked to have come from a dozen different places, some boards painted, some raw. The table was covered with piles of clothes and baskets that seemed to be full of jewellery and shiny objects.

Jake saw the amazement on Poacher's face. What was this place?

–Old signal box, Ralph said, like he knew their thoughts. –Outside stairs got smashed long ago. No other way up here. Leastways, not one the seccas know about. So I can hide up here in plain view.

–And all this stuff? Poacher gestured towards the baskets and the piles of clothes.

–From the warehouse. Abandoned stuff. You saw the luggage. From when the New Wall went up.

Jake stared. What did he mean?

–It wasn't like they teach it in schools, Ralph said. –The English people didn't want it and a lot of people died. Innocent people. Their luggage was taken off them. Punishment for going. But the Coalition wouldn't destroy it because property is sacred, ain't it. He winked, then went on. –So they stuffed it in that warehouse. That was thirty years ago, more. Now it's what I live on.

–So you're a thief, Davie said.

–And you're not? Ralph said. –I'm an Outwalker. If I don't steal, I die. These things: their owners are dead or gone. But sometimes I can help people. He looked around at them all. –Better to live for the living, eh? Now he was opening small tubs and mixing things in bowls. He gave Davie a spoonful of honey. –Good for your cough. And before you sleep, you'll drink some thyme tea.

There was something about this room that Jake hadn't felt about anywhere for a long time. First he didn't know what that was, and then he did. This room was a home. Jake hadn't been anywhere that felt like this since the day his parents died, and it made him feel sad.

The kettle sang and Ralph turned off the gas. –You with the dog, come here, he said, and gave Jake a tub. –Smell that.

The orange paste smelled sweet and like it had curry in it.

–For your dog, Ralph said. –Nasty wound. I'm going to sedate him and clean it properly. Then you'll put this paste on it.

Ralph cleared a space around Jet, crouched down and lifted up his head. His hands were big, fingers red and rough, but he was gentle. He slipped something into Jet's mouth, held his jaw closed to make him swallow.

–What was it? Davie said.

–A plant. Help him to be quiet now.

–What plant? Davie said.

–You're a quizzy one. Valerian. All-Heal.

Quickly Ralph shaved the fur around the wound on Jet's shoulder. Then he dipped a piece of cotton wool into the boiled water. Carefully he cleaned the torn flesh. This time Jet barely opened his eyes. Last of all, Ralph cooled Jet's paws and ears with a damp cloth.

Ralph spoke to Jake then. –Wash your hands, and put

the paste on the wound. He needs to sleep now. No moving him, not at all, for forty-eight hours. Kill him if you do.

Jake washed his hands with the soap and spoke gentle words to Jet as he spread the paste over the wound, but Jet made no movement. Ralph covered Jet with a blanket, leaving the wound uncovered.

–Done all we can, he said. –Hope he's a fighter.

Jake watched his dog. Saw the faint shift of his fur with each breath, watched for his eyelids flickering, his paws twitching: watched for his dreaming. But Jet was in a different kind of sleep now, and he was still as still. Tiredness pulsed through Jake's body but he was afraid to close his eyes.

Poacher turned from the window. –Hubbers have gone. Scar woman, blond Surfer, they just driven off in their Jeep.

Jake looked about the room, seeing it but not seeing it. Ollie was near the stove, humming a tune. Davie sat at the small table with the black box and the wires, headphones down over his head. He was completely still, concentrating.

Ralph went over to the bed and looked at Cass. He spoke with Swift. Aliya sat near, her arms round her knees still. It was like all these things were happening in another room. In his room, there was only him and Jet.

Nothing else mattered now.

Jet had tried to save him. Had killed the other dog, because the other dog would have killed Jake. He'd saved Jake. And now Jake might not be able to save him.

He wanted to cry, but he knew if he started, he wouldn't be able to stop. And that wouldn't help Jet. His eyes were so heavy. He'd just close them for a minute . . .

*

The air was still and bright. From where he sat, he could see that the sea had gone far out, and high above, birds wheeled and cried. Along the tideline was bladderwrack, and driftwood, and pieces of plastic, colours faded, morphed by the sea, and jellyfish washed up, gritted with sand. Birds with slender red bills ran along the sea's edge, then rose in a pattern, their kaleidoscope wings breaking the light when Jet ran towards them.

Someone was singing a song. And across the blue water were hills, mountains, like shadows of themselves, and behind, in the green of the bay, a church, some ruins, a line of small houses, and in one of the houses a lit stove and food cooking, somehow Jake knew this, could smell the food, and two figures not quite made out clearly because they might be older or they might be younger.

But what was clear was that they were waiting, and one of them shouted for him, and when he came in with Jet, they would all sit down and eat food and Jet would turn around three times and curl up to sleep beside the stove.

–Hey! A voice pressed into his dream, broke into the sea air. Jake opened his eyes.

The wide beach was gone, and Jet wasn't running at all, but still lying on the floor, his coat dirty, fur matted with blood.

–Hey, the voice said again. –It's us! They mean us!

Ollie stopped his humming and Poacher was on his feet.

It was Davie, shouting and coughing, and he was standing now, headphones still clamped to his head. Reaching round the black box, Ralph yanked out the headphone lead and a radio voice filled the room.

. . . *Hub forces tracked them to a freightyard in the*

north-east. Although the gang appear to have fled the yard, a hub spokesman said the hub forces were closing in. The gang, thought to be made up of at least a dozen renegade young people from Home Academies around the country, used illicit drugs to lure the lowlifers to their deaths deep below the London Tube system. Seventy-eight are dead already, but emergency services warn that the final death toll is likely to be higher . . .

–No! Aliya had her hand over her mouth. She was white as a sheet.

Another twenty-three remain in a critical condition. It is not known yet whether this is the same gang that were responsible for the murder last week of the London security guard. As yet, the gang's motive is unclear, but senior Coalition spokesman Noel Knight suggested the massacre might be part of a lowlifer turf war. Mr Knight stressed that the gang was very dangerous and should on no account be approached. He urged anyone who believed they had seen the gang to text LOWLIFERS to the following number . . .

–Switch it off, Poacher said. Davie flicked a switch and the room went quiet. No one moved, no one spoke.

A picture flashed through Jake's mind of the Hadleys. He hadn't thought about them since the day he escaped. But he pictured them now sitting in their kitchen and listening to this news and knowing that he was one of the renegades. Mr Hadley turning to Mrs Hadley and saying: –I told you so; and her just looking sad. He remembered how sure he was, the day he escaped from the Home Academy, that they would take him in as their son, give Jet a place by the fire.

That was in another life now.

Ollie picked up his knife again and went on chopping

vegetables, but silently, urgently, like he was racing somebody. No humming.

–Hubbers got us pegged as their scapegoats. Swift's voice was bitter. –Got us blamed for their dirty work.

–So you can believe me now, Aliya said. Her voice was calm and clear. –You wouldn't listen to me in the Mail Rail shop. You smashed my mobile. But now it's been on the radio. Seventy-eight dead. Some of them will be my friends . . .

Jake heard the break in her voice.

The room was quiet, then Poacher spoke. –We had yer wrong, girl, and I reckon we gotta apologize.

Thirty-eight

The whole gang sat at Ralph's long table and ate Ollie's food – hot potatoes with butter and vegetables with cheese melted over – while Aliya told them why she had run away from her home. She sat with her hands out on the table in front of her, and spoke in the flat voice that Jake recognized, because he'd heard it in the Home Academy. It was the voice you spoke in when something hurt nearly too much to tell.

–I've already told you that my mother is Minister for Borders: in charge of keeping people inside England and keeping people out.

She stopped, took a drink of water, and they waited. Then she went on, her fingers picking at the wood grain in the table.

–I used to feel proud of her. I thought she was keeping England safe. But then I met Gaz, and I joined the Catchpitters. Began to hear about what my mother didn't say, as well as what she did say. They always call them incidents. 'Unfortunate incidents'. She waved her fingers in the air, to put in speech marks. –Did you hear it just now? On the radio? They say stuff like 'Three people drowned. Unfortunate incident'.

–What d'you mean, incidents? Swift said.

–Incidents aren't accidents, Aliya said. –It's what they say when they kill people. It's the word they use. 'Unfortunate incident off the south coast involving three adult migrants'.

'Unfortunate incident on the Anglo-Scottish border involving seven migrant children and a dog'. Mostly they manage to keep those stories out of the news. That's part of my mum's job too.

Then she told them about the memo. –Show them the notes, Jake, she said. And she explained it to the gang, as she'd explained it to Jake earlier.

–We were witnesses to what happened at the meet, she said. –That's why they have to catch us. To stop us saying what really happened.

They blindfolded Aliya, tied her hands and feet, pushed her to her knees. They told her not to speak and not to move. Ralph dropped the blinds at the windows and Poacher lit a fire, a tiny one, in a shallow metal bowl. Then they made her stand up on her own, just like they'd done to him. Only this time Jake was standing with the gang, and this time he understood.

It took Aliya three goes to get up. She grazed her forehead on the floorboards and cut her lip, but she didn't cry out.

–Untie her, Poacher said, and when the blindfold and the ropes were off, he stepped forward. –Aliya Khan, you have proved yerself in the MailRail and today, in the freightyard, and you've earned yer place as an Outwalker. From now on, we stand with you, and you stand with us.

Aliya stood very still, swaying a little, eyes down, mouth serious. Perhaps she didn't want to become part of the gang. Perhaps she was angry. What would happen then?

But then she lifted her head and turned to look at Jake, and for the first time he saw her smile.

–Now we got ter give you a mark, Poacher said. –Your

first, cos you ain't never been cut fer a chip. And when you got it, you belong with us. So bow yer head.

Around him, the others fell into sleep. Jake listened as their breathing settled. Davie had drunk Ralph's tea and he was coughing less. Aliya lay with her back to Jake and he could see the small circle on her neck.

–You did good, Aliya, he whispered, and he felt proud.

Jet lay in one corner. Jake brought a bowl of cold water, set it down on the floorboards. Wetting a cloth, he washed first Jet's paws and then his ears, to bring the fever down. He checked the wound. It seemed the same. –Hey, boy, he whispered. But Jet was motionless, lost in his fever, and Jake lay down beside him, covering himself with one of Ralph's old blankets.

–Gonna rest you up, he whispered to Jet, –and get you to a good place.

A remote place, high in the hills, Poacher had told them. They'd set off in the evening, the day after tomorrow, once Jet was out of danger and it was safe to go. An Outwalker house. He'd been there before. Two women, who would take them in and keep them safe till they could cross into Scotland.

Jake's thoughts raced. He couldn't sleep. Again he saw the guard dog lunge for Jet. Again he heard Scar woman's voice, its cold hatred like broken glass, sharp and shrill.

–Stop it, he told himself. –Sleep.

Seated on a chair and still as a stone, Ralph kept watch, looking out into the freightyard night. The moon was up, and in its light Jake could see Ralph's profile. His skin was silver and his hair shone in a river over his shoulders. He looked the same age as Jake imagined his grandparents to be.

Jake closed his eyes. He imagined his grandparents in their place. The house by water. Added in some sheep – black ones – in a field, and pictured a shed with tools on the wall, sawdust, and dark corners. His grandfather at work on something and there, with her back to him, another figure, wearing the old cardigan he loved, patched and darned. As his breath steadied into sleep, from the shadows his mother turned towards him.

Jake jolted awake. A roaring engine noise filled the room. He opened his eyes, heart banging. It was still dark. A swathe of light swung in through the windows across the room, and then away. The roaring died away, then rose again. It was coming for them, hunting them out. He sat up, panic beating through him.

A hand on his shoulder. Poacher.

–Hubbers. Keep yer head down.

They waited, hearts in their mouths, as the Land Rovers roared through. Waited for one to stop, for the hubbers to get out, Tasers ready, batons lifted. But the roaring went on, deeper into the yard, engines revving past, and then the noise was gone and it was quiet again.

Jake looked around, as if the noise and the light might have hurt someone. They were all there. Swift on the bed, beside Cass. Poacher back crouched in the midst of the rest of them, looking out of the window. Ollie's lips were moving silently, and Jake saw him make a cross sign over himself.

A movement on the far side caught his eye: Ralph, headphones on, listening to the old radio, muttering something. His hand turning a dial. What was he doing? Hubbers pouring into the yard, and he was listening to the radio?

–Ralph, Poacher called, but the older man didn't look up.

Just went on muttering. Maybe he was angry, Jake thought. Angry with them for bringing all this trouble.

–Twelve Land Rovers, Ollie said. –Maybe eight hubbers in each. Nearly a hundred hubbers. On the radio, they said we'd left the yard.

–Maybe they said it on purpose. To fool us, Aliya said. –Maybe they knew, all along, that we were in here.

Poacher stood up. –That many, we ain't got a hope. No point staying on here. They'll search every inch . . .

Out of the corner of his eye, Jake saw Ralph clamp his headphones tight to his ears, tip his chair forward, like he wanted to block out everything, everybody.

–Likely they'll catch us this time, but we ain't gonna make it easy. So get yer stuff on but don' rush it. We run when we're ready.

He clapped his hands together, then everyone was moving, pulling on boots, rucksacks. Jake got his stuff on fast, zipped up his jacket. Ollie was ready, and Aliya, and Swift was lifting Cass into a blanket sling she'd knotted and slung across her chest. Only Davie wasn't moving yet, but kneeling at the window still, and rocking slightly.

Jake bent down to Jet. No movement. Not even the tip of his tail. Jake shook his head. He wasn't going to think about it, cos if he thought, he'd stop. If he thought, he'd lie down by his dog and never get up again.

–Course you're coming with me, Jet boy, he said, and he grabbed at a blanket. –I'm gonna do you a sling, like Swift. Safe as houses.

–Gotta go, Poacher called, and Jake was knotting the blanket corners, his fingers clumsy with nerves, when Ralph shouted out:

–Yo! Stop there!

Jake paused, looked round. Ralph's craggy old Outwalker face was cracked wide in a grin, and he grabbed his cap and flung it away, so that his grey ponytail swung around his head.

–Too late, Ralph. They're at yer door, and we gotta be outta here. There was a warning in Poacher's voice the whole gang could hear. A warning that said: *Don't try to stop us. Don't try.* –Ollie, Davie, get the ladder down! he said.

But before they could move, Ralph was there in front of it. –Hold your horses, lads and lasses. Cos I've got you one hell of a ride out!

They didn't have long to get to the rendezvous, and the bikers wouldn't hang around if they were late. Too risky. A footpath in the woods just outside the freightyard. Ralph would take them past the fence, show them where to go.

–That what you were doing with the black box? Davie said.

Ralph nodded. –CB Radio, he said. –Old tech. Nobody uses it now, so hubbers don't check those frequencies.

–But you do, Davie said, and Ralph grinned.

–The bikers: they Outwalkers? Poacher said.

Ralph put his hand to his heart. –Old friends. Used to ride with them. I'd trust them with my life.

–Where can they take us to? Poacher said.

–Best bit, Ralph said. –They're gonna take you right to the border. Bloke called Tom. Only thing is, Jet . . . He turned to Jake, and Jake knew what he was going to say.

They ran past the buildings and through the high weeds, the sunrise dazzling them, nettles stinging the backs of their hands, catching their cheeks, bramble runners whipping at their ankles.

Jake saw Davie flinch, hand to his eye. Behind him, Aliya bit back a gasp. But Jake felt nothing. He moved in a fog, his hands empty, and his heart torn. Behind him, up in that high room, his dog lay wounded, maybe dying, and he was running away.

They'd gone past the last warehouse and stopped at the edge of the undergrowth. Ralph pointed.

–There's where we're headed. Bikers'll be here in ten minutes. The perimeter fence, gates to the left, and beyond it: trees. In there.

Jake saw his mum and his dad in their car at the bottom of the river. He saw JoJo and the other boys waking in the morning to his empty bed. He saw Jet lying on the floor of that high room. He hadn't said goodbye to any of them. He just left JoJo, and now he'd just left Jet and he felt cold to the bones. The rising sun blasted his eyes, and he felt cold as ice.

His mum's voice. *You and Jet, always.*

–How are we getting out? he said.

Ralph pointed to a patch of brambles. –Tunnel. Goes underneath the fence. Footpath just the other side.

Jake nodded. –They'll be here in ten minutes, you said. I got to do something. I'll see you there. And before anyone could stop him, he had turned and was running back with the sun behind him.

Jet hadn't moved. Jake found the bowl of water and the cloth and wetted his ears and his paws.

–Hey, boy, he said. –I got to say goodbye. But Ralph's promised me: he's going to look after you. He's the old tall fella. Knows loads about getting dogs well.

He stood up and went over to the radio table, found a scrap of paper, nub of pencil. He wrote on it: *Jet. Mr and*

Mrs Gillies. Applecross. Scotland. And he slipped it underneath the radio. He stroked Jet's head. –Get strong, boy, he said, and he wasn't certain, but he thought he felt Jet lift his head a little.

He couldn't help it then. He sobbed. He buried his face in Jet's fur, like he'd done since he was little, and he howled with the pain of it, sharp around his heart and pulling his chest into a knot.

He lifted his face, wiped the back of his sleeve over it. There was no time now. Easing his fingers gently under Jet's chin, he undid his collar and pulled it free. He wrapped it twice round his wrist and buckled it close. –Now I got something of you with me, he said. –Me and you, Jet. Always.

He checked and listened before he set off. No sounds, no movements. No hubbers here yet. Then out through the smashed car and he was running back to the gang. The sun dazzled, but he knew that ahead were the high weeds, and the patch of brambles. He was in time. Wrapped around his wrist, Jet's collar was still warm. He held it in to him, protective.

The woman came from nowhere.

Jake stopped, backed up a few steps, and she was walking towards him, smiling. The scar on her cheek seemed to glow.

–Well, well. Look who we've got here. Mr Jacob Riley, I believe, and she laughed. –Oh yes, we know who you are. And who your parents were.

Jake tried to think. On either side of him, containers were stacked three to the sky. No gaps between them. He could run back the way he'd come, but that would bring her nearer Jet.

–We know what you're like, Scar woman went on. –We got quite a character reference for you. Mr and Mrs Hadley. Do you remember them? Nice couple.

Or he could try and get past her. But he didn't rate his chances. Not when she had all those weapons strapped to her. Her fingers were on her Taser already and he knew she would use it.

–I wouldn't try anything, she said, like she knew what was in his mind. –It's not nice, being hit twice by a Taser. Can be fatal, though I'd hope not, because I really would like to know what's in your little head. What lies your mummy and daddy might have told you, for instance.

She tilted her head, peered at him. –But I remember you now. You're the same boy I saw on the escalator. I felt sorry for you. Big mistake, that was.

–You killed people, Jake blurted out. –You killed those people in the Tube station.

She smiled. –Such an awful loss of life. Still, we learned a great deal from them, and you got the blame. Won't be long now before the vaccine is safe enough for everyone.

Jake clenched his jaw. This woman and the hubber with her had killed Martha. But he had to keep thinking, because he was running out of time.

–So, she said, and she was stepping towards him, and pulling the Taser from its holster, –enough chat. I need to know where Aliya Khan is. And I need to know now.

Jake darted to one side, pulled at the levers on a container door. Locked tight. He tried the next. The same. Scar woman walked steadily towards him. No need to hurry. She had him trapped. Jake's heart was beating fit to bust.

He got to the stack of containers. They looked forty feet high at least.

–I wouldn't try it. We've got you surrounded, Master Riley. Her voice was oily smooth. –You've had your bit of freedom. Time to come in now.

Last chance. Last try. He reached again for the door lever, this time holding on to it, using it like he'd use a jut of rock on a rockface, to pull himself upwards. Then, if he kicked up with his leg, he could shove his boot into the narrow space between the locked lever and the door and twist his foot round to make a foot jam. Foot jam. The word swung into his head. His father's voice. *Good move, Jakey boy. Now make it tell.*

He pulled himself up, reached again, grabbed higher, foot-jammed, pulled up again. Scar woman was running at him, she was shaking the door lever, pointing the Taser. Ten feet up and climbing, Jake waited for the shot, the pain. Waited to fall.

–Stupid boy! she shouted, and the door lever rattled. –Stupid lowlife scum! A few questions, that's all. Then he heard her call in for support and he knew she wasn't going to fire.

He reached the top, and he was up and running at once. The whole yard was visible from here, hubbers down the far end like a swarm of black ants. He heard a Land Rover gunning its engine, saw ants pile into it, saw it drive this way. They were coming for him.

A gap between containers and a twenty foot drop. He leaped and cleared it. A second gap, and a third. Jake's breath was loud and ragged, but he knew he would have heard the bikers' engines if they'd arrived, and he hadn't heard them yet. The last container, and just ahead the perimeter fence. Pulling his jacket sleeves down to protect his hands, he slid down the door levers like a fireman down a pole and dived for the weeds. On his belly, elbowing through, he got to the patch of brambles.

Somewhere behind him, Scar woman was yelling curses, yelling for the hubbers to get down here. But Jake knew she'd lost him. He had a chance.

He looked around. The undergrowth was so dense that it was hard to see anything. Spiders' webs smeared across his face. Flies buzzed in his hair.

Where was the tunnel?

Then he heard them: the low rumble of motorbikes. The bikers. Another minute, two at the most, before Swift and Cass and the whole gang were helmeted up and gone.

Ahead of him, a patch of clearer earth. He scrambled over and saw what he'd been hunting for: a rusty sheet of corrugated iron lying flat to the earth.

He was into the tunnel seconds later, pulling the iron sheet back over, just room enough to turn himself and crawl forward. No torch, and there was earth in his eyes, his mouth. Blindly he crawled, feeling the tunnel drop down, then rise, and he was pushing up the cover at the far side, heaving himself out.

He looked around. Trees and more trees, and bird noises, rustlings. But no bikes, no human voices. No sign of his gang. Sweat ran down his back. There was no time left.

He ran, straight ahead up the hill, crashing through the trees, and then he was stumbling out on to a broad green path.

Except no sign of the gang, just a man who lifted his gun and pointed it straight at Jake's chest.

Thirty-nine

Jake dropped to his knees, and the gun followed him. It was pointing at his head now. The man was as wide as he was tall, and he was dressed in black leather with a balaclava over his head, so Jake could only see his eyes: cold, blue, unblinking eyes.

Jake's stomach turned over and he thought he would be sick.

Still pointing the gun, the man took a step towards him. Jake put his hands above his head.

A voice from the trees shouted: –Don't shoot, Monster! It's the boy. It's Jake!

And there was Ralph, running out, ponytail swishing from side to side. He pulled Jake to his feet and, to Jake's surprise, hugged him.

–Thought you were a goner, man. Thought the hubbers had got you.

–They nearly did, Jake said. His voice came out wobbly.

–I'll look after your dog. I promise, Ralph said, and he clapped the balaclava man on the back. –Jake, meet Monster. He's your ride out.

Monster's cold blue eyes crinkled to a smile, and he slipped the gun into his belt, picked two motorbike helmets out of the grass, and passed one to Jake. –Come on, he said in a soft voice. –You're late.

Jake could hear the Land Rovers screaming up the freightyard again. It was the second time he'd escaped from under Scar woman's nose – she'd be crazy with rage.

Monster gave him a biker's jacket, big enough he could wear it over his own. It smelled of cigarettes and sweat. And thick leather gloves, for hands twice Jake's size. Monster took some duct tape from his pocket and taped the gloves firm round Jake's wrists.

–How long will it take? Jake said.

–Should be two hours . . . Monster told him.

They were only two hours from the border! He could be in Scotland today!

–Unless we find trouble, Monster went on. –But we got moves for that, if trouble happens.

Monster didn't seem to hurry, but for a big man, he moved quickly. He led Jake to a small clearing, only a few feet away. Just one motorbike. An old-style one with lots of black and chrome, and high handlebars. Monster showed him where to sit and how to put his feet on the pegs, and the grab bar behind.

–Where are the others? Jake said, and Monster nodded towards the bottom of the hill. He climbed on to the bike, released the brake, put a finger to his lips, and they free-wheeled silently down the hill.

At the bottom, the others were waiting, already mounted, in their borrowed helmets and borrowed jackets. He was glad to see them, but itchy to go: the Land Rovers would be on them if they didn't move.

–Did you say goodbye? Swift said.

He nodded.

–Good. And he saw her whisper something and he glimpsed Cass, harnessed on somehow, in front of her.

–Ready? Monster said. Jake nodded. –Because we're not stopping unless we have to. Too dangerous.

He raised his arm, and the six bikers kicked their bikes into action and their engine roar filled the air. Down the footpath they rode, a posse of bikes, like they were cowboys from one of his mum and dad's old films.

Monster had the widest shoulders Jake had ever seen. He was like a rock, and Jake held onto him for all he was worth.

They rode out of the woods, alongside some fields and on to a wide, empty road. An ordinary road. A lived-on road. Houses, shops, fast food joints: Regal Sandwiches, Angel Blinds, a bike shop, Ming Kitchen, Anglo Pizza, a park, a school. It looked like the life Jake used to have. A sign read:

Gateshead 1 mile
Newcastle 2 miles

The bikes split up, leaving space between them. For a moment Jake felt scared – he didn't want to lose the gang again. But he guessed it was for safety. Six separate bikes would have a better chance of escaping. He squashed his fear down again.

The roar of the bike thrummed through his body and the wind filled his head. His fear for Jet, for the lowlifers, his rage at the Coalition, his longing that was Scotland, the gang, even his grief: they all fell away beneath the throaty purr of the engine, the rush of wind tugging his head in the crash helmet, the world going by. There was just the bike, and Monster, and him.

The road got bigger, and they were weaving round an

underpass, and then up and on to a bridge high above a river. On both sides more bridges. A train chugged by above on one, and far below Jake could see the river, wide and green. The air smelled of fish and ozone. Then up the hill they rode, to a tall statue of a grey stone man. A few people were on the streets. Jake saw a boy in school uniform, head lost in his phone. Could have been him a year before. A queue outside a food bank already. Jake couldn't see any of the other bikes now, but Monster seemed to know where he was going.

On through the waking city and out the other side they rode, and as they left the city behind, Jake felt the bike surge forward. Monster was stepping on it. There was some traffic, but the bike was a wave; it was a dolphin, riding the road. It slipped and turned, carving slick around the cars and lorries, hugging the curves.

He could smell the countryside. He could smell the undergrowth, and the green crops. The early sun lit up the fresh green. The air grew sweeter, then cooler. He could taste the salt in it, then there it was: the sea. No borders, nothing to stop it coming and going. All he could see was the blue line of it, but that was enough.

They were going faster than Jake had ever been in his life and he wanted to shout out, yell into the wind. He was heading for Scotland and the hubbers would never catch him now.

Monster powered down the narrow coast roads, past caravan sites and holiday homes. The beaches stretched as far as Jake could see: yellow sand and green-grey water, and birds. Last year he dug sandcastles with his mum, played Frisbee with his dad. Last year Jet chased seagulls along the sand.

But as they rode on, the beach changed. No birds, and

the sand turned grey, the sea brown. The road turned in from the coast here and the hedges became high barbed wire fences, signs posted all along: FRACK FOR THE FUTURE, NORTHUMBERLAND. Surveillance cameras on high poles pointed in to the fields. KEEP OUT. DANGER. TOXIC WASTE. The air smelled metallic and strange.

Beyond the barbed wire was a vast brown field, and dug into the field were concrete pools like huge swimming pools, brimming with grey water. Rising above, a red drill rig. Further on, a line of low bunker buildings with washing strung beyond, a line of picnic tables in front. Three people in blue and red coveralls and cropped hair sat at a table and they turned and stared out of grey faces as the bike went past.

Monster slowed the bike down and brought it to a stop beside a ruined castle. He turned round, lifted his visor. –You OK? Cos you're shaking.

Jake looked at his hands. Monster was right. –It's not because of the bike, he said.

–You seen a fracking field before?

Jake shook his head.

–I got a message from the others. We're making a stop. On account of a helicopter. Anyway, take a minute. I need a pee. Keep your helmet on.

Jake walked over to the info board. It showed a picture of how the castle might have been five hundred years ago. Underneath, it read:

'The castle's history is England's history. Hundreds of years in its construction, besieged by the Scots in 1327, fought over for centuries, now it is peaceful, protected by the New Wall.'

But Jake couldn't shake the fracking field from his mind,

or the three people sitting at the table. It was quiet here, but it wasn't peaceful. Still people getting hurt. Still the bad happening. He thought of Jet, wounded and suffering. Ralph might not be able to save him, however hard he tried. And if he couldn't, then Jet would die without Jake there. Jake turned away from the castle and its info board, and he stood beside the bike and tried to think of nothing at all till Monster returned.

On they went, and Monster kept to the small roads. More empty beaches, more ruined castles. No sign of any hubbers. Then Monster slowed the bike right down. Ahead Jake saw a give way sign and he could see moors beyond. Monster lifted his visor, called back: –I'm gonna gun the engine soon as we turn. So hold on.

The surge pulled straight through Jake's body, like a plane taking off. He gripped Monster's waist and held on, the two of them sitting high and the gears singing higher and higher.

Monster's mood had changed. Jake could feel it. Then he saw the black speck in the sky: the helicopter. It was flying very high, but if he could see it, then he guessed it could see them.

The bike slowed to turn. A green sign read:

Monster swerved the bike right and they thundered down the lane. Two minutes later they were streaking along a causeway with a sky so big it looked as if it would swallow them up. They rode past dunes and then they were on to the island, fields of sheep, a car park, houses, gift shops, cafes, people.

People who looked at the bike and looked away; people who had no idea that Jake was a fugitive in his own country, wanted by the hub police. He was glad of the crash helmet, to hide his face.

The streets were narrow now, and Monster rode more slowly. Somewhere above them, Jake could hear the chug-chug sound of the helicopter. Out the far side of the village and they rode, with the sea on their right, towards a castle on a crag. Boats leaned, beached in the mud, and holiday-makers stood against the sea for photos, in another world from Jake's. Monster rode on till he reached a line of large upturned wooden boats, their keels pitched in black towards the sky, a couple of men slouching beside them, staring out to sea.

As Monster slowed the bike to walking pace, a door opened in one of the boats and with his feet down for balance, Monster rode the bike inside and the door shut behind them.

The boat shed was crowded and hot, everybody crammed in around the bikes. It smelled of fish and petrol; the smell turned Jake's stomach. Storm lanterns threw long shadows over everything. The gang had pushed old tyres, orange buoys, a pile of fish nets, to the sides and in one corner Poacher and Swift sat in a huddle on a pair of plastic fish boxes. Coils of rope and yellow oilskins hung from nails, and Swift had spread an oilskin smock on the ground for Cass.

Jake counted. All the gang and four bikers. The two men slouching outside must be lookouts. Aliya gave him a thumbs up from the far side of the shed. Someone passed him a plastic box full of sandwiches.

Jake hadn't felt hungry on the bike, but now he was famished. He took a sandwich, bit in. Cheese and chutney. Just like his dad used to make, crusts cut off and everything.

–Hungry, dog boy? Davie said.

Jake took another bite. It was like tasting home. He finished the first sandwich and took another, then a third. He wished he could eat for ever.

He lifted his wrist and felt the smooth leather on his cheek. It smelled of Jet.

In the half-silence of the shed, the helicopter noise got louder.

–Have they seen us? Jake said.

Davie shrugged. –We'll know, soon enough.

It sounded as if it was right above them, a whirring, urgent roar. Jake could feel the violence in the air, and he fought a rising panic.

They waited.

The bikers had their hands on their belts; Poacher too, and Swift, ready to draw their knives and fight. Then the roaring lifted away, and another minute and it was quiet again. Only the tourists' voices outside. They waited five minutes, and another five, and still the air stayed silent. Then a nod from Monster and the bikers did up their jackets.

–We're off, Monster said. –We're going to be decoys. Helicopters are hunting for bikes, so we'll draw 'em away. We'll aim for the land border and throw 'em off.

–What'll we do? Swift asked.

–Nothing for now, another of the bikers said. –Food's

on the table, and tea. No light when it gets dark, and don't nobody go outside, OK?

–Don't answer for anybody, Monster said, –unless they knock five times. Like this. And he rapped a beat on the side of his bike. –Sit tight. Someone'll come for you.

One by one the bikers went, and Poacher locked the door behind them.

Cass stood up from the oilskin and came over. She was wobbly on her feet, as if the tiny piece of strength she used to have was draining away again. Tentatively she put her hand out towards Jake. Surprised, he waited. Cass didn't really touch anyone except Swift.

With a single fingertip, she touched the collar, and looked up at his face.

–She wants to hold it, Ollie said. –Cos it's Jet's. That right, Cass?

Cass kept her finger to the collar.

–OK. Jake unbuckled it and put the coil of it on the ground in front of her. –Here you go.

Carefully Cass picked the collar up. She held it as if it might break. Placing it on her oilskin, she unfurled it, keeping it flat with both hands down. Then she picked it up at one end and, just as Jake had, put it against her face and shut her eyes.

After a few minutes she was asleep, and Jake was staring at the collar. Something was catching the light. Not the buckle, but something on the inside leather.

Gently, without touching Cass, he took it back and held it up to the light. There, set inside a small hole inside the collar, was a tiny metal disc, an oval about the size of his little fingernail. Bending the collar away from it, Jake prised it off, a drop of hard glue still stuck to one side. He turned it over in his palm. The collar already had a name tag, so what was it?

He looked at the collar more closely. His dad had bought it only a few months before the accident. Jake remembered because they'd added their phone number to the name tag. –Should have done it years ago, his dad had said. But this disc looked like somebody had hollowed out a space for it, with something like a kitchen knife maybe, then glued in the disc. And that somebody must have been either his mum or his dad.

–Davie? Jake said. –Look at this. It was stuck into Jet's collar.

Davie turned the disc over in his hand as Jake had done, squinting at it.

–It's hinged, Davie said, and running his nail down the length of it, he pressed. The disc fell open and inside was the thinnest electronic gizmo Jake had ever seen. It was smooth except for two tiny indentations, and when Davie held it closer to a lamp, Jake saw that one was coloured red, and one green.

Jake shook his head. –What on earth . . .

–I think it's for you, dog boy, Davie said. –Reckon your mum and dad got something to tell you.

Forty

Jake didn't want to know. Didn't want to find out what his mum and dad had hidden so carefully. He wanted to shut his ears and be back on the motorbike, the wind and the noise driving everything out, thoughts and feelings. But everybody was waiting.

He pressed his fingernail into the disc's tiny green indentation.

Something tingled against his palm; and into the room, like she was there and alive, and he could touch her, his mother spoke, her voice clear as day. She spoke his name.

'Jake. If you're listening to this, that means we're both dead.'

Poacher grabbed his arms to stop him falling, and sat him down on an upturned crate. Jake's breath was unsteady, his heart thumping. He'd been right. It hadn't been an accident.

'Before we say why, your dad and I need to tell you that we love you very much. The thing we've always wanted, since you were born, has always been for you to be safe, and to be amongst those who'll love you well. We hope, since you've found this message, that you're with Jet, and that he's a comfort. We hope you're with your grandparents. Or with friends. We love you, Jake.'

His mother's voice was unsteady. Jake felt as if his heart would break. Outside the shed there was the sound of children laughing. Inside you could hear a pin drop. On the recording, Jake's mother took a deep breath. The gang listened on.

'We're going to speak quickly, Jakey, because perhaps your life is in danger, perhaps you haven't much time, and what we have to say is very important. Important for the whole country. You'll have a task to do once you've heard this message, just as important as our task as scientists. So make sure you're ready to listen, Jake, and when you're sure, go on.'

Jake pressed the red indentation and the recording stopped.

–Play it, Jake. We ain't got time, Poacher said.

–Dunno if I can, Jake said, because he couldn't bear it. He didn't want their task. He wanted *them*. He wanted his mum and his dad. He wanted Jet.

He looked up. His gang were watching him. Maybe they were his family now. Maybe that was enough.

–Jake . . . Poacher said, and Davie whispered, –Dog boy.

–Go on, Jake, Swift said, and she made a circle on her palm, and placed the point inside.

Jake pressed the green indentation again.

'You know we're scientists. You know we work at the Co-Labs. Originally we were developing a treatment for cancer: a tiny machine called a nanorobot that could combat leukaemia. When the Coalition realized what our technology could do, they ordered us to stop our work on cancer. Instead they made us work on something else, and they made us sign the Official Secrets Act so we couldn't speak to anybody about what we were doing. But we're going to tell you now . . .'

Jake heard it, the catch in her voice. Like she was just taking a breath, but she wasn't. After a moment there was the sound of papers rustling, and she cleared her throat and went on.

'The Coalition made us work on a vaccine to combat the virus. Once it was successfully trialled, the Coalition said they would make sure every English citizen got the vaccine for free. It would contain a nano-microchip, and it would protect us all. A government looking after its people. That's what everyone would think.'

His mum cleared her voice again, and when she went on, her voice sounded higher, like it was hard to speak.

'But when we began our work, we realized that there isn't any virus. It's all made up. A made-up story by the Coalition. There's no danger in the countryside from any infected animal, and we're in no danger from any living thing in this country, except ourselves. The Coalition has made up a pretend virus, so they can invent a pretend vaccine. Vacplus, they're calling it.'

His mum stopped and just whispered, Jake heard her say, 'I can't, Jonny.' There was a slight scuffle in the sound, and the sound of papers, and then his dad's voice.

'So if there's no virus, Jakey, you may be asking, well then, what's Vacplus for? And why does the Coalition still want to inject a nano-microchip into us all? What's it for? What's it to protect us all against? And you might be asking why your parents agreed to carry on developing it.

'Well, it's not for curing anything. But at first we believed them when they told us that its primary use would be to deliver medication, to eliminate illness, by changing the expression of the genetic structure, and all that good stuff. And it could be used to do that. That's the kind of research we had been doing into cancer. But we know now that's not what the Coalition really want to do with it. They don't want to use it to save people's lives; they want to use it to control people's lives. Control how we behave, and even to shut people down.

'Here's why they want to inject everybody. Every single one of us. Vacplus will do everything the old hub chip does, but a thousand times better. But unlike the hub chip, you won't be able to get rid of it. It's a non-removable tracking system, telling the Coalition where you are, what you're doing, how you're feeling. But it's more than that. With Vacplus, the Coalition will be able to decide who becomes ill, and who doesn't. Who can have children and who can't. They'll be able to control where you live and how you live.

'In a year from now it will be ready to trial. And once it's deemed safe, then everyone in England will be injected. And once it's inside you, you'll never get it out. It'll go with you to the grave. They told us we were developing something that would be life-giving. But our fear is that they'll use it to deliver death.'

Jake felt numb. It was too much to take in. But his dad's voice went on.

'There isn't time to tell you how we came to know this. Or how we came to realize it wasn't going to be used for good. We haven't been too good at keeping that quiet. Maybe we should have played along better. But after we'd begun working on this, Jakey, our lives got a whole lot more dangerous . . .'

Jake shook his head. No. He didn't want this. They were dead already and now he could hear them and they sounded as alive as the people outside this shed. But they weren't. They were dead, and they were telling him it was no accident. He put his hands around his head. He couldn't bear to hear his dad's voice, and he couldn't bear for it to stop.

His dad's voice went on explaining.

'The line between curing and controlling is a fine one. By the time we realized what we were doing for the Coalition, we'd stepped over it. We tried to step back, but by now we'll have paid for that with our lives. An "accident" of some kind, probably.'

There was a pause, and his dad cleared his throat. Jake wondered where they'd recorded this. At work, in the Co-Labs? At home? Had he been sleeping upstairs when they made this? In the pause, he heard his mum's voice. Not the words, just the sounds, very quiet. His heart hurt in his chest, and he crossed his arms around himself. Then his dad began again, speaking the terrible words in his calmest, saddest voice, but speaking now in broken phrases, like it was hard to get the words out.

'If you're listening to this, then it may be too late . . . to stop it. If you've been injected, then it *is* too late. But . . . if they haven't started yet . . . then the only way to stop them will be to destroy the Co-Labs. So, Jakey . . . Jakey, we're asking you to do what we've failed to. Get this disc out of England. English people must be told. They must know what the Coalition is doing, and then maybe—'

–No! Jake's voice was a scream. He couldn't bear it any longer. –Stop! He stabbed at the red indentation to turn it off, but his hands were shaking and he couldn't make it work.

–Give me, Davie said, and he took the disc. He stilled the voices and put the disc back in Jake's hand.

Jake was shaking and he couldn't stop. His parents were dead, but they were speaking to him, and he wanted to listen to their voices for ever. But what they were telling him was worse than anything he'd imagined.

Poacher had a hand on his shoulder, and Ollie was rubbing his back between his shoulder blades. But it was Aliya who knelt down in front of him and took his hand. Then he shook more and more, so his teeth chattered.

–An unfortunate incident? he said to her.

She nodded, and he could see her eyes were full of tears. –I'm so sorry, Jake, she said, and she cried for him, the tears he couldn't cry himself.

Everything was muffled and there was a ringing noise in his ears. He let them help him down on to the floor, and he let them put oilskins over him, because he was still shaking. He let them feed him some hot, sweet tea. He didn't know what to do with his arms, with his eyes. He didn't know what to say. He wanted Jet. He needed Jet. But Jet was fighting his own battle.

Aliya sat down in the other corner. He saw her wipe her eyes.

–What're you crying about? He could hear that his voice was harsh, but it was like someone else was speaking his words.

–I'm sorry, she said.

–Wasn't you that killed them. It was your mother.

He saw her flinch. He knew his words were knives and he didn't care. His parents were dead in their graves and hers were still alive.

Her mother had killed his mother.

–Would the Minister for Borders say sorry, if she was here?

Aliya had her hands over her ears, her knees up to her chest. She was silent.

–Stop it, Jake. Poacher's voice.

–Would she say it? Jake said. He knew he was shouting, but he couldn't help himself. –Would she?

–I said stop. Poacher's hand was pressed over Jake's mouth, damming his words. –I ain't one fer speeches, but you need one, so listen up. You're in shock an' yer gonna say things cos o' that. But Aliya, she's an Outwalker now. The gang needs her and she's been brave, just like you have. You didn't make your parents into scientists and she didn't make her mum into what she is. But you both got to live with what they've done, an' it's hard fer her too.

Poacher took his hand away and Jake curled down on to the floor. His body felt like iron. Cold and hard and heavy. Around him, the others sorted out floor space and coverings.

–I reckon we'll be here till dark, Swift said, –so everyone lie down, get some rest. And listen to me. You're going to be really tired. But we have to cross that border tonight, and this time it's not just for us, but for everybody's sake. All the bona fides out there, and everyone you've ever known, all the children in the Home Academies, your friends, all the people on the streets and in the towns and the villages and the country, and in the cities. All of them. We've got to get across that border for them now, as well for ourselves, and give that disc and that memo to someone in Scotland that can help our people down here.

All those people outside this shed on their holidays, Jake thought: they'd be shocked if they could see inside. A gang of kids, grubby, dog-tired, and in clothes that were so dirty; they'd likely walk away, given half a chance. And all those holidaymakers would be even more shocked if they knew these kids were planning to cross the border and leave England tonight.

But the most shocking thing of the lot, Jake reckoned they wouldn't believe. The most shocking thing was that the Coalition, their caring government, didn't care about them at all. Not only that, but it might even want to kill them off, if they didn't fit the Coalition's picture.

His dad's words, from that breakfast time: *You are nothing to the Coalition, Jake.*

He clenched his fist. Now he could feel the disc in his palm. He'd forgotten it was there. Around him, the gang was quiet, sleep coming over them like a flood. Only Poacher sat up awake, on watch.

Cass slept with the collar beside her. Gently Jake lifted it away. He turned it wrong way out and set the disc back into the hole in the leather: no glue this time, but it seemed tight enough. He wound the collar round his wrist again and fastened the buckle, feeling the leather grow warm against his skin.

He looked across at Aliya's sleeping face. She looked like a child, and only a child, in this sleep. He felt the truth of Poacher's words, and a blush of shame rushed to his face. She'd been as brave as him. And she'd lost her mother too. A different loss. A different pain, but a terrible one.

–I'm sorry, Aliya, he whispered.

Forty-one

Jake was awake when the rap on the door came – five times, like Monster said.

Poacher opened the door to a very tall man. From where Jake lay, he seemed to be all elbows and knees, and he was dressed in strange clothes. Checked trousers that only came to his knees, then long, hairy socks, and a yellow tie and a checked waistcoat, and a cap on his head.

–They're hunting for you, the tall man said. –Roadblocks everywhere. So come quickly, and quietly.

Jake had woken Aliya, crouched down beside her, taken her hand. He'd said: –You lost your mum too. I'm sorry. Then before she could say anything, he'd gone to wake Ollie.

Now it was nearly dark, a fine drizzle falling. The tall man led the way, and the gang stumbled behind him. More than once Jake tripped, slipping on rocks and sinking into boggy ground.

–Half a mile, the tall man had said, –then we'll reach my Jeep. The man spoke out of the back of his throat, like someone in one of Jake's mum's old black and white films. It was quite hard to understand him.

–Upper-class, Aliya whispered to him.

They were going to Berwick. That's what the tall man told them. Berwick was two miles from the border, but they would get on a boat there and cross by sea, not by land. And when they got into Scotland, they were to phone a number, which he made them all memorize and swear not to tell anyone. The person who replied would help them.

–Aren't there smugglers in Berwick? Aliya said.

–An awful lot of them, yes, the man said as they climbed into the Jeep. –Along Pier Road. They're jolly dangerous. Knifings and such. But I'm taking you to a lady friend. She's a good egg.

Jammed up against the Jeep window, Jake watched the dark and wondered what a good egg was. He guessed it meant someone you liked. The tall man drove without headlights over the sand and the Jeep bucked and bounced.

They were very near the border, only a few miles left to go, but Jake felt so weary, he didn't care. He'd slept for a while in the shed, but something had woken him, a sleep-shout, or a bird maybe, and he hadn't been able to sleep again. He seemed to have been journeying for ever, since that day he escaped from the Home Academy, and for so long the border had been so far away that it'd seemed like a mirage. Now it was so close, he didn't know if he believed escape was possible any more. Maybe his grandparents were dead. Maybe Scotland would be as terrible as England. And what about the task he had now, the task his parents had given him? Jake shook his head. It didn't seem believable. It wasn't like real life, it was like something you saw in old films. And what if Scottish people didn't believe them, about the nano-microchip and all the dead lowlifers?

He rubbed a finger over Jet's collar. What about Jet? He shook the thought away. All the questions, all the grief, all the unknowing overwhelmed him, and silently, into the Jeep's cold hard window, he wept for helplessness.

The Jeep swerved to the left and came to a stop. They'd been driving, Jake guessed, for nearly half an hour.

–We're on roads from here, the tall man said. –Much more dangerous. There are a couple of tarps under your feet. Spread them out. Get underneath, as low as you can, and make sure you're fully covered.

The Jeep drove on. It was hot and smelly and uncomfortable. The tarps smelled of fish worse than the boat shed. In the dark, Jake couldn't see anybody else's face, and nobody spoke. But he could sense their fear and he knew his own.

A knee pressed into his back and someone was lying on his leg. Davie was tapping, tapping, all his nerves in his fingers. Jake knew it helped him stay calm, but it made Jake more nervous. He didn't dare say anything, though, and he didn't dare move.

Suddenly the Jeep slammed on its brakes and everyone was thrown forward. The tall man said quietly to them: –Roadblock. Keep covered, and don't make a sound.

Outside, voices shouted something. The sound of a window buzzing down.

–Good evening, gentlemen. The tall man sounded even posher now, like the King, even. –Doing a good job here.

–Purpose of your journey, sir? The reply was curt.

–A little business to transact, Jake heard the tall man say. –Personal business.

–Destination?

–Just to Berwick.

–We'll need to see inside your vehicle, sir, the voice said, and Jake saw flickers of torch beam, prying at the edges of the tarpaulin.

–What are you looking for? The tall man's voice sounded curious, but not worried.

–Please open up your vehicle, the voice said.

Jake tried to breathe, but there was a tightness in his

chest. –Let us not be caught, he pleaded. –Let us not be caught.

–I would rather not disclose whom I have in here, the tall man said.

Jake heard Ollie stifle a gasp. Was the man going to betray them all?

–Matter of national security, sir. I'm sure you understand, the hubber said. –ID please. And open up your vehicle.

The tall man lowered his voice, and Jake imagined the hubber crouching down at the window to hear.

–Do you know who I am? I guarantee that if you insist on this, my friend, then you will live out the rest of your working life scrubbing the latrines. My journey too is a matter of national security. The person I am transporting must remain unseen, for your sake as well as hers. Were you to see her, I regret to say it would be the end of your career. The Coalition would regard you as a liability henceforth, and could not risk leaving you in post. A bit of a speech, but do you understand me?

Jake could still see the torch beam playing along the edges of the tarpaulin. –Sorry, sir. Though he didn't sound it. –Got my orders. ID please. And open up.

–As you wish. Jake heard the tall man rummage for something.

What should they do, when the hubber found them? Run? Or give up finally? Jake held his breath.

–I'll need yours too, of course, the tall man said, –so I can explain my failure. My superiors in Whitehall will want your name. I report directly to the Minister for Borders, Mrs Ina Khan. I'm sure you understand.

Jake heard Aliya's gasp. Her mother. Of course, it would be her mother.

The hubber was silent. Jake could feel the gang around him, all of them tense, waiting. Then the hubber's voice again but loud now, commanding.

–Hurry up, please. Drive on. And he slammed his hand twice on the roof of the Jeep. It sounded like a gun going off.

He was letting them past!

The tall man started the engine again and they were through the roadblock and driving on.

–Nice one, Davie said. –That told him.

–Glad to be of service, the tall man said.

Street lights filtered under the tarpaulin and Jake guessed they were driving into the town. The Jeep was going slowly, turning now left, now right, and turning again, until at last they came to a stop.

–Don't move yet, the tall man said. –People coming.

The engine ticked and the gang waited. Jake heard the swish of cars going past, then the sound of people laughing. Grown-up laughter, and he remembered his parents sitting in the kitchen with some beer and laughing with friends. He'd go in, pretending he wanted a drink of water. It seemed to him, lying under that tarpaulin, that it was a different boy who'd opened that door to laughter. The boy lying under this tarpaulin would never be that child again. He wasn't a grown-up, but he'd gone beyond his childhood since his parents died.

The laughter came closer, passed by, died away. But into the silence came another noise. Sirens. And the blare of a tannoy.

Hubbers.

The noise was getting louder. They were coming this way.

–Up! Get up! Fear was in the tall man's voice. The gang scrambled up from under the tarpaulin, stiff and aching.

–Listen, he said. They'll be here in a minute. Down that street, about fifty yards, number sixty-nine. Knock on the door. A woman will answer, a friend of mine. You can trust her. She's got a yacht. She'll take you over the border. She's very rich, so nobody suspects her.

Jake heard the click of the door lock.

–Quick, get out, the tall man said. –And jolly good luck, he called after them as they ran, full pelt, down the road.

A terrace of houses. Jake glimpsed the numbers. Thirty-five . . . forty-three . . . sixty-five . . . then there was a beautiful house set back from the road with a high front wall and big gates. A doorway was set into the wall, and on the door: sixty-nine. This was it.

–I'll go, Poacher said, and quickly he pushed the gate open and stepped through. The gang waited, backs pressed against the wall. Cass hid in her sister's shadow. Jake heard the tap of Davie's drumming fingers, saw Ollie make the cross sign again. He could smell the dampness of the old wall. He could smell roses. He heard Poacher's footsteps on the gravel drive, heard him clear his throat before he knocked on the door.

–Hurry up, he heard Swift mutter.

But before Poacher could knock there was the sound of the tannoy, blasting through the air, booming all around them. And this time there was no mistaking the voice. It was Scar woman and the words were very clear:

–ALIYA KHAN. ALIYA KHAN. WE ARE HERE TO HELP. THIS GANG IS DANGEROUS. GIVE YOURSELF UP. WE WILL TAKE YOU TO SAFETY.

–No! It's her! Jake felt Aliya's hand on his wrist, gripping him as if the hubbers were already pulling her away.

Then Poacher's feet on the gravel, running, urgent, and he was back with them on the street.

–We're outta time, Poacher said. And Jake could feel the hubbers now, the rumble in the ground from the heavy hub vans.

–In here! It was Ollie's voice from across the street. An alleyway with a sign over in gold lettering that Jake could just read in the thin moonlight: *The Church of Our Lady and St Oswald.*

They ran into the alleyway, pushing the big iron gate shut behind them, Ollie leading the way, Jake and Davie bringing up the rear. From the dark Jake and Davie watched a hub van roll to a stop, its headlights blasting the street in light. They saw hubbers tumble out, six Jake counted, helmets on, Tasers ready. And they saw them pile through the doorway of number sixty-nine.

Three minutes later and the hubbers were out, two of them with a woman between them. She was in stockinged feet and she seemed to have trouble walking. They had her by the elbows and were half dragging, half lifting her to the van. The moonlight caught on a string of pearls around her neck. This was the tall man's friend, Jake knew, the woman with the yacht who was to take them across the border.

–Lord, Davie breathed, fear in his voice. Because she had not left her house willingly, that much was clear to them.

As the hubbers pulled the woman to the back of the van, Jake glimpsed her face. There was blood on her cheek, and her mouth was open in an 'O' of shock. For a flash of a second, their eyes met – Jake could have sworn it – then the back of the van was opened and the hubbers threw her in and climbed in after her.

Jake watched in horror. She'd been arrested because of them. The hubbers had beaten her up. What would they do to her in the hub station?

Then Poacher was there, pulling Jake's arm, tugging Davie away. –Come on, he whispered.

Forty-two

The church door was locked, but beyond it was a little garden and at the end of the garden, a statue of Mary. Little spotlights lit up her long blue dress and her hands lifted up to heaven. The gang all stared at her, and she stared up at the black sky.

–Maybe she'll put in a word for us, Ollie said.

–D'you believe that? Jake said.

Ollie shrugged. –My dad's a Catholic, so he does.

–The woman in the house, she knew we were coming, Poacher said. –An' the hubbers, they'll get that out of her quick enough. They'd already started before they got her in the van. It'll be a fist here, truncheon there. Her pearls won't last long. An' then they'll be back fer us.

–We could make a run for it, now the hub van's gone, Ollie said.

–Too risky, Poacher said. –They'll be back any second.

–So what we going to do? Jake said.

–Do like Ollie says. Call up Mary, or Jesus, Davie said.

–Shut up, Davie, Swift said. –We gotta think.

But Davie went on. –Jesus had a way with storms, didn't he, Ollie? We could—

Then he stopped. Someone was coming towards them, walking firmly, unhurriedly. A woman, Jake thought, until the figure got closer, and he saw it was a man wearing a dress and a pair of Doc Martens.

–Be ready to run, Poacher murmured.

Then they saw the cross hanging round his neck.

–It's a priest, Davie said, and Jake heard wonder in his voice.

–Good evening to you. I'm glad you've found my little sanctuary.

–Sanctuary? Aliya said.

–I think so. And you . . . He swept his arm round to include all of them –I think you may be the answer to my prayers.

–We ain't any person's answer to nothing, Poacher said. –An' we gotta go. His voice sounded dangerous, angry. He took a step closer to the priest and Jake saw he had one hand on his belt, ready to pull out his knife. –Anybody asks, we ain't bin here, all right? Then he turned away, and gestured for the rest of them to follow.

–Hang on, Poacher. That was Swift's voice. Then she spoke to the priest. –You don't know who we are. So what d'you mean?

The priest stopped. He looked up to the sky, then down at his feet. Then he gave a little nod to himself and looked at them. –I believe you've been sent to me. To help.

–Sent by who? Swift said, suspicious. –Why should we trust you?

–Follow me, and I'll explain.

–Come on, Swift, Poacher said. –We gotta go; and the gang was turning to him when a beam of light lit up the night sky overhead, and there was the sound of the tannoy voice again.

–Quick, the priest said. –My house is over there; and he pointed to a door in the corner of the garden.

Poacher was still moving towards the street, but Swift shook her head.

–They'll catch us at once, she said. –I'm following him. Nothing to lose. And without waiting for Poacher to agree, she followed after the priest, hugging Cass so close they seemed to Jake like one person. Poacher only paused for a moment, then he nodded, and they all followed Swift.

The priest took them through the door into a house that smelled of cabbage, and closed the door behind them.

–Tell me nothing, then I have nothing to lie about. Don't speak, just nod or shake your head. Are you running from the hubbers? And are you needing a boat?

And when he saw their nods, he lifted a dark cape from a hook on the back of the door and picked up a red velvet bag from the side table that jinked as he slipped it into his pocket.

–The chance I've been praying for, in this benighted land, he murmured, and then, to them: –I have a way out through the back here. I was after taking a walk to the seafront. Do you want to come with me?

The priest's voice was soft and he spoke his strange words in a lilting accent Jake had never heard before. And although he walked briskly, under the electric light Jake saw that the priest was an old man whose head shone, and whose eyebrows were white.

The priest seemed to glide, not walk, and Jake had to jog to keep up. The gang followed him along stone passages and old alleyways too narrow for any hub van, down the hillside, through ramparts from another time when other kinds of walls were built.

They came to the seafront, the sea just beyond, its breakers white in the moonlight.

The priest handed the red velvet bag to Swift. –Wait in the car park, he said, and he pointed to it. –The hubbers will be a while getting there. I'm after a man to take you across and I know where I'll be finding him. But be careful. There's dangerous fellas about. Smugglers. Don't take a lift from them. They're as bad as the hubbers. They care about no one.

Gently he put his hand on Cass's head.

–I'll be back.

Then he was gone.

The gang stood in the corner furthest from the lamplight. Behind them in the town they could hear the hubbers' vans, and the tannoy calling Aliya out, again and again. Jake looked round at her. She had her eyes on the ground, her mouth pinched to a line.

Five minutes they stood on the grass at the edge of the car park, and then a white van drove in and a man in oilskins got out. He looked over at the gang, then walked across, purposeful.

–He must be the one, Ollie said. –The priest's man. He looks like he's come to find us.

The man stood a few feet away. –You're needing a boat, he said. He had a nice face. Friendly.

–You from the priest? Poacher said.

The man hesitated. –Yeah, he said. –Yeah, that's me. The priest told me you needed something, he elaborated.

–We need to get across the border, Swift said. –Now.

–So I'm your man, the man said.

–Where's the priest? Poacher said.

–He's on his way, the man said. –But no time to waste, those hubbers on their way too. He pointed. –Boat's just down on that beach. Don't suppose you've got anything to help with my costs? Mobiles, Nikes, pads? He said it hesitantly, like he was embarrassed to ask.

–I don't trust him, Davie whispered. –I don't think he is the priest's man. I think he's bluffing.

–No choice, Swift said. –Got to trust him; and already she was taking the red velvet bag from her pocket, passing it to him. –The priest gave us this.

The man thumbed through it quickly, and when he looked up his face had changed. He didn't look friendly any more. –This a joke? he said. –All you got? There are more hubbers in town than I've ever seen before. D'you know how dangerous it is for me, just being in this car park?

–Swift! Davie whispered. –He's not the priest's man. He's a smuggler.

Searchlights lurched across the sky above the town. Then the noise Jake had been dreading: the thrub of a helicopter.

But Swift waved Davie down. –We're out of time. The priest isn't back. We got no choice.

–How much d'you need? Poacher said.

The man counted round the gang. –Seven of you. He nodded towards Cass, in Swift's arms. –Do you the little hinny for half, cos I'm nice like that, long as she shares on the life jacket. But my best price: it's more than double what's in this bag. He shook it so it tinkled.

–We've got nothing else, Swift said. –Please, we have to cross the border tonight. My sister's very ill. She needs medical help. We can't get it in England. We'll make it worth your while later. But if they catch us . . .

–Come on. The smuggler's voice was soft. –Everybody's got something else they can offer. Something valuable.

Swift was standing oddly, like her legs didn't connect properly to her body. Jake shivered.

The smuggler went on, his voice like a caress now. –Everybody's got something. Something they really didn't want to lose, but . . .

Ollie put his hand on Swift's arm, and she didn't shake him off, but covered it with her own and dropped her head on to his shoulder. It was as if she'd finally given up.

–You can take me. It was Aliya, and before anyone could do anything, she stepped forward. –I'll be your price. You can hand me in, if you take the others to Scotland.

There was a moment of total quiet. Davie crumpled to the ground, a small, collapsed shape, but nobody else moved.

–There's a reward for my return, Aliya said. –A big reward. You can claim it.

The smuggler stared at her, like he didn't understand.

–My name is Aliya Khan, she said. –I'm Ina Khan's daughter.

Then everything happened at once. Poacher, Swift, Jake, and Ollie, and the smuggler too: all of them lunged towards her. All of them shouting.

–No! NO! Jake was yelling at the top of his lungs.

Swift grabbed Aliya, but the smuggler was there too. He pulled something from his pocket.

–You move, I'll shoot her, he said, and he held the gun steady at Aliya's head. –I've done it before. Don't think I won't.

Jake felt as if ice had been poured into his veins. He made to run at the man, thinking if he went low and fast he could shove his arm down before he could fire. There were lots of them, they could overpower him, pull Aliya back.

But Ollie grabbed at him, held him. –Don't! He'll kill her.

–Aliya! Poacher shouted. –What have you done?

Now the smuggler was dragging her across the car park, banging on the side of the van. –Open it up, Benno.

And another man got out, and like vampires leaning over their prey, the two of them bundled Aliya into the back, locked the door and climbed into the cab.

–Aliya! Jake yelled, and he shook off Ollie's hold, and was across the car park to the van, one hand against the rear window to brace, the other pulling and pulling at the rear door handle.

Through the window's small square her face, wild with tears, stared out at him. She put her hand to the glass, so that it met his, palm to palm, fingertip to fingertip. The engine roared and the van started moving, headlights off but gathering speed, and Jake was running to keep up, running to keep sight of her.

–We'll rescue you! he shouted. –I'll rescue you! You're an Outwalker! Always!

Then the van was gone, away into the English night.

Forty-three

Everything went quiet. That's how it seemed. Like the world around them held its breath. The hubbers' sirens, the tannoy, the vans: they all just stopped.

–No, Jake cried, and he sank down and pressed his hands on to the wet tarmac, pressed as hard as he could for the pain it gave, because at least the pain stopped the thoughts for a few moments.

He could hear the sea. It was so close, just across the grass and over the beach. A soft sound, a gentle sound. He shut his eyes and wished he never had to open them again.

–Jake? It was Poacher's voice, but gentle. Poacher crouching down next to him, pulling Jake's beanie from his head, and lifting his hands away from the ground.

–Yer spoke good words to her. Good words. But you ain't gonna be able to rescue her if yer give up now.

Then Poacher fetched Swift from where she sat, and Davie and Ollie, and when the priest returned, they were a gang again. Sad, hopeless nearly, but a gang.

The priest was running, and he was alone. Out of breath, he bent forward, gasping. In the moon glow his bald head shone.

–Thank God you're still here, he said. –I saw the van. I know them that own it well enough.

–They took Aliya, Ollie said.

–Aliya? She's one of you? the priest said.

Ollie nodded.

–She's the girl they're hunting for, the priest said, like that explained everything.

–They took her at gunpoint, and we couldn't . . . Ollie's voice cracked.

The priest looked down at the ground, thinking. –Now listen, he said. –We can't rescue your friend Aliya now. If we try to, they'll catch the lot of you. The hubbers are already on Pier Road. I just came past them. They'll be here in minutes. But I've got an idea.

–Your man with the boat, Swift said. –We need him right now.

–I'm afraid he can't help us, the priest said. –So—

–So get lost, Poacher said. –We gotta run, cos they ain't gonna catch us jest standing here.

–No indeed. I've a far better idea than that, the priest said.

The priest took them out to the boat in a rubber dinghy, across a sea that was smooth black glass and silver. Behind them, searchlights crossed the sky.

The priest pulled on the oars and the dinghy surged forward. Jake's life jacket was sticky to touch. It smelled like the boat shed. He trailed his fingers in the water. It felt so cold, it burned. He pictured Aliya in the van, Aliya with the blond Surfer, Aliya facing her mother. He wished the water hurt his fingers more.

–I used to be a fisherman when there was fish to be had. Same as those smugglers, the priest said. –No fish left, so now it's people.

Ollie sat on one side of Jake and Swift on the other, Cass buckled in to her life jacket. Cass seemed so small on Swift's lap, it was as if she was shrinking away, and in the moonlight Jake could see the bones in her face set tight against her skin. She seemed to be getting more fragile by the day now.

In the front sat Davie, peering across the black sea. –Do you know the way? he said, and the priest laughed.

–North is the way, he said. –Two miles from here and we'll be in Scotland. Across the border. And I know these waters like the back of my hand.

–So we'll be safe? Davie said.

–The priest shook his head. He spoke in snatches, between the pull on the oars. –Safe from rocks and currents, and the hubbers' patrol boats are still moored. But not safe from the people that are after you. I'd say they're not ordinary hubbers, and they'll have more than patrol boats to chase you with.

–Listen, Swift said. –It's very important we get to Scotland tonight, and that we deliver something to the Scottish government. Aliya knows that too. If they force her to tell them . . .

Swift didn't finish, but everyone knew what she meant. Aliya was strong-willed, but who knew what the Coalition might do to her, to make her speak.

The priest was silent a moment, just the forward and backward motion of his shoulders as he rowed. Then he seemed to nod to himself, like a decision come to.

–So I'm after taking you to someone I know, across the border in Scotland. Someone I can trust absolutely. But the journey won't be a walk in the park. It'll be a couple of hours in the boat, and the weather's set fair tonight. But the hubbers'll be out hunting.

–We ain't chipped, Poacher said. –Not any more.

–But I am, the priest said, –and they only need the one to find us.

–The smugglers will've shopped us by now, Poacher said. –I thought they were your men. The ones you'd gone fer.

–Ah, the priest said. –I understand.

–So we could always cut yer chip out. Drop it in the sea, Poacher said. –Done it often enough, do it by moonlight, I reckon. That'll sort 'em tracking yer.

–No. The priest was pulling even harder on the oars now, and he spoke the words between the strokes. –My flock . . . is here . . . You cut me . . . I can't return . . . But I know this sea . . . and you don't . . . You won't make it without me.

–Better pray then, Davie said. He looked back at the gang seated in the boat behind him and Jake saw that his face was dead serious.

The priest nodded. –Yes, all of you might pray, he said.

The only sound was the splash of the oars till they reached the boat, but Jake reckoned everyone was doing like him, and praying to any god they could believe in.

They climbed up the metal steps and into the fishing boat. The priest moved quickly, like a man who was as easy on the water as he was on the land. He sent Swift and Cass down the narrow steps to a cabin below and ordered Poacher to come with him into the small glassed-in room he called the bridge. He pointed to Jake and Ollie and Davie.

–You three: lookouts. Anything with a light, anything moving towards us, you shout, he said.

–It's the smugglers' boat, this, Poacher said, –isn't it?

Jake couldn't see the priest's face, but he could hear him smiling as he answered. –'Tis. You paid your passage. Or your friend did. I'm just helping you along a bit.

The engine started, a deep rumble in the heart of the

boat. The priest put the boat into gear and it surged forward. Gripping the side, Jake stared across the sea, tears streaking down his cheeks. The boat smelled like his life jacket, like a hundred thousand fish had died in it, and he was glad to have the wind in his face. The boat showed no lights and the priest steered on into the darkness. Only sometimes, briefly, Poacher's small penlight dimpled the black so that the priest could read the compass, swinging for its true north, and the map spread out beside him.

In broad reaches, the priest swung the boat one way and then the other, cutting a long, angled wake across the water. Behind them, the lights of Berwick grew smaller, the sounds of the town fainter. The water stayed dark and the sky stayed black. Jake eased his grip. He was finding his sea legs. And in spite of his sadness, he felt a spark of hope.

They were so close now. Perhaps. Perhaps.

–Jake? It was Ollie calling above the noise of the boat and the wind. –When I see my dad, first thing, I'm going to get him cook for us all. Spaghetti, I reckon. Spaghetti with clams, since we're on the sea. *Spaghetti alla vongole.*

Jake heard the spark in Ollie's voice too, and he remembered all those weeks back, when Ollie told him his dad was the best cook in the world. When they'd sat in the sun outside the abandoned hospital.

–I had spaghetti for my birthday once. Proper dried spaghetti, imported from Italy. But I've never eaten clams, Jake said. –Be my first time.

And he saw Jet, strong again, and he pictured Aliya sitting next to him, arguing about something, and the spark grew stronger.

The helicopter noise seemed to come from nowhere.

No time to warn anyone. It was deafening, the din beating at them, its beam swinging over the black water. Then the searchlight found the boat, lighting them up in a cold, white spot of light: everything, everyone picked out in its merciless glare.

–Looks like the smugglers got their price for us, Ollie shouted.

The priest swung the wheel and the boat lurched out of the light, but in seconds the helicopter found them again. Booming down, they heard the voice Jake dreaded. Scar woman's voice.

–We have weapons, and we will use them . . . Give yourselves up, or we sink this vessel . . .

–You have nowhere left to hide . . . I repeat, give yourselves up, or we sink this vessel . . .

–Come out and stand with your hands in the air . . . I repeat, stand with your hands in the air.

–We have weapons and we will use them.

The helicopter dropped lower. The wind from its blades rushed at them; the noise blasted.

Swift came to the top of the steps, and Jake saw Poacher shake his head, his shoulders slumped. Next to Jake, Ollie stared at the helicopter. He looked as angry as Jake felt, but what good could their anger do now?

–They'll shoot us anyway, Jake shouted to Ollie. –They've got Aliya, so nothing to stop them.

–Even more reason not to surrender, Ollie returned, but there was fear in his face.

–Hold on to your hats, the priest yelled out to them. We'll give them a run for their money. And he swung the boat sideways, its engine shrieking, zigzagging over and over to avoid that bright white eye of light. But each time they lost the helicopter, it found them again, and Scar woman's voice roared down at them:

–You cannot escape. Surrender. You have nothing to fear.

He should just jump. He could swim for it. The life jacket would keep him afloat, and the tide might pull him over the border. He leaned over the black sea.

–Don't! Ollie yelled, grabbing at Jake's shoulder. –They'll pick you out like a fly in the water.

But Jake shook himself away. He'd planted one foot on the rail when the air exploded with machine-gun gunfire and the sea blistered, cut into a thousand flurries below him. He dropped to the deck floor as the priest threw the boat the other way, then swung it again. But there was no hope, the priest must know that. They didn't stand a chance against a helicopter, and machine guns, and Scar woman.

–Surrender, or we'll come and take you.

Scar woman's voice, calm and collected. And as the helicopter lifted away, they knew it wasn't for long. The priest found his course again and the boat steadied. Jake and Ollie got to their feet and joined the others on the bridge. They weren't any safer in there, but at least they were standing together. They all watched the helicopter, a giant insect hovering above, waiting to destroy them. All except Davie.

–What you doing? Jake said, because under the glare of the helicopter's searchlight, he saw him rummaging amongst the maps on the shelf. –Bit late to change our route, he called.

–Got it! Davie shouted, and he grabbed something, like a long, thin torch, and pushed open the bridge door.

–*Porca vacca!* You crazy? Ollie shouted.

–Davie, stop! Poacher said.

But Davie ignored him and stepped out on to the deck.

Forty-four

They saw Davie at once from the helicopter and Scar woman's voice boomed down again.

–*Hands in the air. We have you in our sights.*

–*Hands in the air now!*

And Davie did lift one hand. Held it high and still, no trace of a twitch. A small scrap of a boy standing stock-still under the searchlight, except for one arm pointing high to the sky; pointing the long, thin torch towards the helicopter so that a thin green beam stretched into the sky. The helicopter noise grew louder, deafening. Again Davie pointed, and again and again.

–What's he doing? Ollie shouted.

Because it looked like the helicopter was going to drop straight on to the boat. Closer it came and Jake could feel the air vibrate beneath it. Then it swerved away.

–Yo! Davie's voice, triumphant.

He kept the green beam pointed, and the helicopter was veering this way and that, lighting up the sea, and the wave froth away to one side of them, then catching the boat in its lights, then swinging away again.

Something was very wrong with the helicopter now. It was veering crazily, juddering out of control, its swings getting wilder.

It was heading straight down towards the sea, lighting the dark water to a glistening white. And they heard

Scar woman's voice again, but yelling this time, terrified:

–Pull her up, for god's sake. Pull her up! We're going down. We're going—

The helicopter hit the sea. A huge crash of water rose in the air with deafening sound. Inside the bridge, they all ducked instinctively as an explosion blew the helicopter apart, an orange ball of fire rising from it and bits of plastic and glass showering all about them.

Davie screamed, and in the light from the explosion Jake glimpsed him, crouched down, scrabbling himself into a locker, the torch still in his hand.

The boat yawed and rolled from side to side with the pull of the massive machine sinking down below the water. The helicopter rotors slipped underneath. Then silence. Some lights glowed green below the surface, then dimmer and dimmer, until they were gone and there was only black sea and the soft sound of the boat engine.

The gang were silent.

The priest's voice: –Hold tight now.

And a great rolling wash came and lifted the fishing boat up and down. Then the waves subsided and the sea was calm again. The priest slowed the engine. Bits of wreckage tapped at the side of the boat.

–I feel sick, Swift said. –We've just killed them. Haven't we?

–They'd have killed us, Poacher said.

–I'm going to circle round, the priest said. –Shine your torches. Look for survivors.

Jake shone his torch at the sea, but he didn't want to find anybody.

–I hope they're drowned, Ollie said.

*

The sea had swallowed the helicopter crew. There was nothing and nobody to be found.

They found Davie still huddled in the locker. Crouching down to him, Poacher shone his torch. Davie was white-faced and his teeth were chattering. His eyes were like two black holes. He'd taken off his life jacket and it lay on the deck. He was rocking back and forth, back and forth, one hand swiping his head, again and again.

–Lo, though we walk through the valley of the shadow of death . . . lo, though we walk through the valley of the shadow of death . . . lo, though we walk . . .

–Hey, brother, Poacher said, and gently he put his big hand over Davie's. –Be still.

–I didn't mean to . . . I only wanted to stop them, Davie said. –To stop her voice, her horrible voice . . .

–Be still, brother. She was bad; she was bad and you stopped her.

–You saved us, Davie. There was awe in Ollie's voice. –You brought the helicopter down. You dazzled them with the laser and they crashed. It was amazing.

–But I didn't mean to. I just wanted to stop her voice. I just wanted her to be quiet. It was only a laser pointer.

The priest handed Poacher the wheel and came over and crouched down, put his hand on Davie's back. –They were trying to kill us, the priest said. –If they'd caught us, they would have killed us, no question.

–But now I've killed them. Now it's on me.

–No. The priest's voice was stern. –It's not on you. He picked up Davie's life jacket; gently he put it back on him, easing Davie's shivering arms through the armholes. –You acted in self-defence, he said. –You didn't intend to kill them. God sees your intention, and your intention was good. He turned to Ollie. –Take him down to the cabin. Get him warm and stay with him. We owe him our lives.

Swift touched Ollie's arm as he turned to go down. –Watch his hands, she said. –Don't let him hurt himself.

Poacher stared over the wheel of the boat. –How much further? he called.

And the priest pointed into the dark. –Over there. Those lights. That's where we're headed.

Jake stared, and then he saw them: pinpricks in the darkness.

–That's Scotland, the priest said.

The next minutes seemed like hours.

Straining their eyes into the night, watching the sea, listening for the engine beat of a boat or a helicopter, all the time expecting something sharp through the air, or the boom of a tannoy voice that was coming for them, coming to catch them.

But nothing stopped them. Not police, not hubbers, not the blond Surfer, not Scar woman risen from the wreckage of the helicopter.

First Jake saw a little bunch of lights. They drew closer and he saw a harbour wall. Then houses behind. A few street lights. A village.

–Doesn't look very different from England, Ollie said. –Hope this is right.

–I'll bring us up alongside, the priest called out. –One of you, jump out with that rope. Make it fast to a ring, doesn't matter how.

–That's you, Jake, Poacher said. –You're the climber. You're good with ropes.

The fishing boat slipped silently alongside the jetty. Jake

climbed up a ladder set into the harbour wall, found a ring set into the stone and tied the rope as the priest had told him. He stood and felt the ground beneath his feet.

Same sky, same stars, same wind, same moon. But Scottish ground.

Ollie came and stood beside him, and then Poacher, then Davie, then Swift and Cass.

Such a churn of feelings swept over Jake that he wanted to laugh and cry together. Martha should be there with them, and Aliya, and Jet should be by his side. No one spoke, and Jake was glad of the quiet. After the last hours in England, it was hard to believe there was nobody hunting them, nobody trying to kill them. He breathed deep, filling his lungs, feeling his feet on the solid Scottish ground.

Then the priest was pulling his cape around him, beckoning, and they were walking.

–It's not far. But if we meet anyone, the priest said, –then you're my church choir. We're on a trip.

–Have you heard Ollie sing! Swift said. When she grinned, she crinkled her eyes. Jake had never seen that before. It felt so good to laugh.

The priest took them up a lane and across the grass along a path, down past a terrace of houses. 'Sea's Reach' and 'Journey's End', Jake read on the plaques by the front doors.

They saw no one. Only lights on the insides of drawn curtains, and sometimes a voice, the noise of a screen: ordinary noise. People-in-their-homes kind of noise. A cat crossed their path: *black as Jet*, Jake thought. It stared at them, then slunk silently into the undergrowth.

Beyond the terrace stood a single, white-painted house standing alone on the cliff. The priest faced the door.

–It might be she's moved by now, he said. –Or she's . . . It's forty years. I haven't seen her in forty years, so. Not since the Wall. He lifted his hand to the door knocker, then lowered it again. –She'll understand, he said. –She'll know why . . . She will know.

–Just knock, Swift said, but her voice gentle.

The priest ran a hand over his face. Then he knocked.

There was no sound inside the cottage. The priest tried to smile at them, but Jake could tell he was worried. The silence went on. Only the gentle lap of the sea, glistening beneath the moon.

–I guess she's not home, Ollie said. –What do we do now?

And then a light came on in the porch and the door opened. A woman stood there.

Her hair was short and grey and she had a direct gaze and the bluest eyes. She wore jeans, and a sweater with a brooch pinned to it that caught the light: a hare, running.

She saw the gang standing behind him, but the person she stared at, really stared at, was the priest.

–It's you, she said finally.

–We need your help, the priest said.

Forty-five

Jake was warm, his body was light, his hands, his feet tingling. His head was heavy on the soft pillow. The pillow smelled of the wind. It smelled of home.

He was in the garden, Jet was chasing a ball. Jake picked it up, and threw.

The ball flew dream-high, but something was trapping him, holding his arms, smothering him. He twisted, fighting to free himself.

–Madonna! Cut it out. Ollie's voice. And something kicked him hard in the side.

He remembered. He was safe. He could sleep now. No hubbers, no Scar woman, no blond Surfer.

He lay quiet, exhausted. They'd done it.

The woman had taken them into her house. She made them take off their boots and their jackets, made them queue up to wash their hands and their faces, priest too. Then she brought in extra chairs and sat them at her kitchen table and made them beans on toast and hot tea. The kitchen had a shelf with little jars with labels, and photos on the fridge. It had flowers in a jug and a bowl full of apples and oranges. Jake's chair had a small, heart-shaped hole carved in its back.

The woman poured for herself and the priest two tumblers of whisky, and the priest said to her: –Auld lang syne, Cathleen.

She didn't reply, but she gave him a look, the kind of look Jake's mum used to give his dad sometimes. –So, she said, –how come a gang of filthy children and a man I haven't seen in forty years need my help at ten o'clock on a Wednesday evening?

The priest lifted his glass – Jake smelled the sweet smoky smell of the whisky – took a sip and then he said: –These children have come a very long way. And they need to speak to the Scottish government on a matter of international importance. So we'd be grateful for the use of your phone.

She laughed, the woman.

Cathleen. She said to the priest: –You always did have a sense of your own importance.

But then Swift told their story, right from the start, and the woman didn't laugh after that. She made some notes, but mostly she just listened. She was one of those people you couldn't tell from her face what she was thinking. But when Swift spoke about the lowlifers and about Martha, then Jake saw her put her hand to her mouth, and she got up out of her chair and started banging down saucepans and plates in the sink.

Jake unwound Jet's collar from his wrist and flipped the disc out from its safe place. He knew they'd have to listen to it, but he couldn't. He couldn't bear to hear his parents' voices again. Not yet.

He went outside. Sat on a bench on the grass beyond the house and looked at the sea and the sky in the moonlight. The black cat found him and butted its head against his legs. He felt shaky, and he felt sick. Above all, he felt tired as tired as tired, like he could sleep for ever and never wake up. He wanted never to wake up.

After a while, Ollie joined him, and they sat together

on the bench listening to the dark sea. The village was very quiet. A van roaring down a street nearby almost had them both out of their seats and running for cover when they stopped, remembering.

–We're in Scotland, Ollie said, breathing hard. –No hub police.

They sat down again and went on watching the cat.

–A doctor's coming tomorrow to see Cass, Ollie said. –And there's going to be a team coming to speak to the rest of us. From Edinburgh.

The cat moved into the shadows by the wall. It crouched, quivering, ready to pounce.

–A team?

–It's what Cathleen said. She didn't say what it meant.

But Jake knew what Ollie was saying.

They'd done it. Crossed the border, escaped from England. That was all they'd dreamed of, for all these weeks, what they'd risked their lives for. That's what Martha had died for, and Jet was probably dying for, and Aliya sacrificed herself for. And now grown-ups were taking control. Taking over.

So what would happen to their gang?

Nobody could answer these questions. He'd gone to bed with them still in his head. They all had.

Outside, the birds had started up. Jake watched a line of light dance across the ceiling. The priest and Cathleen were talking in the kitchen still, first her voice, then his, then hers again. A steady thread of sound, comfortable, familiar.

As the day came, slowly the room emerged. The others were still sleeping, Ollie and Davie and Poacher. A sofa, a black stove, in the corner a TV screen. There were shelves above Jake's head, lined with books. Photos too, old ones.

Cathleen as a young woman with friends; with her parents, maybe; holding hands with a young man, not much older than Poacher, Jake guessed.

Something about the young man was familiar, and he peered closer.

–Oh, he said, because it was the priest.

The priest cooked them porridge for breakfast. There was maple syrup and cream to pour into it. They all ate ravenously while Cathleen explained what would happen when the team of intelligence agents arrived.

–It's called interrogation, she said. They'll probably talk to us first. Then you. They'll ask you a lot of questions. They have to, so they're sure they understand things properly. So they can work out what to do.

–We can tell them what they gotta do, Davie said.

–It's not as simple as that, Cathleen said. –But you don't have to answer anything that you don't want to. I'll be in the room with you, or Angus–

–Angus? said Ollie.

–That's me, said the priest. Father Angus to you.

So then they all said their names. It was safe to, now. The priest shook hands with all of them, saying, –Pleased to meet you, Poacher; or –Pleased to meet you, Davie. Which was strange, after the night, but he looked like he really meant it.

–So, as I was saying, Cathleen said when the introductions were over, –in the interrogation, one of us will be there with you to make sure you're OK.

The doctor arrived for Cass. She came with her doctor's bag and a kind, serious, doctor face and she smiled at the rest of them before she followed Swift upstairs. When she came down again, her face was more serious, and she spoke for a while on a mobile. After that, she checked the gang all out, one by one, listened to their lungs and their hearts and put a strong cuff around their arms and pumped it up, asked them to show her any bruises or cuts and shook her head over what they showed her. Got some medicine out of her bag for Davie's cough.

–I'm asking no questions about how you got here, she said, –but . . . and Jake saw tears in her eyes. She blinked them away. –Plenty of rest, good food, some sunshine if we can manage it here in bonny Scotland, she continued. –That's all you need. Stay brave.

The team came soon after. A roar in the sky, louder and louder, and Cathleen calling to them all to stay inside. Poacher slumped on the sofa while Ollie, Jake, Swift and Davie watched through the front-room window. They came in a helicopter, four of them, in dark suits with dark glasses and short hair. The helicopter landed in the open space near Jake's bench, whipping the grass flat, and the team jumped down and ran below the blades and over to the house.

They came with identical rucksacks and they didn't smile. One ran round to the back of the house, and one stayed outside the front door. Jake realized, with a tremble in his stomach, that she wore body armour and had a gun. The other two came inside.

Davie peered round the door into the kitchen. –They're, like, padded out with gear, he whispered. –A woman and a man. One's got a holdall, one's got a briefcase. The bloke's huge. He hasn't got any neck. An' the woman's got studs up her ear.

–No-Neck and Studs. That's what we can call them,

Jake said. He felt better, giving them nicknames. Made them less scary.

–My mum used to have studs in her ear, Ollie said. –Four of them. She'd twizzle one when she was reading, or watching TV.

Father Angus came in. –They want Jake, he said.

–On my own? Jake said.

–It should be all of us, or none, Ollie said. –That's right, isn't it, Poacher?

–Should be, if we're Outwalkers. But we ain't outside now. We're inside. Different rules.

–They want Jake on his own, Father Angus repeated.

In the kitchen, Studs was tapping something on a pad. She had short blonde hair and she still wore her sunglasses, though the sun wasn't shining in the kitchen. No-Neck was pulling things out of the holdall. Davie was right; he was built like a boulder.

On the kitchen table were the notes Jake had made of Aliya's memo, and the disc from Jet's collar. At the other end of the kitchen, Cathleen had her back to the room, making tea.

When Studs looked up, Jake saw the surprise on her face.

–Blimey. You really are a kid, she said. –Better be something good. Your call got us up in the middle of the fricking night.

–Siddown, No-Neck said to Jake, and he swung a kitchen chair on to the middle of the floor. Jake sat on it, his back to Cathleen, facing Studs.

Studs looked down at her pad again. –Introductions, she said. –I'm Jill. He's Jack. Your name is Jacob Riley, she said.

Jake nodded.

–Please say so then. For the record.

–My name is Jacob Riley, Jake said.

–Right. Here's how it goes. We decide what's important, and we ask the questions. You answer them. Got it? Studs's voice was clipped, like she didn't want to waste any breath.

–Yeah, Jake said, but he wondered what he'd done wrong already.

–Our time is precious, Studs said, picking up the disc. She bit her nails, Jake noticed. –We've been ordered to drop vital tasks back in Edinburgh to fly down here today, thanks to your friend here, calling in her favour last night. So while I question you, my colleague is going to evaluate this disc. She looked down at her pad, then up again. –Ms Cathleen Dewey will stay in here with us, but she will not participate in the interrogation.

–Actually I will, if I need to. Cathleen's voice was steely behind him. –Whatever you think, we have a duty of care under Scottish law towards this boy, both of us. And I won't hesitate to suspend the interrogation if he asks me to. Or if I judge you to be breaching the law.

Jake saw Studs's eyebrows go up a bit. –Fine, she said. She leaned in towards No-Neck, whispering. Jake had butterflies in his stomach. He looked round at Cathleen.

–All right? she mouthed, and he nodded.

No-Neck took the disc and his holdall into Cathleen's utility room and shut the door. Studs scrolled on her pad, reading through something. It was quiet in the kitchen. Cathleen set cups of tea on the table in front of them; she'd put sugar in Jake's, and the sweetness startled him.

Studs questioned him for about half an hour – Jake could see the time tick by on the kitchen clock. Sometimes she let him finish his answer, others she cut him off with the next question. The Home Academy, how had he escaped? Any others with him? How had he found the gang? How had he evaded the hub police? How did they cut out the hub chip? Did he still have it? On and on, the questions went. What about his parents? What did he know about their jobs? When did they die? How did they die?

–In a car. But not an accident, he said. He shut his eyes and he saw them again, their faces against the car window. –An 'incident'.

–Have you killed anyone? Studs sounded bored, uninterested. –Where did you hide the disc? How did you meet the girl? How did you know who she was? When did she give you the memo details?

Jake felt dizzy. His fingers, his legs were tingling. He made fists to dig his nails into his palms, to bring his mind clear again. He answered her questions as best he could, but his head was in another place. He was on the floor in the Home Academy hall again, the Headteacher's voice dinning into his brain, and lots of other voices were dinning too. Mrs Hadley's, and the Food Bank woman, and Scar woman, and the ticker tape, and the newsreaders. *Not your home. Not your home. Disgusting, lowlife scum.*

Studs's voice drove on, mercilessly. How did you get to the border? Names, please. Places, please. But you escaped, didn't you? And you escaped again? How many hubbers chasing you? How many?

–Stop! Enough! Cathleen marched down the kitchen and stood between Jake and Studs. –He's a child, for god's sake. Look at him. What are you accusing him of? Or any of them?

Studs scrolled back on the pad. –You tell me, she said quietly. –This is what I've heard so far. Over the last month or so this gang of children has travelled the whole way up England without any phones, or other tech, or money. They've evaded hubbers, stolen Coalition top-secret info, and killed three hub police, plus a helicopter pilot and a security guard. Accurate so far?

–We didn't kill the secca. He fell off an escalator, Jake said. –And the hubber on the MailRail—

–All right. Studs interrupted him. –I'm not concerned with the rights and wrongs. Just whether these people died.

–Yeah, Jake said in a quiet voice. –They did. And Martha died too.

Studs ignored this. –Then yesterday. Our intel was telling us—

–Your what? Cathleen said.

–Our intel. Intelligence. According to our information, Berwick was locked down yesterday evening. Completely roadblocked and flooded with hub police. We've only seen that once before along the border. For a major political fugitive. So we knew something big was kicking off over there. Miraculously your little gang gets in to Berwick and you manage to find somebody, a priest no less, to skipper a fishing boat to get you over the border, out of the clutches of the hub police?

Her voice went up at the end of the last sentence, and it sounded like a question. So Jake answered her.

–He found us more than we found him. We were in the church garden. You should ask him.

–Oh, we will, Studs said. –Don't worry.

She swiped to a different page, took a sip of water.

–To sum up, she said, –English surveillance is second to none. Hub chips, CCTV, a vigorous and well-trained hub police force. England's borders are extremely – aggressively

– well-policed. The New Wall is virtually impassable from the south. And yet, here you are, six of you, and you're children. You've made it over the border on the first time of asking and you're all in one piece.

Jake said nothing. It did sound a bit unlikely, the way she said it, but he didn't understand why she didn't believe him.

–So, Studs said, –to be plain, we're wondering if this little gang, and in particular you, Jacob Riley, had some assistance from on high. And I don't mean from God.

–You're saying Jake is a spy, Cathleen said, –aren't you? You're saying they're all spies, the whole gang . . .

Studs pushed her pad away from her and sat back in her chair.

Cathleen leaned forward now. –And that's why you're being so aggressive with this child. That's why you're treating him like he's guilty. Like he's the bad one . . .

Studs put a hand up. –Not spies. More like stooges.

–A stooge? Jake said.

–They've risked everything, Cathleen said. –One of them killed, another captured, and you're treating them like they're evil. Like they're on a mission to destroy us.

–Stooges are people, kids in your case, set up as fall guys, Studs said. –You've been briefed for your mission and sent over by the Coalition to provoke us into action. Her voice was even and Jake noticed that she didn't correct anything else Cathleen said.

Jake stared at her. She thought the gang were her enemies. How could she believe that? They'd told her what had happened.

Her voice drilled into him, with its calm, reasonable, horrible words. –Because who would suspect a boy? she went on. –You fooled the priest. Disillusioned with his Coalition government, he was desperate to believe you. Jumped at the chance, didn't he? To help you? And after all, who would suspect a gang of kids? It's like children being used as suicide bombers . . .

Jake tried to keep his face calm, but inside he was boiling with anger and with despair. He'd lost so much, his heart just felt hollow. His mum and dad murdered, Martha dead. Jet wounded and still in England. Aliya captured and sent back to London, to her mother. And this woman was telling him he was part of a Coalition plot. That they all were.

Studs was still talking. –So we'd take action. Bomb their facility, probably. Only way to know we'd stopped it. And then the English Coalition would have all the excuses it needed to retaliate. And it would do that with full force. All those thousands working in the so-called fracking fields, and so-called picking fields, trained up, weaponed up. Ready to strike north and take Scotland back. They've wanted to do that for years. Decades . . .

There was a noise from the utility room, like a roaring shout, and the door was wrenched open, and No-Neck came pounding into the kitchen, breathless, and slapped something down on the kitchen table in front of her.

–You gotta listen to this disc, he said. –Now.

Forty-six

–Watch the news tonight, guys, said Studs before the team left.

So they all crammed into Cathleen's tiny living room, three of them squashed on the sofa, Jake and Ollie on the floor, Ollie's long legs folded up beneath him. Even Cass came down to watch, sitting on Swift's lap. Jake didn't know if she'd changed in the last day, or if it was just that he was looking at her properly for the first time, now they'd crossed the border and stopped running. But he saw how her eyes were far too big for her face and he saw the dark rings beneath her eyes, and he saw how pale she was. So pale, it was like you could see through to her bones.

He gave her Jet's collar to hold.

On the screen, a slick newswoman, checking her pad. Then she looked out to the camera.

Tonight, in breaking news, a successful drone strike on a secret scientific and military complex across the English border. We hope to have a statement from the Defence Minister.

–Yo! Davie was on his feet, and Ollie too, shouting at the screen. –Yo! That was us! Outwalkers are top!

–Keep it down, Poacher said. –Watch.

And there it was, filmed from above, a line of low, white buildings on fire. The camera zoomed in and they saw fire engines spraying water, and flames that leaped to the sky.

Over the top of the footage, the presenter's voice went on:

It is believed that new intelligence led to the targeting of this facility in the south-west of England. Satellite images suggest that the strike was successful in destroying the facility entirely, and with the fire spreading to all parts within minutes, loss of life cannot be ruled out. Fire crews were unable to reach the fire quickly due to the extreme security surrounding it.

An initial statement from the Scottish Foreign Office denies Scottish agency in the drone strike, though it states that the Scottish government had recently become aware of a "very real threat" posed by the facility. For this reason, the Foreign Office statement says it cannot, at this time, condemn the action, though Foreign Secretary Hamish Alexander says that of course any loss of life is regrettable, and he is aware that the action will carry serious international consequences.

We will bring any updates as they occur. And we will return to this story later in the programme when we will have the Defence Minister here to respond to events. Meanwhile, in other news . . .

Cathleen turned the volume down. Poacher turned to Swift and high-fived her, and Ollie and Davie were on their feet again, jumping up and down.

–We did that, Poacher said. –That drone strike, it was down ter us. Our gang. Jake? he said. –That was you!

–Yeah, Jake said. He tried to smile. It was good, wasn't it? That they'd destroyed the Co-Labs, and the nano-microchip vaccine that wasn't a vaccine, and the ways to switch people on and off, like his parents had said. So why did he feel so bad?

–You've started something much bigger than you know, Father Angus said. –Bigger than this drone strike. You've started something for the English people.

–They'll blame it all on Scotland, or lowlifers, or these kids. They'll say it's destroyed their ability to protect their people, not their ambition to control them, Cathleen said. –Your Coalition will slam the lid on this so hard the whole island will shake.

–They will. Father Angus nodded. –But I don't think the English people will believe them this time.

Jake pulled off his hoodie. His cheeks were burning. He knew why he felt bad, and he wished he could just sink into the ground. He wanted all of this to end. Or never to have begun.

–You all right? Cathleen said.

–I've been there, Jake said quietly. –In that building.

He could feel Cathleen's stare. –The one on fire? she said.

–Yeah. Those pictures on the screen . . . I could see my parents' lab. The windows: they had flames coming out of them. My dad got special permission for me on 'Take your kids to work' day. And their assistant, Jade, she made me hot chocolate in the laboratory kitchen. She gave me a Curly-Wurly to dip in it.

He saw Jade's face. He saw her big smile and her lipstick and her white coat.

–Jade worked there every day, he said.

Cathleen sat down on the floor next to him. –They don't know whether people died yet, she said. –She might be fine.

–Wages of sin, Davie said in a singsong voice. –Live by the sword, die by the sword.

–Zip it, Davie, Swift said.

–I bet she didn't know anything. I bet she had no idea,

Jake said. –She was kind. He got up, and went to the window. Looked out at the darkness. He just wanted to live in a family, live with his dog, find his grandparents. He didn't want people to die.

–We've got blood on our hands, Ollie said.

–No. It's the Coalition that's got blood on their hands, Swift said.

–Listen to me, all of you. Father Angus's voice was gentle, but it held their attention. –Listen to me, not because I'm a priest, but because I've been around on this planet longer than anyone else. This is a sermon, but just a short one. You know far more than me about all this anyway. But what I do know is this: this Coalition, they're threatening innocent people. Innocent English people, innocent Europeans. Millions of them. Their so-called vaccine: it's a terrible violation, not just of English people's human rights, but Scottish people's too, and beyond. They can't be allowed to succeed. This drone strike, it's a far, far smaller act of violence to prevent a vastly greater one, and it's terrible if any single person is killed, but—

–But it's better than allowing it to continue, Cathleen said. –You've done a good thing, all of you. And a brave thing.

–Even though people probably died? Jake said.

–Even though people probably died, she said.

Later, Ollie cooked up a storm for their supper. He made pizza, and little fried rice balls with cheese in the middle. He made a little speech before they ate.

–You come to Italy, he said to them all, –and then my father will cook pasta for you. In Italy, everyone can afford to eat pasta. And he will cook the best arancini for you. The best food in the world. Now eat. And then he shut his eyes and muttered something under his breath.

Jake ate all the food put on his plate. But he felt a hollowness that food couldn't fill. Everybody else looked serious too, and he guessed they were all feeling the same. Tomorrow they would be split up and they'd all go different ways. Swift and Cass to a hospital in Edinburgh for Cass to start her treatment – Cathleen had an Edinburgh friend for Swift to stay with. Ollie was going to Rome, to be reunited with his father.

Poacher was heading straight back to England. –Plenty more need rescuing. Plenty more to bring over the border, he said as they ate.

–What about the hub police? Father Angus said. –They'll have your description on their screens. They'll lock you up for good if they catch you.

But Poacher only shrugged. –It's what I gotta do, so . . .

That got Davie drumming, his fingers going so fast against the edge of the table, they were like a blur.

–'S all right, Davie, Jake whispered. –Poacher can look after himself.

–A boy needs a place to return to, Poacher, Cathleen said. –And you can always return here. Always.

–Nice one, Poacher said, grinning. –Might need a bed and a plate o' beans at the end, and he bumped knuckles with Swift.

Jake caught the look that passed between Cathleen and Father Angus then, but he didn't know what it meant.

–What about you, Davie? Are you staying in Scotland? It was Father Angus's question.

But Davie didn't answer him. He just shut his eyes and turned his head away, and his fingers went on beating.

Jake saw Cathleen raise her eyebrows at Father Angus, and take another bite of pizza. But it was only when she spoke again that he understood what her look had meant.

–Davie, this is up to you and you don't have to decide right away, because the offer's there for good. For always. But we want to offer you a home here, she said.

–We? Ollie said.

–It may be, Father Angus said, and he was blushing.

Davie was still drumming, but it was a slower riff now. Ollie caught Jake's eye and made a questioning gesture, and Jake shrugged. He didn't know what was happening either. Everyone waited.

–Anyway, Davie, Father Angus said, –whatever you need, we'd be glad if you found it here, made it your home too; and he gave a little nod, as if to say: –There. That clears things up.

Then Davie's fingers stopped drumming, stopped in the middle of a phrase, and he opened his eyes. He kept his gaze fixed down on the table.

–A proper home? he said.

–Yup. Cathleen's voice, quiet and firm.

–Here? With you?

–Yup.

Now he looked up. Looked straight at Cathleen, then straight at Father Angus.

–I ain't . . . He stopped, shook his head, like it was hard to get the right words. –My own room? he said.

–Yup, Cathleen said, and she held his gaze.

–Ain't never had a home before. Not a proper one. Nice one, he said. –Prodigal sons an' all that, eh? And Jake saw Father Angus's grin out of the corner of his eye.

Cathleen pulled ice cream from her freezer, and Ollie

poured hot chocolate sauce over it. Jake dug his spoon in, but he didn't really want it. It was that hollow feeling; and the ice cream wasn't going to fill it. Still, tomorrow he was going to Applecross; tomorrow he'd see his grandparents.

But it would just be him. No gang. No Jet.

He got to his feet, went to the back door. He needed some air. He leaned his head out into the night, feeling the cool, salty air on his face. Tears ran down his face.

A few minutes later Father Angus came and joined him. They looked out towards the black sea.

–I don't know who I belong to any more, Jake said. –Or where.

Poacher disappeared that night, leaving a scrawled note on the kitchen table for them to see in the morning:

Stuff goin off in Inglan cos of us so thers other kids to bring owt now. See ya nex time. Owtwalkers foreva. Gud luk my gang.

Then a helicopter came after breakfast for Swift and Cass and Ollie. It would land in Edinburgh on the roof of the Royal Infirmary. Doctors would take Cass and Swift straight into the hospital, and an official from the Italian Embassy would meet Ollie there and put him on a plane to Italy.

–You're a very special group of kids, Cathleen said. –Let us know when you've arrived safe.

They stood in the hall to say goodbye, the five of them left. Outside, the helicopter blades were already turning. Jake bit his lip. He didn't know how to do this. Out of the corner of his eye he could see Davie shaking his head.

–It's time, Swift said, but Davie shook his head harder, and ran up the stairs.

–The lord bless us and keep us, The lord bless us and keep us . . . he chanted, over and over.

–Davie? Ollie followed him up. Jake could see them through the banisters.

–Give me your hand, Ollie said, and slowly Davie put out his hand. Ollie took it, and on to Davie's palm he made a circle. –You're there, he said, and he put a dot in the middle with his fingertip. –In the middle of us. Outwalkers for ever, like Poacher said.

–For ever? Davie said.

–Yeah, Ollie said, then he ran down the stairs, and he held Jake by the shoulders and kissed him on both cheeks. Jake bit his lip again.

–It's what we do in Italy, my brother, Ollie said, and before Jake could reply, he ran out to the helicopter.

–Stay well, Davie, Swift said, and she put her hand up to salute him, and Davie put his hand up to her.

Swift touched Jake's shoulder. –Jake, she said, and Jake heard the catch in her voice. –Cass has something for you.

Cass held out Jet's collar in her tiny, bony hand, and as Jake took it she stroked his thumb with her finger, three small strokes.

–When he's back, I'll bring him to see you, he said, because it was easier to feel brave for Cass than for himself.

Then the helicopter roared, and they were gone.

*

Now Jake was in a helicopter himself, just him and a bodyguard, strapping themselves in. None of the gang with him, and no Jet. Cathleen and Father Angus waved to him. Father Angus had his arm across her shoulder. The helicopter tore him from the ground and in seconds the land had gone to nothing below: toy fields, toy houses, roads like threads.

–Look! The pilot pointed to the line of the New Wall before the helicopter dipped away north.

Studs had taken a copy of his parents' disc, then given it back to him. It was back in its hiding place on Jet's collar. One day Jake would listen to the end. Perhaps it would be easier when he was with his grandparents.

They flew along a velvet-green valley, low enough that Jake could see the blue shimmer in the loch at one end. Scotland was very beautiful. He closed his eyes again and he must have slept this time because next thing he knew was the pilot's voice in his headphones.

–Five minutes to landing. Fasten seat belts.

The air was colder here, and it smelled different. Across the water were mountains, their tops cut off by clouds. The helicopter seemed to fly almost over the water, hang for a moment, then it landed on a stretch of grass. In front of them, a bay of sand and shingle. The blades slowed and the engine stopped.

The pilot called back. –That their house, d'you reckon?

Jake was running before he knew it. Flying across the sand, scrambling over the shingle, rucksack bumping on his back. Now he was close enough to see the curtains in the windows, close enough to see that the front door was open. Close enough to see that two people sat in the front garden, backs to the wind, backs to him. He stopped. Glanced back. The bodyguard was a long way off. Jake hadn't felt it before, but now he was nervous, butterflies in his stomach.

What if . . .

Stepping quietly, he reached the wall that ran around

the garden and stood silent, looking over. A man and a woman, grey-haired; a tray on the step with a jug of coffee and two mugs. By their feet, a newspaper, weighted against the wind with a stone. On the front page a picture Jake recognized: the Co-Labs in flames, and above it a headline: ACT OF AGGRESSION, OR ACT OF LIBERATION? DRONE STRIKE DESTROYS ENGLISH CO-LABS.

The woman turned towards the sea, and as she turned, Jake saw her profile, and he saw his mother in her face.

He ran towards the gate, fumbled with the latch, tugged it open. He ran up the path, and a few feet from them, he stopped and stood there.

He had travelled so far for this.

On their faces he saw surprise, and he saw shock.

–Jake, his grandpa said. –It's Jake!

Forty-seven

In those first days with his grandparents, one thing was ordinary for Jake, and nearly everything else felt very strange.

The ordinary thing was no phones, no pads. –For your safety, his granny said. –We've been given instructions. No TV either, for now.

But everything else was strange: living in one house, and eating meals at a table, and brushing his teeth with toothpaste, and going to sleep at night time. It was strange to have clean clothes. It was strange to feel so lonely. His grandparents were kind and they didn't ask him much. Only what he liked for tea and if his shoes were comfortable.

His granny washed all his clothes. Twice. He still wasn't allowed in public places, so they didn't go shopping for new ones; instead, she phoned around the village and found other boys' clothes for him to wear. Then she pegged his Outwalker clothes on the line at the side of the house for the wind to blow through. The other boys' clothes fitted fine, but they felt like a borrowed life, and he wore his Outwalker clothes when he could.

Nearly every night Jake would lie in his bed and dream horrible dreams. Of dogs attacking Jet, and of Aliya tied up, and of Martha running towards him but never arriving.

–Bad one again? his grandpa would say sometimes, and he'd sit beside Jake on the bed like Jake's dad used to.

Every day Jake kept thinking he'd see the gang. See

Poacher building a fire on the beach, his hair like crazy snakes, or Swift with Cass in her arms, or Ollie. Once he thought he saw Ollie at the far end of the beach and he ran out, waving his arms. But it was another tall skinny boy with short, dark hair, digging for something.

On the fourth day, somebody phoned with news. Jake's grandpa took the call.

–What did they say? Who was it? Jake asked.

His grandpa read off from his notes. –No word about Poacher, and no word about Aliya. They're monitoring all her mother's statements and her Twitter feed, but she hasn't mentioned her daughter.

It was good news about Poacher, but not about Aliya. It made Jake's dream seem more real.

–Ollie is with his father in Rome. He's sent you a message: 'Hello, my brother. My father wants to meet you and cook you pasta. Come and stay.'

That made Jake smile. –And Cass?

–Responding well to her treatment. Though she has to live in an isolation tent for now.

–Not even Swift allowed in?

–It's a special tent. Even the nurses have to stay outside it, his grandpa said.

–Swift carried Cass all the way up England. She loves Cass more than anything in the world, Jake said.

There was no news about Jet. Jake didn't expect there to be.

On the fifth day he fished his mum's green cardigan from the bottom of his rucksack and gave it to his granny.

–It isn't dirty, cos I haven't worn it. But it's got holes. Mum always wore it for gardening. Then, in case his granny hadn't understood, he said it again: –She always wore it.

His granny held the cardigan close. Finally she gave it back to him. –One day I'll darn the holes, she said.

He understood. It took time to live with losing people.

Everywhere were photos of his mum. From when she was a little girl, right up to him being born. And she was always smiling, like everything was always happy, and everyone was always kind, and there was nothing bad.

–Did they tell you what happened? he said. It was after supper and his granny was standing at the sink.

He couldn't see her face, but she went very still.

She didn't answer, so he went on. –What happened was, their car went off the bridge. Into the river. Coming home from work. It was a Thursday. They said it happened very fast. They told me they didn't suffer any pain.

He wanted his granny to stop standing still. He wanted her to turn around, come and sit beside him.

–Granny? Did you hear me? I said their car went off the bridge, but they didn't feel any pain. It filled up with water, and they couldn't get out, and they drowned. But it happened very fast, and they were together, and they didn't feel any pain. Did you hear me? They didn't feel anything.

His granny still stood at the sink, still stood with her back to him. He wanted to make her turn, make her feel it, like he'd felt it all this time on his own.

–You haven't asked me about them, not you or Grandpa. Why haven't you asked me about them?

He hadn't seen his grandpa come in, but then he was there, sitting down beside him, and his granny turned and she sat down opposite. She put her arms on the table, still wet from washing up. She had hands like his mum's, only they were old. Square-ended fingers. 'Strong hands, and all the better to tickle you with.' That's what his mum used to say.

His granny's hands reached out to him. Somebody was crying; the drops were marking the table in small, dark blots.

–They said not to ask you, his granny said. –They didn't tell us anything. Just said you'd talk to us when you were ready and not to ask.

Jake stared at his granny's hands that were the same as his mother's. He saw them against the car window, pressing and pressing.

–It was an electrical fault that made the car go wrong, he said. –But they didn't feel any pain. They didn't . . .

He stopped. His throat hurt and his eyes ached. He couldn't breathe because his nose was blocked.

–They didn't . . . he said.

His grandpa's arm was across his shoulder, and somebody was crying.

Nobody had cried with him for his mum and dad. Not when they were killed, and not since. Not till now. His grandpa fetched a box of tissues and soon there was a heap of scrumpled white on the table. Jake told them all about it, and the more he spoke, the more he remembered. He told them how when he came home that day, there were hubbers in all the rooms, with these blue gloves on their hands, going through everything. All his parents' things, and then his too. He told them about the trunk and hiding his parents' things in there: the photo, and the cardigan and the knife. He told them about escaping. They laughed about the Home Academy guard dog and the meat wrapped in toilet paper. His granny clapped her hands when he told them about rescuing Jet.

–You're a brave boy, she said, but he said that his parents were the bravest on account of the disc.

–You can hear them if you want to. You can hear Mum and Dad. Then you'll understand about everything. And he took Jet's collar from his wrist and flipped out the disc.

He went outside before they played it. The sun was bright and he sat down first against the house, the warm stone at his back. But he could still hear the voices from inside. A tree stood in the corner of the garden and it didn't take him long to be up amongst its branches, snug in a cruck between two of them. He looked out over the bay towards the mountains of Raasay. The light was clear, and he could see a figure on the far hill and a scrap of shadow that was a dog.

This was where he'd wanted to be. This was the place he'd dreamed of, ever since he left the Home Academy. This was where he'd escaped to. Here, with his grandparents. Here, by this sea, looking over to those mountains. But with every bone in him, he wished Jet was here too, and Ollie sitting beside him dreaming about food. He wished for his gang.

So what you going to do, Jake? His mother's voice inside his head. *What are you going to do about it?*

Jake stayed there, very still, for a long time. He was so still, two blackbirds perched, unconcerned, on the branches near him to pluck the red berries. They were so near to him, he could have reached out and touched them. His grandpa came out and called for him. Later his grandma. He called back to them, and they let him be.

The sun had dropped close to the water and the light was failing by the time he climbed down. The kitchen was dark, but through the sitting-room window came the flickering blue light of the TV. Jake looked in from the outside. His grandparents were watching the news. He couldn't hear what the voices were saying, but there on the screen was the

New Wall, with its barbed wire and CCTV, and hubbers at watching posts with semi-automatics. And there too, right next to the Wall, was a vast crowd of people. They were smiling and waving banners, and holding up their phones. Men and women, old and young. Some were carrying sledge-hammers and pickaxes, and many were carrying children. The hubbers were staring down at the crowd. They were wearing their riot gear, but they weren't shooting.

The screen changed to another crowd, angrier looking, outside Big Ben. There were the hub police again in their riot gear, only this time you couldn't see their faces because they had their visors down, and they held truncheons out in front of them, and some of them held Tasers. This crowd was waving pieces of paper in the air, all of them, every single one, and they were turned towards someone standing on a stepladder, who was speaking with a loud-hailer.

Jake read the news ticker along the bottom of the screen:

English crowds rally to New Wall in peaceful protest . . . Angry scenes outside Coalition Parliament . . . Coalition foreign ministry summons Scottish Ambassador to demand explanation for overnight leaflet drop . . . Thousands of leaflets dropped across England exposing Coalition plans to implant nano-microchips in all citizens . . .

So that's what the crowd was waving. Leaflets dropped from the sky.

–Yes! Jake said. Cos you couldn't put any kind of wall up against those. Not a firewall, not a physical wall. They'd done it. The gang had done it.

Mum, Dad, hope you can see this, he thought.

His grandparents had turned at his voice, and they smiled and beckoned him in.

By the time he sat down the screen had changed again. A line of people sat at a table, facing a room full of journalists. Jake stared at them and his heart pounded.

–Aliya, he whispered.

She was seated at the far end, small against the grown-ups, her head down, hair over her face. But he knew her. Knew her immediately. Beside her sat a woman in a smart suit. Jake knew who she must be. He could see the resemblance. And beside her, also in a smart suit, sat the blond Surfer. There were hubbers at the table too.

Jake barely heard the questions asked, the answers given. He couldn't take his eyes off Aliya. Was she all right? What had they done to her?

The blond Surfer was speaking, and now the hub officer. Then there was a question for Aliya's mother.

–Minister Khan, have you caught the gang that abducted your daughter?

Jake watched Mrs Khan turn towards Aliya, put an arm around her shoulders. He still couldn't see Aliya's face, but he saw her flinch.

Mrs Khan didn't take her eyes off Aliya as she answered the question. –We will leave no stone unturned to apprehend those lowlifers responsible for my daughter's abduction. She has been exposed to a traumatic series of events and I am only glad that she will be able to benefit from the wonderful facilities and expertise provided within our Home Academy system. The doctors have assured us that she will, in time, make a full recovery. Then Mrs Khan squeezed Aliya's shoulders. –You're looking forward to it, aren't you, Aliya?

And, horrified, Jake saw Aliya lift her face to the cameras for the first time, and he saw her smile, and nod.

–No! Jake yelled.

Aliya's voice was small, next to her mother's. –Yes, she said, –I am looking forward to it. Looking forward to being better.

Questions rained down from the journalists. Jake watched Aliya lean into her mother and whisper something, and her mother nod, and turn to the waiting cameras.

–My daughter is exhausted. She will answer no more questions.

And while the journalists turned their attention back to the blond Surfer, Jake saw Aliya push her chair out from the table and stand to leave. But before she turned away, he saw her stare straight out at the camera, for all the world as if she were staring straight out at him, and him alone. And in a gesture that was over in a moment, she scribed a small circle on the table and placed her fingertip at its centre. Then she was gone.

I won't leave her there, Jake thought. *Whatever happens, I'm not leaving her in England.*

Forty-eight

The tide was nearly full and Jake walked along the edge of the water. Out in the bay a few kayakers were paddling out, a couple of windsurfers. He didn't want to think about anything. Not about England, or the New Wall, or the gang. He didn't want to think about his sadness.

He shut his eyes. Bird cries, the break of the tide against the beach, a car starting, faint voices from the village. Why was it that you could hear more clearly if you couldn't see? There was the distant noise of a boat engine, a tiny sound. Opening his eyes, he looked across the water again. There it was, just a dot far out in the bay.

On the far side of the beach, a group of birds was rushing to and fro, orange beaks pecking in the wash. He walked towards them and they took flight between the waves, calling and calling, a panicky, piping sound. He crouched and flicked away some seaweed, black, rubbery stuff, and tiny, translucent creatures jumped this way and that. A crab the size of his fingernail ran sideways. Jake caught it and set it down on his palm. It was white, and on its back it wore a green diamond.

He took off his trainers, rolled up his trousers and walked in up to his knees. The stones were sharp underfoot and the water was cold. Cold enough that if he were to swim in it, he thought it might fill up the whole of his mind.

He didn't know how long he stood in the water for.

Maybe it was only a few minutes. The wind had dropped to nothing. The kayaks had gone and the windsurfers had given up. The boat was still there, a bit bigger now, its engine grown to a chug sound.

His gang was gone, and he didn't know who he was, or what to do, without them. He didn't know how to fill the holes in him, made by all the people who'd gone. His parents. The gang. Jet . . .

He didn't belong here, in this village. He didn't belong in Scotland. Not yet. His grandparents loved him and wanted him here, but there wouldn't be anyone else like him. He saw other children in boats and canoes, and playing on the beach, and hanging around the inn, and he couldn't imagine being friends. They'd ask questions, and he wouldn't know how to answer them. And if he did answer, they'd say he was making it up, or else they'd be freaked out and leave him alone.

A memory came to him, as sharp as if it was from yesterday. He was watching TV with his mother. Except for her old films, she didn't much like watching TV, so that hadn't happened very often. It was a programme about orcas. Killer whales. A mother whale was separated from her calf. She was making these sounds, whistles and clicks, over and over.

–What's she doing? he'd said.

–She's crying, his mother had told him. –Crying for her calf. She's heart-sore.

–Heart-sore. He said it out loud. That was how he felt. His heart was sore.

He could feel the sun on his shoulders. Either his feet had grown used to the cold water, or they'd gone numb, like the rest of him.

The boat sound was larger now, and the dot had become a squat red boat. Not a sailing boat – no mast – and not a fishing boat, he didn't think. It had a square nose and a line of tyres tied round its side as fenders. It stopped out in the bay and Jake heard the sound of a chain giving out. The anchor, he supposed. Because then a small rowing boat was lowered to the water.

Last night he'd dreamed about Aliya. He'd dreamed she was locked in a safe room in the basement of a Home Academy, and he was in the Home Academy too. He was crawling, in the dream, under the dormitory beds to rescue her. At first it was easy, but the bed coverings hung down to the ground and as he crawled beneath each bed, they trapped him, twining round his legs. Then the Father was in the doorway and he spoke Jake's name . . .

The tide was drifting in; he felt its gentle push against his legs. Something fingered round them, and he started and kicked out. But it was only seaweed, and when he saw it for what it was, he kept his ground.

He'd woken sobbing from the nightmare and his grandpa had been there again, beside him, and he'd felt the wash of relief because he was here, in Scotland with his grandparents, not locked away in a Home Academy. Then he'd remembered Aliya, and the nightmare became real again, because he'd heard her mother speak, and somewhere in England Aliya *was* locked away.

Jake watched the rowing boat because, except for birds, there was nothing else to watch. This had to be the quietest place he'd ever been.

Two figures got in. Men, he reckoned, from their size. The smaller one sat in the stern with some luggage beside him. Some bags, a box, maybe. The bigger one began to row, but Jake could tell, even at this distance, that he wasn't used to it. He kept dipping the oars in wrong, and Jake could hear him cursing each time. A voice sounding over the sea. Jake reckoned it was cursing, though he couldn't hear the actual words.

Jake couldn't get the hang of rowing either when his granny took him out, kept putting his oars in wrong and throwing up a spray of water. Catching crabs, his granny called it. Twice he tipped backwards and the boat went round in a circle. Worst of all, his granny just laughed at him. But she made him keep on and he liked it in the end, the leaning forward and dipping down of the oars, then pulling them back through the green water. He liked the tug of the boat with each stroke. He liked it that he couldn't think about anything while he was rowing, only about getting the oars in the water right, and keeping them even, and pulling back smoothly.

The big man in the rowing boat had got the hang too. Not so many splashes now, and the rowing boat came in a straighter line. But it stayed small for ages, a little boat beneath such a big sky, and the mountains behind, and the sea that would take you all the way to Ireland, if you set off swimming. Jake had seen it on his granny's map.

The boat drew nearer, and the man in the stern began waving. Jake could see the swing of his arm. But who was he waving at? Jake looked around. There was no one on the beach except him.

–Hey! The man's voice travelled like a bell-note across the water. There was something familiar about it, but Jake couldn't place it. Closer the boat came. Jake could see the man in the stern more clearly. Baggy black trousers, black coat. Grey hair pulled back to a ponytail. Jake saw it when the man looked round. He stood knee-deep in the sea, mesmerised. Who was it?

Then suddenly he knew, and he waded, not heeding the sharp stones, though they made him catch his breath. He was out of the water and running along the beach, shouting, yelling:

–Ralph! Ralph!

And the rower. He knew the rower too. That leather jacket, that broad back.

–Monster!

And he heard his name returned, Ralph's voice deep like thunder.

–Jake, boy!

Jake's heart leaped. Monster and Ralph! Maybe they'd seen Poacher. Or Aliya! They might have news of her. And in the same moment, his spirit sank. Where was Jet? He'd left Jet in Ralph's care. His dog, so badly wounded, close to death. What was Ralph doing here? Why had he left Jet?

And he felt the thought he couldn't bear to think, and every stone cutting into his feet screamed up at him: Jet is dead.

The boat was close now, but Jake didn't want to see them, or hear the news Ralph had come to tell him. He'd come all this way from England on a boat to tell him, and Jake didn't want to hear it.

The boat was rocking from side to side and the bags and the box on the stern seat had tumbled. Monster's oars had caught a pile of crabs, sending water into the air like diamonds, and he was swearing and splashing, and it would have been funny, except that nothing could be funny now. Not ever.

Why did he have to come? Why couldn't he have sent a message?

Ralph was lifting the bags back on to the seat and now he had his arms beneath the box and Jake could see he was struggling with it, because the box seemed to be moving by itself, and Ralph was trying to keep it steady, keep it on the seat beside him.

They were nearly to the shore and above the sound of the oars splashing, and Monster's curses, there was another noise coming from the boat. A noise Jake didn't understand. Not a noise a man could make. It was like small bird noises, except there wasn't any bird.

Small, urgent yip noises.

Jake stood silent, not daring to call another name, not daring to hope.

Monster rowed on, his big shoulders pulling steady again on the oars. The boat was only yards away, and Ralph was undoing the box.

–Said I'd look after him, din't I? Ralph called. –So I had to get him home to yer.

As the boat pulled to the shore, Ralph lifted the box lid. That second, no more, was the longest in Jake's life. And then from nowhere, from nothing, from out of Jake's despair, a dog leaped.

A black dog; a thin dog now, with a wound on his shoulder that was healing. The dog Jake had thought was dead.

Tumbling out of the boat, into the shallows, Jet bounded towards him, yipping and barking, and then he was leaping up at Jake, licking his face, turning in circles so that the water was thrown against the sunlight in a silver sheen.

And Jake buried his face in Jet's black fur.

–Hey, boy, he said. –We're home.

Acknowledgements

This novel has been made possible with the support of many people, and institutions. My thanks to the University of Northumbria for providing sabbatical time for writing, and to my colleagues for their writerly support. Many thanks also to Arts Council England for their Grants for the Arts Award, which gave me invaluable time to write, and to Claire Malcolm at New Writing North for her help with this.

Two residencies, the first at Hawthornden Castle International Writers' Retreat, and the second at the HALD, the Danish Centre for Writers and Translators as part of their International Residency Programme for Writers, gave me two months of uninterrupted time to write, for which I am enormously grateful.

A considerable portion of this novel was written in the wonderful Pig & Pastry cafe: it's been a great place to write in. Thank you.

Thank you to Dave Wilson, for giving me the low-down on freight trains and their timetabling; and to John Cunningham for introducing me to the world of nano-technologies. Also to the lorry driver at Michaelwood Services on the M5 for his vivid account of life on the road and how freight security is maintained.

Workshops with children in St John's and Waverley Primary Schools, Newcastle, gave me very helpful feedback about the ideas in my story and two great first audiences. Thank you to all of them, and especially to Kelly Bewick and her class at St John's who welcomed me back with open arms the following year. You are all fantastic imaginers and I loved your stories and ideas.

To all at David Fickling Books, thank you for welcoming me so wonderfully; and to Bella Pearson, particular thanks for superb editing.

Thank you to Gillie Russell at Aitken Alexander for most helpful notes on *Outwalkers*.

Thank you to my beloved daughters Eliza and Jesse for their support and opinion. There has been no shortage of either.

To Julia Evans-Turner, Matthew Jamson, Rosa James Kilbane, Elodie Salter, Romy Salter and Alex Turpin: a big thank you for reading the first draft of *Outwalkers* and for giving me such strong responses. Your thoughts and comments have been invaluable, and I have, I think, addressed each one.

To my wonderful agent, Clare Alexander, a most heartfelt thank you, as ever.

Finally I'd like to thank Martin Riley as friend, ally and pacer, for all his thoughts and wisdom about stories, over much coffee and cake, as this story developed. And most of all, thank you to Karen Charlesworth, who has walked the length of the UK with me, literally and metaphorically, and kept me off the straight and narrow in the writing of *Outwalkers*.

Fiona Shaw